THE RED PATH

To TREVOR COLLETT,
I HOPE YOU ENJOY THE
STORY, TOLD....

Mc P. Sh

LEGACY'S ROAD

THE RED PATH

A NOVEL BY
M. DANIEL SMITH

BAY LEDGES PRESS

Published by Bay Ledges Press
www.bayledgespress.com

ISBN (paperback): 978-1-7377843-0-2
ISBN (ebook): 978-1-7377843-1-9

Edited by David Aretha
Book design by Christy Collins, Constellation Book Design

Printed in the United States of America

*I dedicate this novel to my mother, Melva L. Smith,
who read to me, my head in her lap, her soft voice helping
still my over-active mind as I drifted off to sleep.*

PROLOGUE

Philadelphia Suburb, Now

A Legacy, found

A man in his late twenties knelt in an attic of a small house. Dust motes spiraled in slanted rays of sunlight filtered by a dust encrusted window, the glow softening the outlines of his thin face. He gazed into an age-darkened wooden chest, the scent of old leather permeating the still air, released as he removed, then carefully thumbed through dozens of bound journals, carefully stacking them alongside the chest until only one remained, lying on the bottom, with a wide slit punched through its cover. He picked it up, holding it to the light, then turned it over, staring at a thin perforation in the stiff leather backing, surrounded by a dark stain.

He opened it, looking inside the front cover, noting the date inscribed in faded black ink: May, of 1758, making it the oldest of the others pulled from the chest. A collection of twelve generations of memories, passed from father to son or daughter, from mother to daughter or son. Each of their lives described in personal observations, stories, and drawings. He used the edge of his thumb to open the damaged journal at random, the wash of late-afternoon light falling across age-yellowed paper, highlighting a drawing of a woman in a long dress with tight waistcoat, arms at her side, hair coiled in a thick braid atop her head, shoulders turned slightly away as she looked back, lips parted as if wanting to tell him her story.

As he stared at her image, a creak from two-hundred-year-old wooden stair-treads below let him know he'd broken his promise to Sinclair, his wife of five years, to bring the chest down from the attic, adding it to a pile of personal belongings waiting for movers to arrive the next morning. The sound of her disappointed sigh as she reached the bottom of a pull-down ladder caught his ear, followed by her grunt of effort as she climbed the treads with thick swollen legs and aching back, entering the final trimester of a first pregnancy.

Sinclair came over and stopped behind him, reaching down, her fingers gently tracing through curls of dark hair on his bowed neck. "David—are you okay?"

He nodded, then closed the journal, putting it back in the chest along with all the others. "Sorry—for not having brought this down earlier." He resealed it, thick metal latches snapping into place. "It's just that—this is an *incredible* treasure."

David knew his wife, deathly afraid of spiders, had rarely came up into the attic. Knew she had never opened the ancient chest, stored away in the family home signed over to them by her father as a wedding gift, shortly before he passed away. He looked up at Sinclair, taking in her delicate face, framed by high cheekbones beneath wide-set, light-gray eyes, with full lips posed above a narrow jaw, a faint cleft in its center. Named by her father after a family relative, she'd told him of going outside as a child, the two of them lying on a blanket, staring up at the stars as he spun fanciful tales about their ancestors. She carried his grandchild now, soon to arrive, who would never hear his grandfather's deep, gravelly voice, sharing their family's history.

David sighed, then got to his feet. He picked up the heavy chest, edging around Sinclair's outthrust belly as he moved toward the top of the ladder, his lips pursed, wishing he knew more about his own family's history, no one left alive to fill in the missing pages. Then a smile broadened his lips as he realized the birth of their child would tie his bloodline to Sinclair's, making him part of her family legacy, one written down in the journals, life by life, beginning with the very first one.

CHAPTER ONE

Ohio Basin hillside, late November 1758

Aftermath

A British officer lay on a battlefield, eyes closed against the press of heat from a midday sun on his soot-stained face. He could hear the moans of his men as they cried out in pain, joined by French soldiers in a mixed chorus of young voices and old. The rage-soaked shouts of men in combat now reduced to pitiful cries of wounded men in need. Others, their lives in steady drain, whispered pleas for the touch of a mother's hand on their grimed faces. All, in plaintive call with stories to tell, in want of someone, anyone, to hear their final words.

The officer's name was Harold Knutt; a second lieutenant in his Majesty's Third Foot, arrived in the American Colonies six months earlier, assigned to a British expeditionary group with orders to force French armies from lands to the west of the colony of Pennsylvania. He'd had little time to acclimate, tossed into the grind of combat with several battles behind him now; the most recent one ending with over a thousand French-born souls left dead or dying over the span of an hour. Half that number now under guard, most unable to stand, their heads down, the image of dispirited men. Distraught, defeated, and hungry.

A surge of nausea forced him onto his side; a wash of bile spilled across the shell-battered ground. Tears flowed from eyes the color of the sky as he relived the horror of what he'd seen and done: his officer's pistol thrust out, trigger pulled, aimed at a young, freckle-faced French soldier with bayonet-tipped musket leveled for a fatal stroke. A jolting thud as a finger-wide ball of lead shattered the boys jaw, gnawing through flesh, teeth, and bone, his head framed in a soft halo of light-brown curls as he fell onto his back. The empty pistol dropped, hand filled with the hilt of his officer's sword, blade raised to deter another soldier's savage-eyed thrust, the honed edge of fine English steel dragged across the side of his assailant's neck, releasing a fan of blood that fogged the air between them. His hand, arm, and face painted red from the heart-pumped spray.

Harold heaved once again then rolled onto his back and looked up at a cloudless sky, grateful to be alive as the churn of his emotions began to drain away. With a tired sigh he forced himself to his feet, knowing it was time to face his responsibilities as an officer. He gazed across the battlefield; eyes drawn to small clusters of women in plain clothing as they drifted among the wounded of both armies.

They were camp followers, coming together from both sides of the conflict to tend to the living. Binding the wounds of those they could save, offering words of compassion and comfort of a gentle touch to any beyond help. They drifted between huddled groups of broken soldiers, each treated with the same gentle care as the next, no matter the color of their blood-stained uniform.

As Harold looked across the thousand-pace stretch of shell-torn hillside he could hear a slow shuffle of weary heels through blood-matted grass as his second in command came to make his report. Sergeant Major Scott, a stocky, broad-shouldered man whose weary face appeared before him, set in stony consideration, a tired wave of hand offered in salute. "One hundred and twenty-four of ours, sir, gone or going. Twice that number, wounded, though likely to survive. Two dozen of those in danger of losing an arm or leg." The grizzled veteran sighed. "Over a thousand dead on the other side of the ledger." He hesitated, then cleared his throat as he shook his head. "They—wouldn't surrender, sir. Not even when it turned to *shite* against them."

Harold nodded, his face set in a tight-lipped expression. "Hunger makes men desperate, Sergeant Major, and desperate men are—difficult to reason with."

The older man shrugged. "Cost us more than it should have, sir." Then he stared at the ground, his toe nosing the edge of a dark pool of blood; the French soldier who'd left it there lying several paces away, face down, hands stretched out before him, death-stiffened fingers clinging onto twists of coarse grass. The weary veteran shook his head again, a tired sigh let slip. "Though far less than it might of."

Scott looked over at the lean-framed young officer he'd mentored over the past few months, noting the look of exhaustion on his narrow face. "Another victory in hand, sir, due to your masterful plan." He swept his dark-brown eyes across scattered knots of dead and dying soldiers. "Though what happened here was nothing more than a slaughter of good men." Scott leaned to one side, spitting a thin stream of tobacco juice onto the ground, careful to avoid the pool of drying blood. "On both sides, sir."

Harold nodded, making a mental note of the casualties his second had described, storing them away for later review when he could find a balance between feelings of intense grief and the exhilaration of having survived another dance with death. He surveyed the field, littered with lines of unstrung men, aware death would come for him one day. Relieved he'd earned the right to see another one through.

Scott saluted again then walked away, leaving Harold to look past the expanse of blood-soaked ground; memories of when he'd first arrived at the port city of Philadelphia six months earlier rising to the surface of his battle-weary mind. It seemed a lifetime ago, measured against what he'd been through, learned, and written down in his journals as he'd made his way through a vast and boundless land.

CHAPTER TWO

Western Pennsylvania, Late Spring, 1758

Six Months Earlier, Military Encampment

Harold stood waist-deep in a river, his unbound hair soaking wet, hanging in thick black strings over broad shoulders. A strong current tugged against his thighs as he looked up at the sky; a half-moon in rise joined by a handful of stars beginning to wink into existence. The whispering rush of water around his lower body blended with the cooing of doves in their roosts, along with a steady thrum from a thick swarm of mosquitoes hovering just above his head.

Harold was embarrassed, the voracious insects having forced him to flee the company of the one hundred soldiers under his command. One hundred pairs of eyes watching with grins on their faces as he'd dashed away from flame-centered circles of men, palms damp with a mixture of blood and sweat, daubed from endless slaps at insects feasting on every inch of exposed skin. A nearby river had offered refuge from the relentless assault, where he'd stopped at the edge of its bank and hastily removed his expensive officer's boots, tri-cornered hat, and British officer's jacket, along with a leather-bound journal kept in an inside pocket. Then he'd launched himself with outstretched arms into the dark water; its cold embrace providing a welcome respite from the itchy press of shirt and pants clinging to his over-heated, sweaty skin.

As Harold cleared the surface, cries of derisive laughter filled his ears, along with the whir of tiny wings in hover. Now back on his feet, he stared up at the moon, contemplating his next move.

"They're as much a part of the land as are the trees." Sergeant Major Scott stood on the riverbank, thirty-five years of age, over half spent in his Majesty's service. He reached down and helped Harold up the steep bank. "The locals use a cedar resin and bear fat mixture to coat the skin. A more fragrant balm available to officers upon request, though at a steep price. The rest of us having to make do with the other, though a serviceable enough blend." Scott reached out, offering Harold a small tin, a grin lighting up his face when the young officer opened it then quickly turned his head away, put off by the rancid smell.

The sound of mosquitoes in rapid approach convinced Harold to grit his teeth and daub some of the noxious ointment on his neck, cheeks, and forehead, aware he was still in a period of dazed adjustment, having left England via the river-port city of Bristol two months ago, stuffed aboard a transport ship with a hundred replacements for the better part of a month before reaching the port of Philadelphia. Once disembarked, a uniformed man with a harried air of authority had checked off his name, then directed him to squeeze into a wagon stuffed with other newly commissioned officers. His journey through dense woodlands came to its end at the edge of a vast military encampment, where he'd spent the past two days in a swirl of acclimation under the ever-watchful eye of the Sergeant Major.

Harold, unable to ignore the itching on his face, rubbed his cheeks, his fingers re-stained by the odorous salve. "The other officers, they made no mention to me of it. I mean, no one's told me anything at all about—"

Scott leaned in, fixing his young officer with a dark-eyed nod of his head. "A lesson there for you, sir. Better to learn the lay of the land from us lowly rankers before the mission begins."

"Mission?" Harold stared back. "No one mentioned anything about a mission."

The Sergeant Major shook his head and sighed. "The primary mission of returning one Second Lieutenant Knutt, fresh from recent arrival in the colonies, back in one piece to—wherever it is you hail from, sir. God willing." Scott grinned once more, his teeth a light shade of gray in the moonlight reflecting from the dark surface of the river.

Harold gathered himself. "Yes, Sergeant Major. Quite right. God's will and all that."

"You sound less than committed to the phrase, sir." Scott squinted. "Protestant, I imagine, like our good King George?"

Harold nodded. "Yes."

The older man shrugged, his wide shoulders rising and falling as he stepped forward and helped Harold into his officer's coat, the journal slipping out, picked up by Scott and handed back. "Catholic myself, sir, not that the uniform cares. Or the French and their native allies either, along with most of the colonists, if the truth be told."

"Or the mosquitoes." Harold lowered his hands, the balm an adequate, if temporary, solution.

Scott smoothed the lines of Harold's coat, then handed him his hat. "Aye, sir. The mossies are an issue at times, but you'll get used to them soon enough." He paused. "If you live that long, what with all the other things waiting to plant you in the ground. Or barrel of brine homeward bound in your case, sir, having purchased yourself a shiny new commission."

Scott stepped back and gave Harold a brief nod, then turned away, leading his bite-swollen officer back to the encampment, dotted with a blaze of campfires surrounded by segregated knots of Colonist and

English soldiers, their sweaty faces pressed close to the large rings of flame, seeking a delicate balance between acrid drift of thick smoke and burn from snapping embers, or leaning back, forced to endure the ceaseless, prickling assault of the mossies.

The two men rejoined the army, woven from disparate threads bound in common cause to try and dislodge the French forces of King Louis and their native allies from a series of forts lying further to the west. Their own ruler, King George II, firm in the belief the land belonging to his citizens. The leaders of both empires eager to spill blood, lives, and small mountains of coin attempting to control the vast and valuable wilderness territory while turning a deaf ear and blind eye to the ancestral claims of its native inhabitants.

A thin mist drifted just above the ground, Harold with a sullen look on his swollen face as he stared at his morning meal: a mound of unidentified slop plopped into a dented metal bowl appearing to be a mix of gray meat and crumbled fire-cakes, along with a sprinkle of dried herbs the local camp-followers put into every meal to help ward off dysentery. Harold sighed as he shoveled a spoonful into his mouth, gnawing it into pieces small enough to swallow, fed along his protesting throat, delivered to his stomach as if lumps of coal to fuel his inner furnace.

The younger men under his command endured their inedible breakfast in resigned silence while the more experienced rankers opined as to the type, origin, and age of the various animal parts. Those like himself, whose uniforms were of recent issue and unmarked by stains of sweat, muck, or blood, stared at the noxious glop in their bowls with crestfallen faces.

Harold, sitting on a large log a dozen paces away from his men, blinked his eyes as a pungent cloud of smoke slipped past, his lids sore from numerous bites of mossies the night before. He barely noticed the taste of the rancid meat, having applied a thick layer of soldiers' balm to face, neck, back of hands, and upper lip, preventing his being able to smell anything else. A result he was thankful for as he choked down the rest of his loathsome meal.

Once finished, Harold opened his officer's jacket and removed a leather-bound journal, used to make observations, capture thoughts, or make drawings of his men, crafting images of them in various poses. Some with smiles on their faces, others walking around with thoughtful looks or shaded frowns. A few, sitting alone, staring with vacant eyes. Each of their moods portrayed based on length of time in service, with Harold choosing to copy Sergeant Major Scott's stoic expression whenever around the men, doing his best to match that of the aged veteran, a man held in high esteem by the soldiers under his immediate authority.

Harold looked up as Scott came over, the Sergeant Major's jacket adorned with a line of chevrons stitched along both sleeves, denoting fifteen years of service to the crown. The older man came to attention and saluted, then relaxed at a nod from Harold. "Sir. The men will need to stand to attention this morning; it being the fifteenth of the month, with mandatory company-wide muster." Scott watched as Harold started to put his journal away. "Not yet, sir. We can wait for the piper's signal before forming up. More than enough time to finish your bit of writing."

Harold nodded. "Yes, Sergeant Major. Of course." He started to return to his journal, then looked up, Scott still standing there, a considered look on his face, bowl clasped in his wide, short-fingered hand. Harold sighed, snapping the journal shut and leaning back. "I'm missing something of importance, again. Correct, Sergeant Major?"

"A minor detail, sir. Barely worth the mention of."

Harold frowned. "You know I'm not yet a proper officer, Sergeant Major. As do the men."

Scott knelt, a grimace of discomfort tightening the lines of his face as he bent his legs. He placed his bowl beside Harold's, then reached down and began to readjust a buckle on one of his boots. "They'd not agree with you, sir. Nor would I. You've performed better than most of the new officers I've worked with over the years. The men and I are appreciative of your willingness to observe without need of making— undue comments."

Harold slipped the journal back into an inside pocket of his officer's coat. "The minor detail, Sergeant Major?"

"My father had a foxhound, sir, with a good nose." Scott grinned. "And an *observant* mind, eager to the training and quick to the trail."

"Another lesson, Sergeant Major?"

"No, sir. Just a moment of personal reflect." Scott looked over, his eyes a match to the color of the sun-bronzed tone of his face and hands. He was a brawny, thick-chested Scotsman, broad in the face with a square jaw, divided by a deep cleft in its center. A spray of thin creases spread from the corners of his eyes, testament to his extensive service record, with the past three years spent soldiering in the western reaches of the Pennsylvania Colony. His thick hands and wrists were heavily scarred, proof of a history of hard-fought campaigns throughout far-flung corners of the British Empire. A handful of newer ones acquired in recent attempts made to try and force French troops from their perch on lands near the border of the Ohio basin, resulting in varying degrees of defeat for the mixed English and Colonial forces.

Scott continued, a wistful note underlying the baritone sound of his deep voice. "We tried him, the hound, sir. Several times. Had the will to trail and corner, but not to go in on the kill."

Harold nodded. "His name?"

"He was a red foxhound, sir."

"I meant his *given* name."

Scott twisted around, a bewildered look on his face. "He didn't have one, sir. None given until they've proven out. Which this one—well, he just never did."

"So, only a pet then, for you to play—" Harold cut off his response as Scott shook his head, responding in a thick Scottish accent.

"A *pet*, sir? Nae. The poor beastie was put down. No room for an animal that canna earn its keep. Margin's wee enow on a small croft as it is, without carry of dead weight. Same goes with livestock. People too, blood kin or no. Cut loose to seek their fortunes elsewhere if they've no mind to the trudge and drudge of turning over soil, planting, reaping, and the endless shoveling of *shite*."

Harold closed his eyes, heart-sick at the thought of the dog's death. "And I would be the—hound in this scenario. Trained, but not yet tested."

A wide smile creased Robert's weathered face. "No worries, sir. You'll do fine." His thick accent faded away.

Harold shook his head. "And if I *fail* the men under my command, Sergeant Major? Will you mark me as unfit for the duty?"

"Of course not, sir. You're an officer." Scott paused; his head turning to one side, a stream of brown tobacco juice hitting the ground beside his boot. "Besides, the Frenchie's or their heathen allies will put paid to you soon enough if you're incapable of command. Leaving you stuffed in a barrel of brine in the hold of a slow boat back to—?" The Sergeant Major looked at Harold, his head cocked to one side.

Harold responded in a soft tone. "Bristol."

"There you are sir. Back to Bristol for a proper burial and well-attended send off, no doubt. Another hero home, receiving the warm embrace of Mother England. A reminder to citizens in attendance of the Empire's vast reach around the globe in spin. India, Africa, Burma, or God-cursed Asia, along with the rest of our far-flung colonies. Yourself having volunteered to take part in the King's grand adventures, praised by parent's and admiring throng for having given your all."

Harold pursed his lips. "A rather macabre observation, Sergeant Major."

"Isn't it though?" Scott looked across the mist-veiled encampment, his voice firm, hands clenched. "People dying in the tens of thousands, from the promotion of one side over another."

Harold smirked. "An exaggeration, Sergeant Major. Our service losses are far less than that."

Scott turned and stared at him. "People, Second Lieutenant Knutt, late of Bristol. Men, women, *and* children, be they dark-skinned—or of a lighter cast. Unfortunates all, caught living on the wrong side of lines of demarcation drawn in black ink on maps in London. Then painted in red on ground trod by good men like us, wielding bayonets, or blades, dripping with the blood of innocents. Soldiering on, bearing the flag of Britain to wherever the Crown points a finger, bidding us go."

Harold lowered his head, staring at the ground, a weave of crushed grass and mud knit together by the metal-studded heels of British boots. The fecal odor from slit trenches used as latrines, mixed with acrid smoke from dozens of fires, leaving a visible stain in the air. He lifted his head as the sound of a fife signaled the companies to stand to attention. "I concede your point of view, Sergeant Major, based as it is on your many years of faithful service."

Scott got to his feet, burying another grunt of pain beneath a soft curse. He gathered himself, making an adjustment to the hang of his coat. "We are to form up then, sir?"

"Yes." Harold got to his feet, then hesitated. "As to the detail mentioned, when you first approached?"

Scott cocked an eyebrow. "Your fly, sir. You've managed to button it up out of order." Harold looked down, his face reddening as the Sergeant Major turned and walked away.

As he corrected the error, with a concerned look on his face, Harold wondered whether he would be able to join in the killing of men, when the time for it arrived.

CHAPTER THREE

Bristol, England, Late Winter, 1757

Commitment to a Distant Cause

Harold's heartbeat thudded in his ears as the words he's just uttered made their way to where his father stood, a scarred hand hooked across the back of a wooden chair. The former soldier, thin faced, wide of shoulder with silver-gray hair, stared back as his large ears cupped the words from the stuffy air of his study. A look of anger painted his lips as he took in their meaning. "*What* did you just say?"

Harold tried to match the stern look in his father's light-gray eyes, poised above an aquiline nose, his lean face bearing a wide scar on one cheek, earned in a military campaign when a much younger man. He failed in the attempt, staring at the floor, a gleam of nascent tears forming in the corners of his eyes, sign of an unpracticed rebel. "I am enlisted. In his Majesty's Royal Army."

"You are *not*." His father stepped toward his office desk, then stopped, his son's voice rising in denial of his authority.

"I *am*, Father. Departure on the morrow for officer training. Then off to wherever—"

"You *will* not." The old soldier spun around; his countenance shadowed. "I did not raise you to be meat for their grind. Sating the appetite of men who couldn't find their way to the proper end of a musket, or sword." He stared at Harold, angled rays of sunlight highlighting the scar earned from service during the Spanish siege of Gibraltar. His anger, fully blossomed, formed itself around a fierce glare, as if carved from shards of sea-ice, centered in his age-faded eyes. "I *forbid* it."

Harold stepped forward, steadying his voice. "I'm already signed. There is no turning back."

His father scoffed in dismissal. "You've not yet reached the age of determination."

"I have, Father. Middle of this month just passed. I signed the forms then." Harold hesitated, then stiffened his will, knowing it was his right as an English citizen to do his duty. "There's *nothing* you can do to stop me. Nothing at all."

His father turned and pointed at the door. "Go then and *be* nothing. You're on their books now. No longer on mine."

ᑯᗕᔈ

The officer in command of the training facility nodded in deference to a bull-headed sergeant who stepped forward, suggesting to a line of nervous young officer candidates they should reconnoiter a specific part of their lower anatomies with their heads. Further explanation offered that if they could not find the target assigned them, it was due to their heads already being in said orifice.

Harold stood at attention, eyes front, arms at his side, jaw clenched against an urge to laugh or cry. Both emotions circled the inner wall of his mind like rats in search of an exit, his inner wolf in stir, rising to swallow them whole. It is only a game, he reminded himself, played with rigid rules, but fair. One designed to separate the wheat from the chaff.

The retching from a fellow trainee, slumped forward on his knees in a sign of weakness, brought an instant and brutal rebuke from the sergeant, the flow of his coarse invective turned by the bone-deep ache of Harold's fatigue into a warm wind, lulling him into a peaceful place. A blow to the side of his head for losing focus sent him face first into the muck of the trampled parade ground, where he lay for a moment before scrambling to his feet.

He'd expected a physical reprimand at some point during the fourteen-hour day, the thick-shouldered, bull-necked sergeant eager to deliver a dose of motherly attention to each recruit in turn. The scarred-faced veteran, hated beyond Satan himself during tortuous run, walk, and crawl activities, then loved beyond all measure of the word when gracing them with a nod at the end of each day and a: "Well done, lads. I'll make officers of you yet. For God, Country, and the King! Hurrah!"

Harold bent down and helped his semi-conscious comrade back to his unsteady feet, the two of them clinging to one another as they shared the misery of a rain-sodden trudge back to the barracks, followed by the promise of another cold meal and dreamless sleep ahead.

৩৩

Harold stood at attention; a normal state of being, his back braced, heels at the mark, head erect, eyes focused straight ahead. He released his mind to wander at will as his ears focused on the tone of words from the officer who was speaking, trusting them to let him know when to refocus.

"Be at ease, Second Lieutenant Knutt." The officer, a major in rank and responsible for the latest group of new trainees, smiled as he stretched out his hand in an offer of respect. Harold shook it, noting the man's grip was as firm as the surface of one of the twelve-pound cannonballs each officer candidate had carried with them over the past few weeks; ordered to treat it with a mother's love. "Munitions," the proper response to the question; "What is more important than breath, blood, and healthy bowels?"

"You have a ripe assignment. With my former group in the American colonies, leading the way against the French and their irascible heathens."

Harold eased his stance, a quick nod and requisite thin smile offered in reply, his lips pressed tight against any outward expression of emotion. His ultimate destination was unimportant; achieving the rank of lieutenant all that mattered.

The officer glanced at the sergeant who leaned in, his voice soft. "Answer the Major, lad."

Harold stiffened. "Thank you, sir. Honored, sir. Will do my best to make you proud. Sir."

The major nodded. "You have six days' leave before mobbing to the replacement depot at Bristol. Good luck to you, Second Lieutenant Knutt."

Harold's salute was as crisp as the fit of his new uniform. He stepped back, spun in a half-circle, then exited the Major's office.

രൈൻ

"You *will* see him before you leave." Harold's mother reached up, adjusting the fit of Harold's uniform, its lines tightened by the increased thickness of his shoulders. She looked into his light-blue eyes, a match to her own. "I will not abide you parting on angry terms."

Harold frowned, taking his mother's hands in his. "Father seemed clear as to his feelings. Both before I left for training and then again, upon my return."

His mother shook her head, her deep red hair showing the first signs of gray. It framed her narrow face, a spray of fine freckles on her cheeks. "He is in *pain*, Harry, seeing you in the same position he was in, long ago. Knowing what lies before you, himself still suffering the effects of his injuries, on the outside and in, wanting more for you than his father offered him."

Harold squeezed his mother's hands, slightly, her skin cool to his touch. "I respect his opinion, Mother, as always, despite his—well seasoned words concerning my decision. And there's no diminishment of my regard for his parental authority. But it is *my* decision. My freeborn right to choose the course of my life."

His father's deep voice responded from behind. "You chose the first step, son, but your toe is now in the trap. What comes next is not freedom of choice, but a slow pull down into the quagmire." He stood in the doorway of his study, a grim look in his eyes, voice filled with concern for his son's future. "You're to be tossed into the churn of other men's ambitions, in mix with the blood and bones of naive boys looking to escape their self-imagined prisons of familial duty and obedience to—"

Harold cut his father off. "I will have no more of this conversation between us, sir." He kept his tone calm, lessons in obedient disagreement driven deep into his marrow by the vigilant attention of the sergeant at the training facility. "I answered a call to serve. To aid in the carving out a greater British Empire from what promises to be an immense and valuable wilderness. One with limitless supply of raw goods, and countless sources of reliable waterpower. More than enough to transform our economy into the largest in the civilized world." Harold squared his shoulders, his face set in a firm look. "I, for one, am proud to support the realm and our intrepid colonists in this divine adventure throughout the New World."

His father waved a hand in the air, the two outside fingers missing due to one of several injuries suffered in prior service to the crown. "You're blinded by the glint of sun on bayonets, son, arrayed in lines 'fore the fortunate few in mount of a horse, stationed well behind the firing lines, isolated from the face-to-face slaughter of men to come. Watching through glass lenses and brass tubes from a distance, as soldiers tear at one another, earning bits of colored ribbon attached to polished metal. Sent out again, and again, until disease, fester of wound, or sudden death leaves them buried 'neath the bloody muck."

Harold's father stepped fully into the room and pulled a pipe from a waistcoat pocket. He carefully stuffed the bowl, lit it with a phosphor and inhaled, holding his breath for a moment before sighing; a thick halo of smoke released, ringing his head. "You're fortunate. Or more to the point, your mother is fortunate. The army will return your remains in a sealed cask for proper burial, however much of you is left after the damage done to your body by shellfire, or native knives."

"Richard! You will stop this! I—cannae stand it!" Harold's mother slipped into her ancestral accent; her family having sprung from Scottish Highlander heritage. She stepped between the two of them, her cheeks in full blush, thin lips pressed in a quivering line. "I will'na hae this memory to carry wi'me these next few months."

She cut Richard a glare as she left the room in a scurry of skirts, the study door slammed behind, the two men left in a silence as thick as the morning fog in Bristol Harbor. Harold's father shifted his stance, then lowered his voice. "You will be two years or more gone, before ever seeing home again."

"*If* I see home again, as you were kind enough to point out."

His father shrugged as he removed the pipe from between his lips. "Odds stacked against you, for certain." He studied the curl of smoke as it rose from the bowl carved out of briar. "It's a hard journey, no matter which game-board your piece lands on. Better off in the American colonies than those in Africa. Or the god-forsaken Middle East. Far fewer diseases to deal with across the Atlantic; most of those the ones carried over on every ship that's departed here over the past hundred and fifty years or more." Richard paused, then sighed. "All those countless thousands of native people made to suffer the deadly consequences. Poor bastards."

Harold straightened to his full height. "An unproven suspicion, proffered by those in opposition to the Crown's plan. Postulating unfounded opinions as to origin of diseases, placed in seditious publications meant to interfere with the people's support of our God given right to pursue a reasonable expansion into a world having much to offer. One with more than enough room for all."

"Well said." Richard placed the pipe stem to his lips and inhaled, bringing the bowl to glow, followed by another smoke-filled exhalation. "Are they *your* words?"

Harold sniffed, the resinous scent of the tobacco enticing. "Is the leaf in your pipe a product of *your* garden?" The comment drew a thin smile from his father.

"A valid point, one of many I've come to rely on you having made over the past few years." Richard leaned back; his long arms crossed as he tapped the stem of the pipe against the corner of his lips. "I will miss such insightful observations. And you, as well."

Harold hesitated, caught off guard by his father's change in demeanor. "I never meant to disappoint you, Father. Had rather hoped you would be proud of my choice, in support of the realm."

Richard shrugged. "Same words I once offered *my* father, over several lifetimes ago when measured against the burden to a soldier's soul, losing so many close friends during desperate moments when—" He sighed, letting the rest of his thought drift away. "There will be challenges ahead. Ones I'm not able to prepare you for; the divide between son and father one not easily crossed."

Harold stared back, his father's openness a shock. He eased his stance, leaning against the sill of a window. "As too the divide between Bristol and the colonies."

"True. And another point in your favor." His father emptied the bowl of his pipe with a solid rap against the side of a clay container, then placed it in his coat pocket. He looked over at the face of a large grandfather clock, listening as the seconds ticked off with each swing of its brass pendulum. "When do you have to leave? Is there time enough for a round at the local ale-house?"

Harold hesitated a moment before nodding. "Yes, Father. There is."

CHAPTER FOUR

Military Engagement, Late June 1758

Glade, Painted Red

Harold stared at the back of his hands, the skin covered in rust-red flakes of dried blood that fell away as he flexed his fingers beneath the intense heat of a mid-day sun. He turned them over and gazed at his palms, coated in a sticky layer of dark-red blood that reflected the sunlight as if still infused with the elixir of life. The gore placed there from having helped collect the scattered remains of three soldiers: two of them young men, new to the colonies and inexperienced in the art of warfare, and the other a middle-aged ranker recently demoted from sergeant to corporal. Their attackers having left their mortal remains strewn throughout a small clearing, ambushed on their way back from a forward observation position. The transgressors, according to the handful of native guides who'd scouted the local area, a party of French irregulars in company with their own native allies.

"Drink, sir?" Sergeant Major Scott leaned down and offered Harold a small flask. The young officer looked at it, hesitated a moment then took it, raising it to his lips. The potent smell burned his nostrils as he dared a tentative swallow, gagging as the locally brewed whiskey squeezed the air from his lungs as he struggled to keep it down. Scott recovered the flask, a cork stopper shoved into place as he slipped it back into a pocket in his uniform. "Not gonna lose your breakfast, are you, sir?"

Harold wiped his mouth, overwhelmed by the stench of heat-bloated body parts. A thick cloud of flies hovered above the blood-splattered ground, creating a shimmer of iridescent green that drew the eyes of the recovery force, made up of British regulars and Colonial militia. A handful of Iroquois scouts rested in the shade of a thick grove of hardwood trees a dozen paces away, hands held over their mouths as they traded comments to hide their grins as they noted the looks of distress on the younger soldiers' faces. Newly exposed to violent death, standing in huddled groups, staring at what remained of the slaughtered men, stacked in three gory piles.

Harold closed his eyes, his voice thin, hands trembling despite his best efforts to hide his shock. "How could this have happened? They were so close." He opened his eyes, gazing at the dismembered remains. "They were—almost back. Almost back to our lines."

"Relaxed their guard, sir. Got careless, forgetting what they'd been taught." Scott turned his head and spit into a pool of blood surrounding a mound of gray and yellow viscera, scattering a cloud of flies for a moment before they settled back down. "Best time for it, sir, no matter which side of the tossed coin you're on, when it finally lands." Scott spun about and glared at a handful of young soldiers standing nearby with shovels and gunny sacks on their shoulders. A dozen others, older men with experience stood further back, stationed along the edge of the glade, ordered there to provide security. "Finish getting your comrades gathered up, lads." He paused, gritting his teeth. "And mind you take care to match every piece to the same bag, as best you can. Same as you'd want done were the situation reversed." Scott lowered his voice, speaking to Harold. "Not that it matters much in the end, sir. A hole's a hole for us bloody footies." He noted the grim expression on the young officer's face, along with a vacant expression in his light-colored eyes. "No disrespect intended, sir. *My* words, not yours."

Harold forced himself to his feet, then squared his shoulders. "None taken, Sergeant Major. Carry on."

Scott motioned with his hand toward the remnants of the three soldiers. "A truer description of this senseless butchery—has never been spoke, sir." He reached up and removed his hat, scratching his fingers through a short, rough-cut stubble of red hair starting to go over to gray along the sides. He reset it, then shot a glare at a young soldier who was reluctant to pick up one of the decapitated heads. "*Goddamn it, lad*! He willna *bite* ya!" He softened his tone. "Just get him in the bag, son, along with the rest of him."

Harold moved away, careful to stay clear of the native scouts tucked into shadowy pockets between a mix of hard and softwood trees. A grim smile puckered the line of his lips as he worked out the twist of meaning in Scott's words. Quite so, he thought to himself, we're all but carrion, in the end.

General's Quarters, Main Encampment

"Your report on the event was thorough, Lieutenant. The body of it—extremely detailed, one might say." The leader of the English force, General Aidyn MacLean, a tall man with a thin build and of an age with Sergeant Major Scott, aimed a piercing gaze at his young Second Lieutenant. Then he glanced over at Scott, nodding at a bottle of port sitting on a small table beneath an overhanging flap of canvas. "Do pour, Sergeant Major—one for us all."

Scott complied, downing his in a quick swallow then begging permission to leave, dismissed with a short wave of the general's hand. Aidyn looked at Harold, who was holding his glass, staring at it. "You do not imbibe, Lieutenant Knutt?"

Harold looked at the polished metal cup in his hand; the dark, red liquid reflecting his eyes. He shook his head. "If you will allow it, sir, I prefer not to—at this time."

"Understood, Lieutenant. Dreadful event, the ambuscade. A bad sign, happening this early in the year, promising trouble for us in the weeks ahead, the Frenchie's sending men this far forward to test our—"

"They were Wabanaki scouts, sir, along with a handful of irregulars. That's what our Iroquois scouts were saying to each other, while our men were busy recovering the—remains."

"You could understand them? I thought they spoke their own language when amongst themselves."

Harold nodded. "As do I, sir."

Aidyn cocked his head. "With fluency, Second Lieutenant?"

"Not yet, sir, though I do have an ear for languages. With French, Spanish, German, and Italian well in hand, along with a decent grasp of Scot's Gaelic, coming from my mother's side. Not that any of those are of much use here, sir, except the French."

Aidyn pointed at a chair, indicating Harold should sit, noting the look of exhaustion in the young man's face. He nodded, encouraging him to continue. Harold leaned back, hands in his lap, trying his best not to yawn or close his eyes. "My mother insisted on an education in languages, my father in full agree as he often transacted with clients throughout the continent. Exceptions made during the occasional outbreak of hostilities." Harold hesitated. "I apologize if I've overstepped my position, General."

The senior officer eyed him as he sipped his drink. "Not at all, Lieutenant. We are a shade or two beyond strict adherence to formality here, being at the tip of the blade as it were." The General's accent revealed a hint of lowland Scottish heritage. He was nearing middle-age, known among his men as a solid leader with a reputation for having an open mind when it came to seeking his subordinate's thoughts regarding strategic decisions. Unlike the myopic blindness of their former commander, responsible for leading them to disaster, insisting on use of European tactics against those of the French irregulars and their native allies, encountered in the thick woodlands in western Pennsylvania. The enemy forces, flexible in strategy with soldiers hidden behind trees and rocks; firing from dense cover at lines of English troops standing in the open, kind enough to wear bright red uniforms with white straps, providing excellent targets for a hail of musket balls and deadly flights of arrows.

Aidyn narrowed his wide-set eyes, set beneath thick, bristly eyebrows. "No doubt your father might have been carrying on a bit of trade *during* some of those outbreaks as well." His full lips widened in a lop-sided grin, tugged down a bit on one side by a thin scar on his chin. "Not that any of us gives a fig about that. It's how we've managed to survive in some measure of comfort ourselves, far from the pleasures of home. Trading, at times, with both sides against the middle." He nodded at a bottle of French brandy sitting on the table then reached up and scratched under the edge of his powdered wig. "You'll ignore that last bit as the heat, along with the news of this recent event, have loosened my tongue."

"Of course, sir." Harold waited a moment, then pressed on. "It's the second time you've used that expression." He waited for the General to look over. "*Event*, sir, to describe the butchery that happened this day."

Aidyn considered, then shrugged his thin shoulders. "It *is* an event to me, Lieutenant, my being removed from the *immediacy* of it, the men killed known in name and rank, not spirit and spit."

Harold bowed his head. "I did not mean to presume indifference on your part, sir."

"Quite right, Lieutenant. Think nothing of it." Aidyn paused, looking at the glass in his young officer's hand. "Are you certain you will not join me?" He held his own out, touching it to Harold's as he cleared his throat and made a toast. "To the glory of the British Empire, stacked on the back of three fine men, made to suffer the consequences for their service sworn to King and Country, in dangerous lands abroad."

On the March

The encampment was a bustle of activity. Tents rolled and lashed; support poles gathered into sheaves of dull-pointed spears. Latrine trenches filled in, along with dozens of fire pits. Large wagons packed with belongings, goods, and a vast array of necessities crucial for supporting an army in the field. The supplies carefully stacked in the center with makeshift awnings stretched above, providing a measure of protection from the elements for those too sick or injured to join the march on foot.

Harold stood in the center of a group of one-hundred men, most of them experienced English soldiers and Colonist militia, assigned by the General to lead an advance well ahead of the main body to protect them from ambush, as well as to secure several water crossings further along their line of march. A mix of native scouts and colonial irregulars were guiding them; a quiet group of hard-eyed men made up of hunters and fur-trappers who drifted through the shadowed woods to either side of the main column.

Sergeant Major Scott and the rest of the British soldiers had changed out of their standard uniforms into an assortment of drab clothing, matching the colonial militia's less conspicuous attire. Harold, encouraged by Scott to do the same, found the increased freedom of movement provided by the loose-fitting garb to be a welcome relief. He also liked the hefty weight of a large, hand-forged knife strapped to his side, a gift from the leader of the Colonial forces, Colonel George O'Malley: a bear of a man. Tall, with broad shoulders over a narrow waist, and thickly muscled arms and legs. The Colonial officer had presented it with a wide smile beneath dark brown eyes, calling it a Pennsylvania toothpick as he removed a wide-brim hat, wiping his forehead with a hand the size of a small ham. Harold noted he wore his hair close-cropped, in the same style as that of Sergeant Major Scott and most of the more experienced English and Colonial soldiers.

When Harold asked him why he kept his hair shorn down to the scalp, the Colonel reached over and grabbed him by his ponytail, giving it a sharp tug before letting go, a tight grin on his thick lips. "Removes a point of leverage, helping to keep your head on your neck. The savages will use a man's hair to yank his head back, exposing throat to their blade. Best to keep it short, or make certain it's queued in a knot and tucked under your hat."

Harold looked up as the large officer came over, having finished his consultation with the guides. "The first water crossing is but a few leagues ahead. There should be no enemy activity there, their scouts having left their mark on us with the recent killings, returning with tales of our continued encampment."

Harold pursed his lips, eyes narrowed in thought. "Might they not have left men posted at the crossing, suspecting we could be on the move?" He stared up at the taller officer, missing Sergeant Scott's slight roll of eyes.

George nodded, giving the question a moment of due deliberation before responding. "The Frenchies won't easily accept the possibility. They trust their scouts but have a low opinion of *our* capabilities. The disasters of the past painting us as weak-minded and hard-headed, fighting out in the open despite a heavy cost paid in blood." He frowned for a moment, rubbing a scar on his lower wrist, then brightened. "Though our new commander knows what needs be done to turn things on their heel. No doubt he'll devise better strategies as we go along, with God's grace."

Scott nodded in agreement while making the sign of the cross. "Aye, the General rose from the ranks alongside me, many years ago, starting out as a second lieutenant like yourself, sir." The veteran soldier grinned. "The men sensing a change in the wind since he's been given

command. Able to feel it through the cloud of mossies, left behind."
Scott looked at George, exchanging a grim smile as he nudged Harold
with his elbow. "At least *their* bite is mild, compared to that of the lead
balls and feathered shafts we'll soon be facing."

George turned away, rejoining the forward element of men. Scott
glanced down at the officer's pistol Harold carried in a fold of oiled
leather, strapped across his waist. He lowered his voice. "Mind you
check the priming of your piece, sir, making certain to keep it wrapped.
The air is humid hereabouts, so best to keep a weather eye out." Harold
nodded, his lips drawn tight in tension, despite the other two men's
loose chatter.

First Crossing

The air was still, without the least hint of a breeze. The sound of running water revealed itself with a steady hiss along the banks of the
first crossing, its level raised by recent rains. The muddy banks were
unmarked, showing no evidence of tracks left behind by man or beast
as native scouts stared into the thick growth across the watery barrier,
hands clenched on weapons of war, eyes fixed in hooded gazes. The rest
of the column came up from behind, compressed into nervous knots
of men, aware their lives might be in the balance. Then they waited on
the young British officer's decision, named by the General to command
the advance force.

Harold studied the crossing, aware of the tension from the men
around him. He turned to Scott and George. "The General's orders to
me were clear. To secure the crossings on *both* sides."

Colonel O'Malley shrugged. "Those are *your* orders, Lieutenant."
He paused. "What are *ours*?"

Harold hesitated, uncertain as to what he should do. Scott stepped
forward, his eyes on the far bank. "Sir. You made mention of sending
two small parties of men, one upriver and the other down, to cross and

make a reconnaissance before committing the main column. With a doubled firing line formed here, ready to fire in support should any trouble arise."

Harold let a soft sigh slip from through his lips. "Thank you, Sergeant Major Scott." He turned to George. "Colonel O'Malley, please direct the men under your command to do so. We shall proceed once your scouts have made certain the far side is clear of enemy forces."

"An excellent plan, Second Lieutenant Knutt." Colonel O'Malley nodded, then waved his hand at the mixed group of Iroquois and colonist scouts, the men splitting into two groups as they slipped away into the shadows.

Harold watched in nervous silence as Sergeant Major Scott placed the veteran soldiers into position along the edge of the streambank where they knelt, muskets primed and readied to fire as another line of men moved into place behind them, standing, forming a concentrated force of arms should the need for support arise. He lowered his voice, calling out to Scott, drawing his attention. "Make certain to take care, Sergeant Major." Harold blushed, adding: "Careful aim, that is, to avoid any harm to our own men."

The stocky soldier grinned, then turned his head, spitting a stream of tobacco juice into the water. Harold lowered his voice even further. "And I'd like to thank you, Sergeant Major, for your—"

"Quick response to your orders, sir? In support of a sound plan of action, expecting the best of outcomes while preparing for the worst?" Scott smiled, wiping his lips with the back of a scarred hand. "Just doing my duty, sir."

Third Crossing

The first crossing proved clear, as did the second. The advance party reached the third one late the next morning, their scouts reporting back that a large French force awaited them there, encamped on the far side.

Harold, joined by George and Scott, carefully made their way forward, staring in silence at thin columns of smoke from dozens of fires that reached up, tickling the dark-gray underbelly of thick clouds hanging low overhead, pregnant with the promise of rain.

Harold held his mixed force back in a dense section of woods, forming them into a defensible position between two large outcrops of rock. He moved away from the temporary encampment, finding a level spot between two large oaks where he knelt, stick in hand, staring at a section of forest floor he'd cleared of leaves. He knew a direct assault across the waterway would cost them dearly once their main force arrived and engaged with the enemy. The land on the far side of the waist deep river rose in a steep angle to the top of a thickly forested slope, providing a huge advantage to the enemy force. Their casualties would be high, with lines of soldiers decimated by French cannonade long before they could fight their way across the swift current and make their way to the top of the rise. Their own artillery ineffective to support them, due to the height of the opposing hillside. He pursed his lips as he used the stick to draw out a representation of the proposed battlefield, aware he would need to find a way to force a crossing with his small group of men in order to disrupt the deadly trap the French had waiting for General Aidyn.

Colonel O'Malley approached the inexperienced British officer, prepared to offer him a bit of seasoned advice, the general having made it clear the young man was to lead the advance force in name only, with himself making any final decisions on how and when to maneuver, supported by advice from Sergeant Major Scott.

"I trust the two of you will help guide the lad, keeping him in check while he gets a feel for the land and how to maneuver through it." Aidyn studied a small hand-drawn map based on detailed discussions with Colonel O'Malley and his group of local guides. "I will need this officer later on, when we are face to face with the French at their fort, standing in line formation." He folded the map and handed it to George. "Make certain to allow our young Second Lieutenant to lead, as is his right as the senior British officer, though it will be *you* holding the reins."

Harold nodded as Colonel O'Malley came up and leaned against one of large oaks. Then he returned to a study of the battleplan he'd worked out. It was based in part on tactics practiced in the squared confines of a large wooden box, one he'd assembled in the backyard of his family's manor when a child. His younger brother, Jackson, two years his junior, always in attendance, allowed to share command of the English troops.

The box, filled with sand, small rocks, and sticks, provided a perfect background for maneuvering of miniature soldiers placed in defined offensive or defensive positions. The two of them having pooled their earnings from work in the family warehouses, the monies used to acquire an enormous collection of lead figurines made up of stalwart foot soldiers forming linked lines of infantry, along with handfuls of individual officers on horseback, each one hand-painted with narrowed-eye exactitude.

Maneuvering the lines of men allowed the two of them to recreate each battle of every campaign recorded in a collection of military history books provided them by a doting uncle. Their father's younger brother, named Thomas, a small, thin-framed man, eager to spend time with his nephews discussing military encounters, working out how best to overcome the rare defeats while maximizing the outcome of numerous victories. Their minds focused on minimizing losses on their own side while inflicting them against handfuls of acorns and small pebbles serving as hordes of enemy forces in tightly bunched formations, advancing against stern-faced lines of English troops, refusing to break. Soldiers stepping forward into gaps in the front line as comrades fell before them, each man firing three times a minute as the foe swarmed in.

Twelve Years Earlier, Family Knutt Manor, Bristol

Harold pursed his lips as he carefully measured the three-deep line of infantry soldiers, their placement checked against a detailed drawing in the book held in his hand.

"They are out of position." His younger brother, Jackson, had come up from behind. He leaned in, his thin chin pressing against the top of Harold's shoulder, who slid to one side, easing the pressure. The evasive movement immediately taken advantage of by his brother, his hand outstretched to make an adjustment to the line of figurines, stopping when Harold coughed.

"It's a study of an *actual* battle, Jackie. Without our creating an *alternative* outcome. The officers there that day, unaware of the enemy forces in approach from beyond the hills, based on the history of the battle. As written."

Jackson frowned. "It shouldn't matter. Common sense enough of a guide as to where to station the lines, further up the hillside in staggered formation, providing—"

"Yes, Jackie, agreed. But again, that's *not* the lesson I intended to study this day."

The younger boy leaned back, hands clasped, head angled down. "I can't help myself, Harry, in seeing everything so clearly. It's—like a chessboard, the moves each side should make, obvious."

"Yes, Jackie. To you, they are. But not to all. Which is why I, and now you, are here to recreate the battle as it occurred, ending with the English forces overwhelmed by the enemy due to the lack of vision by their commanding officer."

Jackie frowned; his hands formed into small fists at his side. "What gain is there in a study of *failure?*"

Harold looked at his brother, noting his narrow jawline, a match to their mothers, along with his reed-thin build; ever a worry whenever the two of them would wrestle. Himself in constant fear a bone might be snapped, or a tendon torn, with Jackie ever heedless of potential for injury, throwing himself with wild-eyed abandon into the fray.

"You see the board, Jackie, but not into the mind of your opponent. You never do. Same as with chess. Your grasp of the game, far greater than others. Beyond that of our father." Harold paused. "And mine."

"Not true, Harry!" Jackson touched him on his broad shoulder. "You still can beat me, two out of five times. So far." Jackson looked up. "I'm only better because you've taught me everything you know." His eyes, light gray like their father's, gleamed as he tilted his head to one side. "You helped me to gain an advantage, in letting me start out by standing on your shoulders."

Harold reached over and tousled his brother's fine hair, streaked through with red strands tucked among mousy brown. "Fair enough, Jackie, and I accept the compliment, despite the fact you were born with a quicker mind than me."

Jackson nodded, then pursed his lips and pointed at the lead figure of an officer on a mount. "So, the game this day is to play out a losing strategy, due to the commander's failure to ascertain the disparity of forces in play. Those of his own, in measure against the unseen enemy."

"Yes." Harold grinned. "And the lesson we are to learn?"

Jackson stared at the book in Harold's hand. "I know it's not in there. Not in the after-action reports."

Harold tapped a finger against the side of his head, then reached over and did the same to Jackson. "You need to learn to see things from other people's perspective, Jackie. Not seeing them as your opponents, but picturing the battlefield through *their* eyes, understanding how they have come to their decision of when to defend, or to attack. To understand your adversary as well as yourself. Or come as close to it as you can."

"How?" Jackson tilted his head. "I mean, if they've not written their thoughts down, or if they've died during the engagement, how am I to discover—"

Harold leaned forward and looked into his brother's eyes. "By use of empathy, and intuition. In putting yourself in their shoes, sandals, or unshod feet and considering how they were feeling as they come to the field. Whether over-confident, frightened, sick, tired, or under duress due to any of a dozen other circumstances. By learning to use your *other* senses, Jackie. The ones most people don't realize they have, lying close to hand."

Jackson's expression brightened. "Like when we play war games against your friends, beating them soundly, with you knowing where they're going to be heading and the two of us lying in wait to ambush them." He gave his older brother a warm smile. "You and I, the two Knutt boys, ever victorious."

"Yes, Jackie. You and I, against the world."

Jackson lowered his eyes, then reached out and placed his hand on his brother's lower arm. "I know I'm smarter than you, Harry. But when it comes to being a leader, I'm more like them." He nodded at the officers. "Focused on my own capabilities, without appreciating those players on the other side of the gameboard. Like you said, it's a weakness in my game."

Harold pursed his lips. "Didn't say it like that, Jackie. Not exactly."

"But it's true." Jackson let go of his brother's arm. "And that's why you'll be a great leader someday. Because you do see things from both sides. From *all* sides. Finding an advantage, every time."

ᴔᴇᴧ

Harold sighed, the conversation with his brother a whisper in his ears. He could almost feel the press of Jackie's fingers on his lower arm as he focused on the drawing on the shadowed ground. The mock-up of the crossing was filled with various objects placed in representation of the forces on both sides, allowing him to consider every possibility from the viewpoint of the enemy commander.

"We're the pebbles, I take it." George's voice came from over Harold's shoulder as the large man leaned down, his thick arms crossed on his chest, head canted to one side as he stared at the ground. "And the Frenchies—are the acorns."

Harold nodded. "Yes. And the small spruce cones off to one side represent your mix of native and local guides, along with most of your irregulars."

"Moving upriver to cross over, if I read the ground correctly. Then heading inland to there." George pointed across the river to the top of the ridge.

Harold nodded. "Your fur trappers mentioned a place upstream where they can move across at night. Fires to be kept blazing here—" He reached out and tapped the center of the cleared space with a finger. "—as a signal to the French of our intention to wait for our main force to arrive. A diversion, one that should allow our advance force, once across the river, to circle around the rise of land, coming in from behind the enemy's upper defensive line where their cannons have been placed, just below the crest of the hill, providing clear sightlines down into the crossing and the false enemy encampment just back of the river, across the way." He saw a look of confusion start to spread across the colonial officer's face. "It only holds half their force, left in bivouac to draw us into the killing ground, before fading away uphill, joining the main line of resistance above."

Harold paused, giving the Colonel time to absorb the plan. When he continued, his voice was steady, confident in tone. "Once in position, our advance group will take cover until two hours before break of day, positioned to attack the upper camp once we begin crossing down here and receive fire from the French sentries. Then our advance force will attack the enemy by surprise, seizing the cannons and using them to suppress the French effort to retake them, while we cross the river here, making a rapid advance through the French encampment, charging uphill to join our men above. The bypassed French soldiers will be forced to form up to make their own advance, ending up caught in a deadly hail of shellfire from their own guns, along with musket fire from our relief force here, on our side of the river, harassing the French while they try to form up."

Harold looked up with a grin, his wide-brimmed hat shadowing his face as he checked George's expression, getting a slow nod of appreciation in return. "It is to be a dual assault, made on their second line of defense from front and rear. The bulk of their force across the river left behind to—wither on the vine."

George shrugged. "And how, pray tell, are the spruce-cones going to accomplish their assigned role, stumbling around in the dark of a moonless night?"

Harold chuckled, his voice relaxed. "By removal of their blindfolds."

George gave Harold an incredulous look. "*Blindfolds?*"

"Exactly. I've directed Sergeant Major Scott to pair the advance party with our British regulars. The blind being led by the sighted, if you will. A strategy used by a Dutch force some years ago, attempting the same thing as us."

George shook his head, eyes wide in amazement at the plan. "Winning their battle, I take it?"

"Actually, no." Harold pursed his lips. "The night crossing worked out well enough, but support from the second force crossing the next day faltered, leaving the first group exposed." Harold stared at the diagram. "All of them killed or captured."

O'Malley cocked an eyebrow. "Leading you to make this attempt now, in order to prove it would have worked?"

"Yes. With our main element attacking at night, well before dawn."

George studied the lines drawn in the dirt, understanding flooding his mind. "Using the same method; blindfolds kept on during the day to improve vision at night, gaining an advantage for us."

"Providing the advantage of surprise for *both* groups, making a coordinated assault."

Scott walked up and waited until Harold noticed him, then saluted. "I have the men paired off, sir. Our regulars leading the advance party around in their blinders to the slit trenches and back again, assisting them with their ablutions. It is a—humorous diversion, the men's attention turned from what lies before them." Scott hesitated. "Before us all, sir."

Harold nodded. "Get them settled down, Sergeant Major. Blindfolds kept on until well after dark, when they will sit up this night with no fires, only those we'll keep burning in the woods just back of the crossing, away from the river. The men made to stay awake so they'll sleep on the morrow. Once night falls again, the ranging group will move upriver and cross. Then we will remove our own blindfolds and make ready to force the crossing before dawn, next day."

◦℮〜

The air was still, the treetops motionless, branches draped over the far edge of a narrow section of the river, its flow slowed by ten large trees fallen across it from the near bank. Their thick trunks, with large, splayed limbs still attached to stumps cut partway through, holding the thick trees in place, creating the beginnings of a natural dam. The advance force crossed the river, weapons and clothing held over their heads until they reached the opposite bank. Ten men with saws in their hands followed close behind and began falling a like number of trees from the opposite side of the river. They ignored the advance force, who quickly dressed then moved inland, heading toward the rise of land beyond. By the time they had cleared the area, ten more large trees were lying in the water, joined to their brethren across the way in limb-tipped embrace.

⌒e⌒

"It's time. Get them up." Harold started to move past George and Scott, heading to the bank of the river past dozens of burnt-out faux campfires, thin trails of smoke rising in desultory columns of gray. George stared, blindfold removed, amazed at the details he was able to make out, his eyes fully adjusted to the low light. We are owls, he thought to himself, ready for a silent swoop across the water to feast on mice dressed in white uniforms. He reached out and touched the young English officer on his arm, his voice soft. "You will not be leading us."

Harold spun around, mouth open to protest, cut off before he could utter a word when Scott leaned in and whispered in his ear. "We have decided it, the two of us. You are to remain here to lead a relief column if needed, while directing aimed fire across the river from a doubled line of men where it may do the most harm to the Frenchies as they stumble from their tents and form up in pursuit of us, once we have rushed through their encampment."

Harold kept his voice low, facing the two men, a determined look on his face. "I am in *command*, and responsible for leading my men- "

"You are in command *here*, Second Lieutenant Knutt." George let go of Harold's arm and stepped back. "Responsible to lead us through this attempt of a restorative victory in honor of some weak-kneed Dutchies over the—" He paused; his head angled as he looked at Harold. "You never said who it was they were fighting against."

Harold frowned, his pride pricked, though he forced himself to consider the change in plan, seeing it through the other men's more experienced eyes. "Us, I mean, the English. Over a hundred years ago."

George nodded; the gesture mirrored by Scott. "Then you must remain here and make certain *we* do not falter, as happened to them. The two of us will lead the first wave through their encampment on the run, while you and the rest of the men keep the pressure on them from here."

Scott nodded in agreement. "We will not stop, sir, until we have cleared the lower ground in a rush uphill to their second line of defense. The bypassed soldiers, roused from their sleep, will start forming up, with you pestering them with a bit of lead while we join the advance group and prepare the Frenchies cannons for a repulse of their assault."

O'Malley gave Harold a firm grip on his shoulder, getting a solemn faced nod of agreement. The large man smiled. "Once we begin firing the big guns, you can cross, taking care to stay well back from the bottom of the slope. We'll be using canister rounds with short fuses, firing into their formations as they move to dislodge us. So, make certain to direct your group to pick their targets with care, marking officers as the priority."

"Targeting of officers goes against any standard of—" Harold paused, appreciating the odds stacked against them. "I—understand." He looked both men in the eyes. "I would not have failed you, or the men, in leading the way."

Scott grinned, reaching out and clasping the young officer's upper arm. "Noted, sir. And your time will come to front the line, but not now. We are heavily outnumbered, and this is to be a movement made at rapid pace, needing a light and responsive touch on the reins held here. Sir."

Harold nodded, then looked down at the ground, every detail revealed as if viewed on an overcast morning, though daybreak was a good two hours away. He sighed, accepting his responsibility to lead from behind. "The water should have dropped below your knees, with things having gone as planned upriver with our intrepid beaver brigade. Go slowly, taking care not to splash, alerting their sentries. You should be able to pass through their camp before they know what is happening."

"Yes. And then make a dash to their upper defenses, leaving those bypassed to stew in the bucket of hellfire they designed for us." Colonel O'Malley motioned to Sergeant Scott, who headed back into the woods to gather the men.

Bloody Crossing

The rank odor of burnt gunpowder mingled with that of spilled blood, drifting across the ground in a thick mist that nosed against an angled slope leading to the top of the ridgeline above.

Harold stood at the bottom, having picked his way between small holes punched into the ground by French cannon shells, filling with muddy water from a steady rain that had started falling since break of day. Dozens of bodies in white uniforms lay strewn about, as if toys dropped from the careless hands of bored children, some of them landing in the limbs of trees bordering the edge of thick woods just beyond the boot trampled earth of the enemy encampment.

As he passed through the carnage, Harold's mind grew numb from grief, seeing the dead soldiers as sons, husbands, fathers, or friends, posed in unnatural angles, their legs and arms flung to the sides or curled beneath shattered chests in stiffened embrace. He knew they had gone to their deaths having awoken from dreams of home as his men passed through their camp. Rising to their feet, most only half-dressed, coming face to face with the nightmare of close-quarter violence as shells began falling amongst them.

A wave of nausea rose from within, Harold forced to swallow it down, his eyes filled with tears at the horror he'd unleashed. A whirlwind of devastation, spun from his creative mind, proving this was no longer a game played by bored brothers in a sandbox filled with lead figures, but one where men and boys had died in a wilderness they did not know or have any love for.

He felt a rush of shame flood across his face as several of his men, standing guard over a host of enemy prisoners, turned, and saluted him. Then they began to cheer, hats removed and held up in waves of blue and red colors, knowing a great victory had just occurred. The man who'd led them to and through it, passing before them. Harold clamped a tight-lipped smile in place, hat in hand, raised in recognition of the honor being shown, the men's cheers repeated by soldiers stationed further up the hill in a rush of hurrahs, echoing a name Harold realized was meant for him. His stomach turned inside out as he slipped beneath the branches of a fir tree and vomited, shoulders shaking, soul shattered by the words: *"Red Fox! Red Fox! Hero of the bloody crossing!"*

The commanding officer of the French force stared back at Harold, his eyes dark, without expression, face drained of color due to the solid overcast. George and Scott had fallen in beside him as he approached the group of senior French officers; a huddle of depressed looking men standing beneath a waxed cloth overhang, out of the rain. They were silent, heads bowed in respect, unlike their commander who stood stiff backed with a shocked look in his eyes, as if unable to process how the tide of certain victory had so quickly turned against him.

Harold stepped forward and gave the higher ranked officer a polite nod. Then he squared his shoulders and addressed the commander in flawless French, with a tone of confidence he did not feel. "I am Second Lieutenant Harold Knutt, of his Majesty's Second Foot. You have my assurance we will follow all protocols regarding your personal security and that of your men. We are treating your wounded alongside our own. My request made yesterday to our main force to send surgeons forward. Word will be sent to your commander once we reach your main fortifications, arrangements made for your parole, once sworn to a cessation of personal military activities against British, Colonial, or allied native forces."

The French officer stepped forward, a thin smile on his lips. "We have *already* sent word to our commander, letting him know of your— unorthodox crossing. No doubt he will soon arrive, offering you as warm a welcome in return."

Harold heard George cough. He turned his head, watching as the large man smiled, his long arm raised then brought down. A group of native guides and irregulars stepped out of the woods, leading three men in white uniforms, their hands tied before them, heads hung in shame. Harold looked at the French officer. "It appears our capable allies came across these fine fellows and invited them here to enjoy our hospitality."

The French officer considered a moment, then offered Harold his sword, prepared to accept defeat. He was middle-aged, slightly built, with dark eyes that searched Harold's face as if trying to understand how this youthful, low-ranked English officer had come to be standing before him. "I will concede victory to you, one that is well-deserved."

"I am at your service, sir." Harold bowed his head slightly, respectful of the superior rank of the officer, whose uniform bore the insignia of a colonel.

The other man gave him another thin-lipped smile. "You are to be commended for your excellent command of our language. Your accent is—almost clean enough to fool the ear."

Harold smiled back, aware his French was far superior to the officer's English. "You will agree to my terms?"

The French commander waved a hand. "Of course, as is the prac- tice between *civilized* men, serving their countries according to the established rules of organized conflict." The much shorter man stared up at George, a sneer on his thin lips. "Unlike what happened to *some* of our officers, taken captive during past campaigns and butchered by those—outside the direct oversight of English military authority."

Harold gave the impolite man a cold smile, interceding before George could respond to the insult, aware of the large man's stiffening posture. "The papers of parole will be drawn up; copies readied for dispatch to each of our military registries with signatures affixed and witnessed, according to the proscribed exchange of officers captured during armed conflict."

"Yes, yes." The defeated Frenchman waved his hand in dismissal. "You are quite diligent in your duties. Let us proceed." He started to turn away, stopping when Harold called out, responding in French, his voice tight with anger.

"Your name, sir, and rank, as is the protocol between leaders meeting to discuss terms. *And* to accept one side's surrender, which has not been formerly offered—*or* accepted." Harold noted the flicker of a grin on Scott's face from the corner of his eye, knowing the veteran soldier understood the tone, if not the full meaning of his response to the defeated officer's rude behavior.

The small Frenchman drew himself up to his full height, still several inches shorter than Harold, his response made in English, with a heavy accent. "I am Colonel Francois de Rigaud, son of Pierre de Riguad, marquis de Vaudreuil-Cavagnial, Governor General of New France. I offer you my conditional surrender, Lieutenant. As you have so—eloquently requested."

"*Second* Lieutenant Harold Knutt. Sir."

The colonel returned a warm smile, his eyes filled with icy anger. "My most humble apologies. You have my conditional surrender, *Second* Lieutenant—Harold Knutt."

Harold repressed a smile of his own, aware he'd just added a new chapter to his story.

Madonna, Standing in the Sun

A soft gleam of coppery-gold drew Harold's eye; result of a ray of sunlight slipping between overhanging clouds, fanning across a loose spiral of red hair that framed the cheek of a tall woman in a plain dress and tight waistcoat, her face angled to the side as she spoke with a wounded soldier, sitting on the ground beside her while she tended to his wounds. She was one of a dozen colonial camp followers sent forward in haste to provide support to English and French surgeons in repair of bodies damaged by iron shards, lead balls, and honed steel blades.

Harold stopped in his tracks, struck by the sight of her blood-smudged cheek, full lips poised beneath the bluest eyes he'd ever seen. She was of a height with him, a strip of linen around her forehead that struggled to contain a thick braid of flaxen hair, twisted in a tight spiral atop her head, a beam of sunlight painting her cheekbones in a half-halo of soft light.

"Madonna," Harold whispered, unable to look away, even as she felt the pressure of his stare and glanced over, then returned to dressing the wounded soldier's arm, nationality unknown as he was bare to the waist, wearing the same white colored pants as were his own.

Scott came up from behind and stopped, noting his young officer's attention was elsewhere. He waited a few moments, then coughed, his face set in a stoic expression as Harold turned around. "Sir, the General sent a rider forward with orders for your immediate return to the main column." He pointed across the river. "He's waiting on the far bank with a spare mount, hoping you will know how to ride. Sir."

"Thank you, Sergeant Major. I am—familiar with the process." Harold's eyes widened as he considered Scott's words. "But what about the disposition of—"

"Two officers of the line have been ordered forward to shoulder your responsibilities, sir. We will be under their orders the moment you cross over and are relieved of your command."

"Then I should make haste to do so." Harold paused. "And I thank you again, Sergeant Major, for your constructive advice and support during these past few days."

"Just following orders, sir. Your orders, and *damn* good ones they've been." Scott waited until Harold turned away, letting him take one step before coughing again, bringing him to a stop. "If you will allow a suggestion, sir. A bit of professional advice, as it were."

Harold nodded, not willing to turn around, knowing he would be unable to prevent another searching stare made in the woman's direction. "Yes, Sergeant Major?"

"About you making haste, sir. I strongly suggest you do *not*. You should comport yourself as the commanding officer in charge of a mixed force. One having made a successful crossing against a numerically superior force, dug in with cannon. An impossible task, accomplished with few losses on our side and a complete rout of our foe." Scott paused, taking a moment to spit, watching as it ran into a bloody footprint. "I would strongly suggest you cross the river with a proud, if not entirely haughty stride, going up to those officers and accepting from them the acclaim you so richly deserve. As is your *privilege* as an officer, and responsibility as a leader of men, reflecting that self-same glory back onto the shoulders of those you've sent into battle. Sir."

Harold nodded, then moved ahead until he reached the trampled edge of the riverbank. He stared across its steady flow, then squared his shoulders and, with his eyes focused straight ahead, ignored the thick guide rope set up as he made his way across, a satisfied look on his weary face.

CHAPTER FIVE

Encampment, Bloody Crossing, End Of July 1758

Promotion to the Rear

"*Damnable* luck, of the *best* kind." The General's face lit up in a blaze of pleasure. "Victory, snatched from the jaws of what might have been a terrible defeat." Aidyn moved away from a map hanging from a tripod support, small weights attached to its bottom to keep it steady against the press of his finger. He stared at Harold with narrowed eyes. "Did you consider the full range of consequences should the attack from the forward element sent behind the enemy's second line have failed to occur as planned?"

Harold waited two heartbeats before he answered. "I knew the guides sent to cross upriver were familiar with the ground, holding an advantage in being able to see through the thick woods. I expected them to be in position well before our own advance at the main crossing."

"A risk. One that could have ended in disaster." The General hesitated as he noted a satisfied look that fell into place on Harold's face. "You have something *further* to add, Second Lieutenant Knutt?"

"I do, sir. The advance party sent a runner back to the woodcutters

I'd deployed at the upper crossing, waiting there before returning to report that all had gone as planned."

Aidyn angled his head. "Woodcutters?"

"Men sent upstream to fall trees across the narrowest section of the river, slowing its flow and helping to lower the depth of the—"

"*Damnable* good plan! *Well done*, Lieutenant Knutt."

"Sir?" Harold's face showed his confusion at the General's error in misstating his rank.

"You've been promoted, Lieutenant; the commission paid by an— anonymous benefactor, making it a permanent position. No reduction in rank upon separation from service due to injury or, God forbid, your death."

Harold opened then closed his mouth, watching as the General reached for a bottle, removed the cork, and poured a healthy dram of whiskey into two glasses, handing one to him with a nod to drink. Once the glasses were empty, Aidyn grinned. "I'm from humble beginnings, much as yourself. Improvements in my family's financial situation allowed purchase of commissions in his Majesty's army, whenever offered promotion in rank by my commanding officers. Each coming with a steep price to pay. But as they say, rank doth have its privileges."

Harold nodded as he considered how quickly his life had spun about; still a neophyte in the service, having lucked into a victory that could have ended his career, not to mention his life and those of the men who'd cheered him with confidence in their eyes. Seven of them left to stare into the great divide, their faces frozen in horror, or awe, depending on how they came to meet their last moments.

"Lieutenant?" Aidyn kept his voice low, noting his newly promoted officer's reluctant attitude.

"Sir?"

"Do you not agree, Lieutenant Knutt? I seem to remember you mentioning a family business, when we first spoke at length."

"Yes, sir. My father owns a commodities company, with my uncle in partnership."

"To be split among you and your cousins one day, I assume."

"There are no male cousins. And there has never been such an offer made or requested by me."

Aidyn sighed, nodding at Harold with a wry smile. "As is the fate of families with tangible assets and a prodigal son. A decision made whether he is to be left to stand apart as his *own* man, or be bound to familial servitude, toiling evermore in a parent's or relative's shadow."

"You have stated it correctly, sir."

"Enough for now. I can see you're about to collapse from exhaustion. There's a cot in the side tent. You will use of it this night and wake refreshed and ready to go on the morrow. We will begin our march to the French fortification then, enjoying use of the magnificent road they've prepared through the wilderness for us." Aidyn reached out and touched Harold on his upper arm. "There will be time enough once we reach it to discuss next steps. Congratulations again on your victory and well-deserved promotion, Lieutenant Knutt."

Beginning at the End

The English army had finally cleared the last river crossing; thick ropes used to haul their cannons to the top of the ridge, added to those captured from the French. The main body of the allied army was on the move west, along a road cut through the forest by the now defeated French force. When they reached its end, they would meet the enemy on open field, if offered battle. If not, they would lay siege to the fort.

Harold nodded, watching a flurry of activity taking place all around him as Sergeant Major Scott returned from making his morning report, the veteran's voice tight with frustration. "We're to serve as a rear guard for the train of supplies. From a position at its *ass* end, in trod through *shite* from man and beast alike."

Harold smiled. "Thank you, Sergeant Major, for your *earthy* observation." He sighed. "I for one, am not the least displeased by our assignment, and consider it to be a welcome change."

"Of course, sir. As you say." Scott cocked an eyebrow, noting his young officer had focused his full attention on one of the women, huddled amongst a group of camp followers trailing the last of the heavy wagons, six oxen straining to move it up the steep hill of the crossing. The women were a blend of young, middle aged, and old, holding their skirts mid-calf to avoid a thick slurry of mud and dung from dozens of officer's horses and over a hundred and fifty heavily muscled beasts of burden.

A broad smile blossomed on Scott's full lips. "I'm certain there'll be plenty enough going on here at the tail end of the British lion, sir, to occupy your time."

Harold couldn't keep himself from gazing at the tall women standing slightly apart from the others, her unbound hair hanging over wide shoulders, although there was no ray of sunlight this day to highlight its coppery flow. She glanced over, a wry smile showing on her lips as Harold looked away, embarrassed at being caught out, again. He knew the General did not allow fraternization between his Majesty's officers and camp followers, disqualifying him from any chance of approach, though the thought of it as forbidden troubled him.

Harold rubbed his eyes, yawning, tired to the bone from the last two days of endless activity. The General had ordered him to prepare assignments for the rear element of the three-mile-long column; a task that had required him to go over supply manifests, assign column location of dozens of wagons laden down with the various materials needed to support an army in the field, along with responsibility for the proper disposition of the group of soldiers placed under his command, providing security. The ranging force he'd led at the river, being called "bloody crossing" for the slaughter of French infantry that had occurred there, reassigned by the General, sent back to their original platoons.

Harold's assignment to the rear of the line of march had been noted by a group of superior officers, calling him a mother hen to a gaggle of clucking chicks, their disdainful smiles and cocked eyebrows reminding him of his rightful place in the formal military hierarchy; one he was but a junior member of.

"A word, sir. If you'll allow it."

Harold turned toward a female voice at his side; the woman he'd been staring at, again, having made her way over. He stepped back, removed his hat, and bowed. When he straightened up, he fought to keep from blushing in shame. Failing. "Of course, Miss. I'm Second Lieutenant—I mean, I'm now First Lieutenant." He paused; trying to collect himself, his tongue thick in his mouth. "Knutt, Miss. I mean to say, First Lieutenant Knutt, Miss. At your service."

The tall woman with slim build returned a smile that caused the blush on his face to deepen. She looked directly into his eyes. "More a Ma'am, than a Miss, the truth of it be told." She smiled again. "Congratulations, First Lieutenant Harold Knutt, on your recent promotion. One richly deserved, from what I've been told."

Harold nodded. "You are much too kind, Madam."

"Ma'am will do, or Maggie, as I'm known among the women." She paused, turning her eyes on a group of officers on horseback as they passed along the column, their voices loud as they exchanged jibes and japes, amusing themselves with the sound of their own voices. "The lot of us, thank God, ignored by the likes of *them*." She pointed with her chin; her blue eyes narrowed in a condescending sneer. "Until some idiot in this muddling procession does something foolish, leaving men injured and in need of attending to. Those of us with medical experience called forward when the bloody fools remember our true value in this sorry enterprise."

Harold hesitated to respond, thinking he might be one of the officers she was referring to with her tersely worded statement. He cleared his throat, drawing her attention. "Your efforts of late, in providing care of the wounded were remarkable." Harold stared into her eyes, unable to look away, or to stop himself from speaking. "Our wounded, as well those of the French side, have you to thank for their recovery." He blushed again, lowering his eyes. "I mean, of course, *all* those who aided the surgeons. Not only yourself—though you were—"

She reached out and touched him on his forearm, her smile spreading to the corners of her full lips. "I take your meaning, First Lieutenant Knutt."

"My thanks, Madam, or rather Ma'am, as you prefer."

"I would prefer Meghan, if your General's silly rules will allow it." Meghan paused. "And *your* given name?"

"Harold, Ma'am. From Bristol. In England. But I beg you to address me as—"

She cut him off, a perturbed look in her depthless eyes. "Lieutenant. Especially when in public. Because of the General's rules."

Harold nodded; his voice low. "Yes, Ma'am. The rules."

There was a long pause while Harold checked on the disposition his men; a make-shift platoon made up of soldiers with no real experienced in armed conflict, sprinkled in with handfuls of hard-core disciplinary cases whose backs had felt the lash. They marched in two long, thin lines on both sides of the heavy wagons, exchanging ribald comments with sick or wounded soldiers, unable to walk. The bawdy back and forth brought a look of concern to the newly commissioned First Lieutenant's face.

Meghan noticed his frown. "You seem troubled, Lieutenant Knutt. Is it there anything you require from our medical stores?"

"I'm fine. Was only a passing thought." Harold bowed his head. "I must return to my duties, Ma'am, unless there is something further you require of me."

Meghan bowed her head. "I only wanted to let you know that your performance at the crossing was remarkable. A great victory, achieved due to your strategic plan and courageous efforts in battle."

Harold could feel the warmth returning to his face. "They were somewhat less than courageous, Ma'am, with me safely positioned in the rear, directing relief where needed and little more. It was Sergeant Major Scott and Colonel O'Malley who led—"

"Colonel 0'Malley was kind enough to fill me in on the—salient details of your contribution, the morning after the assault. Held in strict military confidence, I can assure you."

"He—should not have done so, Ma'am."

Meghan tiled her head to one side. "It was due to a request from me to him, Lieutenant. Your intense stare in my direction as you were preparing to turn over your command, of such—intensity, it provoked a need to seek out information from the Colonel, as to your identity."

Harold, surprised by her direct approach, regarded her with a growing awareness of her intelligence and thoughtful disposition. "My apologies, Ma'am, to both you and the Colonel. As to my untoward attention that morning, I beg your forgiveness, as I never meant to cause any measure of—"

"There's no need to apologize, Lieutenant Knutt. You were simply a victim of biology. A common enough affliction in people, I can assure you. Whether one is in—Bristol, or *here*, people being much the same the world over, Lieutenant Knutt. Would you not agree?" Meghan grinned, then turned away, skirts gathered in her work-stained hands, revealing her lower legs as she headed back to the end of the column.

Harold was unable to look away, following her with his eyes as she rejoined the rest of the women, who immediately surrounded her, their voices clear in the still air, offering comments that caused some of the hard-case soldiers nearby to blush and look away. A voice at his shoulder startled him, requiring all his inner will not to react in surprise.

Scott leaned in. "She's a right bonny lass. Would you nae agree, sir?"

"She is *definitely* that, Sergeant Major." Harold turned and looked at the world-worn visage of his subordinate. "And, as such, I find myself placed in an uncomfortable position, the men no doubt having marked our discourse. News of it soon to reach the ears of our commander, carried there by officers eager to see me ground under their heels."

Scott turned his head and spit, then wiped his lips with the back of his hand as he stared over at the slow-moving procession. "She's George O'Malley's sister, sir. Last name of Patterson, still using her married name. Her husband and son, seven years of age, lost in a settlement raid, two years ago. Herself taken by the natives, then ransomed back to her brother." He gave Harold a sly grin. "She's been with him on every campaign, since. And, as she is related to the commanding officer of the Colonial militia, plus a lady of impeccable repute, she is *exempt* from the General's list of rules, sir."

"I see." Harold gazed over at the group of women as they disappeared around a turn in the wheel-battered trail. "The only question remaining now is—am I?"

Scott shrugged, then spit again. "There's the rub, sir, so to speak, leaving you to decide if the risk is worth the reward in daring to plumb the depth of the water before you." Scott reached out, clasping the younger man's shoulder, his voice shifting to Scottish Gaelic. "A bheil ios agad ciamar a ni thu snamhr?"

"Aye, Sergeant Major." Harold nodded. "I do indeed know how to swim."

CHAPTER SIX

Outside French Fort, Mid-August 1758

Waiting in Line

An open plain, baked solid by a steady wind under bright sunlight and covered in thick clumps of grass and tangled knots of stunted trees, created a difficult advance for foot-soldiers and officers on horseback. Artillerymen, stationed on both ends of the battleground, knelt behind large guns with squinted eyes, making final adjustments in elevation, prepared to light fuses. The cannons kept silent, for now.

Long lines of soldiers in uniforms, their muskets shouldered, stood at both ends, each man quietly assessing their odds of survival, considering the possibility of a fate worse than death; left maimed in body, missing a leg or an arm. Officers on horseback held their position slightly behind, hands tugging on reins to check anxious steeds as they evaluated the need to show fearlessness in battle against whispers of self-preservation that, left unchecked, might lead to charge of cowardice. They knew their careers hung in the balance, with future rise in rank based on their own performance and that of the men assigned them. The same deliberations made by the two commanders, standing in mirrored pose at each end of the thousand pace field.

Harold's company, three lines of soldiers in red and white kit, were part of a long battleline formed of flesh and blood. They stood in close ranks on the extreme right of the battleground, as seen from the English commander's position, Harold assigned to defend the flank, his men positioned on a steep slope, one hundred strong, close to the edge of a thick forest framed by a massive outcrop of white limestone.

Harold stared at the enemy formation, noting the French forces outnumbered them two to one, despite the loss of their advance force and artillery pieces at the bloody crossing. The French infantry were joined by a large contingent of their native allies, now massing in the shadows of the bordering woods, their war cries slipping through the heated air as paint-faced warriors expressed their eagerness to feast on the far end of his company of dedicated, though increasingly nervous men.

Harold forced himself to appear relaxed; prepared for his first real taste of battle against a foe met face to face. His own life held little value, when measured against potential failure to lead them with resolve. Scott leaned over, his shoulder touching Harold's, his voice kept low while he scanned the line of their men with veteran eyes, measuring their morale.

"I did not question your decision to make a late-night requisition of several, small-bore cannons, sir. Nor raise my eyebrow when you had the men place them, along with a stash of cannister shells and powder, on top of the outcrop of rock lying between here and yonder thick wood line." Scott turned his head and spit. "Nor did I ask the reason for your order to the men for release of their bayonets from their hesitant grasp. The steel blades, firmly lashed to the ends of long poles, now stashed on the upper ledges of said rock. And I have no doubt you've some plan in mind to deal with the what-ifs and how-to-dos that come along with the chaos of battle, once joined. But the men and I *are* wondering as to the placement of tar-daubed logs along our assigned section of the line, believing you have gone mad from the heat."

Harold swallowed the knot of trepidation in his throat, a grim smile finding his lips. "The false cannons and men pretending to man them are meant to encourage the swarm of native foes in howling approach to stay as far into the woods as possible, before curling around the edge of the rock fortress on our immediate right. As well as to help bend the flank of the French lines, currently in steady advance, suggesting they move a wee bit further to our left. A move they should be happy to comply with, hoping to break our line so their native allies can swarm us under from the right flank. At least—that is what I'd be planning to do if I were their commander."

Scott shook his head, another stream of tobacco juice let to paint the ground, his jaw working on a large chaw in his mouth, a sign of his own nervous anticipation of the fight to come. He frowned, wiping his lips with the back of a brown-stained hand. "Another of your *sandbox strategies*, then."

Harold nodded, keeping his eyes fixed on the shimmer of light reflecting from hundreds of polished steel bayonets as they drew near. "With an original twist, Sergeant Major. One of my very own."

Scott joined him in watching as the enemy advanced in silent lock-step, officer's shouting orders, intent on maintaining the integrity of the bunched formation. "Like use of the woodcutters to lower the river at bloody crossing."

Harold checked on the disposition of his own men, noting their hands clenched on rifles without bayonets attached, their expressions revealing uneasiness at not having a half-meter length of honed steel to meet the enemy's eventual charge. He shrugged, swallowing a knot of fear, his stomach contracting as the line of white uniforms resolved into individual faces, closing to within two hundred paces. "More or less. The outcrop intended for use as a fortress of final repulse. The cannons we left positioned there last night, high enough to provide for plunging fire into the enemy's flank once they've closed the distance."

Scott released a long sigh. "*If* they follow your plan as expected. A risky decision, if you don't mind my saying so, sir."

"It is, Sergeant Major." Harold looked over from the side of his eyes. "*If* our men waver, refusing to follow my lead when the moment to execute my plan arrives."

Scott clenched his jaw, his eyes glaring as he gave Harold a hard look. "I assure you they'll obey your orders, sir, or feel the *tip* of my boot up their fear tightened *arses*."

The two men returned their attention to the front, eyes drawn to lines of grim-faced soldiers downrange. Then Harold shifted his attention to the gleam of the polished steel swords as officers on horseback waved them in the air, their voices raised, encouraging their men as they continued the long march uphill, cannons beginning to sing out from each end of the long field.

Scott leaned in, his lips touching Harold's ear, barely heard above the background noise of the battle. "Going exactly as you planned, sir, with the Frenchies shifting to avoid our false cannonades." The sound of musket fire rippled along the first line of red-jacketed soldiers; a buzzing swarm of lead bees sent in the direction of their white-flocked foes, slapping into chests, abdomens, thighs, arms, and faces. Another round soon followed, after a measured count of twenty seconds as the English lines played another chorus. Lead balls began to arrive in return, most of them peppering the ground with small pockets of dust, well short of their marks. British and colonist soldiers busying themselves in plucking at twists of paper tubes filled with pre-measured powder, and musket ball. Rammed home by steel rods, held in fingers stained with black-powder residue.

The two armies, now fully joined on the field of battle, stopped and traded volleys of musket fire, the buzzing whine of balls mingled with sounds of men screaming in anger or pain. Their howling punctuated by the dull thud of cannons, a whimpering of shells slipping through the air, arriving in geysers of earth that erupted in gray blossoms of death, sprouting between and among lines of men in steady march into the chaos in build. Puffs of gray-black smoke drifted above the mayhem as cannister shells exploded in the air, showering men with a rain of hot fragments slipping into stern-faced soldiers, their uniforms stained dark red as handfuls of them grimaced, falling in twists of torn bodies onto the ground, the lines of men following behind stepping over them as they marched on, replacements slipping into place, urged forward by officer's commands to fill the gaps, as spatters of dirt and pieces of former comrades fell in a gory mist on their heads and shoulders.

Harold nodded, unable to speak, throat shut tight from the sight of the carnage, noting his men had their weapons leveled, waiting for Scott to give the command to fire. Their eyes fixed on the Sergeant Major's arm as he raised, then brought it down. A sheet of smoke erupting as an unseen wave of lead balls slapped into the enemy line. Scott leaned in again, shouting above the screams of wounded men coming from the twice bloodied company of English soldiers stationed to the left of their own section of the line. Grime-faced men were cursing as they focused on reloading, waiting for the order to fire at the advancing enemy who were unable to match the disciplined pace of the British, volley for volley.

Scott shouted, his hand against Harold's ear. "When do we begin our slide to the rock pile?"

Harold twisted away from the horrible sight of shattered bodies being stepped over by stoic faced men in white uniforms, his section of the front line ignored for the moment by the enemy as they approached across the smoke-wreathed, pock-marked field. He swallowed twice before managing to respond, his throat bone-dry despite Scott's sage advice to breathe through his nose. Adrenalin gnawed at his will to stay in place, his body eager for release to rush forward into the approaching storm. Then the mindless reaction fell away, Harold feeling his brother's hand on his arm, his high-pitched voice in his ear, whispering he was going to be a great leader of men, scouring away the mindless hate and bowel loosening fear from his veins, leaving him poised on his instinct's call of when to react.

He twisted his neck, speaking into Scott's cupped ear. "Soon. Once the platoon to our left moves back, their officer failing to let us know we should join in the action, leaving us critically exposed."

Scott pulled back slightly, staring at Harold, a shocked look on his face. "Why would you think such a thing? No officer would do that to another."

Harold clenched his jaw as he looked to his left. "One of them would, in needing to deal with someone like me, considered a threat to their advancement in rank."

"You seriously believe that will happen?" Scott tilted his head, eyes wide as he stared at Harold.

"It just did. *Look!*" Harold pointed at the formation of men on both ends of the battlefield, seeing them as if placed in a box of sand, pieces moved by his finger, sliding into place. Both men watched as the wall of men to their left dissolved in an organized scramble up the slope, moving into their designated fallback position. Their officer, astride his horse, waving his sword about his head as he ordered them to form into line.

"May God *damn* his soul to *hell!*" Scott called out to their own men to hold, their eyes filled with questions, panicked looks breaking out on their faces. A few of the younger soldiers stood motionless, with stains of urine down their pant legs, no shame aimed their way by the more experienced soldiers, holding down both ends of the steadfast line.

"We go—*now!*" Harold stepped forward, turning his back to the foe and facing his men. "The natives will be here soon, so make haste, as if in mindless fear, racing for the shelter of the rock outcrop as we discussed last night. Once through the split in the face, climb to the top of the first ledge wall and recover the wooden shafts tipped with your bayonets, then prepare to repel the native force when they follow us in."

The men rushed to comply, effecting a realistic pretense of panicked flight as a loud howling erupted from the near edge of woods, the sound raising the hair on Harold's arms and neck as war whoops pierced the air. The noise, designed to break the will of men lined up shoulder to shoulder, served to amplify the pace of men pretending to run for their lives toward the questionable promise of shelter provided by the narrowed entrance of a crevice in the face of the large cliff.

Harold stayed to the rear of the strung-out line of retreating soldiers; his voice in steady encouragement to the last of his men as they rushed past. He followed behind, feeling the thud of leather-shod feet closing in behind him, using all his resolve to keep from taking a quick glance back at the native warriors as they began to close the distance. Scott had left with the first of the men, already at the sanctuary, his distinctive voice heard sending men aloft at selected spots along the narrow ravine that bisected the body of the immense limestone edifice.

Harold had fashioned the plan in order to deny the horrific price his men would have ended up paying due to a superior officer's jealousy of his success at the bloody crossing. It had happened before, in battles recreated with his brother, Jackson, with support pulled or delayed by one officer to another to further advancement of a career. And it had just happened here. Harold followed his men into the pinched throat of the crevice; Scott's hand offered from the top of a chest-high wall of ledge, pulling him up.

᥆ᦕᦓ

The natives were in a state of disarray. Not shock, their warrior minds refusing to bend to thought of failure as they milled about, searching for a way past the deadly probe of steel into their tawny flesh from the bayonet-tipped poles. The steel penetrated their hands, forearms, necks, and shoulders, leaving wounds impossible to ignore, despite the native's adrenaline surge that urged them on in howling waves, determined to climb the walls to close with their enemy.

Massed rifles, thrust out from between the wall of improvised spears, fired point-blank into the seething horde, sending lead balls hissing into the condensed wall of tawny skinned bodies; the heads of Harold's men wreathed in a dense cloud of smoke. Native men died by the dozens as bullets tore their way through flesh with wet slaps, mixed with the crack of fractured bones and shouts of pain forced past taut lips.

Harold waved his arms; a sword in one hand, pistol in the other. "*Fall back!* Back to the next section of ledge. Bring the *wounded* with you. Drop the spears if you need to, and wait to reload after you reach the top, not before." Scott echoed Harold's orders, his arms in a rapid wave above his head, the men's attention drawn to them through the clouds of drifting smoke. The leaders among the native force noted the motion as well and called out to one another through the din, forming into a thick knot of men who came on the run.

The soldiers pulled back, climbing the white shoulder of blood-stained rock in a flow of red and white uniforms, heading to their preassigned position where they quickly reassembled in two lines, half of them standing with bayonet tipped shafts at the ready, while other men knelt between them, muskets reloaded and leveled, waiting on the native's charge.

Harold felt a wash of pride run through him as he watched his men perform as if of one mind, following his plan. Their faith in him a gift far greater than any he'd ever known. This, he told himself, tears in his eyes, running with his arm wrapped around a wounded man's waist, was why leaders of men in battle were willing to give their souls to the waging of war.

Scott came along the line in check of each man's eyes, measuring their morale, a pleased look on his face when he stopped beside Harold. "It will be a slaughter when they come. For *them*, not us. The men ready to meet it." Scott was red-faced, his breathing strained from having carried a wounded man up the sloped rise. He coughed, then turned his head, a stream of brown splattering the bone-white limestone beside his feet.

Harold wiped his brow, wincing as he did so, a slice in the skin from a musket ball that had grazed him. He ignored another wound, received from a metal arrowhead that had slipped beneath the lining of his coat, its honed edge pressed in place by a wide leather strap over his back, slicing along his shoulder in a searing line. The shaft had jostled free, along with a decent amount of his blood, his physical condition worsened by exertions made in assisting wounded men up the slope. "I hope they decide to pull back." Harold paused, listening to the sound of war cries coming from below the lip of the limestone ledge. "Otherwise, it *will* be a bloodbath."

Scott glanced at him. "Maybe you should go down and let *them* know that." He looked back over his shoulder, his eyes on a group of soldiers gathered around two small bore cannons, deemed of little military use for the General's primary defensive position. The innovative officer standing beside him having left a requisition form behind during a furtive mid-night mission to the supply depot, the guns brought to the rocky redoubt, made a vital part of his innovative plan. "We're as ready as can be, sir. Next move is theirs."

"And they've just now begun it." Harold shivered, his gaze drawn to the faces of a host of angry men as they poured up and over the first ledge, their eyes wide, expecting to be able to over-whelm their red-coated enemy, who'd fled their defensive position in seeming disarray. Ululating cries for revenge rang out, the natives shrieking in anger as they came on, eager to atone for the damage done to them at the first ledge. Wails of dismay sounded as a wall of lead pellets chewed into them, their head-long rush knocked back, repulsed for a moment before their leaders howled, eyes filled with bloodlust, urging the others to head for the center of the line of men, intent on killing the officer who was standing there, ready to receive them, sword in his hand, exhorting his men to stand firm.

Harold blinked his eyes as he struggled to free himself from the grasp of a warrior, the man's hands clamped to the front of his officer's coat. He closed his eyes as a blanket of warm blood splashed against his face, result of a gaping wound he'd opened in the native's throat with a desperate, back-hand slash of his sword as the rush of warriors threw themselves against their line, battering their way past the bayonet tipped shafts with expertly wielded war clubs, his men fighting back with knives, bare hands, and teeth. Those in the back line, their muskets reloaded, had thrust the muzzles between uniforms in front, pulling the triggers, helping to blunt the attack. The muskets pulled back to reload once more, the line standing firm in the close-quarter melee between wild-eyed men.

Harold shoved his dying assailant away, using the handle of his sword to break the grip of the man's fingers clenched on his blood-soaked coat. A young soldier threw himself forward, knocking Harold to one side, using his body to shield his leader, intercepting one of the abandoned shafts flung by a warrior, the bayonet passing through the soldier's abdomen, the honed point slamming into Harold's side as a war club descended, crushing the impaled boy's head. The warrior delivering the blow howled in dismay at having missed his chance to kill the man he was after, pulling back his arm, the club raised to lash out again when a musket ball punched through his painted cheek. Two soldiers stepped forward, one shoving away the wounded native's body while the other pulled Harold behind him, another of the discarded spears flashing forward, the young man taking the blow in his lower thigh, then smashing his fist into the warrior's nose, flattening it. Two more men in blood-stained uniforms came forward, their voices calling out for other men to rally to their leader's defense.

Harold struggled to get out from under the press of dying and wounded men lying atop him. Heeled boots pressed against his chest, his lower legs pinned down, as a dozen men shoved past, answering the call to come forward. Young and old alike, determined men all, willing to sacrifice their lives to save his. He shouted for them to reform the line, knowing they would need to retreat to open a firing lane so the small-bore cannons could sweep the sea of warriors away with a devastating cloud of dozens of lead balls from their muzzles.

The men ignored him, cursing with wild-eyed effort as they parried the warclubs and probe of steel-tipped shafts they'd been forced to leave behind, placing themselves between an equally motivated foe, fixated on removing the man responsible for the slaughter of so many of their own. Scott's voice came in a roar to reform, his large hands grasping Harold by the shoulders, hauling him out from beneath the collapsed body of the young soldier with broken skull, and the other young boy named Ramsey, who was writhing in pain as he lashed out with the haft of a broken spear, his leg still pinioned by the steel point. Two other men, veterans, reached down and pulled the boy back, tossing him beside Harold, just behind the reformed line. A knot of mindless, raving soldiers continued to tear at the natives, ignoring Scott's order to clear the way for the anxious cannoneers poised over their pieces, fuses ready for igniting.

"Give them time to disengage!" Harold screamed, trying to make himself heard above the sounds of men tearing away at one another.

"Get them back before—" The sound of Scott's command to fire was drowned beneath an ear-shattering crack of noise as the cannons fired from close range. The bull-whip snap deafened the ears of the men on the edges of the heaving line, two wide holes punched through the mix of combatants struggling hand to hand, painted skin pressed against pale white while the object of their mutual attention stared with shocked eyes as bodies were turned into a cloudy haze of tattered flesh, blood, and splinters of bone.

Harold tried to sit up, Scott's hands holding him down as another man tore open his officer's coat, the brass buttons sent flying, his blood-soaked shirt ripped apart, exposing his wound, a small gash oozing blood. "You've been struck through, laddie." Scott's lips were in his ear, the roar of men's voices starting to drop as the smoke slowly cleared, revealing the terrible damage caused by the volley, with dozens of bodies strewn about as if handfuls of colorful shells lying on a surf-drenched beach.

Harold reached out and removed Scott's hands, half-sitting up, having trouble breathing, the blow having struck him in his right side, just beneath his ribs, the wind driven from him by the impact. He reached into his coat's inner pocket and touched his journal, realizing it had saved him from a more serious wound. The boy who'd sacrificed his life, absorbing most of the killing blow, lay beside him, looking up at the sky with sightless eyes, his fair hair fanned by a gentle breeze, his story having come to an end. Young Ramsey, lying on his other side, reached over and took Harold's hand, squeezing it before he passed out, his lifeblood slowly draining away onto the gore-stained rock.

Aftermath at Bloody Rock

Harold was sitting up, coat and white linen shirt removed, the long shallow cut in his upper back exposed to the air, his fair skin covered in a thin sheet of drying blood from the arrowhead that had sliced into him, early in the fight. The wound was beginning to ache, the layer of muscles singing in pain as he struggled to take in a deep breath, causing him to wince, his lower right-side bruised, the cut in his upper abdomen still oozing blood. Harold held his journal in his hands, staring at the cover where the point of the tossed bayonet tipped spear had penetrated, passing all the way through, leaving a thumb-wide slit in its back cover, stained black with his blood.

Harold remembered how the men around him, Scott included, had stared down with doleful eyes, thinking him struck through, gasps of amazement breaking out when he'd sat up, very much alive. Several men crossed themselves, unaware the journal had saved his life; a misunderstanding he would have explained to them had his eyes not rolled up in his head as the world went gray, then dark. Now fully recovered, he watched as his men moved out in front of him, checking the contorted bodies of natives with cautious prod of musket barrels, bayonets gratefully reattached, searching for signs of life. A few were using words he'd given them; simple phrases in French, most natives able to understand them.

Harold listened to their voices, soft-edged with respect being shown to their vanquished enemy, offering them opportunity to surrender with their honor still intact. Most of the wounded natives accepted with thankful nods, stretchers used to carry those unable to walk to pockets of shade, or escorted there by guiding hands on their shoulders, if able to make it by foot. Some of those who'd managed to survive the carnage shrugged off the friendly approaches with stoic expressions; their hands secured with twists of leather, then led away.

The smallbore cannons had been brutally effective. Two rounds of cannister shells each, fired into the center of the native's bunched formation as they'd pressed ahead. dozens of men in buckskin garb scythed down, including a handful of his own who were unable or unwilling to claw their way free. The storm of their heated emotions had drained away, as if water from a cracked bowl, leaving those on the native side who could manage it, to stumble away in desperate flight from the scene of horror; refuge sought in the woods below. Harold could hear their angry shouts, filled with bitter frustration, as they moved away through the thick canopy of trees.

The cannons, repositioned forward along the edge of a rise overlooking the open battlefield below, had sent dozens of volleys of short-fused shells into the exposed flanks of French soldiers as they struggled uphill, the thud from the guns sounding to Harold's cotton-shocked eardrums like the slow heartbeat of a great beast, reaching out to feast on the bunched groups of men in white.

Scott came over and looked down at his twice wounded officer. He gently probed the edges of his own wound, a thick clot of blood congealed on his lower forearm, product of a deflected blow from a hatchet, wielded by a large warrior with murderous intent. A jab of a wide-bladed knife, given him by Colonel O'Malley, finding the warrior's heart, ending the personal conflict as the native's brown eyes widened in surprise before he slumped to the ground, as if shocked at the outcome. Scott sat down beside Harold, waiting to give him a report on casualties, knowing the young man was still working his way back from the shock of having barely survived his first brush with sudden and violent death.

"I've done a horrible thing this day, Sergeant Major." Harold's voice was a thin whisper. He tried to lift his arm and failed, left to stare as it fell back across his legs, looking no different to him than any of those torn from men's torsos, scattered on the ground before him in a litter of gore spread across the red-painted dome of white stone.

Scott kept his voice even, ignoring the comment. "The third cannon, placed behind cover in the pinch of the ravine below, put paid to any ambitions they might have had for making another rush. Risky, for the men volunteering to man it, though it worked out just as you promised them; the natives' attention kept focused on us."

"Murder." Harold's voice was a mumble. "Senseless murder. On both sides. None of it making any difference." He looked over. "My hands are stained with the blood of every man killed this day. Or left wounded, unto death."

Scott looked over his shoulder and waved a handful of stern-faced soldiers away, their muskets leveled to protect their wounded leader. "Enough of that, sir. You dinna start it, only finished it best you knew how. And it was a near thing at that, considering the long odds we faced." He reached up and gently clasped his young officer by the back of his neck, careful to avoid the wound in his shoulder. "Nid ydych yn llotrudd, dim ond dyn a ddaliwyd rhwng dewis gwael a gwaeth."

Harold nodded as the words began to form in his pain-dulled mind. "I'm no murderer, agreed. But as to a choice made between bad or worse options, it seems a man should build something better with his ambitions—than this." He looked straight ahead; eyes filling with tears. "My father was right. I'm being drawn further into the grind, each day. Losing pieces of myself, of my soul, in trying to survive. Unable to find the good in what I caused to happen here." Harold shook his head as he looked across the blood-stained ground, dozens of bodies lying where they'd fallen.

Scott released his hand, his fingers resting on the thin shoulder of his officer, knowing he'd lost significant weight since the bloody crossing. "Your decisions today saved far more lives than it might have cost us. Every step along the way, just as you'd foreseen and prepared for. There's good can be found here, laddie, if you'll but open your mind and see the truth of it. Sir." Scott slipped a metal flask from his pocket, dented from the blow of a war club during the close-quarter fight. He removed the cork and took a sip, washing away a film of dust and grime that coated his mouth. "Here ya go, son. A bit of mother's milk to help ease your ache."

Harold complied, his hand shaking. Scott took back the battered flask, stoppered it, then tossed it to one of the men standing guard.

"Mind I get that back when you've emptied it, gentlemen." He got to his feet, thick hands on his hips, trying to ease the stiffness gripping his lower back. "Now that the Frenchies are in full retreat, I'm off to report to the General. I'll be letting him know you've received two wounds, sir, but are of sound enough mind to issue orders." He gave Harold a firm stare. "Correct, sir?" He waited until Harold nodded. "Then I'll be back shortly with wagons and a surgeon, along with others to tend to the wounded, on both sides."

Harold tried to stand to return Scott's salute, unable to do so, his legs not yet up to the task. He gave him a wave of hand in dismissal, his eyes following the short, wide-shouldered man as he moved away.

ഗൈ

"You just had to insert yourself into the fray." Meghan jabbed a large needle into and through Harold's torn flesh; a strand of boiled horsehair tugged through, closing the last raw-edged gap in the long surface wound caused by the honed edge of an arrowhead. She tied off the suture, clipping the ends with a small pair of scissors.

Harold was the last of the wounded in need of attention. Meghan, in company with a doctor and a handful of camp followers, had arrived with bags of surgical supplies in hand, sent by Scott to try and save as many lives as possible; grievously wounded natives included. Meghan administered to the natives with firm set jaw, her eyes ice-cold until finished, then she'd worked her way over to Harold, finding him sitting in the shade of a large tree, shirt off, coat lying at his side, a journal in his hands, having insisted on being the last of her patients.

"Take my hand and I'll help you to your feet. You can lean on me while I get you back to the encampment." Harold let Meghan pull him up, her arm firm around his waist, his draped over her shoulder, needing a moment to recover his vision as the world shifted through various shades of gray before returning to full color again. When they reached the shattered field below, a wagon with wounded men passed by, their voices ringing out in a loud cheer, shouting the name given their leader. *Red Fox! Red Fox!* Harold winced on hearing it, having to force himself to wave his free hand in return, the gesture met with hurrahs from those able to join in. Once the wagon moved out of sight, he sagged, his legs trembling, Meghan helping him to one side of the path, stopping behind a small mound of earth.

She whispered in his ear, letting Harold know it was okay to let go, cradling him as his legs collapsed. She eased him to the ground where tall grass waved in a light breeze, sheltering them from sight. He looked at her, his face pale from exhaustion, blood loss, and residual shock. "I'm sorry. For sustain of the wounds. For all of it. For the wounded and dead on both sides."

"There's no need to apologize." Meghan's voice softened. "I was being less than serious, Harold. You're an officer and must lead from the front when called upon to do so." She stopped talking, concerned as she saw him start to slip further into shock. "Lieutenant?" When he didn't reply she leaned in, checking his eyes for sign of a concussion. His pupils looked normal; his pulse beneath the press of her fingers on his neck rapid and shallow, his skin gone pale. "Harold? Talk to me. It will help. I know, having once been where you are now."

Harold remained silent, beyond reaction to external stimuli, as if floating in a cove of storm-tossed foam, unable to reach the shore. He lost sight of Meghan's face as he recalled the scenes of gore, the sound of her voice pleading with him turned into screams of mutilated men, their bodies in pieces due to his lethal plan. A blow to his cheek jolted him away from the darkness he was slipping into.

Meghan pleaded with him to return. "*Harold!* Listen to me. *Squeeze* my hand. It's vital you come back. I know what you're going through. I went through it myself. Look at me. *See* me!"

The tone of Meghan's voice compelled Harold to reach for her with an outstretched hand, trying to drag his emotionally waterlogged body from the sluggish flow of his melancholia. His shoulders began to shudder with grief; his heart overwhelmed, aching for release of the burden he carried. He slipped his arms around her, ignoring the pain of his wound, clinging to her as if she were the only ray of sunlight left in a world grown dark.

Consequences of Command

"You broke the line." A major in an immaculate uniform looked at Harold, his eyes aimed in a focused stare, thin shoulders drawn up, his demeanor in full huff. Harold forced himself to remain standing at full attention, his back ramrod straight, the line of stitches in his shoulder tugging at the dried edges of his wound beneath an unstained officer's coat, provided him by Scott. He didn't bother offering a response, knowing the statement stood on its own as an accusation. "You requisitioned artillery without following proper protocols, denying its contribution, limited as it was, for use in repulse of enemy forces."

The major, in the middle of a spittle-laden harangue, had a nasal, high-pitched voice. An impeccable, white-dusted wig perched on his narrow head above an expansive brow and pair of small, beady brown eyes, close set on either side of a long, aquiline nose, giving him the appearance of a cross-eyed crow. "In doing so, you caused the loss of unit cohesiveness which might easily have led to defeat of—"

"Enough, Major Sanderson." The General's voice cut through the background murmur of officers crowding his command tent. "You are dismissed, along with the rest of you, excluding First Lieutenant Knutt and his second." Aidyn waited until the sentries escorted the small army of staff officers beyond earshot, then stared at the two men left behind; the young officer in a wobbling attempt to stand at attention, and Scott, yawning, in a relaxed pose with a smile on his lips. Aidyn frowned.

"Something humorous on your mind, Sergeant Major?"

Scott gave Aidyn a look that bordered on familiarity. "Not at all, General. We are discussing dereliction of duty. A *hanging* offense, as I recall. Nothing in that to smile about." Scott paused. "Sir."

Aidyn glowered, attempting to work up righteous anger, failing to do so, shrugging his shoulders and nodding. "I take it you have something you'd like to add?"

"I do, General, though I am with a terrible thirst. If I might have a wee dram of Agua Vitae to wash it down with, sir?"

"Get on with it, Sergeant Major. I haven't all day to finish this up so my military strategist can begin working on a plan to take the enemy fort, lying beyond yon hill." Aidyn waved a hand in Harold's direction. "You may stand at ease, Lieutenant."

Harold relaxed his posture slightly, aware the mood in the tent had shifted. He loosened his gaze, watching as Scott came over with a bottle and three small glasses pinched between the fingers of his other hand. The veteran poured a healthy dose of liquor into the General's glass, then one of his own; a smaller amount delivered into Harold's, Scott aware residual shock and loss of blood would strengthen the effect of the alcohol. The ranker sat the bottle down then raised his glass, giving Aidyn a firm stare.

"I will not toast to a victory as brutal as this one has been, offering instead a toast to a battle well fought, with courage and conviction on *both* sides. Particularly by the company anchoring one end of the line."

"Well said, Sergeant Major Scott. Here, here." The two men touched their glasses to Harold's, then bottomed them. Harold took a tentative sip; a crease of pain in the corner of his eyes as he raised his arm to do so, the row of stitches Meghan had used to pull his torn flesh back together again tugged by the motion. The smaller wound in his side had settled into a dull ache, with heavy bruising beginning to take effect. A perforation of skin and muscle noted, Meghan leaning in to sniff it for odor of intestinal gasses before closing it up with several stitches.

The General looked over, having noted the wince on Harold's face. "I was told you had suffered a wound, Lieutenant. Two, if I recall correctly."

Harold forced himself to speak. "Of little concern, sir." He paused. "And well attended to."

Aidyn pressed in. "Their cause?"

"A deflected arrow, just along the back of my shoulder, sir." Harold paused, the image of the pinioned boy's eyes haunting his thoughts. "The other, but a graze. A few dozen of my men suffering much worse than I."

"If you'd held your assigned position, it would have been much worse. For us all." The General considered for a moment. "Why didn't you pull back when ordered to do so by Major Sandersen?"

Harold took a deep breath, held it a moment, letting the dull ache ease before letting it out. "I did not—receive any order to that effect, sir. Not from Major Sandersen or First Lieutenant Pearson, stationed on my left flank, in line of battle."

Sergeant Scott opened his mouth to intercede, closing it at a hand motion from Aidyn. "You must have been aware of his order to withdraw. Could you not have signaled for clarification of orders from our now deceased Lieutenant Pearson?"

"The Lieutenant may have assumed I'd join in when his company pulled back, sir. He never looked in my direction. He seemed—preoccupied, as my hand signals to him were not responded to."

Aidyn stared at Harold, his eyes in a fixed gaze. "So, you remained in in your assigned position as ordered by Major Sandersen, until allied enemy forces began to move on your exposed right flank, forcing you to seek a more tenable position of resistance to the enemy's advance."

Harold returned the General's look, his voice low, feeling a wave of heat come over him. "Not at all, sir. I had planned to move to a prepared position in the rocks once forced there by superior numbers of native forces. Assuming they would appear from that quarter at some point during the battle, trying to over-whelm my section of the line in order to turn our flank."

Aidyn narrowed his eyes, lips pursed, the empty glass in his hand forgotten for the moment. "A move *some* might consider imprudent, having abandoned your position without orders. A court-martial offense."

"Yes, sir." Harold stiffened his shoulders, feeling several of the upper stitches pulling apart, a trickle of blood running down his spine.

Aidyn looked over at Scott, who was reaching to refill his glass. "Sergeant Major, do you have anything to add to Lieutenant Knutt's account?"

Scott nodded, his feet set apart, shoulders squared, looking straight ahead. "Lieutenant Knutt, faced with a reasonable possibility of over-whelming enemy forces moving to envelope his flank, successfully deployed his men to a more defensible position from where he was able to significantly reduce their numbers by use of properly requisitioned and pre-positioned artillery. He then supported our forces in the field, directing the gunners to concentrate their fire into the exposed flank of the enemy's main assault forces, helping to break their lines, leading to a significant loss of their men, forcing their retreat from the battle." Scott inhaled, then burped. Loudly. "Sir."

"Leading to another satisfying victory for us, delivered by actions taken by our young officer, creating an—inconvenient situation for me to have to deal with. Once again." The General walked over to the entrance of the command tent, taking a moment to look outside before spinning around and giving Harold a firm stare. "You have far fewer enemies on the *French* side, Lieutenant Knutt, than *here*. Though one of them managed to find an odd way to die in the action. The former and—much preoccupied First Lieutenant Pearson who was shot in the back while fleeing the field of battle, well out in front of his own men." Aidyn paused, frowning. "As likely from an errant English ball, as French, I would imagine."

Harold started to sway, then caught himself. "If I'd not left my position, sir, I might have been able to prevent the breaking of the line."

Aidyn scoffed. "The natives would have annihilated you, creating wide-scale havoc with their skill at close in fighting. We'd have suffered much worse and done far less damage in return if not for your unorthodox plan. Which leads me back to my comment regarding you having created a problem for me that will soon need sorting out." The general looked at Scott. "Would you not agree, Sergeant Major?"

"Assuredly so, General." Scott offered and poured Aidyn another glassful of whiskey. "The lad has a streak of—unpredictability in him. Better suited to a bit of detached duty, I should think, tasked with leading a comingled group of colonial irregulars, along with local and native scouts, and perhaps a few of our more experienced troops, staying well out ahead of our primary force. To locate and make penetration into enemy positions, wreaking a measure of havoc thereabouts."

"Yes!" Aidyn held out his glass, waiting for Scott to touch his to it. "Removing our Lieutenant from the highly organized, baked in chaos I have to deal with *here*." He frowned. "Within my *own* chain of command, not that it was any different when the two of *us* were coming through, Sergeant Major. Back when I was the rash young officer and you a recently promoted ranker." Aidyn paused, staring at the wood-planked floor of his command tent. "At least I wasn't some politico *fop*, my father buying my way to a higher level of command than I was qualified for. Like—" He shook his head, looking over at the closed flap of the tent, then stopped.

Scott nodded. "Why we suffered so in the beginning, sir. Over here. Led to disaster by Braddock, though young Washington learned a valuable lesson from the fiasco at the Forks, leading the retreat, saving hundreds of lives." Scott and the general stared at each other for a long moment, then nodded, silent as they recalled early expeditions made against the French. A series of abject failures occurring during the first three years of the conflict, going up against the unorthodox fighting style the natives used then taught to the open-minded leaders of the French forces.

Harold stared at the two of them. "I'm—not to be hung, sir? Or flogged?"

Aidyn shrugged. "Not at all, Lieutenant, though I *will* punish you for leaving your position without orders, even if done under compelling circumstances. There is to be no formal commendation from me, along with any subsequent rise in rank. Due in most part to you having pre-planned the repulse made at the bloody rock, as the rankers are calling it. An action that, had you dared suggest of it beforehand, I would *not* have countenanced."

Scott poured himself another drink, then glanced at the general, getting a shake of his head. He held up his glass, studying the chestnut brown color for a moment, before taking a sip. "Which would have left our company pressed between a rock and a hard place. Damned in the doing. Doubly damned in not."

Aidyn gave him a cutting glare. "Are you quite done, Sergeant Major Scott?"

"Better hung for stealing of a cow, then a sheep." Scott returned a wide grin, recalling how Aidyn had stood side by side with him in far flung colonies of the British Empire; himself a fresh-faced sergeant of the line, along with a much younger and still damp behind his ears, Second Lieutenant. The two of them soon becoming dependent on each other while they learned painful lessons, while following the rigid rules of a deadly game. Aidyn, provided opportunity for purchase of multiple commissions due to the death of a wealthy uncle, had earned his way in blood up the chain of command. Recently placed in charge of the expeditionary force, just as the tide was starting to turn in England's favor. Scott aware that Aidyn would make good use of the innate talents of the young, but deadly officer, whose head was stuffed full of innovative ideas, along with the will required to accomplish any task in assign.

⌒℮⌒

"How long before you have to leave?" Meghan stared at Harold, her eyes reflecting the glow from a small fire centered in a ring of stones. They were sitting on a large log, just outside the cozy confines of a small hut. It had been crafted from wooden pallets erected by a group of native scouts, the men insistent on provision of private shelters for the immense colonial office they called Brother Bear, and his sister, who was a close friend of the young officer they'd named Red Fox. The taciturn warriors were openly bonded to both leaders by mutual respect, eager to provide security patrols in the local area from their nearby campsites, where they spent their time between missions.

Harold hesitated, looking into the dancing light of the fire. "I am not at liberty to answer that question, no matter that it might cost me the pleasure of your acquaintance."

Meghan tightened her lips. "The price of my—acquaintance is not in the balance. I only ask because I have come to enjoy our time together. My brother feeling the same way. Both of us holding you in high esteem, welcoming your attendance in our rustic setting." A snap of an ember from the bed of coals arched into the cool night air, landing near Harold's boot. He crushed it beneath his heel; a thin spiral of gray smoke rising, lost to a slight breeze in gentle nudge back toward civilization.

Harold's thoughts turned to the riverside port of Bristol where, God willing, he would one day step ashore again, should he manage to survive. The brush with death had caused a cloud that still hung over him, his mood withdrawn, causing the General to become perturbed at his lack of eagerness to reenter the fray, demanding from him a strategic solution. One Harold had complied with, now ordered to bring it into action on the morrow, though his heart remained heavy, in no mood to see it carried out.

Meghan reached over and stirred the coals with a stick. "Can you at least tell me if—"

"No." Harold's tone was curt. He watched as a frown slipped across Meghan's full lips, then turned into a pout of frustration. He sighed. "Tomorrow. Mid-morning. A turn to the east, then circle to the north to try and cut off the enemy fort from upriver approach, severing their lines of communications and resupply by water."

"How will that be possible? I mean—we have no ships here."

"The French do, so we will—requisition them. Use them to form an English navy, while our army sits in siege. The goods captured will resupply our forces while the French sit inside their fort, watching it happen. A plan I helped devise, the General ordering me to lead it." Harold dropped his voice. "He called me an—uncommon man. The General."

Meghan looked up. "And so you are, Harold."

"As too yourself, Meghan, according to conversations with your brother." Harold hesitated. "Without his having shared *any* personal information on your behalf, only his words of pride in regard to your intellect and caring nature."

Meghan grinned. "Then you do not yet know the *half* of what I'm capable of." She stood up and ducked into the hut while Harold scrambled to his feet, hat in hand, uncertain of his next move. Her voice called out from within the small enclosure. "I will be out in a moment. You *do* play chess, correct? I seem to recall my brother mentioning something to that effect during our own conversations. About *you*."

"I have *some* experience, though it's been ages since—" He lowered his voice as she stepped out with a thick rectangular case in her hands, its surface comprised of alternately colored squares of hardwood forming one half of a playing surface, with the chess pieces contained within.

"This belonged to my brother, once. Mine now, until he wins it back. Though *that* will never happen. Not as long as I still have my wits about me." Meghan paused, a feral smile on her lips. "He plays as if fawn in a meadow, while the wolf watches from the edge of the woods, contemplating its next meal."

Harold angled his head. "And I'm to be another innocent animal, posed before your vulpine leer?"

Meghan settled down onto the log, finding a level spot where she could rest the case, her long legs folded alongside her as she leaned in, setting up the board. Harold watched as she removed an assortment of figurines; the black pieces carved from an exotic wood, the white from ivory. Each of the two kings and queens wearing gold inlays, forming crowns.

"It is a magnificent piece of artisanship." Harold sat down then reached out, holding up two of the pieces, admiring them in the light from the fire. "They look old. The ivory, well-aged."

"It belonged to my father. To *our* father, who handed it down to George. Who then lost it to me. A foolish wager." She glanced across the board at Harold, a sly grin on her face. "My brother's ass-wide pride prevented him from avoiding such a rash decision, unable to fathom how I could best him—ten games in a row."

Harold started to speak, then stopped as Meghan looked at him, waiting for him to continue. He shrugged. "I hesitate to ask his level of skill, not wanting to suggest any diminishment of your own."

"George was more than a match to our father, who was himself a man with a reputation for knowing the game." Meghan paused, a pained look on her face. "He wouldn't play with me, my father. Not after I finally beat him." She shook her head, her eyes lowered. "He forbade me from ever playing again."

"Yet here you are, chess board in hand."

Meghan shrugged. "My brother defied him, not for the first time, moving our games to the stables, teaching me a few new strategies." She shrugged, her shoulders rising and falling, copper hair shimmering in the light from the fire. "Not that I ever used them. Preferred devising my own."

Harold felt himself drawn closer to the woman he'd come to admire for her forthright approach, along with her gentleness in caring for the wounded, and ability to express herself with firmly held opinions on a host of subjects, academic and pedestrian. "You profess to having a killer attitude at chess, though I wonder if you're only trying to subvert my will to win."

Meghan looked over at him, the lashes of her light-colored eyes fluttering as she gave him a devilish smile. "Are you *susceptible* to subversion, Lieutenant Knutt?" She angled her head, the light reflecting from her eyes. "Perhaps I *am* stretching the hide a bit, but I assure you—I know my way around the board."

Harold arranged himself opposite her, one of his legs brushing against Meghan's as she held out her hands, long fingers closed around a pawn of each color. He reached out and placed his hand on hers, the warmth of her skin inviting, as was the firm pressure of her leg on his, still there. Harold smiled as he held on for a moment before letting go, looking at the black pawn, satisfied at having made his choice.

⌀℮∩

"You're an opponent with no lack of interesting moves." Meghan reached out, chin in one hand, eyes narrowed as she began to set up for a third game. They each had earned one victory, the winner of the next allowed to crow as champion, if only for a single night. Their first match ending in a protracted win for Meghan, though Harold had come within a move of managing a draw. The second had become a slashing affair, pieces sacrificed to speed; each of them acting and reacting with slicing advance or cunning retreat, trying to lure the other into subtle traps. The game coming to a close with a series of deft moves by Harold, his Knight at an offset angle to her King's back; Meghan forced into a sullen surrender.

As she finished resetting her side of the board, Meghan glanced over at Harold, knowing he was still trying to regain his emotional balance from the carnage at Bloody Rock. Aware that once their final contest was over, he would beg his leave, returning to the main encampment in the valley below. Harold felt her eyes on him and leaned back. "I learned some of those moves from my brother, back when I was first teaching him the game. Each of his early losses increased his understanding, until I became the student and he, the master."

Meghan glanced at Harold as she made the opening move. "He is— younger than you?" Harold nodded, Meghan seeing a look of disquiet slide across his face, decided to press on. "By how great a divide?"

Harold decided on use of an unorthodox approach learned from his brother. "Two years, less a month. Jackie. Jackson Thomas—named after my Uncle."

"Does he also ache to join the service?" Meghan slid another piece into place, expanding her possibilities for attack or defense.

"He passed away when I was thirteen. A brighter light—I've never seen again. Far beyond any measure of my own, Jackie glowing with promise, pushing me in all areas of academic study. Asking questions I was constantly scrambling to find the answers to." Harold shook his head, a thin smile on his lips. "I taught him how to read when he was turning three, having just learned myself. Jackie needing only the first gentle shove, then running ahead to a promising future."

Meghan reached over, hand on his. "I'm sorry—at your loss. It must have been a great blow to both you and your parents."

Harold lowered his eyes. "Was a fever, took him from us. Sore throat and mild cough in the morning, with a rattle of lung and high fever in the afternoon. Gone—during the night, with nothing we could do. Like that." He snapped his fingers. "Like a candle flame snuffed out by a gust of wind."

Knutt Homestead, Bristol

"Why can't I go with you?" Jackson stared at Harold with a shocked look on his pale face. "I won't get in your way!"

"You will—as you *always* do, unable to resist the barbed comment or off-putting remark. Your constant utterance of cutting observations causing me no end of—" Harold paused, easing his tone. "I'm not much in favor with my friends as it, of late, having to defend you against physical rebuff due to your frequent and much too pointed insults." Harold placed his hands on his brother's shoulders, fingers soft on his thin bones; Jackie eleven years old and yet to hit his growth. "I'll be back before you finish reading our latest book on military campaigns. Then you can tell me how you'd have handled things better, with losses reduced by finding the perfect strategy, as you always do."

"Like the one you're using now, with divert and distract, as if I'm but a child?"

"But you *are*, Jackie. A child, *still*." Their mother's voice floated into the conversation, her hand coming to rest on the back of the younger son's head, fingers tugging gently on his ponytail, fine hair bound in a black ribbon. She pulled it away from his neck, landing a quick press of her lips on his warm skin. "Besides, you've a bit of a peswch bach on you this morning. Best stay in and keep warm by the fireplace. Your brother will be back soon, and you'll just have to abide his absence as best ye can."

Harold watched as his brother stomped away. He started to call out to him, his mother's finger touching his lips. "You run along to your friend's house and be sure to give my regards to his dear mother." She paused, a smile on her face. "And his twin sister as well—if you happen to *see* her there."

Harold fled the kitchen steps before the blush on his face gave him away, returning several hours later to find Jackson in bed, his face beaded in sweat. Restless, in an unsettled sleep. A thick book of military campaigns lay on the bed, opened to a description of a battle, no doubt searched through to discover a means to a bloodless victory, fever, or no. The doctor sent for, unable to make his way there; tied up with dozens of cases with similar symptoms. Another fever of unknown origin in a ravenous feast of lives throughout the densely packed communities just outside the seaport of Bristol. People young and old alike, struck down at random.

✺

It was dark outside, wind in a howl against the eaves, rattling the panes of glass in an upstairs bedroom window where Jackson lay in feverish repose. Harold had been moved into the study, kept away from the bedroom shared with his brother. He stood in the doorway, eyes on Jackson who seemed to be in midst of a dream, his hands working beneath the covers, lips in motion beneath a flutter of eyelids.

Their mother was downstairs, replacing fever warmed water in a basin with cool, used to bathe Jack's heated brow. Their father in his office, in a slow pace, unlit pipe in one hand, invoices he was unable to focus on in the other, used as props to hide his deep concern.

Harold went over and sat down, gazing at Jackie, seeing his brother as if he were a baby bird, fallen from its nest, narrow chest in shallow pulse, arms trembling as if featherless wings. Harold leaned in, elbows bent, struggling to find his balance in a world gone to spin. "I'm here, Jackie. It's me, your brother—Harry." The whisper in return painted a thin smile on his lips.

"Redundant—superfluous—as if it could be—anyone else." A long pause ensued as Jackie tried to swallow. "You promised to return, and now have done so. We shall go out—in a moment. I've an idea—to show you."

"In the morning, Jackie. You'll be right as sunshine by then. You'll see."

"Is it night?" Jackson tried to turn his head, a moan slipping from between clenched lips. "It hurts, Harry. My neck—and throat. Hurts so much."

Harold reached out and dampened a corner of a small towel, then placed it against his brother's cracked lips. He watched in anguish as Jackie tried to pull the moisture from it, another moan of pain reward for the effort made. "Here, I'll squeeze some into you."

"Want tea—not water. A blend of those herbs Mother likes to—"

When there were no more words, Harold's felt his throat constrict, his heart skipping a beat, "Jackson" He touched his brother's chest, a flutter of heartbeat still there, followed by a slow rising sigh of breath, then soft release. He stood up to summon their mother when Jackie reached out, clutching his wrist in a claw formed of heated flesh, his voice growing stronger. "Can you hear them, Harry—from just over the hill? The sound of buglers, calling the men to stand the line. Are you coming with me? We need to go. I need to find the General. To explain how—"

A sudden gust rattled the windows, causing the bedside candle to flicker. Jackie's eyes fell open in an expression of awe at something only he could see. Harold leaned down, pressing his ear against his brother's chest, his intrepid heart grown still. Their mother came in, standing over him, her hand on his neck, head bowed, her tears landing on Harold's cheek, mixing with his own.

"You're in check." Meghan's voice was as soft as her fingers touch on the back of Harold's hand. "Checkmate—in two moves."

Harold stirred himself, refocusing on the game. "I—" He stared at the board; the placement of pieces and next moves clearly defined. He reached out and tipped his King. "I concede the victory—to a brilliant strategist."

"We will not count it." Meghan lowered her voice. "Though I *would've* had you, no matter what stratagem you might have selected in defense."

Harold stared across the board-width space between them, Meghan's eyes open to his gaze, both knowing it would be his decision as to the next move made. Harold considered the pledge made to her a week ago, rejected with a gentle shake of her head. He recalled how close his death had been in the recent battle, causing a sudden realignment of moral position, unable to face the thought of going to his maker without having shared the loving embrace of a woman. He reached out and gently swept the pieces to one side of the board, then leaned over and kissed her. His fingers on her neck, eyes closed as he lost himself in the promise of her heated response.

Meghan finally broke away. She stood up, taking Harold's hand in hers, pulling him to his feet. With her hip pressed against his, she led him over to the small hut. The blaze of the fire had died down to small flames, matching the flicker of lights from a hundred campfires glowing down in the valley below, as if a field of fireflies in search for a mate.

CHAPTER SEVEN

Ohio River Basin, Late-August 1758

Ripples on Water

The waters of a wide river slipped through a narrowed section, squeezed between two ridges, creating a swirl of eddies indicating hidden rocks lying in wait just below the surface. The ripples provided a signal for cautious approach for a heavily laden boat moving downriver with the strong current, forced to hug the westernmost bank until a sharp turn could be made at the last moment to avoid the underwater shoal.

The vessel slid out from beneath an early morning mist, ghosting along, four oarsmen to a side, their long sweeps raised, ready to dip and pull when ordered to do so by their thin-framed captain: an older man who leaned over one side, his eyes on the near bank, looking for his marker.

The men at the rudder and oars knew the next move needed, the boat sitting deep in the water, laden down with vital resupplies for the French fort a few leagues downriver. The bow lookout, one arm draped across a small-bore swivel gun, leaned over the prow, eyes searching the depths. He jerked his head back as a flash of movement reflected back from the dark water, startled as a shadow dropped into place beside him with a thud of leather clad feet.

Harold, having relaxed his hold on the limb of a thick oak tree overhanging the river, gained his balance after a three meter drop, along with a dozen of his men. They landed on the deck of the wide boat as it passed beneath, taking up positions beside three crewmen on its upper deck; one manning the rudder station, with a man each at the stern and bow gun positions. Eight more sailors sat perched on benches several feet lower than the raised section of the upper deck, manning the oars, waiting for an order to pull. It was an order they would not receive, the helmsman's throat squeezed by the firm fingers of Master Sergeant Scott, his knife pressed to the soft skin below the man's eye in a pointed suggestion he should remain silent.

Harold's force overcame the two sailors at the fore and aft gun stations without a struggle, their pistols aimed at the rest of the crew. Harold nodded at the captain, who gave an order to his men to set about their task of pulling the boat away from the shoals, the helmsman released, leaning into the rudder pole until they were clear.

"Well done, Sergeant Major." Harold kept his voice low, a grin on his face, teeth a line of white in his soot-darkened face. "A fine piece of pirating, though I prefer to think of it as a commandeering of enemy shipping."

Scott shrugged, sweat beading his forehead. "Without a letter of marque from the King."

Harold widened his smile. "But under the orders of an officer of his Majesty's army. So—no hangman's noose for us."

Scott raised his hand, stirring the air with a blunt finger, his voice a match to Harold's light-hearted tone. "Yay."

Harold turned and pointed at the now ex-captain of the captured vessel. The man stepped forward without a shred of fear on his tanned face, waiting to find out his fate. "We will deposit your men near the fort, without any harm coming to them. They will convey a message to its commander that we will intercept *all* shipments, heading downriver or up. Our main force is now less than a day's march away, prepared to offer reasonable terms. Once accepted, you and the other captains will have the return of your boats. Undamaged, if possible." Harold paused. "I assume you are a—hired merchant?" The other man nodded; his eyebrows raised, a pair of hazel eyes in steady gaze. Harold nodded, a wry grin on his lips. "I take it you have a question?"

The tall man with gray-salted dark hair and beard whispered in reply, careful to prevent the other men from hearing it. "You're keeping me aboard. Why?"

Harold leaned in. "I require something from you in my promise to return your boat, *if* you're willing to provide it."

The captain considered a moment, then smirked. "You don't know how to pilot a boat such as this. One with sails."

Scott leaned over, his hand closing on the older man's upper shoulder. "You have the right of it. Our leader is a fair man and will keep his word. You've little to lose and much to gain in this deal. What say you?"

The captain shrugged. "Where am I to begin?"

Harold gave him a considered look. "Why—at the beginning, of course."

The captain smiled, then reached out, finger pointed. "The left side of the ship is called the port. The right side, the starboard."

An English Port, Arrived

Aidyn strode along a newly built pier to where Harold stood in conversation with the captain of a large scow tied to a temporary dock, assembled just downstream from the French fort. The area around the hastily constructed port was a beehive of activity as men moved goods from the holds of captured boats to wagons loaded down with tons of food and military supplies, seized from a host of bewildered captains; an English ensign raised at the last possible moment after a purposeful approach.

Sergeant Major Scott, in command of the first boat captured a month earlier, stood alongside Harold, watching as the General came up, a pleased smile on his weathered face. Aidyn came to a stop, returning the other men's salutes. "Do you have the wine I ordered?"

Harold reached down and pulled two bottles from a haversack; the bright light of the noonday sun swallowed by the dark-red liquid within. "Compliments of the French commander of yon fort. A fine vintage. Exquisite blend."

"I take it you have sampled it." Aidyn frowned.

"Nary a drop, General." Harold shook his head. "But I have seen a similarly labeled product moved between seller and buyer—in my previous incarnation."

"Your father's mercantile company, no doubt."

Harold nodded. "The same, sir."

Aidyn noticed his young officer's quick glance toward a rise of hills and dismissed him with a wave of a hand, releasing him to shore duty, watching with a smile on his face as Harold cleared a tangled line of wagons, then broke into a sprint toward the rise beyond the encampment. Aidyn turned and looked at Scott. "You have outperformed every expectation, Sergeant Major. Another mission completed with *great* results. I commend both you and your—salty crew members."

Scott shrugged. "Thank you, sir. It's been our pleasure, believe me. Beats slogging through the muck and mire, listening for the whistle of ball, or hiss of an arrow."

"A temporary post, Sergeant Major." Aidyn stepped aside as several men carrying supplies passed by. "Do not let your sea-legs get the best of you. Once a footie, always a footie."

"Sir." Scott waited, knowing Aidyn had something on his mind. He didn't have to wait long, Aidyn lowering his voice after the men had moved further along the dock.

"Tell me, Vice-Admiral of the fleet—how is our Admiral doing? Has this latest duty helped lighten his previous mood?"

"A bit, sir, though he does still find the occasional distance to stare into, burdened as yet by want of fair treatment for all."

Aidyn sniffed. "As do I, Sergeant Major. As do any of us bearing the burden of decisions made as to what needs doing and when. Comes along with the braid—and promise of a barrel of brine for the long journey home."

"Sir."

Aidyn sighed. "You do not agree, Sergeant Major?"

Scott shook his head. "He's an unusual sort of soldier, sir. More than willing to play the game, though not yet hardened to the reality that comes hand in hand with every soldier's journey. The hard realization that all stories end, in time." He paused. "Some, coming along earlier than others."

"So, you claim he is still a—sandbox soldier, then."

"Sir?" Scott gave Aidyn a considered look.

Aidyn leaned back against the side of the large boat and crossed his arms. "Our young officer related his fascination, one evening, with stories of men in war. Of becoming a student of the game as a child, with insight gained from reading everything he could lay hands on having to do with the movement of men in battle. Of how and when to maneuver, using feints and counter moves based on an opponent's reactions, weaving the disparate threads from hundreds of recorded battles into a single rope. Now using that knowledge *here*, helping to check our opponent's ability to respond." Aidyn paused, returning Scott's quiet gaze. "With a potentially *fatal* blindness to his game, one keeping him from opening up to his—full range of capabilities."

"Sir." Scott looked away, Aidyn sighed once more, shaking his head.

"Speak freely, Robert. We're alone for the moment, and you know as much of me as I do of you."

Scott looked down at the side of the dock for a moment, staring at the water curling underneath. "As to the lad's ability to light a fire in his men, I've never seen anyone better, not even yourself. And, as far as his own capabilities go, he's only in need of the proper match to ignite his inner passion for battle. There will come a day when he'll discover it, releasing the same devil all men carry deep inside their bellies. Buried a bit deeper in this one, but it's there, hidden behind his eyes. And I, for one, pray never to see it fully revealed."

Aidyn reflected on what the man he'd shared many a soldier's fire with had just said. He knew the greatest favor he could do for his young officer would be to release him from his term of service, sending him back to England with promotion and assignment as an instructor at an officer's school. But he needed him here to help drive the French to negotiation of a treaty, an effort requiring every man, every advantage, every one of thousands of British soldiers and colonist militiamen in order to wrest control of what promised to become a rich and bountiful British colony. To defend it from any who would stand in their way, including native tribes in support of two powerful nations, engaged in conflicts around the globe.

Shore Duty

Meghan and Harold's embrace took place in front of the entire entourage of camp-followers, the two of them no longer concerned with others knowing of their close relationship. Affairs on the red path of war viewed through the lens of imminent death from disease, accident, or result of armed conflict. Meghan, swept off her feet by the strength of Harold's arms, laughed with tears in her eyes as she released two weeks of tension.

Every casualty, with injuries suffered in securing the river-wide blockade, bringing a tightness to her throat as she watched them come ashore on litters. Harold, granted shore leave twice over the past six weeks, finding her, then the two of them beating a hasty retreat to the small campsite set up well outside the environs of the main camp.

They were there now, an outdoor fire banked against a curved wall of stones, its heat reflected onto their bodies, entwined in spent pose. A thick woolen blanket lay beside them, ready to cover them up once they'd recovered their strength, the air beginning to cool as evening approached.

Meghan ran her fingers through Harold's hair, a satisfied smile on her lips. "You're bringing about a bloodless cessation of hostilities, one that will shove the poxy bastards back to their frog-ponds across the ocean. Their *savages* left to our native allies to deal with."

Harold listened to the deep-seated anger in Meghan's voice. He was aware of parts of her story, George having told him of the loss of her husband and young son, a grievous wound that had damaged her to the core. Meghan's anger, whenever it arose, would move him to a silent reflection of her pain, unable to help her heal from the injuries done to her body, mind, and soul. "I'm only following the General's orders, the men deserving most of the credit, taking to the mission like—"

"Ducks to water?" Meghan leaned in and kissed him.

Harold responded, then pulled away, looking into her eyes, lost in their depths. "I was resisting the *obvious* reference."

Meghan reached out and toyed with a curl of his unbound hair, dangling over his shoulder. "I'm glad you weren't resistant to *my* reference, when I asked if you'd returned to assault my fortress."

Harold grinned, then leaned in and kissed the end of her perfect nose. "Never have barred gates been approached with such eagerness to force them apart, only to discover how little effort was required to make a penetration."

"You suggest I am a *wanton* woman?" Meghan angled her head.

Harold gave her a lecherous smile. "I sense you might be wanting *more*."

"You *would* think that—" Harold cut off Meghan's response, his lips on hers, his hands, roughened by hours of hauling ropes attached to sails, grasping her firm body with focused intensity, touching her, caressing her, delivering them both to the edge of passion, then beyond.

ᴼᴇᴧ

"My sister—she is of an *agreeable* nature of late." George looked at Harold, a grin on his broad face. "Distinct change from a few days ago, shortly before your return to port." He sighed, leaning back, resting on a log beside the fire ring in front of Meghan's small shelter. "She wields a sharp tongue, when out of sorts. Fortunate for you, always managing to miss it. Her sour mood coming back upon your return to command of our naval force."

Harold gave Meghan's brother a wry look. He'd become close with George since Bloody Crossing: a relationship helping to draw colonist militia and English forces together, encouraged by the inclusive attitude of the General, though practiced to a lesser degree by senior members of his staff.

Harold knew George and his men were satisfied with the current situation, the colonial militia relieved at the prospect of earning their pay with lowered risk of injury or worse, due to his innovative tactics. He shrugged. "I am aware of the effect I have on her. It's the same with me, my men having to deal with my heavy mood once back on the river."

"I have difficulty believing that my friend, sensing no heaviness of spirit in you. Something I admire in a comrade-in-arms and possible—" George left the sentence unfinished.

Harold picked up a thin piece of wood, holding it in his hand. "You've cast your arrow into the bushes, in hopes of striking unseen game."

George chuckled. "My ploy has fallen short, seen through by the master strategist, himself."

Harold reached out and stirred the coals, raising a thin trail of sparks, following them with his eyes as they swirled away. "I've proposed, going so far as to suggest making my home here, among people I've come to care for."

George nodded. "And?"

"No *direct* rebuff to my latest offer. And no desire to agree. Yet. A hesitancy on her part noted, requiring a need for continued patience on my part."

George looked at Harold with a serious expression on his face. "As titular head of our family, I can intercede, insisting she comply if you'd like."

Harold slipped a tight grin onto his lips. "Now *that* I would love to witness, if only to measure your how far your head travels—when removed from your thick neck by her sharp tongue."

George nodded. "She is a force of nature, when her inner tempest is set free." He leaned forward, searching Harold's eyes until he dropped his stick into the flames and matched him, stare for stare.

"What is it, George?"

"I can see it. The same fire burning in you, as does in her. As it does in me, at times."

"You vision is unclear, my friend." Harold glanced at the fire, watching the stick as it began to smolder. "I'm unable to find that level of heat when it comes to dealing out death. One that others seem able to call on at will."

"Then I apologize for having overstepped and will admit I'm wrong."

Harold grinned. "No apology asked for or needed, my brother, who we may one day become. It is important we always speak the truth to one another, as we see it to be, no matter what." He looked away, hearing footsteps on the path from the main camp, watching as Meghan returned with a sack of food and two bottles of wine, taken from his share of French stores, recently gained. "Perhaps when I next return from my watery post, I shall visit the topic with your sister, anew." Harold stood up and moved away from the flames, going to meet Meghan.

George followed him with his eyes, his voice a soft whisper. "But I'm not wrong about you, my brother. Not wrong at all. Someday the fire will rise and consume you, as it does all men who trade in the lives of others."

CHAPTER EIGHT

Reflagged English Fort, Mid–September 1758

Vibrations on Land

The French surrendered the fort, with British and French staff officers enjoying a banquet offered by the French commander to General Aidyn and his staff. The defeated host, forced to use goods intercepted by Harold and his armada of small boats, had extended an invitation to the victorious commander and his staff, a customary practice which included officers of high rank on both sides who were enjoying each other's company after a two-month siege. The celebratory feast did not include the presence of the recently demoted First Lieutenant Knutt, no longer Admiral of his Majesty's fleet in the Ohio Valley, disqualifying him from joining the ceremony.

Harold, left to his own source of entertainment, had spent the afternoon engaged in an exchange of pleasantries with Meghan, who was gazing at him with a look of admiration in her depthless eyes.

"You have put a third feather in your cap. From beginning to end, a skilled display of maneuver and riposte." Meghan poured a full measure of confiscated French wine into a confiscated wine glass, touching it to the side of Harold's, the thin, glassy note revealing the exquisite quality of its manufacture.

Harold nodded. "I was lucky. Or rather, *we* were lucky. Sergeant Major Scott and the men performing as if born to the role of pirates."

"I can only imagine the risks you took, especially in the beginning." Meghan looked at him, unable to keep an ache from her heart, the thought of his death more than she could bear.

"We had the benefit of an Acadian captain, excessively eager to show us the—literal ropes. Seems the French military had treated him and the other captains unfairly when conscripting them into maritime service. We treated him as a captive when making our approach, to prevent retribution falling on him once we released the fleet of commercial crafts back to their original owners."

Meghan gave him a quiet look, her eyebrows raised. "A magnanimous gesture."

Harold shrugged. "One the General was happy to agree to, at my suggestion. A matter of respect shown men from mercantile backgrounds, like ours. And a common enough practice during times of international strife."

"You are so—" Meghan forced her lips to close, glancing away, her eyes on a pot of rabbit stew suspended from a metal spit above a glowing bed of coals. The fresh meat a gift from their native allies, eager to provide fresh game and personal security while tucked away from the main encampment.

"What were you about to say?" Harold watched as Meghan busied herself going to tend the stew, the rich scent birthing a grumbling in his stomach. The sight of her body beneath a thin, clinging robe stirred a hunger of another kind within him.

Meghan finished checking on their meal, tasting the stew then sighing. "It's nothing—of any *real* note." She turned around and faced him. "It's only that you desire so to deal—*fairly* with the enemy." Meghan shook her head, her unbound hair shimmering in the sunlight. "I don't mean it that way. Fairness is a reasonable gesture in an honorable man, which you definitely are." She came over and knelt before him, taking his hands, a sad smile on her lips. "It's only that you deal with people, friend and foe alike, so gently—as if they were an extended part of your family. As if you've made them some form of—familial vow."

"Treating them fairly when I can, yes—as you just said. As it should be between—"

Meghan leaned in, gazing into his eyes, her own open, lips parted. "Is there no hunger within you for the deaths of those seeking your *own*?" Her hands squeezed his, to the point of pain. "To give into a desire to end the promotion of butchery on behalf of—of a *greed* driven cause?" She stood up. "It is a *weakness* in you, one that may prove lethal when forced to stand up to the enemy with fire in your eyes, unless you find it within yourself, fanning it to full intensity, if only to protect those you profess to love."

Harold cocked his head, shocked by the abrupt change in Meghan's tone. George had related the story of her capture by native raiders, of the massacre of her family and indignities suffered before he could arrange her release, a few weeks later. A hesitant tale, shared around a campfire shortly before the surrender of the fort, with most of the details left aside. "I understand my view of this is—not your own."

Meghan leaned over, her fingers gently brushing the curve of his cheek. "I mean you no disrespect, Harry. You've accomplished so much, with little enough blood having been shed on *our* side of things." She sighed, shaking her head. "It is only that you are limited by your view of the world, filtered through a life providing few real challenges, until now. One that's adhered to—civilized rules, with your Christian conditioning blinding you with a false reality. The same one I believed in, once, until it was clawed from my heart, torn from my womb, the scales ripped from my eyes, leaving a grievous wound within me that will never heal."

Meghan went over and stirred the stew again, her shoulders tight beneath the thin linen shift she wore. When she turned around, a thin smile painted her lips, cheeks bathed in the soft glow from the fire beneath the seething kettle as she recalled the slaughter of natives at the battle of Bloody Rock. The sight of their torn bodies that day bringing a sensation of joy to her heart. Greater than any felt since seeing the horrific sight of her husband and young son lying dead on the ground in front of her. Refused by her captors to go to them, her hands bound behind her, dragged away into the woods along with several other women. All of them victims of a random raid made against the outer settlements, crowding the border of native hunting lands. "I wonder what it would be like to see it released within you, the flare of mindless anger let loose on those who would take from you all you love—all you are, as happened to me. A mother and wife in morning's light, then grieving parent and widow in the night. Reclaimed by a brother weeks later, returning to my home and kneeling before wooden grave markers, driven deep into the ground."

She looked into his eyes, tears falling from her own. "I do not wish it on you—pain beyond any measure of describe, existing inside me still—with no hope of ever seeing it gone."

Harold, struck silent, had no words to offer that would stem the upwelling of grief from within her. One she hid behind a winsome smile and generous nature as she cared for those in need with an angel's touch and comforting voice. He reached for her, drawn to his feet by her hands, her body cradled in his arms, forehead pressed to his. Cupping her neck, he leaned in with closed eyes, drinking in the scent of her skin and hair, a mix of wood-smoke, natural oils, and sweat. His heart pounded, mirroring her own as their lips joined in ache-filled beat. The stewpot steaming as the flames burned down. The stars above, swept from the sky by a layer of dark clouds racing in from the distant horizon.

CHAPTER NINE

Ohio River Basin, November 1758

Ranging Ahead

The scent of musty leaves permeated the air: a thick fall of oak, mixed with a scattering of beech and birch. It probed the edges of Harold's nostrils, coaxing him into a sneeze, smothered in the crook of his elbow. When Scott glanced over, his bushy eyebrows raised in alarm, Harold nodded then started forward once again. The two of them were on point of a loosely formed column of men; a ranging force made up of native scouts and colonial guides spread out to either side, along with two dozen Colonial and British soldiers, all of them skilled in the hunting of men in woodland environs.

Harold slouched down, a wave of uneasiness creeping over him as his eyes probed a thin layer of fog hovering waist-high above the ground. His caution was rewarded with the buzz-whine snap of a lead ball slicing the air above his head, followed by the thud of a musket close behind. He dropped to the ground; aware he'd led his men into the outspread jaws of a trap. With a quick roll to one side, he cleared the hidden foe's line of sight, tucking his body behind a moss-covered rock. Once he'd caught his breath, he rose to one knee and began probing the gray wall of fog for a target, his pistol leveled.

Several shots thumped out in an echo to the first, coming from a tree-topped ledge some seventy paces ahead. Enough of a response to convince Harold he'd need to pull his force back and prepare them for a coordinated attack, with small knots of men sent to either side of the ledges, circling around and coming in from behind the enemy force lying in wait.

"Crafty bunch, these ones, sir—bit like us." Scott turned his head, spitting on the leaf strewn ground. "They knew we'd be coming in with the fog. Our scouts being spotted when in reconnoiter, the day before."

"It would seem so, Sergeant Major." Harold scanned the woods to either side, noting the ghostly forms of his men as they moved back into defensive positions, careful to maintain strict fire discipline, the enemy left guessing as to their location and number. "Any ideas?"

Scott wiped his lips. "Send someone forward, asking if we might join them for a cuppa tea and a hot meal, then part ways with smiles and handshakes all around." Scott grinned. "You want to do the honors?" Harold opened his mouth to reply, then stopped, turning his head and watching as George slipped up to where they were in a sinuous movement, his large body sliding in between them. Harold nodded a greeting as the big man leaned in, his deep voice reduced to a thin whisper.

"Someone on their side shot early—before we got in too deep. A few others joining in, which means they've not the experience or discipline of our group. Must be a mix of regulars, pressed from the ranks. A scattering of irregulars and scouts in with them, serving as their eyes and ears." George grinned. "Might be their leader has read the same books as you, Lieutenant Knutt. Our orders?"

"Sergeant Major Scott thinks I should go forward, seeking an invitation to join them for tea."

"Capital idea. Could use the warmth of a fire and food, the air here-abouts a bit damp."

Scott pointed with his chin, a movement in front having drawn his eye. "Someone coming to check on the result of the shot that missed you, sir." He leveled his musket, prepared to fire. Harold touched his shoulder, signaling him to wait. The three of them watched as a man in buckskin garb slowly emerged from the mist, wearing stained leggings beneath a faded leather-fringed coat, a thick mat of white hair and long beard sticking out from head and cheeks, framing skin the color of aged walnut.

Once the man reached the spot where Harold had been, he knelt, checking for sign of blood. Finding scuff marks, his eyes trailed them across the ground, locating where his target had rolled to the side. He rose, ready to follow them, then froze in place when he saw the barrel of Scott's musket pointed at his head. The elderly man placed his weapon on the ground and raised his hands in surrender.

The three leaders of the ranging party had moved back a few hundred paces; their captive brought with them, now sitting on a log under guard a dozen paces beyond a temporary firing line as the rest of Harold's force settled in. The surrendered man, a scout for the French, had a genial smile on his face, shaking his head, refusing to divulge any information as to numbers or identity of those holed up on the ridge.

"Options?" Harold gave George and Scott first chance to speak. He waited a few moments, then nodded. "My plan is to probe ahead, finding and fixing the ends of their line with our scouts, then send half our scouts and men to find cover behind the enemy, while the rest of us wait here. Shouting out orders and making noise as if preparing for a direct advance in line formation. Once the remainder of our native scouts locate their flanks and open fire, we'll break into small groups and rush forward, finding cover and firing as the others advance, then do the same. Continuing to close their lines, which should begin to panic due to the pressure from our men coming up from behind and the pressure on their flanks."

"What are we to do with any prisoners taken?" George gave Harold a hard stare. "We're rather thin in numbers—and too far out in front of our primary force for hope of additional support."

Harold swallowed. "I know the decision needed, realizing we cannot be burdened by—" He looked down, his hands trembling. "—must not allow any diversion from our goal of locating their main force, making raids against their supply train."

Scott reached out and touched Harold's upper arm. "Going to need to hear the words, sir." He paused. "Gonna need 'em as an order."

"There are to be—" Harold swallowed again, a sick look on his face, gone pale. "There are to be no prisoners. With no one allowed to escape, telling tales."

George shrugged in acknowledgment, then moved away in a long-legged stride, going over to where the older man they'd captured was sitting, his hoary head angled up in quiet conversation with two younger men, assigned as his guards. The Colonel paused, taking out a large-bladed knife and dragging it across the man's throat, his body left slumped forward, blood gushing out. "Follow me, men. We have our orders. *No* prisoners."

⌒℮⌒

The assault began with deadly precision. The combined effect of loud whoops and gunfire from each end of the ridgeline, combined with aimed fire from along the enemy's front, breaking the enemy force into shattered groups of confused men. Harold's force ambushing them as they came through, split up into dozens of deadly pairs, chasing down men fleeing for their lives. The assault from the front pushed forward, passing through the enemy encampment, herding the survivors into the thud of musket fire, hiss of arrows, war clubs and knives of the scouts and irregulars lying in wait, guided by the screams of men dying as they tried to surrender. A knot of experienced French soldiers made a last stand, creating a swirling melee of noise and movement filling the dense woods with pockets of men hacking at one another, the few who survived, easy enough to track down, their blood-trails staining the floor of the forest.

Harold ended up alone, separated from the others during the fight. He stood atop a steep rise, pistol in hand, freshly reloaded, having used it to drop one of the uniformed French soldiers before they could bayonet George in the back, then becoming entangled in a game of dodge the bayonet, finally able to thrust the tip of his sword into the stomach of a wild-eyed French officer. Scott coming up alongside him, striking the wounded man with the stock of musket to his bewigged head, before sprinting away in chase of another.

Harold felt numb, the whirlwind of close combat having spun him in every direction, his heart racing in his chest as he sucked in deep breaths. A river of sweat ran from forehead to chin, despite the late autumn weather. It had been his first identified kill, the pistol shot having struck the soldier in the back of his head, the man facing away.

Harold looked down at the ground, his instincts having led him to the top of a ridge where his men would reform. He was standing beneath a tall hardwood tree, identified as a beacon, helping to guide his men once they finished their grisly chore.

A slight movement from overhead drew Harold's attention to the limbs above, the soft mutter of a curse in French telling him to drop to the ground and roll away. He resisted the urge, remaining in place, head angled up as if a child prepared to receive his just punishment for the no-quarter order given. His fate hung in the balance, determined by the man lying in wait above, and the quality of his aim.

A pale face described itself from a pocket of breeze-stirred leaves. Harold sighed, a waft of cool air across his neck a pleasure, magnified in intensity as it might be his last. A clunk of metal against wood sounded, followed by the sight of a musket falling from in front. It landed against the base of the deeply rooted tree and discharged, a hiss of lead ball winging its way through the shadowed woods as a thick cloud of smoke drifted away. Another muttered curse in French broke the silence as the youthful face disappeared.

"Show yourself. You'll not be harmed." Harold spoke French, using a rural accent. After a long pause, he opened his mouth to call out again when the soldier's voice shouted, in a clean Parisian accent.

"You *killed* them. Men with *hands* in the air. *Unarmed*, or lying wounded on the ground. You killed them *all*. Every last *one* of them!"

Harold hung his head, the lethargy of leadership with its requisite evils fully borne, his heart weighed down with remorse. He cleaned his accent, matching that of his hidden rival. "We did. My men and I did. On my orders."

"You are the officer in charge?"

Harold didn't answer, a rustle from above indicating the young man might be moving to get a clear shot, with a pistol cocked and aimed. His life once again in another man's hands, fate determined by press of a finger on curved trigger. Harold nodded; eyes aimed down. "I am. To my eternal regret for the decision made, no matter the explanation I might offer—which I shall not."

"You swear—upon your *honor* as an officer—upon your *mortal* soul, that you will not kill *me*?"

Harold nodded. "I do solemnly swear. On my honor as an officer, tarnished though it is. There will be no further deaths, directed by my own hand or any of those under my command. You are under my protection, should you choose to accept it."

"I do not know the proper way to—surrender myself."

Harold stepped forward. "You need not learn now. You are not my prisoner, and free to go. I will point out the direction to you, should you ask it of me."

"And what of your men—and your *savages?*"

"No one will hinder your journey back to your lines. I swear it—again."

There was another long pause, followed by the slip of cloth against tree bark, ending with a thump of feet as they found the ground. The officer, a year or two his junior, straightened up, hazel eyes wide in fear, though he tried to hide it. He came over and presented his pistol, his head bowed as he did so. "I am Lieutenant Pierre de Coulombe, of—"

"Say no more. You are not a prisoner and should keep such details to yourself. This is only a—chance encounter between two soldiers, each giving way to the other."

"I would know your name, sir, if you will indulge my curiosity." The young man relaxed; his moment of truth having passed without lethal consequence. "Your French is—immaculate. You have spent time in Paris, no?"

"I was never that fortunate in my limited travels abroad. As to your first request, I am First Lieutenant Harold Knutt."

The other man's eyes widened in recognition. "*Renard Rouge!*" He shook his head. "I—I had you in my *sights!*"

"Why did you hesitate?"

The young officer blushed, his skin turning dark red. "I confess I could not stop from pissing myself, my fear so great. My hands trembling, losing my grip of the musket I'd recovered from—" The youth shook his head, looking down.

Harold shrugged, a thin smile on his lips. "It happens to us all, the first-time in."

"I would have been a hero, in having claimed you as my first—victory."

"And now you'll never be able to tell the story."

Pierre looked up. "No, I suppose not." He stiffened, standing straight, head high, his eyes filled with pride. "But my instincts were excellent, placing myself where I assumed your forces would gather. Prepared to eliminate the commander—you." He turned his head, looking at the musket. "Which I did not do. To my dying shame."

Harold returned the surrendered pistol. "You will need this, before making your way back."

Pierre eyed the weapon, took it, keeping the barrel pointed at the ground. "I—swore no oath." He hesitated a moment. "But will honor yours."

Harold could hear his men approaching, their calls of satisfaction ringing out from the far side of the steep knoll. Pierre looked around, eyes going wide once again. Harold took him by the shoulder and ushered him away, leading him downhill to a section of thick forest filling a narrow defile. Once there, he pointed toward a stretch of watery marsh. "Follow the slough on through to a stream. Then follow that to the river. Once there, turn upstream, staying close to the bank. You should come to your army within a day or so."

Pierre's eyes showed a level of concern. "How—can you know that?"

Harold sighed. "I often see things from a great height, as if a bird on wing looking down at the world."

"A splendid gift."

"You would think so." Harold bowed his head slightly. "You need to be moving, and quickly. I'll keep my men gathered here for the next few hours, allowing time for you to put distance between us." Harold held out his hand. "Whether our journeys provide for a future meeting or not, I wish you good health, Lieutenant Pierre de Coulombe."

The young French officer nodded, the sound of Harold's men calling out to their leader a signal for him to fade away into the cloak of forest.

A soft voice floated from behind a large rock, Harold brought to a stop, halfway back to the top of the knoll. "You'll order the meal—but take no part in the eating of it." He turned to one side, eyes on Scott as he stepped out, the lower sleeves of the veterans dull-colored coat covered in dark stains. Scott came over and stood beside Harold, his eyes gazing back along the climb his commanding officer had made.

Harold sighed. "I fear I'm not made for this. The killing of men—unprovoked."

Scott frowned. "You ordered it done, in order to remove the ears and eyes of their army by eliminating their forward element—as a *necessity*, so none could return with a warning."

Harold sighed. "He could have ended me. *Twice*."

"Deservedly so, a young man such as himself, still wet behind his ears—able to catch you out unaware." Scott turned and faced Harold, a cool look in his eyes.

Harold noted the lack of formal address from Scott. He knew he'd made a grave mistake, as seen through the older man's eyes. "He will be two days or more getting back. The river will prove to be a hard slog through marsh and backwater bogs. The General will be here by then, and we'll have moved forward to the hills, just there." Harold pointed toward the north, where a line of gray humps bordered the far edge of the riverine basin. "Advantage to the ones reaching them first, securing the higher ground. Which *we* will do, I assure you."

Scott waited, silent, his lips clenched as he stared back. Harold folded first; head angled down; his voice low. "I'll—let the men know what transpired here, Sergeant Major. If deemed necessary, I'll order men to follow the boy and—"

"You will *not*." Scott stepped forward. "If I felt it needed doing, I'd have taken care of it myself, before joining you and the rest of the men." He shrugged, one shoulder lower than the other, an ooze of blood visible through a tear in the upper arm of his coat. "But—in consideration of how the other odd strategies you've come up with have proven out—I'm willing to let this one lay as played." Scott shoved past Harold, heading back to the top of the rise. He took a few steps, then stopped, his words carved out with sharp edges. "Just hope it doesn't end up sinking its teeth in our *arses*." He paused, a final word tossed over his shoulder as he moved away. "Sir."

⌒e⌒

The night was as dark as Harold's mood, overcast beneath a thick layer of clouds, rain holding off while thunder and flashes of lightning toyed with hills in the distance. He lay on his side, curled beneath the roots of the tree where the French officer had lain in wait. The rest of the ranging party had settled into scattered clumps of snoring men, while a handful of sentries kept watch at their posts, half-way down the slope.

Harold sighed, aware the only threat to his men this night would come from ghosts in restless wander, attempting to reclaim life's sweet sauce. He rolled onto his back; his eyes focused on a leaf-filtered sky through the oak limbs overhead, with nary a single star to focus on. Not a single point of light to pin his attention to while his mind drifted through a sea of emotions, filled with moments of shame and guilt. The dead man's face before him, red-lipped wound in his throat, with a questioning look on his whiskered face as he died, his eyes staring as if asking why. A burden to his soul, Harold left to wonder how long he would need to carry it, before letting it slip away.

"Ye canna sleep—the ordered deed a heavy weight upon your shoulders, sir." Scott slid into place beside him, his knees drawn up, elbows angled back, resting on the ground. "Your first real feel of the salt, rubbed deep in the wound. Fearing you might never be let go from it." Scott let out a long sigh, then shook his head. "Would tell you it'll pain you less as you move further along the road, but the sorry truth is—it will only grow stronger, each year passed, until it eats away the better part of your soul—*if* you let it."

Harold sat up, squaring his shoulders, looking at Scott's profile, barely seen against a lighter section of sky on the horizon. "I have become what I swore to fight against. Left standing in front of the mirror, my reflection no different from those men I read about in books, fighting their battles over and again in countless recreations. Trying to wrest good results from bad, failing to do so, every time." He sighed, shaking his head. "Childish games, played as a boy. Hard deaths, now, and I—the cause of them."

Scott opened his mouth and yawned, covering the sound of it with one hand. "The man we—murdered, he had the choice of following up his shot or staying in cover. Was his own fate placed him in our hands this day, or yesterday—the midnight hour just now turning over."

"Some would make claim of it being our destiny. His, now joined with mine."

Scott looked at Harold, his face shadowed by the background arc of sky. "Are those the words you'll have put on the stone placed over you? Bearing his story, along with yours?" Scott snorted. "Along with all the others to come?"

Harold reflected, sitting beside the only man he knew could understand what he was going through. "Have you, in all your years of service—ever had to carry such a load as this? Without an officer's order being given, helping you bear the curse, relieving you of the burden of having to do—what needed to be done?"

Scott hesitated, rubbing the line of his jaw. "A few times—yes. In high mountain passes, outside villages. Young boys met on the trail, herding goats. Killed to prevent them alerting the ones we were after. Each of them an outsized portion of the price paid to get the task done—and the hardest to get over. But you do, in time—get over it." Scott sniffed, then spit to one side. "Once you suffer the loss of a few close friends, taken unaware, butchered while on watch, it helps diminish the rawness comes from killing those who, on another day and in a different place, would be but boys, playing at war. Now left meat on the ground, slaughtered, hands bound behind them, ordered to their deaths by an officer's momentary whim. Our own necks in a noose, left swinging from a limb—for any who couldn't manage the task."

Harold interrupted, his voice a hiss of despair. "I—cannot make it *stop*. The *sight* of it!" He scrubbed the beginning of a whine from his voice. "The careless ease of it. Colonel O'Malley's knife. Of how it went through the old man's throat like parchment paper. One moment—a living soul, sitting there, smile on his face. The next, gone, the light fading from his eyes." Harold swallowed, feeling his stomach flutter in response to the image. "How easily the stroke was made." Harold turned his head, the clouds thickening, barely able to make out the silhouette of the thick trunk of the oak. "George seemed not bothered by it, as if it were no more than a wipe of leaves 'cross the crack of his ass. A careless drag, then toss away of a man's life. For no other reason than to keep him pinned in place, forever silent."

Scott softened his voice. "As happens to our *own*, at the hands of the natives, or the French. It matters not the size, shape, color, or form of the ones in deliver of your final moment. We all end up food for the worms, unless you choose the Viking route—sent off in a twist of smoke and ashes, dancing away in the wind."

"I would gladly choose *either* of those ends—tonight, if only to shed myself—"

"You will, in time, whether still a soldier or not."

Harold hung his head. "Not soon enough."

Scott sighed, then reached over, taking Harold's shoulder in his grasp. He gave it a gentle squeeze. "The days will fly, and you will wonder where they went to, while in contemplation of every hole you ever saw dug, or fiery bier set fire to. So—*cheer up!* Your own moment will arrive, bringing you the peace you feel is deserved." He lifted his hand. "Just know that, were the circumstance reversed—your throat would be as easily slit by slip of cold steel through blood warmed flesh."

"I only wish—"

Scott's voice shifted into a firm tone. "Belay further blather. You've no right to remorse, sir. You signed the forms, then toed the line in swear of a solemn vow made to King and Country. So, pick yourself up by the nape of your neck and—and shake this feeling out, without stopping until your back teeth rattle in your yawp. You've men to lead, and it's for them to follow. Time enough to mourn your innocence lost once home again to England, with a fine lass on your arm, no doubt."

"Then I will—never be rid of this?"

"Was not smoke blowing from my lips, sir." Scott stood up, hands on his lower back, working away at a knot of pain. "You will need to speak with the men before we break camp by dawn. Best get some sleep." He paused, before moving away, his voice barely a whisper. "If you can manage it, son."

Harold nodded, then lay down, listening to the sound of Scott's footsteps as he walked away, the older man's final word penetrating the fog of his thoughts. He shook his head, thinking of his father, wondering how and what he was doing, the day already begun back home in Bristol.

CHAPTER TEN

Ohio Basin Hillside, November 1758

Push to Battle

"They're waiting us out—knowing we are sore pressed in supply, while they're served by their fleet of boats." The General turned away from a map drawn in fine detail. "We hold the reins to a perfect killing ground *if* we can convince them to advance." Aidyn noted a frown on Major Sandersen's pinched face and aimed a curt nod in his direction.

"Yes, Major?"

"I believe it a mistake, sir, the advice given you to let go of the boats we'd recently commandeered. Burning them, a far better plan. Removing—"

Aidyn cut the sallow-faced man off. "Then we must return to that exact moment in time and do so, *now*." He frowned, then gave the fawning man a sour look. "You would do better to provide me one less 'should-have-done' and a few more 'what-we-are-to-do-nows'." Sandersen bowed, then stepped back, his close-set eyes filled with suppressed anger.

Harold opened his mouth to speak, stopping when the General shot him a glare, before ordering everyone to leave. The officers fanned out

of the command tent, going in different directions, Harold at the edge
of the encampment before a runner managed to catch up to him, letting
him know the General had summoned him back. As he followed the
out of breath soldier, Harold knew Aidyn would order him to produce
a plan to break the stalemate, of significant benefit to the French, for
now. Then he smiled; the seed of an idea having already sprouted in
his fertile mind.

ᘒᘎ

Aidyn shook his head as Harold saluted. "It was my decision to release
the boats back to their rightful owners, not yours, Lieutenant. The weight
of it a burden that comes with any leadership position." Aidyn shrugged,
then gave Harold a considered look. "A hard truth you're no doubt aware
of, based on recent events brought to my attention." The older man
paused, his eyes looking away for a long moment before turning back.
"A difficult order to have given, though warranted under the extreme
conditions as were described to me." He paused for a moment. "If not,
your head would be in a noose. Is that understood, Lieutenant Knutt?"

"Yes—sir."

Aidyn held out his arm, a glass placed in his hand with a dram of
whiskey poured in by Scott, who held one in his own hand as well. "I
will hear your plan, Lieutenant—on how we are to force the Frenchies
to come to *us*. I assume you have one in hand, based on your incautious
attempt to voice it earlier, all but guaranteeing a dagger in your back
should it prove viable."

Harold nodded; the criticism deserved. "I do, General. A simple
scheme requiring but a few kegs of powder, along with a handful of casks
filled with lead balls. And several meters of slow-burning fuse. And a
raft, which I will oversee the construction of upriver, well beyond the
range of French patrols."

Aidyn returned a silent stare, his light-blue eyes narrowed beneath bushy brows. "Another stratagem taken from one of your books, I gather."

Harold shook his head, a smug smile on his face. "No, General. This one is *all* mine."

A gentle breeze angled against the relentless slip of a wide river, filling the sail of a raft, an oil-fueled lantern hanging from the bow as the craft drifted with the current. A slight movement of rudder pole helped center it in the flow, a lone sailor standing at the helm, his arm lifted in a casual wave, voice raised to a yell, a slurred stream of guttural French released into a moonlit sky. "A shipment of casks—of the *finest* wine and brandy. Sent from your friends in Ontario to lift the fighting spirits of our—of our *glorious army*. To celebrate another victory over the filthy *English!* To your boats, my friends. Come gather yourselves 'round my humble craft and receive your just rewards for the work done in resupply of our—of our *glorious*—glorious *army!*" The drunk steersman stumbled back out of sight, his voice dwindling away. Soldiers standing watch at their posts near a temporary dock ran to wake the boat captains and their men before the raft and its precious cargo could float past.

A flurry of activity built among the canvas shelters lining the banks, lanterns lit, swinging in the hands of men as they rushed toward a multitude of boats tied up at moorings or lashed alongside the dock. Once there, they leapt in, manning oars, the vessels guided out toward the raft in an angled line to intercept it. Their voices joining that of the drunken captain who was in the middle of a bawdy tavern song, waving one arm, encouraging their spirited efforts.

Harold glanced down, giving a wink to two young soldiers who'd volunteered to come along, willing to join him in the first part of his plan aimed at depriving the French of their supply fleet once again. He'd overseen construction of the large raft along with loading in of three kegs of gunpowder surrounded by a mound of small casks of musket balls. He'd had the carefully positioned munitions covered over with thick tarps, nailed in place, with a series of short fuses gathered in a thick knot. A touch of flame from a lantern would start their measured burn, ending with a devastating explosion, eliminating any watercraft within fifty paces. Time enough for Harold to alert the enemy crews to their danger, with an invitation to leap into the water to avoid the worst of the effects.

⌒℮⌒

George nudged Scott in his shoulder, eliciting a slight wince on the other man's face as he did so, still bothered by a wound suffered during their last mission. A thrust from a French bayonet skewering it to the bone. One of several minor injuries sustained among the advance force, with no deaths on their side of the ledger against that of the entire French force, less one young officer. The General had listened to their report, then ordered the main body of the army forward at a doubled pace until they'd arrived at the top of an imposing slope where they'd encamped and begun preparing fortifications, allowed by the French commander to dig in, then forced to sit back and wait for him to attack. The enemy reluctant to do so, satisfied to wait the siege out. Aidyn hopeful their young strategist's plan would force open the French through the gates of the fort below.

"Our men are in position—the wind in our favor." George kept his voice to a murmur. "All we need do is move forward on the sound of thunder from afar."

The taciturn Sergeant Major clenched his lips. "*If* the lad's plan goes off as designed."

George licked his lips, staring at a sealed clay pot secured in one hand, containing a noxious extract that he and several other infiltrators intended to toss at the sentries patrolling along the boundary of a large munitions and food supply depot, located well behind entrenched lines of French soldiers, providing security. George could tell the men on guard were tired, their feet dragging as they made their way around the perimeter. The second part of Harold's plan ready to proceed as soon as the sentries were driven away, allowing two dozen native scouts and colonist guides to rush in and set kegs of gunpowder. Fuses timed to explode after the raiders cleared the immediate area, the ensuing chaos intended to draw attention away from the first explosion upriver, providing Harold and the two men with him better odds in making their own escape.

George nodded, then looked over at Scott, his face reflecting a glimmer of light from torches lining the perimeter of the supply depot, a grim expression on his lips. "You don't seem happy—at the thought of his success."

The Sergeant Major turned his head to one side, spitting on the ground. "I'm not. For each time he congers up a minor miracle, it's a mark for *and* against him. The other officers above him already scheming to cut his legs out from under him, knowing they can never match him, move for move."

George grinned; his teeth white against the deep tan on his face. "Then release him to me. I'll see him made general of the militia and we'll send you fine lads packing for home."

An owl hoot sounded from the edge of the surrounding woods, signal from a native scout letting George and Scott know they were ready to dispatch the guards as they fled the odorous concoction in the sealed clay pots, joined by a handful of trappers, men who'd cackled with glee while collecting musk glands from over two dozen skunks.

Harold stumbled; his voice heavily slurred as he approached the bow of the raft, singing a song the Acadian captain had taught him during their weeks spent in close confine. He peeked over the near rail, sounding as if he'd already consumed a large amount of the imaginary supply of wine and brandy promised to the crews of the approaching boats, many of them waving their hats in greeting as they drew close. Harold mirrored them, a large mug held to his lips, pretending to drink, then belching, tossing the empty container over his shoulder as a signal for the two men hidden beside him to light the fuses.

"You're too late. I've finished it all. So—so turn around and—and *pull* for shore, as there is no more." Harold attempted a jig, raising a chorus of mock groans and jeers from the approaching supply fleet. The sailors shipped their oars, drifting in and starting to tie up alongside, using the tops of several posts running along the sides. Harold glanced at the middle of the raft, the two young men on their feet, faces tight as they slipped past the rudder post into the river.

"Enjoy what's in the kegs, my friends—but dally not, for the raft and all boats tied up to it will be blown to bits in less than a half-minute. See yourselves over the side and stroke for shore as if your lives depend on it, for they surely do. The Red Fox bids thee a fine fare-the-*well!*"

Harold spun around and dove into the water, staying under for a count of twenty seconds. When he surfaced, he could hear an angry snarl of shocked voices and loud splashes from behind. After a deep inhalation of air, he dove under again, heading across the current, aiming toward the near bank, wanting to get clear of the mayhem about to happen. He stayed submerged until a dull thud reached him, then surfaced, clearing his eyes, the raft and boats gone, his plan having gone off to perfection. He could hear splashing from the near riverbank, along with a muttering of voice and knew his two men had survived; the only twist left in the mission to evade capture with the help of native guides, stationed close by to gather them up.

Harold found the bottom of the riverbed with his feet and waded toward the shadowed bank. Then he stopped; head angled to one side, a pained voice calling out to him in English with heavy accent. "My friend. My fellow captain. A hand—if you will."

Harold recognized the speaker and turned around, making his way back into the current, collecting his former instructor on all things nautical by the back of his water-logged coat, pulling him into the shallows and helping him climb the sloped bank. Once there, he lowered him down, then sat beside him, resting against the trunk of an old pine.

Harold gave the older man a warm smile. "I'm glad you had the sense to join me for an evening swim."

"I recognized you—before we tied up." The Captain attempted a smile in return, his words in French. "Your dancing—is not much improved—since we last—parted." A guttural groan slipped from between the compressed line of his lips.

Harold leaned in; his eyes narrowed in concern. "You're injured?"

The Captain nodded, then closed his eyes, his breathing labored. "A small piece of my—my lady—found me as I cleared the surface—to draw a second breath. Preventing me—from taking another—full breath. Or I would have—beat you to shore."

Harold started to stand. "Let me help you to one of your surgeons. It won't be far. We can follow the riverbank."

The man waved him back down with a motion of his hand, shaking his head. "It is of—small consequence. And I am satisfied to have—caught you up—if only to bid you a bon voyage." There was a long pause as the man wheezed his way through several shortened breaths. "I suspect you—have men nearby—to assist in your escape. You are, after all—the Red—"

Harold heard his friend let go a final breath. He bowed his head, taking a moment to offer him a murmured prayer, easing him on his way. Then, with tears streaming down his cheeks, he closed the older man's eyes, adding another life to the opposite side of the scale. He knew the bill would come due one day, all things brought back to a balance, as his father would say when considering a handful of receipts proving a merchant had cheated him. Then Harold pulled the captain's body back out into the river, committing it to the steady current in honor of his friend's final request, expressed over two months ago. The old mariner, head on crossed arms, staring up at a sea of stars, his voice soft with reflection, offering thoughts on his eventual death.

"A man knows his place in the world, and mine has always been to the water drawn. Ever since a small boy. It speaks to me—with an angel's voice, guiding me past unseen shoals and dark-bodied logs. Though never of any help with pretty women. Left to my own instincts when making an escape from angry husbands, knowing that, whenever ashore, I was on my own."

Harold listened to the angry sounds of men as they struggled to reach shore further down the riverbank, providing the closest thing to an angel's voice to help guide the captain to wherever he would end up. "Have a pleasant journey, my friend." Then he turned about and made his way back to the bank, an owl's hoot in Iroquois accent calling to him, one of his own offered in soft reply. Two native guides stepped out from the edge of woods; hands extended. Harold took their outstretched wrists, letting them pull from the clinging grasp of the river.

CHAPTER ELEVEN

Ohio Basin Hillside, late November 1758

Change in the Weather

The French forces began forming at the bottom of a long slope in massed lines. Uniformed men, decked out in white, standing in front of a dozen bronze cannons hitched to teams of horses, ready to move forward in support of the soldiers when the order came for their advance.

Two weeks had passed since the destruction of their supply boats and devastating raid on their depot. The French commander aware his only hope lay in winning a victory now or end up having to vacate the fort, beginning a monthlong struggle overland to reach Ontario, while under constant assault by the English warrior known as Renard Rouge.

General MacLean lowered a brass telescope, having finished another survey of the enemy formations at the bottom of the long slope. "They do not seem—*pleased.*" He handed the glass to an aide, then sighed. "Dangerous, when a man's back is pressed to a wall. Hunger, a damper to his fear of death, with nothing left to lose." Aidyn fixed Harold with a tight grin. "We have an advantage in food and munitions, though our men are over-burdened with confidence. Which I blame *you* for, Lieutenant. Your string of victories has created a sense of—invincibility in the men."

Aidyn sighed, then lowered his voice. "We're heavily outnumbered and facing a foe who must win today or lose everything. Their commander intent on coming after our store of supplies. A desperate gamble forced upon him, willing to suffer formidable losses due to our advantage in elevation, increasing the effectiveness of our artillery while diminishing his own." He paused, tightened his lips, then shook his head, his silver-gray hair tied into a ponytail with a twist of leather, swinging between his narrow shoulders. "I'd hoped to offer them a mutually agreeable surrender—undermanned as we are with no guarantee of stopping their assault." Aidyn, the lines in his face softened by concern for the lives of his men, looked over at Harold. "I believe we must plan for a retreat. Set about burning our excess supplies and munitions. Valor alone will not be enough for us to win through this day."

"If I may, sir." Harold moved to the battle map and reached out; his finger pressed to its surface. "We must retreat, yes, but as part of an *offensive* plan. Starting here—" He tapped the parchment. "—at what will be our first line of resistance. Formed into our typical three-deep formation, with normal spacing between each man of the front line, but with a shift in the last two rows. Moving them in a diagonal slant. The French commander seeing what will appear to be a solid wall of red, with three times the number of men he believes us to be. The increased spacing helping to reduce our losses from enemy shells."

Aidyn nodded, indicating Harold should continue. "Once their front-line closes to seventy paces, our front line will kneel, with the second row standing, firing as one. The angled lines will allow for the passing forward of loaded muskets from the third line, with the empty ones handed back for reloading. After three rounds of concentrated fire, our men will make a rapid withdrawal up the slope before the French can close to fifty paces to return fire. Reforming again—" Harold moved his finger higher on the map. "—here, where the second line will now become the first, the third becoming the second, and so forth. The same maneuver repeated, with our men in quick retreat each time the enemy closes in. The unorthodox maneuver will reduce their number by half before they reach here—" He tapped his finger a third time. "—where our men will retreat to positions in front of our artillery, all rows kneeling in a solid line just to the front of the cannon muzzles, which will be loaded with sacks of musket balls. Our men will volley fire a final time, then fall back at the sound of a bugle call, taking up defensive positions just behind the cannons, where they will wait while we wither the enemy, now coming on in a massed charge to try and overwhelm our artillery. Our men will then advance, stopping to fire a final round, then meeting the French survivors with bayonets leveled, encouraging their surrender."

The general pursed his lips, considering the idea. "And what of our Colonials and native allies?"

Harold nodded, sliding his finger to one the side of the lower section of the map. "Colonel O'Malley will lead his forces in an attack made from here, coming out from the thick woods to the side of the slope, after we've made our second withdrawal. The French commander will be focused on moving his artillery up to support the advance of their infantry, their range limited due to the steep slope. Our skirmishers will be on them before they can react, scattering them while our native allies move in from both sides of the upper slopes, harassing the flanks of the French infantry lines. The Colonials, once they've spiked the enemy cannons, will move up the hill, staying out of range of our own guns until we've decimated the center of the enemies massed charge. Then they'll advance, completing the encirclement, with calls for the enemy to surrender. Offered and, God-willing—accepted in return."

The general gazed at Harold. "As simple as that?"

Harold nodded. "Nothing ever goes exactly as planned, but we *will* prevail, sir."

Aidyn stared at the map; his eyes narrowed as he reflected on Harold's plan. "A variation of the ranging attack used by your men in the recent forest engagement. Fire and maneuver tactics—though on a much larger scale."

"It *will* work, sir."

"I expect so Lieutenant, leaving me with a dilemma, once again." He turned his attention back down the long slope, marking the enemy's slow movement into position. "What I am to do with you once we win through, as you will be forced into waters over your head, far deeper than any faced in the river below."

"Time enough for that worry at the end of this day, sir. *If* we live to see it through."

Scott glowered at Harold, the young officer having positioned himself a few paces to the front of the company, located in the middle section of the front line. The French infantry was in a slow advance, struggling uphill, worn down from hunger. "You're no good to us there, sir, exposed as you are. Of little value to esprit de corps, with you sopping up stray balls of lead."

"The men must know me as an officer of the line, Sergeant Major—not some child at play with toy soldiers."

"The men must load, fire, and *move* as ordered, sir. They require *nothing* more!"

"I *will* stand with them, Sergeant Major. You'll accept my decision and see to the men, ensuring they follow my orders."

Soldiers on either end of the section of line just behind glanced over, their fingers tight on stock and forearm of muskets. The murmur of their voices turned into a roar of shouts that began to flow along the line, the cheers of a hundred men building to a thousand strong with Harold's company roaring the loudest, their voices creating a wall of sound that flowed to where the enemy forces were marching in tired formations. *"Red Fox! Red Fox! Red Fox!"*

Scott heard the note of confidence in the shouts of the men. Could see the reflection of their love for their officer in the tear-filled, but steady eyes of the young man who'd earned the right to fight and die alongside those who followed him without question. He added his own voice into the mix, his musket raised as he joined in with the massed line of frenzied soldiers as they sent a confident challenge down-slope to lines of desperate men in white coats.

The battle was over; an hour of mindless bloodshed having passed. Days of mass burials and slow recovery from wounds still lying ahead. Harold stared across a field littered with unstrung men, thankful for another day still above ground, his survival and reputation earned at the cost of a thousand lives or more.

As soon as Scott finished his casualty report and walked away, Meghan came over and took his hand, as blood-stained as his own, their fingers formed into a single clenched fist. She leaned her head against his shoulder, her pain-filled eyes focused on the sun as it crawled toward the far horizon through a hazy western sky.

"Tomorrow will be a bonny day." Her voice was husky, brushed with bass notes of sorrow, tears streaming down her blood-stained cheeks. "The sky—clear."

Harold nodded as he leaned his head against hers, a wash of warmth flowing through him as he released his nausea, fatigue, and horror at what he'd seen and done. His need for Meghan the only thing that mattered. His love for her, unconditional, greater than that felt for his men. For those who'd passed or were still alive. Greater than for his family; an impossible distance away. He sighed, bound to his life as an officer for as long as destiny would allow. Bound to the woman at his side for as long as she would have him as a partner in her life.

"Yes, Lassie. It does indeed look to be a braw and bonny day."

CHAPTER TWELVE

Native Village, Mid-Winter 1759

A Change in Scenery

A haze of woodsmoke threaded its way between clumps of undressed trees, the ground covered in a thick carpet of leaves. The acrid scent from dozens of fires hung below an overcast sky, heavy with promise of snow sometime in the night. A line of men in dark leather coats and drab clothing inched their way down a narrow path etched into an angled wall of limestone. Once they reached level ground, they bunched into a thick column and marched toward a large native village, encircled by a high palisade wall formed of pointed logs, their ends embedded deep into the earth.

Harold smiled as a flood of children came out to meet them, chased by a yipping pack of small dogs. Their voices were indistinguishable to him from those of any other youths at play, no less boisterous or shy. Some reached out and touched their clothes, weapons, or hair. Others held back, concerned looks on their round-cheeked faces, hands in a nervous twist.

The children, the product of a group of people who began to filter out through the main gate in the wall of the village, were members of the Mingo tribe, smallest of a handful of others collectively known as the Iroquois nation who were in firm control of the lands of the greater Ohio basin.

Harold lifted his hand and wiped away a line of sweat from under the brim of his officer's hat. He was glad their weeklong journey was behind them, an arduous climb and then difficult descent made through dozens of steep-sided valleys. Twenty-four men and ten sure-footed mules had carefully worked their way through the wilderness on their way to the remote village, under the guidance of several natives and three colonial guides. He grinned as he watched the handlers of the pack animals keeping a tight grasp on the halters of the antsy beasts of burden, struggling to keep control of the animals loaded down with packs of food, military supplies, and a healthy assortment of ceremonial gifts selected for the tribal leaders of the various native groups who were assembling outside the village.

General Aidyn had arranged the gathering in advance. Leaders from the various Iroquois tribes invited to attend a mid-winter conclave to hear his representative's request for their support. A man known to them by his reputation as a proven leader of men in battle and deemed acceptable to speak to them on behalf of the English forces now based at the recently captured French fort upstream.

The leaders had agreed to meet at the Mingo village, under the leadership of a chief with equal reputation as a gifted leader of men. One Aidyn knew his young officer would need to convince to join the English, helping to turn the tide against the French. Sergeant Major Scott having convinced him the man known as Red Fox would be able to sway the natives to their side.

Orders

"I do not see its value, General. The words are but a—meaningless expression. Nay, not even that. Only a foolish nickname. Nothing more." Harold stood at attention, an expression of dismay on his face. "Sir."

"It is a title given *and* earned, *Captain* Knutt. One carrying significant weight with our native allies, who coined it, as well our own men, who repeat it with great fervor. An asset I will use as *I* see fit. Is that understood?"

Harold froze, his face blushing as soon as the promotion in rank had been mentioned by the general. "Begging your pardon, General. I've not been long enough in rank to deserve such rapid advancement in—"

"You'll be representing the British Empire as my emissary. Speaking on my behalf. Doing so with whatever title I care to assign, and I have determined this recent advancement in rank to be justly deserved, provided to the man who will be responsible for making—*reasonable* arrangements to secure pledges of mutual support with the various tribes who will be in attendance. Charged with passing on the promise of my unwavering commitment to honor the claims of those living in the Ohio Basin. Allies instrumental to our being able to keep hold of what we've so recently won. Is that understood, Captain Knutt?"

The general stopped to draw in a breath, one finger raised as a signal for Harold to remain silent. "The French will not stand idly by, allowing us to sit in residence at this strategic locale unattended to. Spring will find an army bearing down on us with thousands of soldiers, supplies in hand, looking to lay siege until we're forced to capitulate. Any additional forces of our own, as well as the goods needed for resupply, having to come overland, exposed to constant raid from marauding bands of French irregulars and their native allies."

Scott brought a decanter of French brandy over and refilled the general's glass. Aidyn drained it, licked his lips, then lowered his finger. Harold waited until given a curt nod. "I—appreciate that, General. Believe me. And will do everything within my power to see it accomplished. Sir."

The general sighed, then lifted his hand and rubbed the space between his eyes, his thick, bushy eyebrows raised in exasperation. "I sense a 'but' about to occur."

Scott cleared his throat. "If I may, sir. I think what Captain Knutt is trying to say is—he does not see himself as others do and would prefer to be less conspicuous in the role assigned him."

Aidyn stared at Harold. "Is that your feeling, Captain Knutt?"

Harold gave Scott a nod of appreciation. "It is, General."

Aidyn smiled, waiting until Harold relaxed, then tossed it aside, his pale-blue eyes hardening into a firm glare. "Then I suggest you get *over* it, Captain. You will lead the assemblage of religious and governmental personages, maintaining strict adherence to my directives. There will be no countenance of complaints among them, or actions taken outside my orders. Nor lack of fervent support for the plan as I have laid it out. Is that understood?"

Both Harold and Scott stiffened to full attention, eyes straight ahead, answering as one. "Yes, General." Aidyn wore a satisfied grin on his lips. "You're dismissed." He waited until the two men closed the door of his office, his voice softening. "And may God continue watching over you both, returning you to me in good health."

Among the Smoke

A middle-aged chieftain named Tawana passed a long-stemmed pipe to Harold, who accepted it with a solemn nod. The native, a middle-aged man of medium height and slender build, was head of the smaller of several tribes Harold was seeking alignment with. A respected leader with a reputation for strong leadership and uncanny vision, Harold knew his support would be crucial in forming a mutually beneficial agreement with the other leaders.

The chief had finished making a speech welcoming the recently arrived men to his village. He stared at Harold with a thin smile on his lips, his dark eyes focused on the ceremonial pipe in the young officer's hands. Harold placed the stem to his lips, wearing a solemn look on his face as he pulled in a tentative draw. The raw-edged smoke clawed at his tongue, then tore through his throat, into his protesting lungs. Harold struggled to hold it in, unprepared for such a harsh invasion. He coughed once, then again, his stomach twisting in protest, a rush of bile reaching the base of his throat, his eyes watering as he quickly passed the pipe to Scott.

A reed-thin man with overly sized false teeth made of ivory, a minister by occupation and one of a handful of Colonial citizens selected to join the group, beamed a smile from a pair of thin, pale lips. "The captain is—considering your words of greeting, Chief Tanawa. Powerful words, from a man known as a wise leader of your people. We are—"

Scott reached over; his fingers pressing the diminutive man's shoulder in an iron grip. The minister closed his mouth around a gasp of pain, his voice stilled while Harold exhaled carefully, finding a tenuous balance between maintenance of a serious demeanor and the look of revulsion struggling to reach his face by his abused lungs. Once he managed to gather his breath, he nodded at the native leader.

"I am honored to have opportunity to exchange words with you, Chief Tawana, and leaders of the tribes of the Iroquois nation." Harold's proper pronunciation of the chief's name and use of his native tongue raised the eyebrows on the nut-brown skin of the man's unlined face.

The chief replied in French, a language all tribes knew and used; trappers and priests having arrived in their lands over a hundred circles of seasons before. Strangers seeking trade of fur for metal goods. Others following close behind, clad in dark robes, seeking to harvest souls from people living in the Ohio Basin, telling fanciful stories around campfires. "I am impressed by your ability to speak our tongue so clearly." Tawana paused; his eyes narrowed in thought. "Yourself, a stranger in our lands."

"As I'm certain your guides informed you, Chief Tawana, their lessons with me were invaluable during our journey here." Harold matched the chief's choice of language, allowing for fluid communication. He glanced at the thin, gangly minister, who was staring back at him with a frown, lost to their exchange with English his only language. Harold tried not to think too poorly of the middle-aged minister of Protestant faith, with limited knowledge of the people inhabiting the basin area, gleaned during several attempts in the past to bring the word of God to natives seeking refuge outside small settlement villages, located on the outskirts of Western Pennsylvania.

Harold gave him a thin smile, then looked back at Chief Tawana. "My friend, Minister Patterson, has been teaching me your history—as he understands it to be. I would enjoy hearing it told directly from you, if willing to share your people's stories with me."

Tawana studied Harold's face closely. "I know some of your history as well. Stories about a man named 'Red Fox' shared up and down the great river, chasing the White-Coat and nipping at their heels until they turn around, then leaping to tear out their throats." He smiled, though Harold noted his expression remained shadowed.

"I bear the title proudly, honoring my native friends who gave it to me, earned on the back of their bravery and skill, along with the Colonial and English soldiers serving alongside me."

The minister leaned forward, having understood the words Renard Rouge. Harold nodded, giving the man permission to speak. "I can attest to the captain's title. One of distinction; richly deserved. As is your own, Chief—Tawana, known in our lands to the east as a great and wise leader. One who might be open to allowing the teachings of—"

Tawana fixed the minister with a sharp gaze, then responded in his native tongue, looking at Harold, waiting for him to translate. Harold gave the minister a measured look as he complied. "The chief asks if this land you speak of was brought with you, carried across the great water on your large ships."

The minister faltered. "I—do not understand. I'm speaking of the land we live on. Where our homes, farms, and settlements are. Along with places of worship, where good people gather to hear the glorious words of God."

Tawana raised an eyebrow, listening to the translation then smiling as he replied, his eyes on the diminutive man as Harold relayed his words. "This land, was it not already lived on by others? Must be poor soil, if left unsettled long before your people arrived."

Harold considered tossing a rescue line to the bewildered man, about to do so when Chief Tawana leaned forward, fixing the minister with a firm smile. "I thank you for your words, my friend." The native leader stood up and addressed all those sitting in a circle within the great lodge, marking the exchange as best they could. "It is time for us to leave off speaking and share a meal together. To begin our journey along a path where our people will remain in control of our ancestral lands. To hunt, farm, build homes on—and defend, should the need arise."

Minister Patterson smiled, his large ivory teeth stained from constant use of tea and tobacco. He nodded his head, unable to follow the leader's words, pleased his own had found a welcome home in the chieftain's ears.

◌

A young native woman, near to Harold's age, reached down and placed a carved bowl filled with thick stew in front of him. He was first of the group of visitors from the east to be served, in recognition of his role as their leader. The woman's hair was bound in a single ebony braid swinging over her shoulder as she leaned down, the ends brushing his cheek, raising a blush on his face.

He turned his head, looking up with a smile of thanks, the food contained within the bowl a mix of seasoned meat and ground corn, a sprinkle of dried mushrooms and herbs added in. The woman returned his smile, dusky-rose colored lips framing her pure-white teeth.

"You are the one they call Red Fox." She spoke to him in French, with a faint trace of her people's accent. Harold nodded; the title accepted without reply. "You are known as a skilled warrior—for the men in red-coats. No?"

"No." Harold paused, knowing his terse reply had thrown her off. "I am only a man, able to see what is in front of him. Nothing more."

"And what do you see in front of you, here" She slipped to the floor of the longhouse, one knee angled alongside his leg, her face highlighted by the glow from a long fire pit.

Harold couldn't help but stare, her features delicate, eyes pools of dark brown, with strands of curled hair circling the edges of perfectly formed ears. He swallowed. "I see a woman—with no name."

"A'neewa. Daughter of Chief Tawana." She shifted into her native tongue. "And you are indeed a fox. Sly, with a slippery tongue." She rose to her feet, starting to turn away, his soft voice stopping her. "I am as much a fox as you are a silent doe."

A'neewa's eyes widened in shock at his use of her given name. "You—have learned our language."

Harold shifted to French, his knowledge of this group's tribal language limited, though he was eager to learn more in service to the general's needs. "The guides your father sent were helpful, as I mentioned to him earlier. They provided lessons as we traveled." Harold waited a moment, seeing A'neewa's eyebrows narrowing above her wide-set eyes, then he continued. "One of them told me about the members of his family. About his father, Chief Tawana. And his older sister, Silent Doe."

A'neewa glanced across the firepit, receiving an inquisitive look from her father, having become aware of their extended exchange. Then she looked down at Harold. "I will leave you to your meal, man with a wagging tongue. Take care you do not chew it off." Her hip brushed against his shoulder as she moved past him, Harold's eyes following her as she slipped through the doorway of the large communal lodge.

Scott leaned against a section of outer palisade wall, his eyes on the fields beyond. The dawn was in steady approach, the edge of the village painted in a wash of gold light as the sun cleared tree-topped hills. He watched a group of young girls at play, noting a gleam of light from metal bracelets on their wrists, one of many cross-culture exchanges seen as he'd made his way through the village. Evident in heat-blackened metal pots suspended above beds of roused coals. Tended by women wearing leather belts, metal buckles displayed around hide and cloth-covered waists, with metal rings on fingers and bands of silver twisted around wrists and upper arms.

Scott wore a wry smile on his face as he considered how the ancestors of the natives might have been able to change history had they only discovered to work with metal. A picture formed in his mind of the original colonists, met by native men with metal-tipped arrows and spears on the briny edge of eastern shorelines.

The stealthy approach of soft-soled shoes caught his attention, his honed instincts ignored, pretending to flinch when a silky voice reached out, caressing his ears. It was the young woman who'd been at the feast the night before, serving Harold and engaging in conversation in French with him, before disappearing, Scott learning she was the head man's daughter.

A'neewa used English, her knowledge of it limited to short words. "You are—Scott. Good friend—to Fox Red."

Scott nodded his head, his reply made in French to ease the flow of their conversation. "I am, though my given name is Robert. Scott is the last name of my family." He spoke slowly, having learned French over the years, using words and phrases picked up in conversation with native allies, and French soldiers captured in battle.

"And your friend, he has a family in your lands—here?"

"He goes by Harold, last name of Knutt. And no, he has none here that I'm aware of." Scott paused, waiting until he saw her nod, noting a hint of a smile on her full lips. "He has one back in England, though." Scott saw her smile fade. "A father and mother. No one else he's ever mentioned. At least—not to me."

A'neewa pursed her full lips. "Someone like him, a named man, must have a woman—somewhere."

Scott grinned. "I agree. A wonderful way to go through life, with a good woman at your side."

A'neewa turned her head, her eyes locked on his. "Where is yours?"

"Home—in England. With my daughter."

A'neewa noticed the slight downturn curl of the stocky man's lips. "The last time you saw them?"

Scott looked away, a look of regret on his face now that the game had turned against him. "More than twelve years ago. No physical contact with either of them. Only the occasional message, by military post."

A'neewa bored in. "Your daughter, growing up without a father around—it would have been difficult for her." She paused, noting as the friend to Red Fox pressed his lips together. "As too, your wife."

"No worries on her end, always capable of finding another man to take care of her. Very much alive, or she was—last time I had a message from her." Scott paused, taking a deep breath, then letting it out slowly, easing the painful memories of a daughter lost to him, last seen as a girl of seven, her small hand clenched in her mother's, uncertain as to the identity of the stranger gazing into her light-gray eyes. "The last time we spoke, she was working her way through a long list of derogatory comments concerning my many shortcomings. Offered me in place of a fond farewell."

Scott reached up, his fingers on a chain around his neck, pulling a silver locket free. He opened it, then held it out so A'neewa could make out the details of a small cameo. "My daughter. With the same eyes and chin as myself, though perfectly tailored to her narrow face. A bonny lass, with quiet mood."

"Much like your own, it would seem." There was a moment of silence as A'neewa watched him slip the locket back beneath his shirt, noting his eyes following the movements of a small army of young girls as they came on a sprint from the edge of woods, hands filled with pinecones, intent on assaulting several older boys, moving across an open field.

Scott sighed. "Her name is Sinclair—not one I would have selected, though the sound of it settled in soon enough upon seeing her face for the first time." He leaned back; a long sigh released forming a trail of fogged air in the cool press of the early morning. "She had just turned a three, a few months before. My first chance to see her, fresh off a boat after a four-year tour of service in Africa. Sent home to England to recover from a nagging injury, before returning to service again. My wife, barely with child when I boarded ship to southern climes, greeting me with my wee child held out as if a bundle of clothing, albeit one with a bright-eyed face, surrounded by curls of dark hair like my own dear mother."

Scott paused, a soft smile warming the corners of his mouth. "Her tiny face—it went into a deep scowl when some boys rushed by in play, causing the carriage to rock as the horse shied away." He shook his head. "Her frown, looking just like my own. The same look at having been disturbed, letting me know for certain she was mine." Scott paused. "I mean to say—there was some question at the time we signed the papers, as to—"

A'neewa shrugged. "We do not judge things like that among my people. A parent to a child is whoever is closest to them when they need holding—or scolding."

"She was a decent enough woman, long used to dealing with coarse brutes like myself." Robert smiled, watching as the boys began chasing the girls back into the edge of the woods. "With a well-honed ability and sharp tongue keeping her safe from all types of dis-reputation."

"A woman of strength—and firm will."

Scott turned, fixing A'neewa with a considered look. "Yes. A woman knowing her own mind, for certain. And heart. Keeping it closed, although she managed to find a bit of room in there to offer a soldier with unhealed wounds—on the inside and out, in flail of moods, drowning my pain with strong drink. Herself willing, and able, to haul me back into the light."

A'neewa nodded. "An angel then, as your people call them."

"Aye, that she was, and had plenty of suitors. Men eager for her personal attention if you will. One, a real jack-a-napes, more in love with his reflection in window or mirror than her. Ended up challenging me to a duel." Scott shook his head. "Foolish thing, that, leaving him bloodied, but not seriously hurt, in a bawling sprawl on the ground. His boon companions looking on in shame."

Scott looked down, studying the ground for a few moments. "She seemed more relieved, than thankful at the result, lending me the comfort of her body in return for the deed. My having released her from the plans of two fathers in regard of her path through life. Her decision to reward me, one I was happy to comply with, leading to me meeting my daughter for the first time, four years later. Letters sent home from foreign posts, asking to be kept apprised of my daughter's welfare, having my pay forwarded to provide for them both, though never responded to. The last one I sent, letting her know I was being sent back to London, prior to reassignment."

"A hard thing to deal with it seems—for you, friend to Red Fox."

"I would prefer it if you would call me Robert—in consideration of our personal conversation, one I've never shared with anyone else."

"Then you must call me A'neewa." She smiled, the stocky man with taciturn features having revealed himself as more than a man in a uniform. "So, my new friend, Robert, your friend, Red Fox—has no woman." A'neewa pursed her lips. "Is it because he prefers to be with men?"

Robert blushed. "He has a woman, A'neewa. One who is every inch as strong as him, in her own way." He hesitated a moment, then continued. "I should mention Captain Knutt is not overly fond of the title given him."

"Why is that, Robert?" A'neewa gave him a measured stare. "Has he not earned it?"

"Yes." Robert nodded. "But the killing of men is not how he measures himself."

"What stick does he prefer to use?"

"One marking the respect earned from those he leads."

A'neewa lowered her eyes, her full lips pursed. "A thirst for respect is a good thing in a chief, friend of Captain Knutt. Pride, in the number of men killed or wives taken, better off found in warriors and not their leader."

The young girls came up at a run, seeking A'neewa's assistance in driving away the boys, their small hands yanking her to her feet, coaxing her to come with them. They ran off laughing, chasing after the boys. Robert watched them go, his heart heavy in his broad chest as he wondered where his daughter was, and what she might be doing. He sighed, recalling the conversation shared with Harold during their trip overland, the two of them sitting around a small fire, the heat from the flames captured by their upheld hands and staring faces.

Firelight framed Robert's face in a soft glow of gold as he stared into the flames, as if able to see in them a place lying beyond the near horizon. He held a silver locket in his hand, open, his thick thumb in a gentle caress of the likeness of a young girl's face. His eyes gleamed as he silently promised himself, they would be together again. Someday, somewhere. A father's prayer, offered on behalf of a soldier's dream.

Harold, sitting across the fire from Robert, looked over, staring at the other man's hand. He used a sharpened stub of a sepia-toned stylus in his fingers, capturing a spider's web of thin scars formed by an old wound on the back of his mentor's hand. The veteran's thumb, bent at a slight angle, slowly rubbed the interior surface of a small locket, hanging from a chain around his neck. It was a ritual the older man performed every day with the arrival of the sun, and the last thing he did every night. Repeated before and after every battle, as if a good luck talisman, helping to keep him alive.

Harold looked down at the page of one of his journals, focused on adding a few more details to the image, having to shake his head as a thick blanket of fatigue weighed down his eyelids. When finished, he stared at the image, added to the other ones drawn over the past few months, along with short stories, and cryptic notes, reminders of what he'd been through, seen, and felt. Memories frozen n place he would look back at some day, should he manage to survive the war.

He was several battles in, thus far, and still no end in sight, knowing he was fortunate to still be in one piece, though battered a bit in mind, body, and spirit. Surrounded by men who'd suffered the same, or worse. Young and old, sharing similar feelings of loneliness, depression, and ache for home. The shock of their survival absorbed as they drifted through the haze of shattered fields of conflict, bodies intact, looks of wonder on soot-blackened faces at having made it through the storm of lead and steel, alive. Others among them wandering off, having lost grasp of their moral roots. Men with blank stares, drinking whatever was near to hand, whenever available, engaged in endless, mumbling conversations with themselves. The same worn-out stories repeated over and again. A few of them, their souls diminished by the repeated experience of violent death, left alone, sitting by themselves in silence while others began to joke and jibe. Quiet men with hard expressions, their hands in constant hone of bayonet or knife as they stared into an abyss no one else dared look into.

Ghosts, Harold thought to himself as he placed an image on the page, a face with hollow eyes and toothless mouth, hanging agape. He flinched as a shadow fell across the parchment, his eyes wide, heartbeat in a flutter. Then he looked up, seeing Scott standing at his shoulder, his thick eyebrows narrowed.

"Friend of yours, sir?"

Harold closed the journal, the stub of stylus held between his fingers. "A shade, nothing more. Just a ghost—drawn to frighten myself."

"The image of the hand placed above—a fine piece of artwork, sir. Detailed and familiar, due to the unique scarring." Scott paused. "Mine, I take it?"

"It is, Sergeant Major. I—felt compelled to capture it." Harold paused, then looked back up. "I hope you don't take it as an intrusion on your privacy. If so, I can easily cross it out."

"Nae, sir. I find it reassuring, knowing someday you'll be sharing memories of my hand with someone who'll ask about the man in attach. Myself, made part of your story, told true." Scott paused, eyes gleaming as he stared into the sunset, the sky gone blue-black and cloudless, with the promise of another cool night. "Though it's not yet complete, sir."

Harold angled his head, staring at the drawing. "It's not?"

"A detail missing. One of—great importance. At least, it is to the owner of said hand." Scott pointed.

Harold nodded. "The object, held between thumb and forefinger."

"That would be it, sir." Scott looked down, measuring the log Harold had selected as a seat. "Mind if I join you, sir?"

Harold nodded as he stared at the picture. "I won't be able to add it in. I should start over again, with the item clearly shown."

Scott removed the chain from his neck, holding it out, watching as the locket swung back and forth. "First time it's been off my neck since—well, since putting it on twelve years ago, this month. Hard to believe that amount of time, passing, with me still above ground and kicking." He handed it to Harold, who held it in his palm, beginning to sketch it. "It opens, sir, with press of a finger on its side." Harold angled it up to the firelight, forefinger on the release, the cover left hanging open.

"The spring give out, a few years back." Scott reached over and used the edge of a dirt-stained fingernail to open it all the way, exposing a carved likeness of a young girl's face, revealed in angled pose, the features rubbed smooth.

Harold realized it must be Scott's wife or daughter, shame flooding through him in never having asked his mentor about his family. He looked up. "Who is she?"

"My little girl. Or she was, when I had that made, twelve years ago. Two of 'em, as exact to my description as the artisan could do. One provided to her, last time we met. With myself left standing on a dock; my daughter sitting in the opposite side of a carriage, with her mother between."

"She's beautiful." Harold squinted. "Has your chin—I think. A bit narrower, but the cleft is there."

Scott smiled. "That it is, sir. Firm chin, and able to take a punch, I'm certain. Like myself."

Harold looked at the cameo. "Do I have your permission to put her likeness in my journal?"

"I would consider it an honor, sir. Done by yourself, and of an age to my daughter, twenty years old, later this month."

Harold rested the locket on his knee, beginning to capture the image. "It must have thrilled her, receiving such a wonderful gift from her father."

"Wouldn't know, sir." A frown creased the lines of Scott's face. "Her mother was the one making the gift of it to her. The bargain struck before my getting to see her again, the day before I sailed off again."

Harold carefully outlined the delicate curve of the child's face, aware of Scott's silence, listening as his mentor made a long, drawn-out sigh, his voice whisper thin as he continued. "Was never allowed to get close to her. Her mother using her as a lever, prying from me whatever monies I'd saved up. Willingly given, just to have a glimpse of my little girl again. To breathe in her scent. Feel the touch of her hand in mine, if only for a moment. Hard to face—the look in her eyes, seeing me as a stranger. No more to her now, than—well, a shade, I suppose."

"She's still part of you." Harold looked over. "And you're no ghost, nor shade. Someday she'll find you and listen to what you've got to say—wanting your story shared with her." He gave Scott a firm nod.

"Hard thing to do, sir, making a promise like that." Scott looked away, staring into the darkness.

"I promise you, she will, Sergeant Major." Harold hesitated. "And would ask that you call me by my given name, Harold, whenever we're alone."

Scott swiveled his head back around. "Hard thing to do—Harold, making a promise like that." He paused, then continued. "And I offer the same request in turn, that you call me Robert."

Harold looked at the man who'd taught him all he knew about being a leader of men. About being a soldier. Shown by the older veteran how to carry himself while still an untried officer, far from home. Molded into the man he'd become, responsible for other men like himself, far away from everything familiar and safe. "I do not make the promise lightly, Robert. But as I hail from Scottish blood, from the same clan as is your own last name, my mother being a Scott by birth, I often see things before they occur, as is the reputation of those hailing from the southern highlands."

"You're claiming—to have the sight?"

Harold nodded. "I am."

Robert shrugged, then lifted a hand, stifling a yawn. "Then good on ya, sir, and keep the locket until you're finished with the drawing, as I'll be turning in." He stood up, then reached down, fingers closed around Harold's upper arm. "I know she'll be in excellent hands, my wee sweet child. My dear little daughter, Sinclair."

ᗡᕪ

Robert watched as the native children continued their playful game of chase, with A'neewa pulled in one direction, then another, used as center pole in a game of touch and runabout. The squeals of joy nudged a hint of a tear to the corners of his eyes as he reflected on moments he'd missed with his own girl, now a woman full grown, if still alive. He pulled the locket from beneath his shirt and opened it, gently rubbing the delicately carved lines of her face beneath the press of his thumb.

A Matter of Duty

Harold stirred as a gust of wind forced its chilled way past a flap of thick hide hanging over a small opening of a narrow lodge, his temporary shelter, barely large enough in width and length to accommodate his lanky frame. Chief Tawana had offered it as a personal favor, the older man letting him know a leader should sleep apart from his men.

Robert had flashed him a wide grin as they parted for the evening, after another fine meal and second round of rank smoke shared among the leaders. Harold, left sleepy-eyed and muddle-headed, making a vague excuse before stumbling off to his private accommodations, asleep as soon as he tucked himself inside the small lodge.

Harold was awake now, still in a fog, one eye pried open as he stared at nubs of dying coals, glowing in the ashes of a small, stone-bordered firepit an arm's reach away. Barely enough heat remained to keep the interior above freezing. He considered tossing a few sticks on the coals, measured against the loss of body heat. Better to fall back asleep, he decided, closing his eyes, drifting off beneath a thick bearskin covering.

Harold woke with a start, his heart in rapid throb; the result of a dream in which the bearskin had suddenly come to life, chasing him into the back of a small cave, its warm breath huffing against his cheek. Still feeling it there, his fear stirring him to roll to one side, his body frozen in place by a soft whisper in his ear.

"I came to see that you are not *too* cold." A'neewa was lying beside him, beneath the bearskin, the side of her face washed by the light from the firepit, several sticks having been placed in a small heap on the dying coals.

Harold drew in a deep breath as he worked out the consequences of his next move. He was certain A'neewa was there with her father's knowledge, if not direct approval. Chief Tawana sending her to gather as much information as possible before negotiating articles of support for the English efforts against the French. He released his breath, his senses alert. "I am, or rather—I *was* warm enough, the bed covering more than adequate."

"And now?" A'neewa slipped one leg between his, her fingers tugging at the buttons of his trousers.

"Perhaps a bit *too* heated." Harold reached down and grasped her hand, bringing a halt to any further exploration.

"Should I *leave*?" A'neewa gave him a soft look, her dark eyes wide, full lips pursed.

"Would you go quietly if I said *yes*?"

A'neewa laughed, then reached out and touched the side of his face. "You do not have a mate. I do not have a mate. Mine lost in a raid—two years ago. You are alone and I am here. What more is there to say?"

"I have a—"

"*Friend*. I know. Your *other* friend, Robert. He told me." A'neewa propped herself up on one elbow, the firelight gleaming on the edge of her breast. "She is not here. And I am. So—"

Harold realized as he looked into A'neewa's dark eyes, her tawny flesh glowing in the building flames, that he and his group of representatives would be guests in the village throughout the next few months, depending on length and severity of the winter weather. He also understood the general's expectations of him were high, his mission of great importance to the Crown. He hovered on a decision of what to do next, aware the daughter of the chief could become an asset or adversary, then reached out, pulling A'neewa's firm body against his, placing himself in destiny's hands.

ᘿᘿ

A small, leather-wrapped ball slipped between the braced legs of a dozen stout men. Half of them of native origin; the rest a mix of one thick-set soldier and a handful of sweat-faced colonists. Robert, a burly wedge with solid girth, was proving to be more than a match to the three warriors determined to move him from his stance.

Harold reached out, using the curved end of his stick to gather in the rock-hard, dry leather sphere, using a series of well-placed taps to guide it around the straining bodies, finding a clear lane to the goal posts, directly ahead; two sticks driven into the ground at one end of a small clearing. He brought the stick back, smiling, ready to score the winning point, when he noticed a small native boy watching from the side, a look of disappointment suddenly turning into a wide smile. Harold turned his head, looking back over his shoulder, aware something bad was about to happen.

A blur of tanned leather and brown skin slammed into him, the end of a wooden stick jabbed under his ribs, driving the wind from his lungs. He collapsed, his vision in a spin, left on the ground watching as

A'neewa recaptured the ball and wheeled around, racing to the opposite end of the field where she sent it between the angled legs of the minister, who dropped his stick, placing both hands over his groin.

The native players on A'neewa's side roared with victory, followed by loud jeers aimed at the colonial men, left with their mouths agape as they stared at Harold, expressions of shock on their faces. Their first win had been in hand, with rights to an evening of wild braggadocio earned until the next day's contest. Lost to them by the man they'd all come to respect for having persuaded Chief Tawana to bring the other leaders into a coalition of support for the English side, against the damnable French.

Harold stood up, his skin on fire from a thick welt beginning to swell from his side. He struggled to regain his breath, left leaning forward, hands on his knees, watching as the winning side spun in a whirling dance, their loud hoots of laughter filling the cold air. Their small, feisty, intrepid leader joining in, lifting her knees high as she celebrated, her head thrown back, a wide smile on her perfect lips.

ᕙᕗ

"Red *Turtle*, more like it." A'neewa rubbed bee's wax onto the discoloration below Harold's damaged ribcage, then tied a strip of linen cloth around his upper waist, binding a warm poultice in place. Her firm hands spared no effort as she pulled the ends tight, Harold grimacing as she did so. "Letting a *woman* catch you up. Stealing your—*moment*. Making it—mine. Victory to me, *Silent Doe*."

Harold muttered beneath his breath, unable to draw a full measure of air into his lungs. A'neewa reached out, taking his chin in her fingers, and staring into his eyes, their color compelling to her, like those of her father. "*What* did you say?"

"More like *Loud Doe*—with *sharp* hooves." Harold coughed, then closed his eyes against the pain, a moan slipping past his clenched lips. "*Ruthless*. Without mercy."

A'neewa shrugged. "And your other woman, is she not the same?"

"My friend is not as—*direct* as you." Harold slumped to the floor of his new lodge, big enough to hold several adults. "Thankfully so." A'neewa repacked her medicinal supplies, placing them with her other things taking up one corner of the lodge, having moved in with him, intent on staying for the duration of his visit.

Tawana had suggested the change in housing, telling Harold a leader of warriors had other responsibilities in need of his attention when part of a tribe, giving Harold a considered look. "A man does not lead by reputation alone, no matter how it has been earned. Any of us are capable of bravery, or cowardice, depending on our will at the time. While those we lead into a fight must see a leader who is confident, strong minded, and calm in battle. Their feelings of doubt or fear, hidden away, deep inside."

Harold knew he had achieved a closer relationship with the native leader than Aidyn had hoped for. He nodded. "Wise words, Chief Tawana." He paused. "But they do not provide an answer as to why I have been moved into a bigger lodge."

Tawana tilted his head to one side, a confused look on his face. "To make room for my daughter." His lips formed into a crooked grin, a scar on his cheek wrinkling into a deep crease. "And you should take another woman, too, increasing your status among my warriors, who have pledged themselves to go on the red path with you when the weather warms."

"*No!*" Harold held up his hand. "I have all I can do to meet *her* needs. I mean—" Harold stopped, uncertain how the chief might react to having his daughter's relationship openly defined.

Tawana chuckled. "Perhaps another woman *would* be too many. My daughter can be—*difficult*, at times, her mother lost in the great sickness.

Raised as if a son to me, as much a daughter." He paused, shaking his head. "She would never listen to the advice of any of my new wives about how to act, preferring to follow her own path."

Harold let out a breath of relief. "Then we're agreed, and I'm pleased to hear your words of advice, as well as to have gained the friendship of your daughter, who I consider to be my equal, in every way."

Tawana nodded, giving Harold a wide grin. "Another thing a leader must have, other than wisdom in battle and the support of his village, is in knowing how to keep balance in his lodge—with his *woman*, where the *real* power lies."

A'neewa looked at Harold, hands on her hips, a satisfied look in her eyes as she surveyed the bandage. "I am your woman here." She leaned in; her lips placed against his ear. "As it should be, even if I must lie down with a man who is not strong enough to hide his pain." Harold reached out, ignoring the agony in his bruised ribs, pulling her into his arms, biting her on the side of her neck, hard enough to cause her to gasp in pain as she reached for his belt. Then she hesitated, trying to maintain a balance between her desire to lie with him and stoic complacency. Losing out to her need for his touch, her inner voice washed away by the rush of warmth spreading throughout her body, aching for his single-minded attention to her needs, aware of the deep void looming ahead once the cold weather broke and the man with pale-blue eyes would leave, returning to his other woman.

The rest of the native leaders had finished discussion of terms, wedged in between feasts, celebrations, and proffer of wampum as gifts with promises made of mutual support for each other's needs. The various tribal representatives, loaded down with gifts from Harold in return, leaving as soon as the weather began to break. The colonials who'd made the trip west, looking east toward home and the families waiting for them there.

A'neewa began to pull away once the celebrations wound down, her comments shorter, holding less warmth, leaving Harold to follow her one morning, finding her sitting by the side of a wide stream. A'neewa refused to face him, head bowed, hands clenched at her side.

Harold knelt beside her, then reached out, ready to pull back as he touched her on the shoulder. "You honor your name, Silent Doe. And I understand why you—"

A'neewa shrugged off his hand. "You know *nothing*." She used her own tongue, letting go of French, the fluidity of it too painful to her ears, knowing she would miss their back-and-forth conversations, sentences interrupted as they finished each other's thoughts.

"Then *tell* me what I am unaware of."

"It won't *change* anything." A'neewa twisted her shoulders, enough so he could see her eyes, slanted in anger as she shifted back to French. "You have been *honest*. *True* to your word." She completed her turn, her hands grasping the front of his coat, pushing him away while holding on, unable to let him go. She leaned in, her forehead touching his, her voice trembling. "*Go!* Return to your other woman before she comes *here* and takes you *back!*"

Harold reached up, cupping her face between his hands, staring into her dark eyes, filled with tears her iron will would not allow release of. "I *will* leave. Soon. As I swore an oath to do to my leader *and* my men. But it was not an oath sworn to *her*. Made clear to me that I must *never* do so again." He tightened his grip as A'neewa tried to pull away, his voice calm. "But I will *never* forget A'neewa, who has taught me far more than the ways of her people."

A'neewa leaned in, her voice soft, filled with notes of sadness that broke Harold's heart. "And I am left with—*what*? Knowing I will never *see* you again. Finding thin comfort in *memories* of you, while you are warm in the arms of—I do not even know her name, this other woman who shares your life."

"Her name is Meghan, and she does not allow herself to share my life. Unable to share herself *fully* with me, or anyone else." Harold sighed. "It is my *duty* I'm sworn to. A'neewa—not her."

"You wish it to be *different*." A'neewa laid her head against his shoulder, studying his eyes, her expression soft. "But she will not be *bent* to your will."

Harold looked away, watching the water as it slid past the edge of the bank. "Her heart is closed. Her pain, buried away, deep within her." He took in a long breath, then released it between pursed lips. "But she freely shares her mind, her thoughts. Her—opinions, strongly voiced." He paused, allowing a grim smile to reach his lips. "As are your *own*."

A'neewa shrugged. "You *like* strong women. They *excite* you." She reached up and touched his forehead. "In *here*." Then she lowered her hand, her finger pressed against his chest. "And *here*." She hesitated a moment, then lowered it again, her voice growing husky. "And—*here*."

Harold felt himself falling into her well-designed trap, knowing it would take all his will to free himself from it, leaving a large piece of his heart with her when it was time to leave. He tossed all thoughts of the future to the side, gathering her in his embrace and bearing her to the ground.

⟆℮⟊

"What does it mean—her name?" A'neewa was sitting beside Harold, fully dressed again, staring into the stream. "How does it look, when made with your little marks?"

Harold shoved leaves aside, exposing the soil. He used a stick to print the letters of Meghan's name. "It means *pearl*, but holds no proper measure of who she is, not in the way your name does." He paused, then continued before A'neewa could respond. "But I *do* have a name for her. One that came into my mind before we knew each other. Madonna, standing in Sun, the way she first appeared to me."

"And *yours*?"

Harold blushed, glancing away. "My given name means—war chief, or leader." He shook his head. "Not that I wished to be either one."

"A name finds a person on the path they are here to walk." A'neewa nodded, growing quiet for a moment, then looked up at Harold. "And *my* name? What does it look like when made into a—word?"

Harold drew it below Meghan's, watching as A'neewa leaned forward, tracing each letter of both their names. She looked back over her shoulder. "We share some of the same marks, as do deer and moose." She paused. "Make *your* marks now."

Harold complied, adding his name above Meghan's. A'neewa studied the letters, head cocked to one side. "May-Gan and I share more tracks than with you."

"True."

A'neewa lowered her eyes, her hands clamped together. "Both of us have suffered loss." She paused. "Was hers also a mate?"

Harold nodded. "Yes. Lost to a raid, along with a son who was seven years of age—or winters, in your measure of a person's life." Harold started to say more, then forced his lips shut.

A'neewa noticed and touched his shoulder. "They took her—those who killed her family. Held her for trade of goods, or to be sold to the French, like happened with me."

Harold shrugged, tossing the stick into the river. "She was ransomed back to her brother, who shared some of what happened to her, knowing my deep feelings for her. Aware I'd pledged my troth and been denied."

A'neewa pursed her lips, a frown on her face. "She—your *Meghan,* would have been beaten, then abused, same as with me. Left with nothing to live for, other than vengeance. Death, preferable to a life of pain. It is why she protects you from herself, knowing she will never have peace—true peace. Not until—" It was A'neewa's turn to cut her words short.

Harold waited a moment, staring at her, seeing the pain in her face. "Until what?"

A'neewa looked at him with a thin smile; a gleam in her eyes reflecting the mid-morning light. "She seeks her revenge, as I did mine for what happened to my village. Hers, still out there, forced upon her by a loss beyond what any man, even you, could understand. Her child butchered, as he would have been. A vision she can *never* forget or forgive. The bodies of her loved ones shown to her before being dragged away, to break her spirit." A'neewa paused, shaking her head from side to side. "It has formed a shadow on her life and will remain with her until she drags those responsible from their lives by the red blade of a knife."

Harold returned a quiet look, eyes wide at the realization that men in combat were not the only ones capable of going to the dark side of their natures; blinded by hate. "Why are you not—?"

A'neewa smiled, a look in her eyes raising the hair on Harold's arms and neck. "Because I *had* my revenge, sliced piece by piece from those who stole everything from me. Everything I loved. So, with the help of some of the men of my village, I took their sight. Removed their tongues, and then their manhood. All of it—*mine.* Burning them alive as they gave me their *will,* moaning in pain, mindless with misery while I watched, rocking in joy, my soul regained. My father finding me, leading me away from those who'd helped me take my vengeance. Bringing me back to his lodge, never to speak to me of what he'd seen done."

Harold closed his journal, then rubbed his eyes, finished detailing observations of recent events, along with images of native life placed in one of his leather-bound volumes; the native village a rich palette to draw from. A'neewa sat beside him, her hands busy as she worked on a deerskin coat, one he suspected was for him though she'd made no comment to that effect.

Harold stared at her; his eyes focused on the flicker of firelight on her cheek, the tip of her tongue revealed as it slipped from the corner of her mouth as she tugged a metal needle through the layers of soft hide.

"What?" A'neewa glanced over. "You have finished making your marks?"

"I have." Harold nodded, leaning back.

"What do they say?"

He opened the journal, pretending to read. "I am watching the beautiful A'neewa as she makes me a fine coat. One that will keep me warm and dry in wind, rain, or snow."

She frowned. "Why would I waste time doing that, for a man who will be leaving me?" A'neewa tossed the coat away, then took the book from his grasp, her eyes searching the page, looking for her name. "It's not *here*. You are not telling the truth—*serpent*."

Harold tapped the side of his head. "The words are in here, where you cannot *see* them." He heard her mutter something beneath her breath, a common occurrence whenever he would tease. "What did you say, Silent Doe?"

"I said a *hatchet* would reveal them soon enough!"

Harold smiled. "Do you have one?"

A'neewa pouted. "No. But I know where to *find* one." She grinned. "And you have to sleep sometime." Then she nestled in against him, holding the journal in her hands as she studied the writing. "It is like—the tracks of many different animals. One following the next, as if they are on the *same* path. Each one leaving something of itself behind so those who follow the trail will be able to see what each one was doing. How they were *feeling* and *thinking*, able to see the world through their eyes."

A'neewa looked up at Harold, eyes wide in sudden awareness. "This is how you are able to leave a trail of thoughts that others can follow." She narrowed her gaze. "This is how your people *know* to make things. *Metal* things. Muskets. Cannons. Steel blades—and tools. Cooking pots and plows. From following marks like *these*, instead of using words passed from mouth to ear, like us. Anyone who learns to use the marks, able to do the same."

Harold stared at A'neewa, amazed at her uncanny ability to see things clearly. He ached at the thought of leaving her; a steep price paid for duty sworn. "In all my years, *never* have I heard it so perfectly described. That is *exactly* what this is." He leaned forward, shifting his legs to provide a place to write, the journal opened to the last page. "There are other uses for it, too. Using different words to form thoughts, speaking to people of nature, philosophy, science, history. And religion."

"I do not have any interest in *that* one." A'neewa fell into a sullen mood, using her own language, her words tight with emotion. "I *heard* the words—read to us from the black books. Those the men in dark robes carried with them, telling us stories about the father who told his children how to behave. Angry, when they would not listen. Sending them away. *Killing* them with the big water, instead of teaching them *how* to listen." She shook her head, her unbound hair a wave of ebony that fell across her shoulders. "Not as the Mother does, helping us find our balance in the world she provides."

Harold, having picked up her native tongue, responded in similar fashion. "Along with constant raids, made against your *own* kind when food is scarce, or claim to hunting or fishing lands are in question. The taking of women, and children, after killing their men."

"*We* do not tell a man how he is to *behave*. Or kill his *children* when they do not."

Harold could feel her body stiffen against him and changed his tone, softening his words, an edge of excitement creeping into his voice as he shifted back to French. "Let me show you something you will *not* have seen before. A way to use the marks to—capture a moment of *beauty*. Of nature if you will. Or anything at all." He took his quill and dipped it into a small vial of ink. "Give me something you have an interest in, and I will *capture* it for you with my marks." He lowered the nib to the parchment, waiting.

A'neewa didn't hesitate. "A *kiss*—between lovers."

Harold closed his eyes, a spasm of pain reaching his heart at the thought of their final kiss, someday soon. Then he relaxed his hand and started scratching out the words flowing from mind to parchment. When finished, he gently blew on the lines of ink, then looked at A'neewa. "There, for as long as the paper lasts and the ink does not fade, what a kiss from A'neewa means to me."

She reached out, her finger poised above the first word as if a bird, hesitant to land. Harold placed his hand on hers, encouraging her to touch the ink, now dry. A'neewa traced each loop and whirl, her eyes intent on how they flowed, as if water in a brook. The rhythm of their curled shapes unlike the letters he'd drawn for her in the dirt. Her finger slipped from one to another and when she reached their end, she looked up. "Make them *speak* to me."

Harold held her hand, moving the tip of her finger as his voice whispered in her ear. "Warm, the press of lip to lip, in parted lines, inviting slip of tongue. Heated breath exchanged in rising anticipation as mouths join, one to another. Time in cease. The only thought—how sweet this moment of pure love, defined."

A'neewa retraced the words, each of them said aloud, assisted by Harold when she faltered, repeating them over again until her voice was the only one needed, committing them to memory as if an ancestral story passed between one generation to the next. She looked up at

Harold. "I will never forget them. They will live with me until I die."
She touched his cheek, then slid her fingers up to the side of his head,
a tearful smile on her face. "I will not need to find a hatchet now."

Harold smiled, bringing her hand to his lips, kissing each finger
before letting go. With a careful tug, he tore the page from the book,
folded it, then pressed it into her palm, closing her fingers around it.
"This is my gift to you, beautiful A'neewa." He avoided a glance at the
coat in puddled form, lying atop the bed they would continue to share
as often as possible, until their final time would come.

A Change of Season

Mules muttered in protest; their sides covered with tightly rolled
bundles of hides the Iroquois nation chiefs had provided for trade of
metal goods, ones they would claim when the tribes gathered to join
the British in their spring offensive against the French. Along with any
war prizes earned along the way.

Chief Tawana came over to Harold, taking his forearm in a firm
grasp, the older man looking deep into Harold's eyes, nodding, then
walking away. A'neewa stood nearby with an expression of boredom on
her face, their relationship having culminated in a vigorous exchange of
physical release before the emotional ties between them had been carefully untangled. Each aware, as the weather begun to warm, of Harold's
imminent departure. Their conversations evolving from personal reflection of their own lives to consideration of the greater world, without.

Harold's views were often in balance with those of A'neewa's, her
vision clear, even when he ranged beyond her ability to understand in
full. Harold amazed at her insight as he listened to her work her way
through to the core of a greater truth.

"The places you describe, they are the same as found here. Large villages inhabited by our people, tied to the balance of the natural world."
A'neewa flashed a frown of impatience when Harold shook his head

in disagreement. "They *must* have the same need within themselves to seek what the Mother has to teach us. To *hear* what she has to say."

"Only a few have such a need, A'neewa. The rest hide from it, living shoulder to shoulder in—small caves, stacked alongside and on top of the other. Afraid to live their lives beyond the reach of squared walls."

A'neewa shook her head, dark eyes on his, frustrated by his refusal to concede the point. "Like those of your people who choose to live in settlement forts, held captive to their fears." She sighed, looking up at the sky. "It would free them, seeing the way *we* live. Make it difficult for them to return to their caves."

Harold sighed, his love for her raised to a new level by her determination to solve the divide between their two cultures. "Many are blinded by fear, A'neewa. By greed and ambition, two bitter poisons, twisting their minds into believing what's formed by man's hand is greater than what nature can provide."

A'neewa gave him an incredulous look, unable to accept that he could not see how simple it was. "This god person—he is but another name for the Great-Mother, who gives *all* to her children."

Harold nodded. "*I* can see that because I'm *here*. But there are many who will never accept your view, standing apart, beyond the mountains. Beyond the edge of the Atlantic, or big water, as you name it. Those who live in a city larger than your village and all the other villages of the Ohio Basin combined. Many more people there, in one place, than are the trees in your forests. All of them ruled by a handful of men, bidding them go forth and claim the earth as if it were their own."

"Then your people should place their leaders outside the village walls. Ignoring their words until they come back into their minds. Or let them walk away, never to be seen again."

Harold shook his head. "You're right. It's *my people* who are wrong." He noted her smile of victory, his heart heavy, realizing the world she knew would one day come to an inevitable end, washed away by countless waves of people moving west. "And I promise to do *everything* possible to open the eyes of those leading my people. Telling them what I've learned from you, A'neewa, daughter of Tawana. Daughter to the Great-Mother herself."

The mules began to move off, Robert wandering away, waiting at the edge of a tall ledge. Harold walked over and touched A'neewa on her shoulder. He half-expected her to turn away and leave without a word, surprised when she faced him, tears in her eyes, placing the coat she'd made for him in his hands, her voice low. "Wear this—and promise to always remember A'neewa."

Harold nodded, then opened the coat, feeling a hard object folded within the soft deerskin. He stared at it: a family bible, weather-worn from harsh treatment at some point in its journey. A'neewa touched his hand. "I think—it belongs to your woman. To Meghan. It holds her name, and three others. My father traded for it with a man from a tribe allied with the French. I—recognized the curled marks of her name." She paused, giving Harold a searching look. "You should return it to her, once you are with her again." Then she walked away, moving with a prideful stride.

Harold held the bible in his hand as if it were a viper, knowing it would end up causing intense pain to another woman he'd come to love. Knew it would cause reflected pain to himself, as well. Then he sighed, took one last look around, and slowly walked away.

CHAPTER THIRTEEN

Upper Section Of The Ohio River, Spring, 1759

The Worm, Turned

Harold left the general's office, located inside the large fort surrendered by the French. He moved past several buildings made up of officers and administration quarters, quickening his pace as he raced across the parade ground to the stables. He recovered his mount, nudging with his heels, urging the large mare into a trot, a hasty salute returned to the soldiers on duty as he passed through the main gate.

Meghan was at their small hut, set up in the hills outside the fort at the top of a steep rise, providing an expansive view down into the encampment with a steady wash of cool, pleasantly scented air. She waved as Harold rode up, apron tied about her waist, her thick mane of red hair pulled back, as beautiful to his eyes as the first time he'd seen her. Their time together since Bloody Crossing had been a rich stew, formed of countless conversations centered on books she'd read as a child in her father's library. Education for his daughter frowned on by the taciturn man, though encouraged by her brother, George.

Meghan's knowledge of art, history, and philosophy was far greater than Harold's, though he could more than hold his own in discussion of common-sense issues, due to hard lessons drilled into him and his brother by their taciturn grandfather during thrice-yearly trips to their mother's family manor in the highlands of southern Scotland. Meghan's firm opinions voiced in daytime discussions on a wide variety of subjects helped to fill the hours between other, equally pleasant exchanges of a more intimate nature.

Meghan came over as he reined in the mare. "Did you remember the bread and wine?" Harold started to lift the reins, as if to turn back toward the fort, then smiled, slipping from the saddle, both items pulled from a saddlebag. "Of course. As promised." He handed them to Meghan, waiting until she turned to head inside before he reached out and pulled her around, into his arms. "I have my orders."

Meghan didn't respond, her eyes on his, jaw clenched. "We are to move out in three days. Advancing to locate the French lines, then return before our native allies arrive, when we will make our main assault on their fortifications upriver as soon as the rest of the boats and barges arrive, overland."

Meghan shook her head as she stepped back, her eyes icy blue. "You sound pleased. Almost *eager* to be on your way—*again*."

"We *both* knew this was coming, the plan put in place months ago, with more of our new allies arriving every day."

She frowned. "*Your* native friends. Nothing more than paint-faced *savages*, to *me!*"

Harold shook his head. "You know I don't—can never share your feelings in that regard." He took a deep breath, letting it out through tightened lips. "And I would remind you of those who protect you *here*, protecting your brother and I, when in the field. Do you regard *them* as savages?"

Meghan shook her head. "They're not from the *same* tribes."

"Neither are those who are arriving."

"But they *have* raided. In the past." She crossed her arms, her face set in a stern expression.

Harold nodded. "Amongst their own kind, yes. But not against the outer settlements, even when attacked in error, having had *nothing* to do with raids made upon the families and friends of those who come seeking their revenge."

"I *know* that. I just can't get *past* it!" Meghan cradled the loaf of bread to her breast, as if holding a nursing child, her shoulders trembling, shaking her head. Harold took her in his arms, remaining silent, waiting for her to regain her balance, knowing she was dealing with memories that still haunted her. She finally relaxed, leaning her head against his chest, her voice muffled by his coat. "Will *all* of them be coming?"

Harold leaned away, finding her eyes. "I told you about A'neewa when I returned your bible. Answered every question asked. And no, she's staying behind with the rest of their women, according to her younger brother, who tracked me down, asking to join our advance group and pledging me his personal protection."

Meghan lowered her gaze. "I'm sorry. That was—unfair. I have no proper claim to jealousy."

"I've offered my troth, soon after we met, before we ever—"

"You needn't *remind* me of it, Harry." Meghan looked away. "The hurt in your eyes lives with me still, in having rejected your generous offer." She turned back, rising to her toes, and kissing him. Taking him by his hand, she led him toward the small hut, the horse left following along.

They lay together, with Harold curled alongside Meghan, his hand cupping her breast. His breath flowed along the curve of her neck; loose strands of burnished coppery hair stirred by its heated current.

He stared into the dwindling flames from their small firepit, the depth of love he felt for her tempered by the anger she was still clinging to, deep inside. He could feel it there, his body pressed against hers. A beast in lurk, with angry eyes, eager to lash out whenever opportunity to do so would next arise.

Repellent to him, based on his own experiences, though accepted as part of who she was, born out of the horror of what she'd gone through, beyond his ability to understand. He knew it would be a challenge to their future together, then decided to let the thought go, holding onto her, his heart open, feeling the beat of her own beneath the press of his hand.

He nosed his way into the spiraled curls of her thick hair, drinking in its oily essence, tinged with scent of wood-smoke, recalling how it had pulled his eyes to her that morning at the crossing. Then he closed his eyes, thoughts in a slow drift as he listened to a coyote calling out in a pale imitation of a wolf, the quavering yips slipping through the midnight air, beneath a thick carpet of stars, scattered overhead.

Eve of Leaving

The air was warm, a long stretch of rain-less weather having wrung it dry, silent brooks no longer murmuring their way through the woods as the Ohio Basin river refused to hug its banks. Harold and Meghan lay outside their small hut, beneath a canopy of stars overseen by a crescent sliver of angled moon. There was no need for words, the two of them silently contemplating tomorrow's separation. Each carrying an equal measure of angst, aware sleep would be difficult to find this final night together. A familiar dance, the same as before. One heading into peril while the other stayed behind, standing a nervous watch.

"I never thanked you." Meghan looked up at Harold, then squeezed his hand. "For the return of it." He nodded, realizing she meant the bible; its spine twisted with dozens of pages torn away from inside a water-stained cover. Her name, written there along with those of husband, son, and infant daughter, barely visible. The letters inscribed in a precise hand, faded by exposure to sun and damp. Difficult to watch as she'd held it in her hands, her eyes wide in shock, unable to speak. A pain Harold had wished to avoid, opening a wound he knew would never heal. George there with him, his arm around his sister's shoulder, lending his support. "Your friend, the native woman, she—"

"A'neewa."

Meghan closed, then opened her eyes. "A'neewa. Yes. She knew the bible was mine." She paused, looking at Harold, a quiet expression on her face. "I never asked how that came to be, her having worked it out—on her own." She twisted around on the blanket, the moonlight in a silver wash across her face. "How would she have been able to do that—to know how to read my name?"

"I'd shown it to her. Written out above her own. The letters scratched with a stick in the dirt."

"She must have appreciated the lesson." Before Harold could respond, Meghan reached out and touched the side of his face. "I mean no tone of jealously, appreciative of the position the general placed you in, there at his dictate. I'm simply curious why she would want me to have it back. There must have been some compelling reason behind her letting go of it."

Harold considered for a moment. "It was a gesture of regard, made through me to a woman she knew I cared for." He sighed. "From a woman I came to care for in return."

Meghan nodded. "Then we shall leave it there, life being what it is, with little enough promise for anything more. Only what one finds and can hold in their heart—or hand."

Harold felt her fingers reach under the blanket, closing around him, gently coaxing him to readiness. His voice dropped into a throaty murmur. "Truer words—have never been spoke." He leaned in and ran his lips along the line of her neck, her earlobe slipped between his teeth, biting hard enough to elicit a gasp of pleasure, wrapped within her pain.

Uneasy Waters

George leaned over and whispered in Harold's ear. "You seem rather unsettled, Captain Knutt. Anything you'd care to share with me and the rest of the men?" They were in a prone position in thick woods, lying behind a small outcrop of rock. Smoke from a host of small fires painting the late-morning air with a filmy curtain, subdued voices in lighthearted exchange of insults, the words unclear, though their intent was easy enough to decipher. Enemy soldiers in encampment, with no awareness their lives were in peril.

Harold's instincts began to kick against his stomach with pointed toes. "I am reminded of a *previous* encounter. Similar in design, though with a different result intended, *this* time around."

"You think it a trap?" When Harold nodded, George buried a curse behind clenched lips. He looked at the young strategist, his thick eyebrows raised, waiting on a command to advance, or withdraw.

⎯⎯⎯

The decision made to pull back, two dozen men in loose-fitting ranging clothes and a like number of natives had quietly regrouped a hundred paces away. Harold gathered most of the men in a loose circle, a handful left standing guard against potential threat. They'd been on the move for two days, passing through tinder-dry woods, streams in listless flow, the air clear, no hint of moisture in it, waking to mornings without any dew on the ground.

Harold, posed on one knee, stared up at the faces of his men, aware the retrograde maneuver had confused them, eager to press ahead and scatter the enemy as before with a sudden assault and accurate fire from cover. As he opened his mouth to let them know the reason behind his decision, a loud thrashing through thick brush from the edge of the woods interrupted him, quickly resolving into blurring movements as several deer rushed past, heads high, noses raised, tasting the air. They spun in tight circles on finding the group of men blocking their path, then selected a new heading and bounded away.

Harold's heart sank, realizing the danger they were in. He turned to Scott, whose expression widened in sudden comprehension. They both turned to the men, their voices raised. *"Fire!* They've *fired* the woods behind us!"

ᔕᘿᔓ

Smoke and flames closed in from behind, spreading rapidly, gnawing through the dry forest beneath clear blue, cloudless skies. The small force of raiders split up into handfuls of nervous men, crouching beneath a thick growth of trees, trapped between a steep-faced ridge on one side where men in white uniforms stood atop it, prepared to fire, and a sprawl of thigh-high grassy marsh on their other side, studded with small knots of alder and birch. A vast expanse of open ground Harold knew would expose them to cannon fire, already raking its length. The thud of deep bass notes sounding out, followed by buzz of shells and crack of explosions as fuses burnt down to the powder inside. Heated iron fragments sprayed the edge of the woods, igniting new fires wherever they landed.

Harold lay beside Scott, the two of them now alone; George and the other men, along with A'neewa's brother, forced away by clouds of dense smoke and walls of flames. Each group left trying to fight their way clear of the deadly trap as best they could. Harold heard hear the rippling sound of musket fire popping away, aware most of his men had gone for the marsh grasses. Their desperate shouts as they searched for cover mingled with cries of pain, most unable to find it. Their calls to one another heard above the growl of cannonballs feasting on limbs of pine and oak before smashing into the matted undergrowth, exploding in ear-shattering blasts, adding to the chaos.

"A good plan—for them." Scott rubbed his eyes clear of tears, the smoke thickening around their position. "Someone must have a copy of one of your books."

Harold shook his head, a wrap of pocket linen stretched across his nose and mouth, knotted behind his neck. He'd dampened it with water from his canteen, helping to allay inhalation of the worst of the smoke, unable to do anything about irritation to his eyes. "Not a chapter known to me. Though the mind behind it is."

Scott pursed his lips, hidden behind his own mask of cloth. "Your young Frenchman, let live, I should imagine."

Harold shrugged his shoulders as he considered their next move, the flames in steady approach. "We can move ahead and try breaking through their firing line, it being the last thing expected of us. Make our run parallel to the flames, using the smoke as cover."

Robert spit, then wiped his mouth. "Risky, if we judge it wrong. But you're right, it's the last thing they'll figure on anyone doing. Anyone with half a brain."

Harold forced a tight-lipped grin, hidden beneath his mask. "There's two of us, so we've got at least one to work with. Enough to win through, Sergeant Major. Surviving to lick our wounds and fight another day."

They rose to their feet, moving in a hunched posture as they followed the tracks of an enormous bear that had passed by. Its small, dark eyes darting from side to side as it hunted for an escape from the flames.

The cannons fell silent as white-coated men on horseback moved along the thin edge of woods, smoke in a thick billow from beneath low-hanging limbs waving in the heated air as if in a sad farewell before erupting in flames. Wounded men lay on the ground, begging for their lives as French lances dipped, probing their shell-torn bodies. A few of those with mortal wounds managed to fire pistols in defiance of death's thunderous approach, snatching white-coated men from their saddles. A valiant effort made to go down fighting, though the battle was all but over, leaving the English force on the wrong side of a one-sided defeat.

Harold lay prone, the soles of Robert's boots inches from his soot-stained face. The sergeant major was lay completely still, staring at the humped backside of a large bear, stretched out before a small clearing. Men in white uniforms waited on the far side atop a rocky hill, outside the reach of flames, having set backfires scorching the ground in front of their position. A body of dark water, dammed by beavers, formed a semicircular ring downwind of the burn, providing an open area perfect for a hail of musket fire to wither any attempt made to escape the deadly trap.

Several deer lay in twists and tangles, their tongues stretched from the sides of their mouths, eyes fixed in death-frozen pose. A sprinkle of other animals shot down as well, the French soldiers using them as target practice, sharpening their aim as they waited for the expected dash of two-legged enemies from the thickening cloud of smoke.

"When the bear breaks, we follow." Robert turned his head and looked at Harold. "We're burnt near enough to a crisp to convince them we're no longer *men*. So a moment or two of surprise might be enough to see us through their line."

Harold could only nod, his eyes wide as he considered how the next few minutes might play out, imagining himself holding a quill, a drop of ink poised on the nib as he prepared to write his final words. He drew in a cloth-filtered breath, wanting to offer his mentor and good friend one last expression of heartfelt thanks. Then the bear rose to its feet, its rage revealed in a loud roar as it bounded forward.

No liquid ever tasted sweeter than the sip of water Harold pulled from a small pool in a moss-covered ledge; a spring forcing its way out through porous limestone. Harold filled a soot-blackened palm and lifted it to his parched lips, then sighed, one of two wishes uttered during the hour-long chase finally granted. The other; a successful escape from their pursuers, dependent on the skill of those in trail, thirsty for vengeance on behalf of comrades lost in the massacre a few months ago.

"You look drained, Robert. We can bide here a while and collect our scattered wits." Harold waited for a reply, then turned, looking at Robert, lying on the ground, hunched against a slope of ledge, his eyes closed, chest slowly rising and falling, as if asleep. He took the linen from his neck, using it to soak up water from the seep, then reached over and touched it to his friend's heat-cracked lips. "Suck on this. It will help restore your strength."

The older man opened his eyes, a glassy look in them, indication something was amiss. "We almost—came away—clean, sir. Our ally. The bear. Drawing their eyes—and aim."

Harold leaned in, touching Robert on the shoulder. "You're hit."

The veteran nodded his head. "Arrow. Low in my back. Still in there. The feathered end—breaking off. When I was rolling—on the ground. Sticking my blade—in the eye of—the one who put it there."

"Save your breath, Robert. Take the water from the cloth. I'll get you more." Harold ran his hand along the back of Robert's coat, a damp spot oozing blood where the shaft had penetrated. He felt a chill in his heart, realizing his mentor's labored breathing was due to a penetration through his lung, the arrow fully embedded. "We will lie here and hope they miss our trail."

Robert drew the moisture from the cloth, Harold re-wetting it, placing it to Robert's lips again, able to predict what the wounded man would say.

"Dinna note—any of 'em—having any—problem moving about. Seemed to have—use of their eyes—and wits." Robert held out the cloth, watching as Harold soaked it again. "We move. Get clear of soft soil. Find rock. Up there." He pointed with his chin, taking the cloth, and sucking it dry, his color improved with the water and rest.

"You'll be killing yourself, making the climb. I'll back track and lead them away. Return at dusk and—"

Robert rolled to his knees; hands pressed on the ground, forcing himself to stand. "No, sir. Not an order—I'll be minding. We move now. Reach the top and—and figure a way to break clear of the noose—being drawn round our sooty necks."

⌖

The tree was a gigantic oak with thick roots, clinging like talons to the top of a prominent ridge. It rose from out of a deep pocket of stone-laden soil, stretching high above the ground, having resisted years of gales from winter storms, providing a natural bastion to seek shelter in.

Harold loosened his arm from around Scott's waist, easing him into position between two of the thicker roots. They'd passed a pool of water near the top of their tortuous climb, quenching their thirsts, and taking a moment for desperately needed rest, each with a serious expression on their faces as they listened to the relaxed voices of native trackers filtering up from the hillside below. A series of careless shouts letting them know it was to be a leisurely pursuit.

Harold leaned back, eyes aimed at the ground, ashamed of his failure to protect his men, their movement into the large wood predicted by the enemy leader. An error on his part, paid for in blood, though none of it his own, he added as he listened to his friend struggle to breathe.

Aware his account was long overdue, with first and final payment to be made at the end of the daylong chase.

Robert called out, his voice a rasp of effort, past the point of caution, knowing their pursuers were less than an hour behind. "Do you have your journal?"

Harold nodded. "I do."

"I would ask—a favor. A letter written—to my daughter."

Harold, knew the odds for delivery of a letter were long as he reached for his journal, tucked away in a leather pouch, wrapped in oiled cloth to protect it from rain and sweat. He removed a small stylus and vial of ink, secured within its leather binding, and started to hand them to Scott who shook his head, his eyes glazed as he pushed them away.

"You will have to—do the words. I canna form them." His hand trembled from loss of blood and recent exertions in climbing the ridge, his voice weak.

"Of course." Harold opened the journal to the last few pages. "I'm ready."

"I will give you—the raw gist. Use your own words—in putting down—my meaning. I need her to know—my feelings. My reason for— having let her go. And not—how her mother has told it to her." There was a long pause as Robert struggled to catch his breath. "You'll do that for me, won't you, Harry?"

Harold angled his head to prevent a tear from staining the page. "I will, Robert." Then he settled back, listening as the man he loved as much as his own father began to speak, wanting his final chapter written down.

⁂

When a long minute passed with no further words uttered, Harold looked over and saw Robert's eyes were open in a fixed gaze, the chain of the locket dangling from a large finger, thumb on the carved face of his daughter, his thick chest motionless, the sturdy heart within, gone still.

Harold finished the scribe of a final line then closed the journal and carefully wrapped it back up, putting it away. There had been moments of strained silence between Robert's pain-filled, drawn-out words while he struggled to find energy to continue. Harold given time enough to structure complete sentences, conveying his friend's final thoughts. He forced himself to his feet, then pulled out a large-bladed knife and began digging a hole between the clutching roots of the immense oak tree.

The top layer of dirt came away without much effort, easy to remove; the layers of stones lying below, less so, interlocked with thick-fingered roots. Harold wedged the blade of his knife under the end of a larger one, trying to lever it loose. It snapped, prompting a curse from his clenched lips, left staring at the hilt for a moment before tossing it away. Then he grabbed the recalcitrant stone and tugged as hard as he could, determined to finish the grave, providing a final resting place worthy of the scarred warrior's sacrifices made in service to King, Country, and boon companions.

A hand found his shoulder, bringing his efforts to a sudden halt, a voice in clean French in his ear. "You need help with that, my friend. *No?*"

Harold lowered his head, then straightened up, facing the man who'd played the better hand. "Your plan, Lieutenant Pierre de Coulombe, was *brutal*. But effective." He wanted to ask how many of his men had survived, then decided to leave the question aside for the moment. "I only ask time enough to finish this task, before—"

The young officer stepped down into the hole beside Harold. "It's Major Coulombe now, the rank recently assigned." He leaned forward, slipping his fingers beneath the edge of the stone. "Allow me to help you. We are both men of honor, after all, when time and—*circumstance* provide."

The two of them worked together while several native scouts and a handful of soldiers gathered around, watching in silence. Two of them eventually came forward, spelling the two officers; the hole quickly deepened as the group of men labored as if they were burying one of their own. They finished as the sun fell out of the western sky, the night in approach promising to be clear and cool, with a half-moon rising in the east.

☙

Harold stared down at Robert's face. He'd placed the silver locket in his friend's hand, his thumb formed into a permanent caress of daughter's face, then secured beneath the folds of his Sergeant's jacket, his tri-cornered hat placed across his face to keep the soil from it. All that remained to finish the burial was to fill the hole with rocks, layered between soil, protecting the grave from probe of bear, or any other beasts in roam.

Harold sighed, satisfied it would be a fitting crypt for the man who'd journeyed far afield, his travels having ended here, atop the high ridge with a magnificent view to the east. Toward England and his daughter, Sinclair.

Pierre came over, placing his hand on Harold's shoulder. "We will take over the duty. There's food and water if you wish to share it." Harold nodded his thanks, then stepped back and watched as the others quickly filled in the hole, placing a large capstone over the top, wedged between the thick roots of the tree.

Once they finished, Harold turned to Pierre, noting the younger man's eyes bore a familiar strain along their edges from the burden of leadership during war. "I thank you, *Major* Pierre de Coulombe, for your forbearance and assistance." Harold slipped his sword and sheath from a branch of a nearby tree and presented it to the young officer. "I—am ready to receive your judgment."

"You may keep your sword, *Red Fox*, as well as the rest of your things." Pierre looked around. "Your officer's pistol?"

"Misplaced, while helping my friend up the hill."

Pierre motioned with one hand. The native scouts conferred, then one of them came forward and offered Harold the recovered weapon. The slim-bodied native glanced at the major, who gave him a nod, then handed the pistol to Harold, speaking with stilted words. "We—share *loss*, your man. Him—*powerful* enemy. You, him—we are not *forget*."

Harold nodded his thanks, appreciative of the honor extended by the native man's use of English to address him. He looked at Pierre with a confused look. "Is it your plan to—*release* me?"

"Not my *original* one, if you'd fallen within range of my pistol, earlier in the fight, down below. I'd have managed to pull the trigger *this* time. But in finding you *here*, preparing to bury your friend, I felt compelled to return the favor once granted *me*."

Harold considered a moment, then looked at the half-circle of men. "What of the consequences to *you*, in releasing me?"

"My men and I are of an accord." Pierre placed his hand on Harold's shoulder and urged him away from the grave. "I ask only that you move *directly* toward your lines."

Harold reached out and took the other's hand. "The world of a soldier is a hard place to abide in, most times. Good men, lost to the vain ambitions of those sitting on their thrones, sent off to march and bleed upon the earth."

Pierre slid a cocked smile into place. "Keeps us in gleam of gold, our chests pinned with such *pretty* ribbons." He stepped back and bowed, offering a wave of his hand as Harold turned to go. Pierre watched in silence until his enemy had moved a dozen paces away, then raised his hands, cupping his mouth. "I suggest you find a *stream*, my friend. Follow it to the *river*. Then head *down* with the current. And may God go with you—*Red Fox*."

Harold forced his way through waist-deep water, beyond the point of physical collapse. His grief at the loss of his friend and men under his command dragging on the last measure of his will. His inner voice urged him to lie down, ceding the nightlong effort to reach friendly lines before morning. A siren call he ached to obey; to lower his weary body into the water, letting it bear him up so his legs could rest.

A young English sentry standing watch on the outer fringe of the English lines, new to the wilderness, serving his first stint of nighttime guard duty, stared into the darkness. He'd drawn the short straw for the second watch, the more experienced soldiers at rest until it would be their turn to stand guard. Their section of the front line bordered a wide body of dark water; a dammed backflow where the young sentry thought a man might set traps for beaver or muskrat. Shallow lines of a slight current stirred its surface, disrupting the reflection of the half-filled moon above. The tranquil scene caused him to raise his free hand, stifling another yawn. Then he blinked his eyes, determined to stay alert, warned what would happen were he to fall asleep. Told natives lurked in the shadows, ready to slip in and cut his throat. And great bears, with ravenous appetites, eager to rise from out of the dark, carving him from stem to stern. Threats made in jest, he said to himself, though he couldn't be completely sure.

He opened his mouth to yawn once more, then stopped, seeing a shadow in the distance, his musket brought to shoulder, hammer pulled back to full cock, the end of his barrel buried in the middle of the ebony shade.

⌒℮〰

A slow movement from the near shoreline drew Harold's semi-conscious attention, his weary eyes forming an image of a man with a musket, the moonlight bright enough to reveal an English uniform. A sentry on duty, Harold realized, releasing a shuddering breath, knowing his journey was near its end. He stopped, in anticipation of an order to announce himself as friend or foe, his left arm raised in a slow wave. A spark of light appeared, his hand flung back, body twisting to one side as an unseen fist struck him from out of the darkness, followed by the muted thud of a discharged musket.

Harold stumbled, his left side gone numb, a voice in the night crying out an order to halt, the rest of the young sentry's words lost as he slipped beneath the dark water.

⌒℮〰

He was back at the crossing. *Bloody Crossing.* The morning after when victory was still a slippery concept to hold onto. She was there, his *Madonna.* His angel, sunlight caressing the side of her face, wisp of red-gold hair on her cheek. Her lips moving, the sound of her husky voice failing to reach his ears. He tried to smile, his body light, as if floating in the backwater's arms. Warm air fell against his face. Vibration of fingers touching him on his neck. He felt pain on his face, a ringing in his ears, and tried to respond, unable to raise his arm to ward off the intrusion.

"*Harold!* Come *back* to me!" Meghan felt the surgeon's hand on her shoulder, shouting at her to leave the dying man in peace. She shrugged it off, her lips against Harold's ear as she stood on the opposite side of his body from the wound in his upper left side. A musket ball having torn through his left hand, then gouging away a thick knot of muscle and flesh from under his armpit, leaving broken ribs behind, added to the injuries suffered, along with blood loss and extreme exhaustion, a combination nudging him to the edge of an abyss.

The surgeon backed away, his attention returning to removal of pieces of cloth and shock-jellied flesh from the exposed wound. He will heal, Meghan told herself, as she watched the surgeon continue his bloody work. "Harold Knutt, you will not *die*. Not if you know what's good for you. I—I *forbid* it!" A jolt of pain surged into Harold's head, along with another loud ringing in his ears. *Unfair,* he thought, *I've done my share and more.* The pain slipped to his chest, his ability to cope overcome as a moan slipped from between his clenched lips.

A hand found his as an angel's voice floated just above the torture someone was doing to the side of his body. "Hold *on* to me, Harold. *Don't* let go. Come back to me, my love."

CHAPTER FOURTEEN

Upper Section Of The Ohio River, Summer 1759

Convalescence

Sunlight was both a blessing and curse to Harold. Of great benefit in helping his damaged body to heal, but unable to drive the shadows of pain from his tortured mind. He leaned back against an outcrop of rock, eyes in an unfocused gaze as he watched draft animals and soldiers mill about in the basin area below, his spirit in agony as he silently counted the faces of men, no longer there.

A shadow grew before him, wide in girth, taking on the form of Meghan's brother, one of the dozen men who'd managed to survive the fiasco of the Big Burn, as the soldiers had named it. The large-bodied officer had been able to gather a scattered group together among the tall marsh grasses, out ahead of the fire. Tucked in among thick clumps of alder, they'd watched as French lancers on horseback came through, chasing fleeing men, their clothes on fire, running in panicked flight, cut down with dip of lance tip or slash of saber.

George led an assault on the riders trailing behind, pistol shots used to punch the startled cavalrymen from their saddles. A handful of horses captured, each loaded with two men aboard, a few more left clinging to stirrups, helped along by the flared-nosed beasts, eyes rolled back in their sockets in fear of the encroaching bands of thick smoke, eager to flee to the further edge of marsh and bog with its promise of refuge from the fire.

Harold had spent the last three weeks in sullen contemplation, sickened by his mistake, one sealing Robert's fate. He was over-burdened by guilt, despite Meghan's reassurances that it was God's will. The general, having come up the hill to absolve him of all blame, saying the same. Harold had nodded, then continued to wallow in remorse, unmoved by the older man's words. He chose to ignore George now, his eyes closed, refusing the feel of warmth from the sunlight on his face as he soaked in a bitter stew.

"Amazing, the view." George was back to his old self, busy in rebuilding his ranging force with men eager to claim a spot alongside the affable man, with a solid reputation for getting things done.

Harold forced a monotonic response. "It provides for good visibility, albeit it one of a forced retreat, in utter defeat, because of me."

"I see it as a strategic *re-disposition* of our advanced forces." George cocked his head, hat in hand, sweat in a bead across his forehead from the effort made from making the steep climb uphill. "Was not the activity *below* I was speaking of, but *you*, in such a persistent and sour mood. Especially when in consideration of your former self, with such a sunny disposition and youthful swagger of *supreme* confidence. Replaced with a bruised pride and battered ego." George gave Harold a hard stare. "A long fall, with further yet to go should you not begin to recover your *original* spirit."

Harold closed his eyes. "I *buried* it. In a grave, alongside Robert."

George lowered his voice, his eyes set in a quiet gaze. "It would have been better to have climbed in *with* him, then. You've been as good as dead, ever since."

"A long walk uphill—for harangue of a failed man." Harold opened his eyes, then sighed, noting the look of genuine concern on his friend's sweaty face. "I'm sorry, George. You deserve better from me."

George sat down and leaned back, his shoulder brushing against Harold's. "Not my intent, friend, to scold *or* cajole. Just stating the lay of the land as found." He turned his head, studying the side of Harold's face, able to see the pain beneath its surface, both physical and spiritual, one well ahead of the other in healing. "I can offer no advice for succor of your wounds. My sister already has you in her excellent care."

"She scolds me, the same as you. In regard of my bout of, as she calls it, melancholia." Harold looked at George. "I've been trying to rationalize my way through this. To measure move against move, trying to discover my error in judgment in having failed to consider how and where a trap might lie in wait. Each time I'm led back to a stark recognition of personal weakness that led to precipitation of the—*event*." He winced, in sudden recall of his gentle upbraiding of the general, months ago, the same word used then to describe the horror of finding men scattered in pieces around a green glade. "Causing the *butchery* of—" He paused, swallowing the bile in his throat, shaking his head, unable to continue.

George leaned over and plucked a blade of grass, placing it in the corner of his mouth. "It *is* war, Harry. As simple as that. And if you're questioning having let go of the young French officer when you first met up, it's a hard truth that in war, as in life, the law of unintended consequences equally applies."

"I am not wallowing from wound to my ego, George. *Or* to my body. And I realize you're wanting to rouse my spirit to its previous level. It's only that the time spent healing allows for an over-abundance of reflection, leaving me in consideration of my role in this—*grand effort*." Harold lifted his good arm and swung it in a small circle over his head. "My role in the greater world, without."

"And where have you landed in your evaluation *of* it? Do you plan to discontinue service to our general? To our *king*?"

"I feel like I have been left standing *outside* my life, having strayed beyond my limited capabilities. Men losing all they have, because of *my* mistake. My lack of humility, blinding me to—" Harold paused, swallowed, then continued. "—having led good men to untimely and horrible deaths."

George laughed, shaking his head, regarding Harold with a wide smile. "And you were hoping to find a *cure* to that affliction?" He reached out, fingers closing on Harold's shoulder, squeezing hard enough to elicit a gasp of pain. "It's one or the other, my friend. Either accept the pain that comes hand in hand with being alive—or lie down for the long sleep. Life is ever in balance between the two, with fate to blame for whichever side we land on once the coin is tossed."

George reached into his coat pocket, pulling Harold's journal out, handing it to him. "I've waited long enough to give you this. Was able to recover it from beneath your coat when they brought you inside the line. It stayed dry while you were in swimming." He paused, his lips pressed in a firm line. "I noticed you were missing the knife I'd provided you." He made another dive into his pocket, retrieving a new one in an oiled sheath. "Take better care not to lose *this* one."

George paused, noting Harold's reluctance to accept either item. "Going to need you back in the fight, my friend. The general's asked me to convey his personal request for your return to service, forthwith. He expects you on the morrow, for a sit down with him and his staff. Until then, remain here enjoying the view below—in whatever mood you choose."

Harold turned his head, watching as the large man walked away. Meghan came out from the hut and gave her brother a kiss on his cheek. Then she walked over, concern in her eyes. "Are you hurt, from his having grabbed you like that? I should look to make certain—"

Harold shook his head. "No. He only wanted to wake me up." He reached up with his arm and took her hand, gently tugging her down in front of him. Then he leaned forward, moving the fall of her copper-gold mane to one side with his nose, his lips pressed against her neck, tears in his eyes, releasing his pain as he grieved the loss of his friend, lying on a distant hill, topped with a tall oak tree. He could feel a rush of warmth flowing from his injured hand and side. It rose through his chest into his neck, then into his mind, the world in spin as he felt himself falling back into the sun-warmed embrace of black-bog waters.

Meghan held onto him, reaching to comfort him, placing her hand on the side of his face. Her eyes widened as she felt the heat in his skin and she called out to her brother, alarmed, as Harold collapsed into her arms.

∽

"You will *not* go. Your hand and side *reek* with discharge of pus!" Meghan glared at Harold, his uninjured hand holding the reins of his mare. She was concerned, her face pinched in concentration as she held the back of her hand to Harold's forehead. His fever was still there, despite her best efforts to reduce it, an entire day passing since he'd fainted in her arms. She knew the surgeon's cleansing of dirt and pieces of fabric from his wounds had failed to prevent infection from setting in. "You're still burning up with fever. No good will come of you falling from horseback, your head cracked open, thick as it is."

Meghan busied herself removing the bandage from the wound to his left hand. The surgeon had already removed the outside finger, still hopeful he could save the one next to it. If not, he might need to remove it as well in order to save the hand. She gasped as pus oozed from between the sutures used to seal the tear in his hand, left behind by a thumb-sized ball of lead. His other wound, still bound in a bandage, of even greater concern; a red-puckered furrow having been plowed through muscle and flesh along the upper left side of his chest, his armpit torn through, with infection finding a deadly roost there as well. Meghan forced a smile onto her lips, leaving the wound in his hand to soak in the sunlight. "It's not *much* worse."

Harold pursed his lips, his energy drained. "I still have eyes—and a *nose*." He stared at his hand, trying to flex his fingers, the swollen flesh preventing it as a wave of pain from the effort washed the color from his sweating face.

Meghan gave him a concerned look. "We may need to let him *attend* to it. The surgeon. And soon. Before it spreads even—"

"No." Harold chose to ignore Meghan's attention, his mood as dark as the day was bright. "It will heal, or not. Both wounds are punishment deserved. For—" His voice trailed away as his eyes rolled back in his head. Meghan gasped in fear, throwing her arms around his waist as he slumped over.

A shadow separated itself from the edge of the woods, moving toward them. Meghan looked up, ready to call out for help when she saw a native woman approach with a large pouch in her hands. "I am—" The other woman started in French, then switched to English. "My name. A'neewa. Have medicine. For him." She held out a leather bundle.

Meghan replied in French. "I'm Meghan. I know of you, A'neewa, daughter of Chief Tawana. Friend to my—" Her voice dissolved as she looked down and stared at Harold's pale face, searching for words to describe her feelings.

A'neewa knelt beside her, helping to support Harold's unconscious frame. "Friend to your man—Red Fox. My brother found me and said the English had wounded him. I came as soon as I heard." She wrinkled her nose, then reached for her bag. "We will need to boil what is in here. It will stop the infection. Help take his fever from him."

Of Herbal Remedy

A spoon found Harold's lips with a mixture of bitter and sweet, more of the former he decided, his tongue recoiling as the medicine slipped down his throat, despite his feeble effort to lift his arm and push the spoon from his mouth. It disappeared, replaced with the edge of a metal cup, delivering a flow of cold tea, eagerly swallowed, his feverish body in desperate need to try and slake a bottomless thirst.

Words began to filter into his ears as he worked his way back to awareness. A waft of pungent smoke washed across his face, drawn into his lungs as he turned his head to the side and tried to force his eyes open. Another failure suffered as a result, a wave of heat rising from within him, bursting against the surface of his forehead, then receding. His thoughts pulled away with it as he fell back into the shadows of a dreamless sleep.

⤚⟨℮⟩⤚

Meghan wiped Harold's forehead with a cloth soaked in cool spring water, clay pots brought in every hour by solemn-faced natives swapping them out in silence. A'neewa was on her knees at Harold's side, her fingers stained green from an herbal paste she'd been applying to his wounds, working the dark, moss-colored potion into puckered flesh lining a row of stitches, straining to hold his swollen flesh together.

Meghan watched as the smaller woman focused on her efforts with eye-narrowed intensity, aware A'neewa had traveled several days without rest upon learning of the injuries to Harold. The two of them had sat up throughout the night, tending to Harold's life-threatening wounds. Meghan amazed at the native woman's strength of will, as her own fatigue had become a heavy blanket, pulling her to the edge of collapse. "Can you save him?" Meghan's voice was a whisper.

A'neewa nodded, clasping the pot of herbal remedy in her hand. "He is releasing his fever. We must keep giving him the liquid. As much as he will swallow. Then we—*you* can start him on clear broth when he wakes up. The mixture reapplied to his wounds again by late morning. Then at midday, and again in the afternoon."

Meghan slipped from her seat, kneeling alongside A'neewa, hip pressed against hers as she touched the back of her hand. "We *both* will. You're staying here, with me, so he will see you when he wakes." She reached out, taking the clay pot from A'neewa. "But you need to sleep, having come so far, so quickly. Use my bed. It's on the floor, but *well* padded."

A'neewa handed her the container, a weary smile on her lips. "You have not seen the inside of a *native* lodge. There is no pad—" She stopped, noting a twinge of pain on Meghan's face, cursing herself for having made the thoughtless comment, aware of what the other woman must have gone through during her period of captivity. "I'm sorry. I did not—"

Meghan lowered her eyes. "No need to apologize. He told me, Harold—that we share a loss in common." She reached out, using a cloth dipped in cold tea to dampen Harold's parted lips, then feeling his forehead to check on his temperature.

A'neewa hesitated, then touched Meghan on her upper arm, a look of admiration on her tawny face, the spill of light from the fire dancing along the ebony line of a thick braid, hanging over her shoulder. "He told me of you. Of the name he gave you. A—native name, like mine." She waited until Meghan turned and looked at her, with a questioning look in her eyes. "Madonna. Standing in Sun. From the time that he first saw you."

Meghan closed her eyes, tears filtered between her full lashes, falling onto her cheeks. When she opened them, her look of vulnerability touched A'neewa's heart. "He—named me that?"

A'neewa nodded. "Said your family name means *pearl*. He saw I did not know the word, so he shared the name he had given to you."

Meghan placed her hand on top of A'neewa's. "Harold told me how much he came to care for you. Of how much he admired you" She hesitated. "I can understand why. You were, and still are, a close friend to him. To us both—Silent Doe."

Harold pulled himself back toward the light, its shimmering surface a golden glow coaxing him to touch it with the tip of an outstretched finger. *Home*, he whispered. *I must be home again*, smiling as he listened to the slow throb of his heartbeat growing stronger in his ears.

Meghan opened her eyes at the sound of flesh on cloth. She saw Harold drag his uninjured hand across his chest, past his shoulder as he reached up. She took his hand, bringing it to her face, his eyes opening, a thin smile on his lips. He touched her cheek, then her hair. A tress of copper-red clenched, then pulled, drawing her to him. Her full lips soft on his own, lost in an upwelling of pure joy. Her hands cupping his neck, tears falling on his pale face.

"How—long?" The effort to speak caused him to recede into the darkness, his will forcing a return.

"Two days." Meghan turned and called out to A'neewa as Harold opened his mouth, his tongue finding one of her tears in the corner of his lips. He tasted it, then sighed. "Salty. We must be—almost home. Almost back to Bristol."

Meghan hesitated to break the spell of his lucid dream. "No, my love. Not there. Still here, in our wee bonny hut. On the hill, just above the fort."

Harold lost his smile. "Robert. He's gone. I killed him." He closed his eyes, his pulse strong beneath the press of Meghan's finger on his wrist.

She sensed he was out of danger. Safe, his energy drained, but alive.

"You told us about Robert when they brought you in. Saying his journey ended on a hill beneath a grand oak. Placed there by your own hand."

"I had—hoped it only a horrible dream." He licked his lips. "Is there water?" Meghan reached for the pot of tea, wetting the linen. "There's tea. And clear broth. Are you hungry?"

"Yes. For stew, not broth. Made from rabbit." Harold licked his lips. "And more tea." His voice sounded stronger, still raspy but thickening in tone.

Meghan nodded, squeezing his hand in hers, tears now in full flow. She released him, then stood up, wiping them away as she went to find A'neewa, letting her know Harold was back.

A Hero, Returned

Two weeks had passed since Harold's injury and recovery from near-death. Meghan and A'neewa had finally allowed him a limited return to duty, approved of and seconded by medical personnel, amazed at their patients' quick and complete recovery. Harold's damaged side almost fully healed, as too the wound to his hand, the treatment with A'neewa's native potion effective in eliminating all signs of the infection that had threatened his life.

Harold flexed his hand, able to feel the missing finger, considering himself fortunate to have lost only the one. His father, as well as the major at the training facility, having both sacrificed an additional digit in support of the Empire's cause. He was moving at a reduced pace, making his way through the large encampment spread out in lines of canvas shelters just outside the fort, feeling drained by the strategy session the general had ordered him to attend. A tedious affair, with each officer on the general's staff asked to voice their opinions on strategy for the upcoming offensive. The general, listened without comment; knowing his force was several weeks away from making another stab north. The native coalition of warriors now on hand, gathered in the local area, in receipt of supplies of food, arms, and trade goods, as promised.

Harold had been invited to meet with the general before the strategy session began, encouraged to offer his own recommendations regarding a plan of action. Aidyn becoming impatient, interrupting Harold's carefully measured remarks with increased frustration.

⟡

"*Damn it*, Captain! I did not order you here to provide a report as if speaking on the *weather*! I seek your *strategic* advice about what the *froggies* are going to do. As well as the capabilities and best use of our native allies."

The sudden outburst generated a grin on George O'Malley's face, standing in for Robert, sitting alongside the general's desk, his muscular arms crossed, bearing the look of a cat who'd swallowed a songbird or two. The large colonial officer in a good mood of late, constantly in escort of A'neewa, squiring her about the encampment once she'd released herself from helping Meghan tend to Harold's injuries.

Harold considered the two of them to be a good pair; each with strong-voiced opinions on a host of subjects, as well as an obvious physical attraction to one another. One they displayed with robust frequency in a small hut of their own, just uphill from the one he and Meghan shared.

He remained standing at ease, waiting out the general's harsh rebuke, appreciative of the worries lying beneath the other's impatience. "I *repeat*, sir—my original suggestion made to you that we forestall formation of strategy until gaining knowledge of the disposition of enemy forces as we are still uncertain of exactly *where* the enemy forces are currently located. Once we send out an advance force, which will include members of our native ally tribes, we can send back information helping to form a plan. One I *strongly* suggest be blended with *their* ideas, and not only in decree of yours."

The general stared at Harold, about to reply when George interrupted. "I *agree!*"

Aidyn swung his attention to the Colonial officer. "You do?" He studied the other man for a moment, then sniffed. "Rather late to the game, Colonel O'Malley."

George grinned. "I've been practicing the study of furtive maneuver with a—native affairs *adviser.* One with considerable expertise on utilization of native talents regarding use of—*penetrative* skills, performed from behind their lines."

Harold tried to keep a smile from his face, and failed, the general taking note of it. Aidyn took his seat, his finger pointed at a bottle of brandy, watching as Harold filled, then handed him a glass. "I am *vexed*, gentlemen. *Undone* by those I trust. As if Caesar himself, but with *two* Brutus's at my side. Or Bruti, I suppose the plural to be." Harold opened his mouth to correct him, stopping when he saw George shake his head. The two of them waited while the general raised then lowered his cup, staring at the latest map drawn by his cartographers. "I'm nothing if not *flexible* in my approach. I will ask all ranking officers to make recommendations, which I will dismiss out of hand. Final plans waiting until I've had opportunity to seek input from Chief Tawana and his allied leaders."

Early evening arrived by the time the other officers completed their presentations, Harold released by the General to continue his rest and rehabilitation, through his wounds were well on their way to recovery, minus the missing finger. He stopped on his way out of the encampment, using a pocket of shadow between two wagons to relieve himself. As he finished and began push his trouser buttons back into their respective holes, a wistful smile found his lips, remembered the morning Robert had pointed out his having missed the mark.

Harold felt like it had happened a lifetime ago, as if a memory from a life lived by a different man. Everything that had happened before his mentor's death, only a dream. A good one, he added, recalling the closeness felt with Robert at the end of their journey together, side by side on the oak-topped hill, sharing the dying man's feelings for a child he'd not seen in over a decade. A new life for him now begun, due to the tireless efforts of A'neewa and Meghan in having brought him back from the edge of night.

As Harold turned to go, a grunt of effort and rustle of cloth on cloth roused his battle-tested instincts. He slipped to one side as a brush of something cold scraped the side of his ear, followed by bruising impact on the slope of his good shoulder, forcing a gasp of pain from his throat. His hand dove to his waist, the hilt of the knife George had given him in his hand, its honed point driven up toward the throat of his assailant. He stopped, the edge of steel puckering the skin of a wide-eyed private, who hands were slowly rising above his head, one of them holding an officer's pistol, the acrid scent of urine from the young man's pants permeating the evening air.

"The weapon, if you will." Harold kept pressure on the handle of the knife, until the pistol was in his injured hand. He lowered the blade. "Your name?"

"John. I mean, Jenkins. I mean—Private John Jenkins. *Sir!*"

"Who put you up to this?"

The young man shook in fear, aware a tree and noose were in the offing. He clenched his jaw, remaining silent.

"I already know." Harold held up the pistol and angled it slightly, a wash of light from a nearby lantern reflecting from the polished wooden handle. An officer's model and expensive, the King's symbol inlaid in silver along the side of its polished, black-walnut grip. He kept an eye on the soldier, though there was nowhere for him to run to should he decide to bolt. Deserters from the encampment providing native trackers an opportunity to fatten their purses, eagerly hunting them down should any dare try and test their skills in the wild. Harold's only interest: determining the leverage applied, then how best to make use of any information gained, bending it to his own advantage.

"What motivation was given as inducement to my assault?"

"Sir?" The young man narrowed his eyes, lost in the exchange.

"The reason provided you, in encouragement of your actions?"

The soldier swallowed; his face beaded with sweat. "Was told the general would pin me a medal himself. For stopping of a—traitor. A spy for the French. Yourself, as it were told to me, sir."

"The plan—should you have succeeded?"

"I was to drag your body—you, into a supply tent." He pointed into the shadows; his voice low. "Just over there."

"And then?"

"Put you in a cask. One of them as is used for officers. Them who are dead, that is."

Harold stared at the handle of the gun. "Sir—" He glanced over, a tight grin on his lips as he took note of the private's look of confusion. "That is how you must *address* me." Harold stepped forward, placing his injured hand on the man's shoulder. "Welcome, Private Jenkins, to his Majesty's mixed band of English and Colonial misfits, detached to advanced field service, along with native scouts. Under the leadership of—the *Red Fox,* himself."

The startled soldier stared back, his mouth agape. "You—you *serve* with him, sir? With the Red Fox, sir?"

"That would, in fact, be *me*." Harold shook his head. "Time in camp, Private?"

"You, sir? You're the—uh—two days, sir. I mean, Captain *Fox*, sir."

Harold sighed. "And the officer who recruited you to this mission?"

"Weren't no toff, sir. I mean, no officer. Sir."

Harold nodded. "Arranged by proxy, I imagine. Targeting you due to—"

"I'm no *poxy*, sir. I ain't *twisted* like that!"

"Through someone *lower* in rank, Private. Perhaps—a sergeant of the line. A man of squarish stature, with a jagged scar on his left cheek." The boy's look of shock was enough to let Harold know he was right. He shook his head, contemplating why Major Sandersen had made his move with such an inexperienced pawn. "How many casks were there in the tent assigned you to use? When shown them by whomever this unnamed sergeant might be."

"Two of 'em. I mean *two*, sir."

"Good. You can count. A definite mark in your favor." Harold paused. "Can you also manage to arrive at a logical conclusion as to the reason for there being *two* containers? Specifically designed for use in shipping bodies home to England?"

"No, sir. I—*two*, sir?" The young man's eyes lit up in clarification. "But I'm no *toff*, sir. I mean—no officer."

Harold hung his head for a moment, then waved for the private to follow as he led him toward the hill where Meghan was waiting on his return.

❧

"*Here?* With *us?* Are you *serious?*" Meghan reached up and felt Harold's forehead. "No sign of fever, so you must be *daft*, bringing the lad *here* instead of hanging him from the nearest limb. I'll go and fetch my brother. *He'll* do what needs to be done."

"Private Jenkins is in *my* charge, and not to be harmed. I've decided

to make him my *aide-de-camp*. To train him up to be a gentleman and—"
Harold turned his head and considered the young soldier, standing at
attention, eyes wide in fear. "—a bit more *informed* than he is at the
moment." He waved his hand in dismissal, watching as Jenkins eagerly
moved outside, well away from the door of the small hut.

Meghan shook her head, having noticed the wince on Harold's face
as he'd motioned the soldier away. "Your wound is bothering you. Let
me take a look."

"It's no more than a bruise. On top of my *good* shoulder and of little
enough consequence, considering the intent of the assault."

"You *have* to report this. And not sweep it beneath the bed. That
bastard Sandersen must *pay* for this! The boy and the sergeant, as *well*!"

Harold shrugged out of his coat; his shirt unbuttoned so Meghan
could assess the damage. He heard her suck in her breath, a soft curse
following as her hands reached for the balm A'neewa had provided,
used to promote healing of scars. Harold's voice cracked with fatigue as
he responded to her vehement reaction. "They coerced him into it. A
false promise of recognition offered, in return for elimination of a spy.
The sergeant acting under the major's lead, their hand badly played."

"Which is why you must—"

"Be *patient*, dear lady. The major will know the game is up when his
pistol is returned to him."

"To what *end*?" Meghan placed a dollop of the mixture along the top
of Harold's shoulder, the damage sustained likely to cause several days
of limited motion, with extensive bruising to his muscles and skin. Her
eyes gleamed with anger, her fingers stiff, causing him some measure of
pain as she rubbed the ointment into his skin.

Harold smiled, watching as the lines of her face softened while she
tended to him. "Revenge is better when served in *small* measures, once
the blood settles a bit with one's adversary backed into a corner."

"Where they become even more *dangerous*, you *idiot*!" Meghan glared at him as she finished, wiping her hands across the hem of her apron. "Sit down and let me feed you." She ladled out two bowls of stew. One, given to him, the other carried toward the doorway, a spoon and Harold's large-bladed knife in her other hand.

"A last meal for the lad, I presume. Followed by his—execution?"

Meghan looked back; her eyes gleaming. "I haven't decided yet." Then she stepped outside.

The General's Office

"The man is not *fit* for such duty." Aidyn shook his head. "*No.* I will not release him to your command." He gave Harold a hard stare. "It's *not* seemly. You, with finger in point, as if to move my men about like pieces on the board."

Harold shrugged, his shoulder still sore, a grimace of pain on his face. "I *need* a personal aide as I am physically diminished *and* mentally strained. My strength not yet fully returned. The private, having recently come to my attention, already proving himself capable of attending to my horse and belongings. And, as a new replacement, there will be no appreciable loss of value to the company he's attached to. So—this is the *optimum* time for his release. To me."

George stepped forward, framing Harold and the young man in question, the three of them forming a wall of reasonable expectation, one the general was having a hard time to resist. The colonel waited for an invitation to speak, a nod in his direction from Aidyn releasing the words he'd carefully rehearsed. "I have found it difficult, sir, these past few weeks, in having to spend so much of my time helping Captain Knutt perform the duties he customarily assumes. It has—reduced my ability to—to—"

"You may *cease* your prepared speech, Colonel O'Malley, well-spoken though it is." Aidyn gave Harold a considered look, then pursed his lips. "I sense there is *more* to this request than I'm being told. And, though it is a *breach* of protocol, I will *agree* to it, pending a word with the private." He waited as the two officers stared back. "*In* private, gentlemen, if you will."

Harold and George stepped outside, moving back from earshot under escort by two sentries, unable to hear any of what transpired behind the door of the General's office. The two of them held their thoughts until Private Jenkins exited, with a grim look on his face. Harold stepped forward; his arms crossed on his chest.

"Are you under my command, Private?" The youth nodded, then swallowed, a host of words pinned in his throat. "Can you *speak*, Private Jenkins?"

"Sir. I mean—*yes*, sir." He paused, his lips shut tight, eyes shifting when George stepped forward, ready to upbraid him for his reticent attitude. Harold reached over and touched his close friend on his broad shoulder. "The general has sworn him to silence, and he will not be made to speak on it." Harold eyed his new protege, nodded once, then turned about, leading him to the stables where his horse needed some gentle grooming, along with a thorough mucking out of its stall.

⁓

Sergeant Schyler slipped a small purse of coins into his inner coat pocket, his eyes cutting to either side as he checked for shadows moving outside the flap of an officer's tent. He exited slowly, then bent down to adjust a buckle on his boot as he searched for sign of observation. None being noted, he dropped a smile into place on his thin lips, his scarred cheek wrinkling as he rose. A large hand landed on his shoulder, fingers in a firm grasp that held him in place. A soft whisper found his ear, the voice recognized, his eyes going wide in fear.

"Picking through pockets again, Sergeant Schyler? Old habits never die, they say. But a rope round your neck will soon put paid to your activities." George bunched the stocky man's uniform in one hand, yanking him to his feet, the much shorter man left standing on tiptoe, the starched collar of his uniform jabbed into his jaw, causing tears of pain to flood from the corners of his eyes.

Harold stepped out from between two tents, with Jenkins in close company. They joined George, the three of them guiding the frightened sergeant away from the encampment. Once they reached a remote section of wood, George released the thief, the red-faced man's hands going to his throat, his beady eyes in swivel from one face to the next.

"It was not on *my* order. It was the—" He shut his mouth, staring at the officer's pistol held in Harold's hand, his face going white as he faced the Red Fox, who gazed back with a relaxed smile on his face.

"I believe this belongs to Major Sandersen." Harold angled the polished wood of the grip, a sliver of sunlight casting a soft glow, revealing a silver inlay. "Handed to my aide, Jenkins. By *you*."

"It was *not*, sir. I *swear*. It were lost by—I mean, I was *not* involved. Never meeting the lad before now. Sir." The heavyset man swallowed, a grimace of fear on his sweaty face. His eyes swung from Harold to George in frantic search of a means of escape and finding none.

Harold shrugged. "I have a dozen soldiers willing to swear they saw you meeting with Private Jenkins. Saw you provide a pistol, *this* pistol, which is a match to a second one, forming a pair, belonging to a highly ranked—"

"It were not *my* plan, *sir*! I am a *victim*, same as *him*!" The frightened sergeant pointed at Jenkins, seeking his validation. "The two of us following orders, as were given us. No idea on my part of how it was to end."

"I have witnesses willing to testify as to seeing a certain major in close contact with yourself in a whispered conversation, with exchange of an object believed by them to be of similar size and shape to this." Harold dangled the pistol once again, holding it in front of the sergeant's fear-filled eyes.

"Was *his* plan, sir. With myself forced into it. Threat made to have me shot for theft of another officer's belongings. I was *not* in on the planning of it, sir. Only in—"

George leaned forward, his voice a hiss of anger. "I'd gut you here and now, leaving you to the worms, were it *up* to me." Harold reached over and moved him back, taking the confessed sergeant by the upper arm and leading him away from the others.

"I have an offer to make you, Sergeant. One that will satisfy *all* sides. Are you willing to agree to my terms?"

"Terms? Sir?"

"Yes, Sergeant. *Terms.* Generous enough, seeing they leave you with your life while allowing the major in question to avoid swinging from a limb, alongside you. I assume you agree. Yes?"

"I *do.* I mean, I *will*, sir! *Anything*—anything you require. You have but to name it. I *swear*!"

"I need only your agreement, clearly stated. To me alone. Without witnesses."

"I *do*, sir. You have my *word*."

"For what it's worth."

"Yes—sir."

"*Good.*" Harold handed him the pistol, the held out his other hand. The sergeant went to grasp it, then stopped when he saw Harold shaking his head. "The purse, if you please." When the stunned man handed it over, Harold stepped back. "You're free to go, making a return of the weapon to the major with my compliments. *My* compliments. Is that clear?"

"It is sir. *Your* compliments. Sir."

Harold waited a moment, then raised his eyebrows, his hand pointed back toward the encampment. "Go. *Now.*" He waited until the relieved man reached the edge of the tree line, then called out to him. Sergeant Schyler turned around, a sick expression on his face, fearing it had all been a ruse and a noose was still in the offing. "Would you care to hazard a guess as to the size of the wager made just now between Colonel O'Malley and myself? Of how soon you will suffer an accident, or a fatal wound? Our good major known for the sewing up of any loose ends."

The defeated man stared back in reply, then turned and walked away, head down, his shoulders set in an angled slump.

CHAPTER FIFTEEN

Upper Section Of The Ohio River, Early Fall 1759

A Coalition in Advance

The campaign against the northern bastions of the French forces in control of the headwaters of the Ohio began with a flotilla of boats and rafts formed into an armada rowed upriver. Filled with men, munitions, and materials to support an army in the field, they took advantage of winds from the south, providing a steady pulse of warm air that filled the sails on the larger crafts, able to overcome the drought-diminished current of the wide river.

General McClean had ordered the expeditionary group, made up of hundreds of native allies along with over five hundred Colonist and English soldiers, to engage and eliminate any forward elements of French forces stationed on the landward approach to the next fortification in line. The balance of the army to join them in a slow march overland, artillery in tow at the end of a two-mile-long line formed of large wagons, weighed down with supplies.

Meghan and A'neewa had tucked themselves away with the contingent of camp followers, the other women quick to accept the native woman, respectful of her intimate knowledge of medicinal roots, herbs, and plants. They were equally impressed by her knife-sharp wit, her pointed comments offered in solemn tones during daylong bouts of ribald gossip. A'neewa's English improved quickly due to the lively give and take sessions, with an occasional explanation needed from Meghan to help her follow the other women's cunning observations regarding the throng of off-duty soldiers always hanging about.

The general sent his aide-de-camp to the two women on the third day of march, extending an invitation for them to join him for dinner that evening. Aidyn was eager to converse with the daughter of the nominal leader of the native forces, as well as the sister of his colonial counterpart, the two women with reputations for strong felt and clearly voiced opinions.

∽∾

"This meal is the last of our fresh provisions. Hardier fare from here on through to the eventual capitulation of the French; once we are able to nudge them from their promontory perch."

A'neewa turned and looked at Meghan, uncertain of most of Aidyn's words, spoken in English with a strong Scottish accent. Meghan raised a finger, delaying any response as she leaned forward and poured more wine in the general's glass. She slid the conversation to French, which she knew Aidyn could speak, when pressed to do so.

"My dear friend, A'neewa and I are pleased to share your company, sir, no matter the quality of provider. Though the wine is of *superb* vintage. A Bordeaux, I surmise, formed from Merlot grapes. Captured, no doubt, during the naval blockade a few months ago."

The general nodded, an impressed expression on his face. "It is. You have an educated palette, Mrs. Patterson. And a keen intellect, too, from what your brother has shared with me. You hail from the city of Philadelphia, as I recall."

Meghan nodded, cutting a glance toward A'neewa to make certain she was able to follow the conversation. After a slight nod in response, she answered the general. "I do. Our family estate located outside the port area. My father having started several businesses there, in trade of commerce with several other businesses owned in common with investors, located back in England. The primary focus being shipment of goods from here to there in cornmeal, wheat, ore, lumber, and coal." She paused, a quiet look in her eyes. "He died. George inheriting, then turning it over to an Uncle to run while he went off and pursued a career in the military."

Aidyn nodded. "A trade made, similar to my own background." He paused. "And that of your friend, Captain Knutt."

Meghan smiled, sampling the wine. "Yes. We're all drawn from a more—*grounded* upbringing, unlike *others* in positions of authority—within your chain of command."

The general nodded, one eyebrow allowed to rise in recognition of the meaning behind Meghan's veiled comment: the reason why Major Sandersen and the rest of his staff officers were not in attendance. "We are, as always, left having to play the cards as *dealt.* Making the best use of the *least* of them."

A'neewa snorted in derision. "A skunk should be removed from beneath a lodge when *first* discovered. It cannot be changed into a *rabbit.*"

Meghan grinned around the edge of her wineglass, noting the smile on their host's face. Aidyn lifted his glass, waiting as the other two did the same, A'neewa hesitant, uncertain what to do. Aidyn smiled, touching his glass to the side of the native woman's. "A toast to our *clear-sighted* ally, seeing us as we *are*, warts and all."

"Here, *here*! Well said." Meghan tipped her glass, then smiled. Aidyn joined her, then quickly refilled their glasses. "I can see why my favorite captain is respective of the opinions of *both* you fine ladies. As am *I*." He picked up a small bell, ringing for the steward to enter with the first course.

ↄℓↄ

Harold frowned as he forced his teeth to close around a black lump of dried meat, trying to work it into pieces small enough to swallow without gagging. An attempt eased by softening it with a dip into a cup of lukewarm tea. He held a black chunk of overbaked bread in his other hand, product of Dutch ovens placed on top of river sand and fire bricks in the hulls of the larger boats, giving it the same treatment, dipping it into the tea as well.

Soldiers passed meals in large buckets between rafts of boats, drawn together, the men perched with elbows on the side rails as they traded good-natured taunts with mixed groups of native allies, colonial militia, and English troops packed in neighboring crafts.

Harold smiled at their exchanges, expressed in a mix of languages. It had been his idea to blend their forces together during the movement north, with cultural boundaries lowered as men took part in strenuous competitions to see which boat would be first to the next outcrop of rock or over-hanging tree.

"Wonder how the women are making out." George mumbled his words around a knot of gristly meat he was doing his best to force down, having to pinch his nose to try and offset the rancid smell.

Harold shrugged, his hunger enough to overcome caution, knowing the meat, while not spoiled, was close enough to put him off. "Food on the march no different for them as us, though the herbs and mushrooms they collect along the trail help improve its flavor. We're *all* suffering deprivation compared to the comfort from our huts on the hill—and their provision of *personal* privacy."

George sighed as he plucked out a wad of gristle from between his teeth with the edge of a broken fingernail. "The wonderful miseries of a soldier's service." He stared over at Jenkins, who was sitting on the opposite side of the boat, a look of satisfaction on his youthful face as he eagerly scraped the last of his second full portion into his mouth.

Jenkins, noticing the other two men's incredulous looks, grinned, wiping his lips. "I find it to be some of the *best* food I've ever had. Far superior to prison stew, made from *rat*." He worked a stray morsel of meat from between his teeth, his eyes narrowed in concentration as he stared for a moment before swallowing it with a wide smile. "*My* mistake. It does seem to have a bit of rat in it, after all."

Harold chuckled, then reached over, touching his cup of strong-brewed tea to the brim of his young aide's.

"You had too much wine. Not enough food." A'neewa held back Meghan's thick mane of hair, the taller woman on her knees, leaning forward, retching again, with nothing left to show for the effort made, her stomach empty. "Unless you are—"

Meghan sat up; the back of her hand lifted to wipe her lips as she glared at A'neewa. "Do not even frame the thought!" She paused, her eyes lowered, voice soft. "Besides, it lies beyond my capability, because of what—" She sighed. "Is but the wine, as you said, and nothing more."

A'neewa nodded, her face a mask of silence, then she stood up and held out her hand, helping Meghan to her feet. The two women stared at one another for a long moment, Meghan the first to turn away. They walked in silence until they reached a small tent, located on the outer circle of where the other camp followers were staying. A'neewa remained outside, starting a fire in a small pit while Meghan busied herself inside. Once the flames had caught, A'neewa leaned back against a thick log, looking up at a sea of stars, picking out the group that made up the Mother, Father, Child, and Deer. She worked her way across the canopy of lights, her eyes tracing lines between them as if they were beads strung on invisible threads, each image known to her since youth.

Meghan coughed from the opposite side of the fire, a wistful smile on her face. "I forget until reminded that you don't see them the same way *we* do. The stars—how they're called in *your* language. Seen in *your* eyes." Meghan came over and settled in beside the solemn-faced woman, the warmth of their body heat shared. She held two books in her hands. "I have these gifts for you, or curses, depending on how you choose to see them." She held one out, an advanced primer on letters and basic words. The other: a book for young children with pictures drawn in simple lines; the words drawn out beneath each one.

Both held collections of stories young children could recite in singsong rhymes, used to educate her own son, Jacob. Read to him when he was young until he was ready to move on to denser tomes. She'd carried them with her ever since his death, a reminder of his sweet face, held between the palms of her hands, gazing into his clear, blue eyes.

A'neewa eyed the two volumes, lips pursed as she considered the offer. She held the larger one open to the flames from the fire, her dark eyes tracing the images as she noted the tracks below. "I know this is how you pass on your knowledge. Your stories. How you teach your young ones." She looked at Meghan. "These are yours? What you used with your own child?"

Meghan had expected the question while she'd been inside the small tent, looking through them, trying to decide if she was doing the right thing. A slip of paper had fallen out from between the pages; a drawing she'd made of her brother's favorite horse, when she was a young girl. An ebony colt with a gray mane and tail, born of a dying mare. One she'd helped to raise, feeding it around the clock for days on end, with limited sleep. The colt having grown into the largest of George's string of exquisite mounts. "Yes, they are. Or were." She teared up, looking away and staring into the fire.

A'neewa found her hand, squeezing it gently. "I honor the gift of yourself *and* your son. It is of *great* value, and I will protect these—"

She raised her free hand, the picture book in it. "—stories, returning them to you when I have captured their meaning."

Meghan smiled; her hand raised, wiping her tears away. "I do not ask for their return, A'neewa. Use them to help unlock a door you will *need* to open so your people can see into the shadows of a world that will one day soon rise before them."

"You will *need* them back, for your brother to use. When he has his children. Yes?" A'neewa tilted her head to one side, confused when Meghan shook her own, her hair shimmering in the glow of the flames.

"There are hundreds of these, spread throughout the settlements. Thousands, in the other colonies. Many—counts of many hands. As many as there are trees in the surrounding forest."

A'neewa pursed her lips, her eyes narrowed in thought. "Like seeds, planted in your children's minds."

Meghan nodded. "Or weeds, depending on how they're used. But for today, they are simply tools for you to have in hand to do the work needed to help protect your people."

"Harold said the same thing to me, the first time we spoke of the power of words, when written down." A'neewa paused, staring at Meghan. "There was sadness in his eyes when he told me, though I did not understand his feelings then." She hesitated, her voice a whisper. "I am beginning to understand them *now*."

Meghan reached out and took her hand. "I fear there is a hard trail coming for you to walk. You and all the rest of the native tribes. No matter which path you take, you will end up being on a hard road. One facing us, as well."

A'neewa stared into the flames as they began to die down, no longer dancing above the bed of glowing embers. There was no need for further words, both women left staring straight ahead, each reflecting on their own vision on what the future would bring.

Tawana slipped back from the edge of a tree line overlooking a small clearing below. His body appeared to move without use of arms or legs, as if a serpent, slithering back to where Harold and George crouched, sheltered by the limbs of a softwood tree. He knelt beside Harold and leaned in, his voice a murmur. "They have over two hands of large tents. Enough to hold *many* men in each one. Soldiers on guard. Others gathered around fires to keep them burning." The chief held out both hands and stared at his fingers as he opened then closed them. "Many soldiers, most asleep. A good place for us to begin this fight, *Red Fox*."

George listened, then leaned away, spitting a stream of brown tobacco juice onto the needle-strewn ground. "They left this ridge we're on *unmanned*. With serious intent, my native ally." He eyed Harold, who nodded, a thoughtful look in his eyes, then nudged him with his shoulder. "Your French friend's plan, I'm thinking. Looking to twist the knife in your side. *Again*."

Tawana narrowed his brows, giving Harold a hard stare. "You have a friend with them?"

Harold sighed. "More of an acquaintance. A young French officer I've had the pleasure, displeasure, and pleasure of meeting before."

The three men crawled forward; Jenkins left behind to keep watch. The reinforced expeditionary mixed group had ended their journey at a series of small foothills a few miles away, the boats leaving to make a hasty return to reconnect with the army, to bring forward another group of soldiers and supplies. They had headed out, irregulars and native scouts sent forward to find and fix the forward defenses of the French troops, following Harold's plan to bring them to battle if conditions were in their favor. Intent on drawing down the number of men they would face when in position to lay siege to a well-fortified bastion, lying over the far horizon.

Tawana frowned, still confused by Harold's remarks about the enemy officer. One of his scouts slipped up from behind, speaking to the chief in their native tongue. Tawana nodded, then looked at Harold. "You understand what he said." It was not a question, as he knew his young friend had become fluent in their tongue.

Harold gave him a nod. "Your scouts have located a group of French forces waiting behind two small hills to the west. Letting you know the rest of our force is prepared to move into place, following my orders." Tawana smiled, his features settled into a patient expression as he waited on the young English officer's next suggestion. Harold shrugged, then provided his thoughts. "You will send word for the men to deploy to either side of the pass between the hills. They will lie in wait until the French come out in a column, then attack them from their flanks."

Tawana narrowed his odd-colored eyes. "Why would the enemy do *that*? Better for them to wait. Make us come against their defenses."

Harold nodded. "True. But once we spring the trap *below*—" He used a finger to point toward the enemy encampment. "—the rest of their forces will come on the run to finish the job."

"Then we will kill them from ambush, as they advance." George joined in the discussion, his voice a deep whisper from the shadows. "After we kill the bastards *here*." He pointed with his chin toward the squared layout of tents below. "Every *whore-born* son of a *bitch*!" George's voice was tight with anger, his fingers on the hilt of his knife, flexing in desire to seek retribution for the men lost at the Big Burn.

Harold sympathized with his friend's thirst for revenge, though he could not agree to the means George meant to attain it, rumors having filtered back to him of unconscionable events that had occurred to wounded French riders during their last action. "*If* they resist."

Tawana noted the exchange between the two men and reached out, Harold's orders given to the scout, then sent on his way with a wave of his hand. He looked at Harold, nudging him on his shoulder. "The men there, in the tents below, will be *difficult* to deal with. We are too few, my friend." He looked over his shoulder, noting the young soldier named Jenkins whose eyes were flicking to all sides in probe of the night for any threat of danger to his commanding officer. The boy had become a shadow twin to Harold's own, always close to his side, determined to protect him with his life.

Harold flashed a grim smile. "There are *no* soldiers in them, Chief Tawana. The tents contain only kegs of powder, surrounded by bags of lead balls."

A look of confusion broke out on the chief's weathered face. "How—can you *know* this?"

"I don't. Not for certain, but sense the tents are a lure to draw us in, with fuses lit by the men at the fires as we attack. Then they will run for cover in the line of rocks just behind the back of where the tents are. More kegs placed there, timed to explode in our faces as we charge after them."

"The spirits—they have *shown* you this?"

George spoke up, his deep voice a muted rumble of thick laughter. "A trick, Chief Tawana. One our wise Red Fox used against *them*. Now intended to be turned back on *us*."

Harold frowned, recalling the death of the Acadian captain at the river. "He—my adversary, is counting on us rushing in, making an attack from the dark. But his plan will fail when their main force advances from between the hills, on hearing the explosions here. They will deliver themselves directly into our ambush, their column torn to pieces as they stumble through the fire-scarred woods."

Tawana was silent as he considered the information. Then he smiled, his teeth a gleam of white in the half-full moon. "You have my support, *Red Fox*. And that of my warriors. It is time to teach the white-coats this is not *their* land." He paused; his voice dropping to a thin whisper. "It belongs to *us*."

A scent of woodsmoke, edged with notes of roasting meat, hung in the late afternoon air. Fires pulsed beneath large metal kettles, filled with an accumulation of vegetables and herbs selected from stores carried in the supply wagons, or found in the edge of woods and fields alongside the trail, tossed into the roiling mix. Camp followers stirred flour in to thicken the broth while off-duty soldiers meandered through the camp in small groups, seeking some measure of respite from the weary drudge of the day. Most of the men, young and old, gravitated toward the rear of the long column, eager to hear the voices of women at their endless labors. A pleasant reminder of happier days.

The women were in fine spirits, turning a large wild boar on a spit above a bed of coals, fat in hissing splatter as it fell into the flames. The meat was almost ready to parcel out to a long line of men standing nearby with empty bowls in hand. The ladies' share of the kill secreted away, along with a dozen hares and two turkeys provided by a band of skilled young native warriors, denied a place with the advance force who were in a deadly prowl, three days or more ahead of the main force.

The general leaned back, pipe in one hand, a glass of sherry in the other. He sat on a small wooden stool outside the opening of a small tent, shared by Meghan and A'neewa. The two women had invited him to join them for dinner in reciprocation of the meal and conversation a few nights earlier. Aidyn, pleased to accept their kind offer, was eager to escape the formal surrounds of his command tent, leaned back, a relaxed smile on his lips as he sat beside a small fire.

"More stew, General?" Meghan held a ladle over his empty bowl, left sitting on top of a small boulder.

Aidyn patted his stomach, a bit wider in girth than he'd like, though still firm to the touch. "I am replete, Madam. Your culinary skills beyond compare with those of my own cook."

"The skill is all A'neewa's, General. And, as I told you last night, I prefer Meghan, when there is no one around to hear you. A request you should find easy enough to grant."

"I thank you, *Meghan*." Aidyn twisted to one side, gazing at the native woman kneeling before a low table, filled with an assortment of roots she was sorting into small piles. She looked over, returning his smile. "And *you*, A'neewa. For your skill and mutual invitation. Well timed, I must say, my patience running thin due to the incessant nattering of my officers, always in a tither about—" He closed his eyes, shaking his head. "Enough that I proffer you both my thanks." Aidyn sighed, giving A'neewa a warm smile, the wine he'd brought, along with the savory scent of the food starting to take effect. "I need not drag my problems to your fire, as your father, Chief Tawana, told me during one of our late-night talks, before he left with the others. He is a—*fascinating* man with clear vision. A good leader, as you well know."

A'neewa cocked her head, her hands busy separating the herbs into bundles. "Have you *heard* from him?"

"Not yet. Though I expect word back on the morrow. We are but three days at most, from reaching our rendezvous point. And please, do call me by my Christian name, Aidyn." He glanced at Meghan, who smiled back. "Or use *Mister MacLean*, when cross with me, if only to provide fair warning."

Meghan's husky voice affected a deep Irish brogue. "Aye, *Aidyn*." She paused; her eyes narrowing. "MacLean—a bonny name and one well known to me. I've kin from the islands along the Firth of Lorn, not that I care to linger in recall of them, being as they're *Scots*."

Aidyn bowed his head, then lifted his glass, effecting a rich Scottish swirl. "To Irish ladies, with sun-kissed hair. Few so brazen, and none so fair." He waited for her to join him in the toast, then lowered his glass, a mischievous grin on his lips. "Why us Scottish lads drink until we're full before daring an approach to Irish lasses, known for their fiery tempers. Wooing, then bedding them. Ensuring Ireland's future, using what lies under our kilts."

"*Mister MacLean*! Too *far*, sir—by *any* measure of decency." Meghan drained her glass, then refilled it again, ignoring a quizzical look from A'neewa, doing the same for Aidyn's empty glass. "Though it is a well-known truth: the Scots' ability to hold their drink, along with a woman's waist in each arm, as well."

A'neewa, unable to work out the meaning of their exchange, the thick accents confusing to her ear, muttered a few words in her own tongue, watching as they looked at her for a translation. "It is an old native saying. Crows announce themselves, while deer remain silent." She noted their blank expressions. "No one wants to *eat* a crow."

Aidyn pursed his lips as he ran the words through for another listen, then lifted his glass. "To *silent* deer. May they live long lives and *prosper*!"

Later, after Aidyn had left, the two women retired for the night. They slipped inside a common bed to share the warmth from each other's bodies. Each left staring up at the pale-white surface of the canvas shelter, shielding them from a broad canopy of countless stars above, knowing they were still out there, like the men they both had come to care for, somewhere over the near horizon, a few days march away.

A'neewa broke the silence first. "When a child and first learning to read—it was your mother who guided you?" She rolled onto her side, head braced in one hand, able to see Meghan's face in profile; light seeping in from beneath a flap of cloth, the fire outside kept going through the night by sentries in slow-paced stroll from pool of light to light, adding sticks to each one as they walked their assigned sections of the large encampment.

"No." Meghan's voice, soft edged, held notes of sadness. "My brother taught me, while *he* was taking lessons. I asked him to show me, using the same books I gave you. He seemed pleased to help me understand what the words meant." Meghan paused. "I learned everything I could from him, throughout our childhood. George opening the door, leading the way. Me, eager to follow close behind."

"Your mother was dead? Your father left alone, without the time to teach you?"

Meghan frowned. "How much happier a story that would be, if true." She sat up, looking straight ahead. "My father was there but unwilling to allow me the same privileges as George. And, as for my mother—she was a ghost. My father having—stolen her spirit. Taking them from others, too. Members of our family. From friends, and even our indentured workers." She turned her head, staring at A'neewa, her face in shadow. "But not from my brother. Or from me. He couldn't pry away the least piece of *our* spirits, no matter how hard he tried. My brother too strong. Or simply too hardheaded." She paused, then grinned. "Like me, I suppose—at times."

"Perhaps your father was *afraid* of him, even as a boy."

A longer pause followed, Meghan finally nodding. "You're right. It *was* because he was afraid of him."

A'neewa bored in, her voice low and measured. "You had no other family? No brother or a sister?"

"No."

"So your father, he had only *one* son as his—hair."

"His heir. Yes." Meghan placed her hand on A'neewa's shoulder. "You see it so clearly. Your vision so—"

A'neewa interrupted. "I have a father *and* a brother too. Younger than me, but as close to me as you are with George. My mother—she became a real ghost, or spirit, as we name them. When I was a small child. Dying during the great sickness, our tribe losing three fingers or more from each family lodge."

Meghan reached out, finding A'neewa's hand and squeezing it. "That must have been a difficult time for you. Left without her, your father—having to raise you." She paused, nodding her head. "I'm certain he treated you better than mine did."

A'neewa shrugged, pulling her hand away. "He is not like your father, but men are men. And I had many women to guide me. *Wise* women, each as much a mother to me as the next." A'neewa sat up, facing Meghan. "We are not the same, as *people*. But we are as *women*, with a need to see into each other. Away from the eyes, the—*energy* of our men. Where we can reveal our feelings, openly. As well as our *truths*." She lowered her voice. "Do you know why your father was reluctant to open to you? Why he gave so much to your brother?"

A sudden revelation gripped Meghan. "My father—I always felt he *detested* me." She stared at A'neewa. "I just never realized it was because I was born a *girl*." Her hand started to tremble. "I could sense his *anger* toward me, but never understood the cause of it. Using *his* to keep *mine* burning. Determined to follow my brother's lead, holding tight to my spirit. To my will. Learning how to read. To ride horses. So I could—"

"Escape."

"*Yes!*" Meghan shook her head. "To escape. Which I did, with my brother's help. He was always there for me, telling my father that I *could* read all the books in his library. His voice kept low, while my father would end up shouting, his hands clenched as if talons. Body shaking in anger as he looked from George to me. Closing his mouth and leaving; a withered man."

"With George left smiling." A'neewa leaned back. "A satisfied look on his face. The same one he wears when moving men from his path with his eyes, forcing them to step aside, as if a great bear, moving without fear."

"Yes. *Exactly*." Meghan leaned forward, looking directly into A'neewa's dark eyes, all but invisible in the dim light within the cloth enclosure. "I see why Harold was so fascinated with you. And still is. Can understand why it took him so long to come back to me, even after he returned. Finding him gazing off into the woods for days on end, as if sensing someone standing there."

"Harold is in love with *you*, Meghan. Has been since he saw you at the place where he discovered his name for you. When he told me about that moment, he said it was like you were—I can recall the word, but do not know the meaning. His *Madonna*. Told me that was how he said he saw you. I could see his love for you shining in his eyes. Pain there as well, hidden beneath his words, telling me about your beauty, about your strength of will." A'neewa paused. "It was clear to me then how much he cared for you. It is as clear to me, *now*."

Meghan shook her head. Her unbound hair framed her face, softening the edges of her cheekbones, backlit by the glow of the fire, outside. "I've—*hurt* him. I *know* that. I'm still *hurting* him, to this day. Unable to love him as he deserves." She hesitated, then turned her head, staring at the thin canvas flap of the doorway. "I should never have gone to him. Never should have introduced myself, opening a door I hoped might lead me to feeling a man's touch. To feel his body—his heat." She looked back. "A terrible mistake made before I came to understand who he was, and still *is*. Unable to fully open to him, even when he stood in full reveal of his love for me, pledging himself, neither one of us able to let go."

"It was not a *mistake*, Meghan. Only your need for something *good* to come from pain. Everything that has come from that—joy *and* pain, has been a *good* thing, for you both. I know Harold has accepted the truth of how you feel. That he is willing to accept you as you are. Frustrated, yes, but strong enough to handle it." A'neewa paused. "As are we both, you and me. As we *must* be, in caring for men in time of war."

Meghan nodded her head. "I know you care for me, A'neewa. I see that. Can *feel* that. But it blinds you to my faults." She waited a heartbeat. "No, not blind. You care for me *despite* my faults. Despite knowing—sensing my inability to love Harold the same way I once loved—*still* love another man." Her voice dropped to a whisper. "*Two* men. My husband and my son. And a daughter, losing her as soon as she arrived. So beautiful. So—innocent."

A'neewa's hand moved to Meghan's upper arm. "Your husband. And your son. George told me they were killed in a raid by native people, though not of *my* tribe."

Meghan nodded, her eyes closed, unable to speak as her grief rose from within, overwhelming her ability to contain it, leaking out of her in tears, along with waves of shuddering breaths. She bowed her head, her hair forming a pocket of loneliness around her upper shoulders, as if an empty shell, emptied of her inner light.

"Tell me their names." A'neewa waited, remaining stoic, as was her nature, aware the other woman had strength enough to find her way back.

"Patrick, my husband. And Jacob—my little Jake." Silence filled the air between them, followed by a deep breath. "And Elizabeth. My little girl, who passed away soon after birth."

A'neewa nodded. "Good names, Patrick and Jacob."

"I love them still, especially my Patrick. Loved him then, more than my heart could take, unable to breathe when he came into a room, until he looked at me with a smile on his beautiful face. His eyes lighting up with happiness."

A'neewa tilted her head, giving Meghan a searching look. "Your brother—he was satisfied with the match?"

"Yes. The two of them were childhood friends. Patrick, a better one to George, willing to follow my brother, granting him pride of place. Never trying to outshine him." Meghan paused; her hands clasped as she looked down. "One of many things I liked about him, along with his gentle spirit. Already drawn to him, long before considering him for a husband. Until forced to make a decision." She looked up, her voice reflective. "It happened just before I turned sixteen."

O'Malley Estate

The stable was in a hushed mood, absorbing a wave of anger as Meghan raged, her feet stomping in anger as she strode across the thick wooden floor, leaving threads of dust in trail. A large stallion, its muscular neck outstretched, nosed the air as it drank in the sharp-edged scent of her feelings. George smiled as he enjoyed the display of his sister's fiery ire; the fierce look in her blue eyes, and long-fingered hands formed in clenched fists as she looked for something to strike, a familiar scene. An innocent pile of hay offered itself up in sacrifice as she gave it a series of sharp-toed kicks, abusing its unresisting body.

"He—he *ordered* me to prepare myself for marriage. As if *chattel*. As if I am his *possession*. To do with as he will. Our *ghost* of a mother, hands wringing in helplessness, hovering in the doorway with an insipid look on her face. Her tears—such *useless* things, hanging from her eyes without the decency to let them flow. Without showing me the least sign of *care*. For her own *daughter*, unable to show support for another *woman*. For *me*!"

The thick floorboards of the stable rattled as Meghan's feet resumed their heavy stamping along their surface. She came over, stopping in front of her brother, who gazed down at her in silence, his thick arms crossed on his massive chest, a half-serious look on his face.

"Well?" Meghan looked up at him. "Aren't you going to *say* something?" She widened her eyes in a glare. "*Do* something?"

"To you?"

"*No*! To *him*!"

George shrugged. "To what end?"

"To stop him from his cursed *plan* of auctioning me off like some prized mare. Ready for the riding of, then bearing of foals. In—" Meghan pulled back as she noted a smile about to bloom on the curled edges of her brother's lips. "*What?*"

"I'm just trying to imagine it, that's all. You, facing a prospective groom with bridle in hand. Him, trying to place the bit in your mouth, without having his arm chewed off by your clacking teeth."

Meghan cursed, her fists hammering his chest as she kicked at his lower legs, unable to move him. Hands and toes left bruised from the effort. Once she'd worn off the sharper edges of her frustration, Meghan stepped back and took a deep breath, then released it. She turned away, her eyes on a beam of light streaming through an open window, filled with golden dust motes, hovering in the cool, springtime air. "What am I to do?"

"Marry." George kept his voice low. "Today or tomorrow, but *soon*. Someone of *your* choosing, not his."

"To what end?" Meghan looked over. "Giving up my freedom just to *chivy*—to *vex* him?" Her anger softened as she stepped away, in consideration of her brother's words, going over to the nearest stall and rubbing the outstretched neck of the stallion. His name was Phoenix; once a motherless colt, brought back from the brink of death by her around-the-clock efforts in feeding him, and rubbing him down. The willful animal nourished by her energy and boundless love. The newborn colt becoming the largest of her brother's impressive herd.

Meghan turned around and leaned against the stall; the stallion's nose coming to rest on her shoulder as she gave his ears a gentle caress. "Or perhaps it would serve to *shove* him one step closer to his grave."

George uncrossed his arms and walked over. He leaned forward, staring into his sister's bright-blue eyes. "Or to affect the *best* outcome for *you*. Providing an escape from the box placed around you since birth. One you've been trying to climb out of, ever since."

"Only so I could force you out of the *way* so I could inherit *all*."

"True." George grinned. "I always thought you might be the first female child to break the traditional mold."

"Stop *teasing*. I need to figure this straight, and you're diverting me from the effort." Meghan walked away, going over to one of the large stable doors, closed against the cold air during the night. She reached out with her toe, nudging one of the wooden wedges lying on the floor, used to secure the doors when open, protecting them from slamming shut due to a sudden gust of wind.

George leaned back; a loose piece of straw sticking out of the corner of his mouth. "How about—one-eyed Slocum? He's of an age. Solid man, with a good head for horseflesh. I'll even stand any dowry our father might ask." A heavy wedge came flying by, missing his broad chest by an inch. "Or perhaps old man Ferguson. You could give him a year of passive riding. Get with child, then kill him off with a few nights of deadly passion. Then all he has would be yours, with no other children left alive to make a claim. Leaving you to inherit."

A second wedge grazed his chest. George turned his head, looking at the stallion, who was staring at a small door in the barn's side, used to come in from the paddock just outside. Its ears pricked forward; a whinny of greeting working its way along its outstretched throat. George smiled. "Patrick's here."

Meghan noted the horse's attentive stare, her mind turned to a reconsideration of Patrick, always seen as a kid brother coming around to help George with whatever needed doing. The two of them, a perfect team. Whether at work on the grounds, or on horseback, heading off in a mad dash along grassy fields, or weaving in and out along the edge of open woods. Each eager to outdo the other, coaxing their steeds into sudden turns or leaps, leaning forward, neck and neck, the title of winner one tossed back and forth as they made their slow return to the stables with joyful expressions wrapped around good-natured jibes. Patrick, whose face had become the thinner one in reaching his maturity. Slim in body, though his thighs were as thick as her brother's. His hands, light on the reins, never in tug. Allowing his mount to have its head. The heels of his boots, bereft of spurs. Gentle, and patient. Patrick.

Meghan smiled. "We were married a week later. George, as our best man and only witness, his own money used to provide a donation to the church. He provided us a dowry too, as promised. More than enough to give us a head start, along with two horses as wedding gifts. One, for riding. The other, for pull of a plow."

A'neewa nodded. "A generous offer. A loving gesture." A'neewa swallowed her next thought: and calculated. She'd come to know George for who he really was: prideful, though generous enough with a compliment or effort made, when there was something of value coming back in return. Someone who cared for himself, first. His sister, second. Everyone else coming in a distant third, Harold included. Though A'neewa knew George was willing to stand slightly behind the other, in order that some of the younger man's unique qualities might be used to enhance the shine of his own.

"*Yes!* As he's *always* been. More father to me than ever was our own."

"And your Patrick? How was he as a father, and as a husband to you?"

Meghan's voice lowered in tone. "He was a good father. Patient with our son, willing to teach him whatever he wanted to learn to do. To teach me as well, when asked. Ready to answer the needs of those who sought out his advice. His knowledge of horses as great—no, greater than was my brother's. Helping us to grow our holdings, expand our fields, while helping others expand their own. All helping all, he would say, encouraging the community we lived in to build a school, and a church. One open to every faith."

Meghan stopped, her eyes wet with tears, voice wavering as she continued. "Patrick led the way, with me instructing the local children, and helping to heal people in need of it. The books I'd read in my father's library having opened doors of knowledge. The natives living in the area, coming into the settlement to trade. Teaching me about any of the natural remedies they were willing to share, adding them to my own."

She paused; her eyes fully open to her past. "It was a wonderful life. Full of joy and hard work, most times. Difficult days, as well, though more than balanced out during evening hours spent together in reflection of how happy we were. Until the day when everything came undone."

Cabin in the Sun

The small door of the house swung partly open, letting in a bright stream of light. Meghan looked over, spotting hundreds of dust motes hanging in the air. They looked exactly like the ones she'd watched in the stable on her family's estate. Her brother's property now, their father having passed away two years earlier. She smiled at the memory of watching the tiny dots of gold, hovering in the still morning air.

The day had arrived with a bright smile, infused with strong sunlight. Grass-green fields in view beyond the doorway, stretched beyond the environs of barn, paddock, and fenced-in back yard. The sound of her husband and young son, splitting wood out front, interrupted now and then by commentary between them. One, still young in body and mind, teaching the other, even younger, in back-and-forth toss of one spontaneous thought after another. A sweet balance found, with moments of laughter threaded between hard work.

Loaves of fresh-baked bread lay on a counter, cooling. Meghan knew the yeasty aroma would soon lead two hungry men inside, in a mad dash upon hearing her laughing call. Eagerly devouring thick slices of bread, butter spread on top in golden streams staining the youngest one's shirt. No scolding needed as he would outgrow it in a few weeks' time, his lean body thrusting higher each day as if a stalk of corn beneath a warm July sun.

A shadow filled the open door, her attention drawn to it; a stranger's face poised in the narrow opening, face painted black. Eyes, as dark, in slow probe of the shadowed interior, a wooden club in his hand. Meghan froze, unable to inhale, hoping it to be only a dream. One she would soon awaken from. Her throat filled with fear as the man stepped toward her, aware nothing would ever be the same again.

A'neewa gathered Meghan into her arms, holding her while the distraught woman processed her pain. No words offered. None needed. Enough to hold her, understanding the enormity of her loss, a hole in her soul no one could repair, not even Harold, despite his earnest wish to do so. A unique pain, that neither woman would ever be free of.

A look of sadness spread across A'neewa's face, aware that vengeance would never be enough to heal the other woman's wound. Knowing as well that she could not divert her friend from walking her path. She closed her eyes, sighing, sensing a hard end lay ahead for everyone involved.

Stain of a Different Color

Harold kept his eyes locked forward; his face frozen in a rigid pose of feigned indifference as his heart recoiled in his chest. His nostrils were filled with the bitter scent of terror coming from a young French soldier that a handful of natives were torturing. A rank odor hung in the air as exposed ropes of intestines were slowly being pulled from a slit in the boy's abdomen, legs kicking in pain, his shoulders tied to a tree. His voice lost from dozens of mindless screams that had stripped his throat raw.

Harold looked around for Jenkins, spotting the young man several paces away, leaning forward, knees on the ground, a pool of vomit spilled between his hands. George stood a few feet away with a hint of a smile on his face, the corners of his mouth lifted in a look of pleasure. Harold swung his gaze to Tawana, who faced him from across a small circle of men, several warriors on either side, his eyes dark, showing keen interest in what was taking place. All of them in various displays of emotion with most of the natives seeming to be impressed at how long the dying youth was able to hold out. A few others, like himself, wanting to look away.

The assault on the false encampment had been anticlimactic; a handful of sentries overpowered before they were aware of native scouts rising behind them from the shadows. Soldiers, sitting around the fires, stunned when a host of leather-clad bodies poured from the edge of the woods, coming on the run. The fuses, lit by the men before they ran for cover in the rocks, kicked from beneath a thin covering of dirt. Knives used to cut them, then turned on the soldiers, their screams echoing in the night. The French forces stationed behind the nearby hills, left to wait, wondering when the thud of explosions would occur, spurring them to come on the run.

Once they'd secured the area, Harold assigned men to reset the fuses, intending to reignite them when the time was right, signaling the French to advance into the ambush being prepared by his own group. Once he finished directing the others, Harold looked for George, the large man gone missing, along with a handful of native scouts.

A warrior came up, letting Tawana and Harold know a small group of men had moved into the near edge of the woods, George with them. Screams of pain helped direct them to where the others had gathered, Jenkins on their heels, the scene that appeared before them one of incredible horror. Harold, feeling the same urge to purge as Jenkins, forced himself to stand erect, uncertain as to his next step. He looked at George, then Tawana. "We *know* where their forces are. This is—*murder*."

George gave Harold a hard stare. "There is a good reason for it, *Captain*. Our allies are part of this endeavor and must be allowed use of their *own* methods in the waging of war."

Tawana, unable to follow their words in English, stared at Harold, seeing the disgust on his face. He stepped forward, drawing his knife across the dying man's throat, ending the useless test of will.

The advance party of men withdrew, dozens of bags stuffed with lead musket balls removed from around the kegs of gunpowder. The ends of fuses lit by a young native who moved like the wind, coming on in a breathless rush, pulled down behind a large rock as the detonation produced a shock wave that tore through the leaves and limbs of the surrounding trees. As the air cleared, the armed party was on the move, heading back down into the valley to join the rest of their force, in position to ambush the enemy as they moved from behind a series of small hills. The combined force eager to feast on the exposed flanks of the column of French soldiers as they passed by, rushing toward the false encampment, ready to crush any survivors of the deadly trap.

♒

War whoops and bitter curses in French, native, and English voices surged through dozens of small openings dotted throughout a charred, log-tumbled wood. The result of a forest fire sometime during the previous year, leaving a maze of dead trees with twisted limbs behind. The open areas, interlaced with thick scrub growth, a perfect killing ground for Harold's group of irregular forces, led by natives eager to secure war prizes from among their fallen foes.

Bewildered men in white uniforms struggled to form into lines, huge gaps left between knots of wide-eyed men, vulnerable to the dart and deadly dash by men highly skilled in close quarter mayhem. Only a few soldiers were able to manage any real defense; closed in tight circles, their heads lifted from muskets as they tried to separate friend from foe. Foreheads shattered by pistol ball, or from war club blows landing from every angle. Men left writhing on the ground, placed there by jab by bayonet, spear, sword, or knife. A gory mélange of bodies scattered in red-centered pools of dark-red blood.

Jenkins removed his bayonet from the abdomen of a young French soldier, tears running in streaks down his ashen cheeks, a forearm long length of polished steel, coated in red from the enemy, slain. The body left lying on the ground, topped by a mop of fair, curly hair, strands stirred by a late morning breeze.

Jenkins spun, instinct letting him know a blow was about to land. He dropped to one knee, watching as Harold stepped in, trapping the musket barrel of the attacker in his left hand, a large knife in his right, moving in an upward thrust, a grizzled-faced sergeant catching the end of it dead-center in his upper abdomen, the wide blade drawn to one side, pulled out, leaving a gaping wound behind. Blood and viscera seeped from between the edge of torn cloth, spelling the veteran soldier's end.

George was somewhere nearby, his voice a lion's roar rising above the high-pitched shrieks of doomed men's voices, screaming their denial of impending death as a swarm of leather-draped, paint-faced demons fell upon them. Muskets dropped to the ground, unfired. Escape, the only thought that mattered. A final one for most, their heads collapsed in with strike of war club or musket stock. No quarter given. No mercy shown.

Harold took a deep breath, sweat pouring into his rapidly blinking eyes as he looked around at intertwined knots of men lying in silent repose on the trampled ground. A fire seethed within him, fueled by an uncaged rage to kill, with strike of fist and stomp of heel. Probe of sword or thrust of knife. He spun, searching to find, then sever strings binding men to their lives. Standing face to face, side by side, or back-to-back, in swirls of friend or foe.

When there were no men left standing, the small battleground left empty as the fight moved away. Harold took in a series of deep breaths, wondering, as he savored the flavor of survival's rarefied air, how he could ever be anything other than a leader of soldiers in battle. As he began to return to himself, he swiped his forearm across his face, wiping away a thick layer of sweat, soot from gunpowder, and other men's blood. "I sense—it would seem—that we've managed to turn the tide."

He glanced to one side, noting a look of horror on Jenkins's pale face, He reached out to him, as the young boys knees beginning to buckle, holding him by the forearm as he slumped to the thick mat of forest floor. Jenkins pulled his arm free of Harold's grasp, his blood-stained fingers pressing the blood-spattered ground, shoulders heaving as he leaned over, moaning, shaking his head from side to side.

Harold checked him for sign of a serious wound, none found. He straightened up, staring at another young boy, in a white uniform with blood-stained wound in his chest, collapsed in a twist of arms and legs, eyes unfocused, looking up at a perfect blue mid-morning sky. Harold reached over, lowering the dead boy's eyelids, aware of the pain Jenkins was going through. Unaffected, with too much death behind him, his own innocence in hundreds of tattered pieces, lost along the way.

"He—were no different than me. Like looking into dark water. As if I had killed my own self." Jenkins' words were soft, no more than a murmur mixed with the muted sound of dying men's voices, filtered through the blood-scented air. Sound of musket and pistol fire in the distance, began to die away as the fight came to a desultory end.

"I—*took* it from him. Everything he had to give. Gone." Jenkins looked up; his face coated with smeared blood. Tears coursed through the splatters of dark red coating his cheeks, his lower arms and backs of his hands painted with the same dark liquid. Stains on his clothing turning into a dull rust-red.

"You did so to save my life. More than once. And to save your own, as well." Harold nodded at the French boy. "His life, part of the price paid to hold onto your own."

"I never done it before. I'm no killer. Not like *you*. Not like the *others*. I could never be like you." Jenkins dropped his eyes. "*Thief,* yes. Brawler, basher, and such, but never a *killer*. Not like you." His voice fell off into a whisper. "Sir."

Harold looked around the thick section of brush laced woods, hard-won experience letting him know the threat of violence had moved past, located somewhere close to hand, a swirl of shouting coming from a line of tall ledges ahead that formed a pocket, edged with tall pines. He knew George would be leading the mopping up, with the native allies following Tawana's orders. Time enough, he said to himself, to ease the youth to as soft a landing as possible.

"You mentioned, on the boat ride upriver, something about the quality of prison fare supplied you. A recollection of having been served rat meat." Harold paused, waiting until Jenkins looked up, a confused look on his face. "You would have been young, to have been put in such a place as that."

Jenkins sat back, using a fire-scorched base of a hardwood tree to lean against. He wiped his tears away with the back of one hand, a smear of water-thinned blood left behind. "Three of us, there were. Like lambs— tossed among wolves. Our backs always to the corner, most times. One of the long termers, taking us under his protect, though his own neck was soon for the stretch. I thought he were trying to find some path to redeem himself, in helping our small lot to survive."

Harold nodded. "A man finds his way to the ending he desires, most times, if given the chance."

Jenkins glanced over at the dead soldier, then sighed. "He saved us—when a food riot broke out. Men, trapped in one large cage, turning into beasts. Food, always in rot. Water, sour with scum. Left to tear at one another with teeth and fingernails. No guards daring to step in. No one to—" Jenkins looked up. "He come up to us, our protector, with bloody hands, his eyes in a dead stare. The three of us in a huddle, with nowhere to go. Trapped in a corner like—like the rats the cooks were always feeding to us." He shook his head. "I knew we were about to die, like it had already happened. I could see it in his face, himself gone to a place—to some place I hope to go to my maker without the *knowing* of."

Harold listened as the sounds in the wood came back into balance. A whir of bird wings swept past his ear, making a swift dip toward crushed brambles, snatching up a cricket resting there, then away to the safety of a limb. Bees began making ruler-edged flights from small blossoms back to colony hives. White clouds began to form, drifting by overhead, daubed across a flawless sky. "You survived. And the others?"

"All of us did. Saved by a miracle." Jenkins looked up, his eyes in soft reflection. "Do you believe in those, sir? In miracles?" When Harold nodded, the boy shook his head and looked down at the ground. "It was a cricket, sir. Come in through a window, between the bars. Hopped onto my shoulder, like he was a parrot sitting on a pirate's shoulder. Not moving." He paused, a thin smile creasing his gore-smeared face. "I cupped it. Held it out to the man about to send us to the hell he were already in. Asked him if he were hungry. If he would like to have it." Jenkins shook his head. "Watched him come back into himself, like he was being poured back inside his body. Like he could see again. Could see us as the boys he was wanting to try and save."

Harold nodded. "You broke the spell. Broke the mirror, reflecting back his hate of everything bad that had ever happened to him, leaving him there, waiting for his life to end."

"He lost the look, with a shake of his head. Lost the will to kill. Took the cricket and held it up, all gentle like, as if it were the most precious thing he'd ever seen. Then he took it over to the window and let it go. When he turned around, he faced the ones left standing, telling them it was over. The killing. The dying. Me, and the other two boys dropping to our knees in prayer, knowing what we'd just seen happen, with our own eyes, was a true miracle. Just like in the good book, sir. And another one happening the next day, when they came and let us three out. Made to sign papers, then put in the army—just like that."

"Ending up here, alongside me, saving *my* life. The miracle, as it were, in repeat."

"Ending up with me taking—" Jenkins pointed. "—his life. Sir." He reached out and snatched a grasshopper with his fingers, holding it up, tears in his eyes. "Look here, sir. Not a proper cricket, but no doubt just as sweet." He smiled, his eyes in pain. Harold nodded, reflecting the same look.

One of the native scouts came running up, sliding to a stop, his dark eyes taking in the scene, a frown on his face. "Chief say you *come*." He spoke in English, giving Harold a hard look. "Men be killed. Tawana say Red Fox to decide."

Harold took Jenkins by the arm, pulling him to his feet. "Take me to him." The native nodded, then spun about, leading them away.

⚮

A thick knot of French soldiers filled a narrow cleft in a steep wall of rock. There was nowhere for them to go, a crowd of hard-eyed men facing them with dark countenances and blood-matted weapons, clenched in eager hands. Harold shouldered his way through the angry colonist militia men who'd sworn to serve him, then parted a sea of natives with a gentle touch on each man's shoulders until he found Tawana, the intrepid chief standing in the center of the opening, in between the surrendered foe and men hungry for revenge. He walked over and grasped the Chieftain's forearm in greeting. "We have won the day. There will be no more shedding of blood. Thank you for holding my people back."

George materialized from the thicket of English and Colonial men, walking up with a limp, his thigh bleeding, a thick coating of blood covering the side of his face, the shoulder of his coat soaked in a black stain. "We finish this. *Now*!" He turned to wave his men to raise their muskets and fire. Tawana stepped forward, placing himself between the French survivors and the Colonial officer.

"*No*. Red Fox has spoken. We will kill *no* more."

George stepped around him, stopping in front of Harold, one of his handmade knives in his hand, the blade red with blood. Harold faced his cold-eyed friend without flinching, while Tawana pulled out his war club, ready to strike. Silence fell around them, Harold ready to die to protect the enemy soldiers, waiting, while his large friend's hate hovered in balance against his solemn duty.

Harold kept his voice silky smooth. "We're done here, Colonel. These men have surrendered. Is that understood?"

George slipped back behind the curtain of his need for revenge, his arm tensing, prepared to strike. Jenkins slipped in, stopping between the two leaders, looking up at George's face, his hand raised, holding the grasshopper he'd caught earlier by its rear legs. "Look, sir. A big, ripe one. Far tastier by far than any cricket ever was." He offered it to George, whose cold eyes barely moved. "You don't care to try it, sir? No?" Jenkins looked at Harold, who shook his head, then he shrugged, popping the large insect into his mouth, chewing with gusto.

The loud crunching brought George around. He stepped back, letting go of his knife, watching as it fell to the ground. He tried to speak, his voice dried out from a lack of water, finally managing to swallow, then clearing his throat. "I will, of course, obey your order, Captain Knutt." He half-saluted, then lowered his arm, head angled toward the ground. "I'm sorry, my friend. Forgive my—"

Harold stepped forward, placing his hand on George's upper arm. "Nothing to forgive, brother. We'll drink to their memory tonight, as soon as we find where the damned *Frenchies* have stored their wine." Harold nodded his thanks to Jenkins, who seemed ready to pass out. He took Tawana by the hand and nudged him forward until they were face to face with Major Pierre de la Coulombe, his sword clenched in his left hand, right arm in a blood-stained bandage, strapped against his chest.

"It's *over*, Major. The battle *and* the war. At least it is for you and your men. We're soon be at your throat in the north, with control of the mouth of the Saint Lawrence in a matter of weeks. Then it will be at an end. Everywhere."

Pierre nodded in agreement though his eyes revealed a yearning to have ended it here, in one last spasm of sinew, bone, and blood. His own friends and comrades lost in a final, mindless orgy of slaughter, to no good end. Harold reached out, grasping him by his forearm, gently squeezing. "I too, Pierre, feel the same. But it's over. And those of us who've survived must now carry on, doing our best to see it's never repeated." He pulled back his hand, holding it in front of him, accepting the other's sword, then returning it to him.

"We will take you prisoner, all of you, doing what we can for the wounded. Help carry out those unable to walk. Do—what must be done for the ones on both sides, too far gone to survive the journey back to our lines."

Pierre sighed. "I had you centered in my sights, earlier. I did *everything* I could to aim true. But providence provided a misfire, saving your life then." He looked at his defeated soldiers. "Saving the lives of my men and myself, now." His legs trembled, knees undone by fatigue and blood loss. He sank to the ground, staring as the assembled group of men dissolved into work parties, going about the mind-numbing effort of recovery of the wounded who would live, while the more experienced men among them attended to those who were near to their ends, the younger soldiers among them tasked with burying the dead of both sides.

CHAPTER SIXTEEN

Promontory Fort, Mid Fall, 1759

A Final Strategy

Lightning tickled the ground, followed by a soft grumble of thunder, close behind. Thick clouds brushed the top of a wide hill, the dark sky providing a black background, highlighted by jagged streaks of lightning, revealed in full glory. Rain hissed through the foothills in a steady march; a gentle breeze trailing behind filled with a mix of clean notes, overlaid with a sweet, pungent odor.

Meghan leaned against Harold, her hand in his, sitting beneath a roof of fluttering canvas. Their small tent, perched on the edge of a hill, lay a mile away from the dark body of an imposing fortress. English forces were encamped between, waiting on its surrender, or use of a wily stratagem plucked from Harold's restless mind to break the stalemate. The two forces left standing their ground. The French, within. The English and colonials, without.

"There is beauty in a storm, balanced on the point of release." Meghan felt the heat of warmth from Harold's body through the thin shirt he wore. Her hand rested on his leg, fingers feeling the lean strength of his body. He didn't respond, his mind twisted at the ends of multiple strings of unspoken thoughts, trying to weave them into a rope strong and long enough to find a way to break the siege. Meghan leaned over, placing her face directly in front of his, the curl of her lashes revealed in an extended flash of bright white light. She looked into his eyes, speaking with a soft Irish accent. "Where be ye, Harold Knutt?"

He leaned forward, kissing her forehead. "*Here*, lassie—with you."

Her lips found his ear with a throaty whisper. "Liar. You are Red Fox, ever on the *prowl*." She leaned back, sighing, resigned to her place in his immediate world, coming in second to his desire to find an end to what might turn out to be his last battle, helping to bring about a satisfactory conclusion to the years-long conflict, one he'd come into a little over a year and a half ago. Meghan tried to avoid thoughts of what might happen when it was over and Harold's home in Bristol reached out with beckoning arms. "I see the storm—and wish to be back in Philadelphia, at my brother's estate. Sitting outside, amid several thousand acres of its lush grounds."

"A bit less than a thousand, according to your brother."

Meghan chose to ignore him. "In a wild gallop—riding bareback on my pick of a hundred or more fine steeds."

"No more than fifty, based on your brother's latest estimate."

Meghan stared at him. "Do you consider it *wise*, tugging the tail of a *lioness?*"

Harold reached around, searching her curves. "I'm safe. No tail."

"But this lioness does have *sharp* teeth." Meghan flashed him a smile, the lightning obliging with another flash of silver-white, highlighting her wide smile. They turned their heads and watched as the wall of water drew close, knowing it would soon force them inside the small tent they were using for shelter.

"As I was saying, I remember taking Phoenix out for a ride one night, when a storm such as this threatened. Riding as fast as possible, the wind

in my hair, a sense of unleashed power in the air. The strength of the
stallion between my legs making me feel as if I could coax it to leave
the ground, carrying me away. My winged steed, become Pegasus. And
I, Achelois. Off to wash away the pains of humanity."

Harold glanced at her; his eyes narrowed. "Never heard of her."

"A minor goddess." Meghan shrugged. "Offering succor to those in
need. Seemed fitting, with me always bringing injured animals' home
to heal and rehabilitate. My father ever in a snit, finding empty stalls
turned into menageries. My brother stayed the switch, insisting it was
a phase and would soon pass, once my head swung 'round to boys."

"Is that why you felt the calling to follow your brother? To heal those
in desperate need of it, myself included. With you to thank for pulling me
back from a long fall to black, because of your skilled administrations."

"Accomplished with A'neewa's help. She's the one who saved your
life." Meghan sighed. "My brother seems quite smitten with her." She
raised a hand, placing it against Harold's lips. "I mean to say, they make
a good coupling, of similar spirits. I only wonder what will come of it,
once this last act of foolishness is over with."

Harold took her hand. "They are both—discerning, when it comes
to letting go, or not. It will be up to them to discover an answer for
themselves."

A moment of silence filled the space between the two of them, mere
inches in measure, but as wide as the sea stretching between Philadelphia
and Bristol, each with the same unspoken question kept from their lips.

A Ride in the Night

Harold stared at the detailed map Aidyn had commissioned, showing
the outer grounds of the large fort, with an inset providing an estimate
as to the layout of the inner defenses. Much of the interior drawing was
based on information bought from a local provider of goods, allowed
entrance now and then with a wagon filled with vital supplies. The

outer environs of the enemy position encompassed a wide plateau to the front, with steep approaches along the three other sides, the land falling away to a river basin below.

Harold pointed at the section of map that represented the approach to the main gates; a wide field, narrowing to the width of the fortress's front wall. "The plan will be to divert their attention to the *fore*, allowing stealthy approach by our forces from the other sides. Our best climbers to toss grappled ropes atop the back section of wall, lightly manned, the least likely avenue of attack. The other two groups will move in from each side, in small teams in dark clothing, placing charges against the walls with fast-burning fuses in order to create a breach. Cannon fire from our main lines will provide covering fire, with air bursts, aimed far away from the horse and rider."

The general studied the map, rubbing his jaw as he considered how the enemy commander would envision the planned diversion. "Why again—the need of horse and rider?"

"To show off the excellent movements of the steed. The display intended to draw the eye of the French comm—"

"Draw a storm of musket balls, more likely." Major Sandersen spoke up, his nasally voice pitched higher than normal, a derisive snort following close behind. "A diversion easily dispatched of, leaving our forces exposed to discovery and subsequent slaughter."

"I beg to disagree." George held his temper, his voice pitched low, though his thoughts ran to going over and shoving his wide-bladed knife up through the other man's weak lower jaw, enjoying the look of shock in his beady eyes as his life slipped away. "Their commander is a noted *equestrian*. Anyone with sense enough to study our intelligence reports would already know that. He will not hazard the beast's health, nor that of the rider, sending parties out to gather them both up instead."

"Yes, Colonel O'Malley." The general nodded. "You have the *right* of it. A plan with small, though *lethal* consequences to the men chosen to perform the assault, if it should fail. Though it will provide for a rapid end to this insufferable stalemate, helping to bring about a complete cessation to this *interminable* war." Aidyn stabbed a finger at Sandersen. "Will *you* volunteer to ride the horse, Major?" Noticing Harold about to speak up, Aidyn froze him in place with a firm glare.

"Sir, I—" Sandersen glanced to either side, eyeing the officers beside him, waiting for one of them to step forward to claim the honor. No one moved, their eyes focused straight ahead. "It would be an *honor* and *privilege*, sir. Except for my being such a—poor rider. As my fellow officers will attest to. And since this—excellent—plan requires an expert's touch upon the reins, then it might be—"

The general nodded to his aide. "Make note of my request and the major's long-winded response in deciding to forego the honor." He looked at the other officers to see if one of them might step forward. None did, leaving him to sigh as he turned and looked at Harold. "It seems you are the one to lead us, once again, Captain Knutt. Am I correct in assuming the steed you will require is one I have grown particularly *fond* of?"

"It is, sir."

"Of course. Leaving me to offer my *fervent* wish that *both* of you return to my service in *one* piece. Or, at the very least—my mount."

∽

"You're an *idiot*. Using my words to conjure up this—this *outrageous* scheme—destined to fail." Meghan stood before him, hands on her hips, fingers flexing as if searching for the knife she carried beneath her skirt, secured to her upper thigh with a thin leather strap. Surprising him the first time he'd found it, though when the strap was revealed, it had proven to be an alluring sight.

Harold was prepared to retreat, though George stood firm beside him, Harold hoping the other would be ally enough to overcome Meghan, if needed. "I understand you're concerned for my safety, but I judge the French will—"

"Is not *your* safety I care one whit for, only that of the innocent *animal*!"

George stepped forward to offer a supportive comment, backing away when his sister fixed him in place with a murderous look in her eyes. He eased further back, hat in hand, then spun about and walked away.

Meghan watched her brother fade into the shadows. "You seem determined to *kill* yourself. To seek a balance of the *scales* you're always speaking of. Thinking the fate of your men lies in *your* hands. You're wrong, Harold. As is that oafish hulk who's just deserted you." Her voice softened, slightly, her eyes gleaming with unshed tears. "I will not wait here until they bring word of your wounding—or *demise*. Or worse, yourself showing up hale and healthy, bringing me news of yet another *grand* victory. Wearing a boyish grin, as if this war is but a fistful of chestnuts tossed in play between friends."

She turned away from the fire, moving into the shadowed woods, head down, shoulders sagging beneath her grief. Harold watching as the woman he loved walked away.

A Mid-Night Ride

The sentry on duty inside the front wall of the French fortress yawned, his eyes squeezed shut with the effort, then yanked open at the sound of his lieutenant's heels beating a measured tattoo along the wooden palisade. He straightened to attention, eyes forward, trying to spot any sign of intrusion on the wide-open field to the fore.

"Keep a sharp eye out, Private. We're bound to face assault within the week. The English general forced to make at least one show of force, before retiring in defeat."

"If I may, sir. Has there been any news from our northern outposts?

Are they coming to our support, bringing additional supplies and men?"

The officer raised an eyebrow, giving the young man a smirk. "Best leave your questions unasked, Private. Better yet, try not to have them at all."

The thudding of hooves from a horse in full gallop sounded from the darkness, along with a loud whoop that drew both men's attention to the stretch of flat land below. A rider appeared from the shadows astride the back of a large stallion, rapidly approaching the wall. Men scurried to form up, their muskets leveled, the rider framed in the sights of their weapons, the sound of hammers brought to full cock radiating along the line.

The lieutenant raised his arm, about to give the order to fire when the rider slipped from the saddle and fell to the ground. He lay there a moment as the soldiers watched in stunned silence, then rose to his feet and called out in a drunken voice, wobbling toward the horse who'd turned back, loping over to nuzzle the man's shoulder.

"To the glorious French soldiers—in pose, above on yon wall." The slur of gutter French was difficult to make out over the rush of men coming on the run to join the sentries, curious to see what the commotion was about. Officers barked out, ordering the men to return to their stations. A few obeyed, most choosing to ignore the commands. The rider, reins in hand, hung his head. "May your aim be as sharp as your wits, as I am undone by grief. My entire family lost to fever while I am here, left unscathed, outside these very walls. A cruel jest, from a cruel and unjust world."

Harold raised his arms as he stepped in front of the horse. "I am ready to receive—" He paused, then turned away, pretending to vomit on the ground, a stagger added into the mix as he did so. "To receive— final judgment—witnessed by my, by my general's *finest* steed. Yours in payment for a—for a quick and painless death." He swayed, lowered his arms, then looked up, a sad smile on his lips. "But *first*—another ride! To show my fine—my excellent *form* in the saddle." He mounted the steed with some difficulty, the saddle sliding from its back, spilling him to the ground. Loud jeering from the soldiers filled the air as he scrambled aboard, bareback.

"Do not *fire*!" A booming voice forced its way through the soldier's laughter; a colonel having climbed to the parapet. "He is a *besotted* fool, though the animal looks to be of superb form. It will make a fine gift for our commander. Form a party from the men manning the other walls and bring the horse to me."

The lieutenant saluted. "And what of the rider, sir?"

"He's of little consequence. Bring him along if he doesn't resist. Perhaps then we'll provide him the release he seeks, pending the commander's approval."

⌒℮⌒

Harold used his legs to guide the horse, the reins let slip from his hands; the bridle dropping to the ground. He wore pants made of thin deerskin, providing as much grip as needed for the smooth gait of the impressive animal. Soldiers' hands reached out, then fell away as the horse changed directions with sudden thrusts of its huge hindquarters, its teeth snapping at the men as they leaped away, the chase soon resolving into a chaotic dance, ending as several artillery shells came whimpering through the clear midnight air, fired from cannons brought to the edge of the English end of the field, passing by to either side, exploding without effect to rider, horse, or the small mob of Frenchmen in chase.

Harold hoped the rest of the plan was proceeding as drawn up, the assault forces now making their furtive approach, with the defender's attention and that of the men chasing him focused on the steed. The men in pursuit started to howl in anger, with those remaining in the fortress seeming to tire of the game, shots thudding out, though none of the lead balls came close enough to raise concern for the steed's continued good health. Harold leaned forward, pressing with his inside leg, turning the thick bodied mount away from the walls.

Two explosions roared from behind as casks of powder kegs placed against the outer walls and covered with bags of sand exploded, tearing open large openings, filled by a stream of warriors and Colonial irregulars, followed closely by a determined charge of hundreds of regular troops. Harold urged the mount into a full gallop as the French soldiers turned back, screams of pain and outrage from within the breached fortress beginning to fill the night air.

୧୧

The victorious men celebrating inside the captured fort fell into a sudden silence, a narrow lane created, one Harold walked through, hat in hand, his uniform back in place. His heart was heavy, carrying the names of the men who'd died in making the assault. Dozens of the overwhelmed defenders having fallen alongside a handful of his own. One name producing a knife thrust of pain to Harold's chest when told of a mortal injury, suffered by Jenkins, lying somewhere ahead in the shadows of the fortress. The joy of success had bled away as he approached the fort, his eyes filling with tears as he came to a knot of solemn-faced men, George centered among them. The large man reached out, touching Harold on his shoulder, then stepped back. Harold knelt beside the dying boy and took his hand, the wounded soldier opening his eyes.

"I'm—sorry, sir. For letting you down. Wanted to—to tell you that. Myself."

"No need for an apology, Private."

"From before, sir. From when we first met." Jenkins' breathing turned into labored gasps, blood filling his punctured lung, the color draining from his freckled face. "I owe you—have owed you a life. Got the chance—to repay it—at Bloody Wood." He smiled, his face going slack, eyes staring into the heavens as the vibrancy of his youth flowed away in a thin trickle of blood oozing from the corner of his mouth, head turned to one side.

Harold reached out and wiped it away, then eased the dying boy into his lap, holding him until his breathing ceased and his valiant heart wound down.

Harold, escorted by George, found Meghan sitting beside A'neewa's at their campsite, the two of them sharing a log seat next to a large rock, reflecting the light from a small fire. A'neewa stood up, coming over, placing her hand on Harold's shoulder, then letting go. She took George by the hand, leading him away.

Harold moved to where Meghan was sitting, her head down, staring into the flames. "I'm sorry—for having worried—"

"The horse?" Meghan's voice was low, barely more than a whisper, turning her head, her eyes finding his, lips pressed together in a thin line.

Harold nodded, a grim look on his face. "Fine. No harm coming to *him*." He paused. "Our losses were light. The French commander and his staff caught in their bedclothes; the fort surrendered before any significant number of casualties could occur."

"Another feather in your cap, then." Meghan tossed a small stick on the coals, causing a spiral of sparks to rise. "You may as well go place a live turkey on your head, its tail-feathers in spread. Parade around the encampment, then use it to provide a fine meal for the men I hear celebrating another of your near bloodless victories. The Red Fox, adding another feather to his cap, enhancing his glorious record."

Harold sighed, knowing from Meghan's monotonic tone that real damage had occurred. "I'm done with such efforts made on the Crown's behalf." He lowered his head. "Done with causing the deaths of men on both sides." He paused, his voice trembling when he spoke. "Jenkins, the last of those sacrificed on the altar of my ego."

Meghan looked up, then rose to her feet. She reached for his hands, taking them in hers, her skin warm, voice softened by pain. "He lowered his shield, cast his sword to the side. Then bowed down, kissed the ground, with a solemn pledge made to never fight again." She grasped the lapels of his officer's coat, pulling him in for a heated kiss, then released him and walked away. Harold left standing alone, watching as she disappeared into the night.

A Promise, Made

"She will soon come to her senses." George nodded. "I *know* my sister. She loves you, only needing time enough to see her way through this."

Harold shrugged as he looked at the ground, using his toe to brush a layer of leaves away. "There's no strategy for making peace with her. I am—in over my head, lost to currents beyond my ken."

George reached out and clapped him on his shoulder. "She'll be all right, you'll see, given time enough to maneuver her way back into a balance."

"I fear time is not an ally, George. She still bears a thirst for—" Harold's voice trailed off.

"Of her need for *revenge*." George stared at him, his demeanor cold, eyes without warmth. "I too *seethe* in wanting the balance paid of the debt owed on *her* behalf *and* mine. For the deaths of a good friend and a dear nephew, lost to *me*. My sister's life bright with promise one moment, then *gone*—" He snapped his fingers. "—like *that*, leading to a life spent seeking to repair the damage done." Harold watched as the other man shrugged his wide shoulders, his face relaxing into a broad smile. "We *all* carry wounds, Harold, inside and out. Some of them wider or deeper than others, with few lucky enough to go through life without suffering them. And more's the pity, there, I suppose."

Harold lowered his head, staring at the ground, his voice low. "I'm left wondering, were her thirst quenched, if she might choose to let go of her own life—in order to be with them?" He looked up for George's answer, the other man already walking away, his words unheard.

$$\sim$$

"You need to let your spirit come back into you, returning with it to who you were, before." A'neewa faced Meghan, her arms crossed on her chest. "It is a hard path, but the one who waits for you at the end is worth the effort."

"Do you think I don't already know that? I *ache* to leave this burden behind." Meghan shook her head, her hair washed, left unbraided, hanging in a red wave, reflecting the morning light. "You seem to have been able to put aside the loss of *your* man, once your revenge was in hand." She paused, hovering between making a plea for help or shoving the request away. "I cannot find its end within me. I've tried and *failed*, my vision blurred by the sight of them: my precious lads. Their faces pale, *eyes* in silent stares—as they lay stretched out, looking into the sun." She reached up and touched the side of her head. "I would use my knife to carve the images from my mind, were that possible."

"So instead, you seek to put a blade to *their* throats. The ones who placed the images *there*."

"*Yes*! I *do*! If given the opportunity—I'd happily *bathe* in their blood!"

A'neewa nodded. "And then you will be *free* of this curse?"

"I'll know the answer once the moment arrives."

A'neewa came over and placed her hand on Meghan's shoulder. "Then I will help you in your search for it."

CHAPTER SEVENTEEN

Promontory Fort, Late Fall, 1759

In Search of Truth

Thick woods, draped in a haze of dense wood-smoke from dozens of fires that were burning in circles dug into the ground, held shadows of native people moving through them in a listless drift between temporary shelters. Their subdued voices murmured in chorus with the soft whimpering of hungry children, stomachs in constant grumble, their large eyes wide in confusion as they trailed behind.

They were allies of the defeated French. Natives, from several northern tribes sequestered by the English in a lightly guarded encampment. Confined there by their oaths and a desperate need for food, forced to wait on promised shipments of goods in trade for their agreement to cessation of hostile activities against colonial settlements. A return to their places of origin a question left to swing in the damp winter air while the English forces took over control of the headwaters of the Ohio River. Both sides hopeful for a resolution of further conflict before winter began its stealthy approach.

A'neewa moved among the huddled groups, doling out herb

medicines to those most in need. Small children clung to her side, their fingers desperately searching through her pockets for scraps of food. None found; all she'd brought with her already plucked out. She continued her walk through the woods, listening to the endless lamentations of women and cursed muttering of men as they expressed their emotions, leaving her feeling as if she were a spider in the center of an enormous web.

"You are daughter to Tawana."

A'neewa turned around, the children at her side having drifted away, coming face to face with a tall native with lean build. "I am."

"Daughter to a chief, no longer our friend." The man leaned in; his breath warm on her cheek. He paused, his dark eyes searching hers. "You were once the woman of Red Fox. Now sharing the bed of the trespasser warrior who wants to steal our land, sicken our people, poison our waters with filthy villages."

A'neewa waited without responding, aware the man had something to ask of her, needing to satisfy his pride before exposing the marrow of his desperate need. The man stepped closer, violating her circle, watching her eyes for a sign of fear. She faced him, her fingers poking through a slit in the pocket of the dress she had on, touching the small knife strapped to her upper thigh, a copy of the one Meghan wore, ready for instant access.

He sniffed her neck, his nostrils flared, jaw clenched in anger. "We are made prisoners here, while the English treat the French soldiers as their friends. The color of their skin binding them as brothers again, leaving us where we were, before."

"You speak the truth."

"Leaving us—*all* of us, as useless weapons tossed aside when no longer needed. While those from your tribe return to stealing from us *all* we have." She waited, sensing he was close to the point of his approach. "Your people are *no* different than us, to the English or the

French, only further away. They will come for *you* as well." He spat on the ground. "They will *eat* your eyes, your hearts, while they swallow your *stories*, steal your *spirits*, leaving you hollowed out." He swung his arm, taking in the remnants of his tribe. "It will not matter how well you *know* them. How often you lie with them, *serving* their needs. They will bleed you, cast you *down*, growing angry when you refuse to give your skin and bones to them as well."

A'neewa stared back, feeling the man's pain. She knew he was right, having seen it herself years ago when a child. Men with white faces wearing strange coverings, coming by river to offer metal for furs. True to their words of friendship and exchange of goods. Followed next by men in dark dresses, holding blocks of leather filled with leaves covered in odd markings. Words, they said, offering to free them from the world the Mother provided, in exchange for one they could not see, touch, or reach, until their deaths. A promise made from behind a serpent's mask, one she could see whenever the robed ones had turned their gaze on her.

She finally nodded, her eyes reflecting a common truth. "That is why I seek those who will listen. To try and bind them to our cause. People whose words are powerful enough for others to hear in their—large villages, where the sun is born again each day. And beyond, to even larger villages across the big water."

The native man turned and spat on the ground. "It will not be enough; our voices drowned beneath the waves. Those who would dare speak for us, made to suffer as we do. Used to the advantage of others, then thrown down."

Meghan looked up, seeing A'neewa standing in the doorway of the small room assigned by General Aidyn's staff to Harold. One she was sharing with him, convinced by her native friend to bow her stiff neck, making amends. Meghan winced. "You were with the French allies. I can see it in your face. You look drained." She pointed to the empty bag hanging from the A'neewa's shoulder. "You took them more of the medicines we've gathered."

A'neewa nodded, then stepped into the small room, sitting down beside Meghan, who was sorting through an assortment of dried roots and herbs. "They were glad to get them, though the need for food is of greater concern. And access to clean water, the spring drawn down by constant demand."

Meghan shrugged. "Has my brother been able to find out when the next shipment of food is due to arrive?"

"Not in comments made to me." A'neewa frowned. "He is not as willing to discuss such matters as before. His thoughts turned to what comes next."

Meghan sighed as she tied a bundle of roots together, adding them to others stacked in a woven basket. "A common affliction it would seem, spreading throughout the entire fort. Each man with the same thought; how to return to life as they knew it, letting go of the madness made normal over the past few years. Though it seems to have gone on forever, when looking back."

A'neewa leaned forward. "That is why we must look *forward* and be *wise* in guiding those we care for, knowing they are not tied to the earth, as are you and I."

Meghan paused, her hands holding another bundle of herbs. "Would you stay with my brother, if asked?"

"No. I will return to my people." A'neewa smiled, hands clasped in her lap. "George is a *good* man but made for a world with challenges I cannot meet. We have satisfied each other's needs, these past few moons. That has been enough for me." She stared at Meghan; the room filled with silence. "You have found your way back to Harold. That is—good?"

"It is." Meghan nodded. "An accommodation made, as you just said, to our mutual needs, though we're a world apart in how we view our individual versions of it." Meghan matched A'neewa's earlier frown. "I do not see Harold being satisfied in the hewing of a life from the edge of a forest, or trapped behind a desk in a dusty corner, moving numbers from one sheet of paper to another." Meghan looked at her friend. "Do you?"

A'neewa gave Meghan a quiet look. "His life force moves him along another path. I saw that in him, when we first met. A light shining from his eyes, wherever he looked. That is why we *need* him. *All* our people. Yours *and* mine. To bridge the river that runs between us. To bring his vision to the *next* war we are to fight, over again, though no one wants to open their eyes to it. Not now."

"You're talking about him returning to England. Taking up your cause from *there*."

"*Our* cause, Meghan. One that will end the cycle of bloodshed on *both* sides of this mindless push and pull, as if twin children forced to share their mother's lap. The Mother will provide enough for all, if we work to find a common path."

Meghan clenched her fingers, the bundle trembling in her hand. "Then I'm right in denying him, despite his promise to stay and make this his home. Right to release him to follow, as you call it, his true path. To let him go and tilt at windmills, hoping for a better result."

A'neewa hesitated, not able to understand most of Meghan's words. She moved forward with deliberation, wanting to stay on the trail. "Yes. As much as it will hurt you both. A greater pain suffered *now*, against a lifetime of small hurts over the rest of your lives. Words of anger from every shadow, draining away the love you share, until it is little more than a dried-out husk."

Meghan nodded, looking down. "I *do* love him. But can never let him hold the anger I carry, knowing it would consume him." She reached up, wiping tears from her eyes. "Why did it have to happen? Why did it have to happen to *me*? To my Patrick? To my sweet-faced Jacob?"

A'neewa shrugged. "It is the way of life. *All* life, without exception. We are born, live, and die as our will and the Mother's path provides. Harold's *still* before him, and you are wise in letting him go to claim it as his own."

Meghan looked up. "And you will help me to seek revenge? Help to slake my thirst for blood, for blood?"

A'neewa nodded. "Yes. I am close to finding the names of those you seek. There is a man who made himself known to me; my questions whispered to him in the shadows soon to bear results."

The native man lifted his head, nose raised as if scenting the air. His skin could feel an icy wind where none should exist. He was sitting inside a lodge made of birch-bark walls, sealed against the weather. His mate glanced over, her hands busy weaving sinews into a single string, a spare for the unstrung bow resting against the wall of their home, shared with their newborn child and the man's son of seven winters.

"What is it, husband?"

He grunted in answer, then returned to sharpening his knife, using a spit-moistened stone to put an edge on the steel. He dismissed the latest sign from the Mother, having felt such chills before in moments of restless stirrings in the night, bringing disquiet into his mind. The old woman he'd gone to, rabbit in hand as payment for her visions, telling him a yellow wolf was stalking him. One he had wronged in the killing of its mate. The rabbit tossed at her feet as he'd stomped away, her words finding no refuge in his ears.

"There was a man who claimed to know *of* them. Having heard the story, told to him by another, in recall of captives traded with the French for transfer to settlements north." The native man speaking was the same one A'neewa had met a few days earlier. He shoved another handful of food into his mouth, his jaws working as he looked at the quiet woman trying to uncover the reason for her questions. He knew she'd been making inquiries of other people in the encampment. Most of those she'd approached had ignored her, though they were eager to accept the food she carried. A few shrugged their shoulders, able to recall faint memories, once settled over a hot meal made with clean water from the new wells, put in by a group of soldiers with experience in such things.

"This man. Does he have a name?"

"Of course." The middle-aged chief of the native group grinned. "For a *price*. Two of the coins with the man's head. The chief of the white-coats."

"Perhaps this man would accept payment of *another* kind."

"I know him. He will not."

A'neewa nodded, then stood up and turned to go. His voice called out. "I will ask him to consider some other thing of value."

She spun around; her eyes hooded in a dark scowl. "I offer him this: his *life,* and food for his family. He will speak with me, or I will go into the dream world and remove the mask from his face, hunting him down, taking from him what I seek: the name and location of those who led a raid, a handful of summers ago, against settlement homes in the valley of the whispering trees."

A'neewa stared at the man who came to the fort to find her, willing to reveal the name of the ones she sought and the last known location of their lodges. She paid him with a large bundle of dried meat and ground meal, her eyes narrowed in thought as she watched him scramble away.

"You believe him." She looked up and shrugged as Meghan came out of the shadows between two buildings. The taller woman stepped forward, her fingers touching A'neewa's shoulder. "I mean—you sense he's speaking the truth, and not only telling a lie to get the coins."

A'neewa reached into her pocket and removed a small pouch, tossing it at Meghan, who caught it. "I paid him with a more *valuable* coin. His life. I used some of those—" She nodded at the pouch. "—to purchase supplies from the supply officer. And yes, he speaks what he *knows* to be the truth. Beyond that, I can offer no opinion."

Meghan slid her fingers into the pouch of coins, counting them with her fingers. "Your approach was very precise. You have a good head for uncovering things that lie hidden in the shadows. With a sharp mind, able to see other's moves before they make them. Our lessons at chess showing similar improvement of late." She studied the other woman's face. "You would do well, living in the settlements. People there would appreciate your natural wisdom and caring nature."

A'neewa smirked. "They would do so to my *face*, while placing small daggers in my back when I turned away."

"Some of them would, yes. But not all."

"Most."

Meghan nodded, conceding the point. "My brother would prevent it."

"Then your brother would be a fool, unable to walk his true path."

Meghan shrugged. "Then you will return to your people."

A'neewa nodded, then turned around as Harold came around the corner of one of the buildings, a look of surprise on his face turning to one of delight. "*A'neewa!* Good to see you. I've missed you at our table, George in a pout of late, drinking far too much to drown his—"

Meghan interrupted. "Harold, stop with your gossiping. We've work to do and you're preventing us from completing it, so make known your reason for interrupting, sir, or I'll have you forcibly removed."

Harold bowed. "As you order, madam. To the point of my coming to find you. The General has relieved me from active duty. Arrangements being made for my return to quarters, outside of Philadelphia."

The two women glanced at one another, concerned expressions on their faces. They both forced the corners of their mouths up into thin smiles as Harold took Meghan's hands, pulling her into an embrace, then turning and doing the same with A'neewa. "There is news of success on *other* fronts. The French have capitulated throughout the entire Ohio Basin." Harold paused, his eyes gleaming with satisfaction and a measure of relief. "The war for us is over, pending signing of a treaty. Until then, an armistice is in place. Hostilities at an end, with forces to remain where they stand. Except for me." He paused, looking at Meghan. "I mean *us*." Then he gave A'neewa a guarded look. "George has also been released, as reward for his exemplary service. An opportunity granted to reset our plans, reflecting on our return to the bosom of civilization's soft embrace."

A'neewa was the first to speak. "That is *wonderful* news, Harold. Has George been told of this?"

Harold shook his head, his eyes lit up in excitement. "Not yet. I came to find you first, to let—well, to let you *both* know."

Meghan reached out and pressed him toward the door leading to their quarters. "Then you must find him, celebrating this wonderful news with your men. Savoring the peace, one you've helped bring about."

Harold grinned, awash in released tension, looking a far different man now than when he'd first arrived on the North American continent, disembarking at the port of Philadelphia. "Yes. Of *course*. We'll come gather you up for a celebratory dinner and dance, the general having invited us to attend." He left the door open as he ran out, his exuberance vibrating in the air. Meghan walked over, closing it, then turned around.

"What am I to do *now*?"

A'neewa crossed her arms on her chest. "We *embrace* the moment, and our *men*. Dress, dine, and dance with them until we fall into bed. Then love them as best we can while we wait to see what tomorrow, and the next day after will bring our way."

⁓

"We've been here but a few weeks. Surely you can wait one more, before making plans to leave." George watched as A'neewa finished packing for her long journey home. She'd put on her native garb, a small pack slung over her shoulder, along with a wide belt fastened around her waist with an assortment of pouches attached, designed to carry items essential to her needs.

A'neewa shrugged. "It is time for me to leave. You can escort me home, or stay here and wave goodbye. You decide. I already have."

George hesitated. "I—cannot go with you. My duty is paused, but not completely withdrawn. If you could but abide here a few more—"

"Goodbye, George. I wish you well."

George stepped aside, his hand half-raised to stop her, his face a mixture of pain and hint of relief as he watched her stride away.

⁓

Harold sipped his tea, eying Meghan, sitting across from him, reading a book. Her hair was bound in a thick braid atop her head, revealing the slim line of her neck. Her skin glowed in the light from a candle resting on a small table. She sighed, closing her book around a strip of blue ribbon.

"You have something to say?"

Harold lowered his cup. "Not to say. More of an inquiry as to your opinion on a matter of—"

Meghan smirked. "It's good you were more direct in your approach when embroiled in the chaos of battle, else you would not be here *now*, plaguing me with circumspect approach."

Harold frowned, setting the teacup on the table. He leaned forward, fixing Meghan in a firm-lipped stare. "I would know your intentions toward me. I am not getting any younger and have little time for women who only want me for my body, and not my mind." Harold shrugged, the corners of his mouth raised in a small grin, though his eyes reflected a more serious emotion.

Meghan looked down, aching to be rid of the beast that haunted the dark recesses of her spirit, biding its time. "I will not be married again. To *any* man. Even *you*, as wonderful a partner as I could hope for."

Harold nodded; his hands clenched between his knees. "Because you still carry—your wound."

"Two of them. Each one without bottom, or sides."

Harold stared at the floor for several moments. When he looked up, his expression had hardened. "I'm to be discharged from service and would know if you will you travel with me to Bristol. If not as my wife, then as an equal partner."

"I cannot, Harold." Meghan widened her eyes, her cheeks reddening. "I *will* not. England to no longer be a friend to us, at the end of this war. The velvet fist of King George soon to come knocking on every door, looking to squeeze a share of what little lifeblood we have left to offer."

Harold stared. "I cannot remain *here*, at the edge of civilization—"

"The edge?" Meghan shook her head in admonishment. "I would see A'neewa's face, hearing that said."

Harold lifted a hand in protestation. "You know I mean no disrespect to the people lying west of us, or those to the north. I recognize their ways are older than are our own, but my statement stands, knowing the tentative balance existing between colonies and King. One I am compelled to return home to try my best to avoid the conflict we both feel making its approach, over the horizon."

"More likely ending up in a return to your father's desk, and uncle's dock, made to move materials and men, aimed in our direction once we dare defy the crown its unjust due. Unless you're planning to return *with* them, helping put us in our place."

Harold swallowed his anger, feeling it rising within. "Just the *opposite*! Planning to go there and then return, preventing that from happening. To caution those in power on *both* sides of the Atlantic against further encroachment into native lands. To offer recognition of their ancestral claims to their territories throughout the Ohio basin, with English forts established to secure against illegal incursions by settlers."

Meghan snorted in derision. "No real difference *there*, the forts themselves becoming a foot on the native people's necks. Their fortified boundaries expanding as if weeds, in constant growth, edging further into the surrounding land to allow increase of commercialism, with expansion of buildings for sellers of goods, traders. Increase of boat traffic, and homes for those who work on them. Becoming small colonies, led by men with greedy eyes in constant gaze to the west. Wanting more. Like swine lined up, snouts buried in troughs full of money, pressed alongside those who will govern our colonial brethren, men no better than are your own."

"Meghan, we're *all* English citizens, with the same rights in assign. Including grant of free and open trade, made along protected sea-lanes, leading to all points of the compass."

"And what of our colonial officers, made to scrape and bow to the English, despite their superior abilities? Despite their knowledge of the land, and tactics learned from the natives?"

Harold held his tongue, understanding the divide between them was wider than words alone could hope to bridge. He stood up, reaching for her hand, waiting until she took it, her skin cool to his touch. "Our days are not our own, at least *mine* are not. Accept my apologies for having broached such a sensitive subject."

Meghan stood up and wrapped her arms around him, looking into his eyes. "Our friend A'neewa provided me excellent advice. To embrace the moment *now*. To embrace my man. To dress, dine, and dance with him until we fall into bed, loving each other as best we can. Waiting on the morrow, and the day after that, seeing what might come our way."

Answers Sought

A'neewa rode a small white mare through a native village, the animal borrowed from Aidyn's personal string of mounts, used to cover in two days what would be a week-long trek between the captured fort and a man who could lead her to Meghan's assailants.

Several throngs of men watched with guarded expressions as she rode up, standing in silent groups while the village women toiled away at endless tasks, shooting well-honed glances at the men from the sharpened corners of their eyes. A'neewa knew they were wondering why the game-poles were empty. She watched as older children tended a meager crop of corn, without the constant stir of dogs underfoot, their younger siblings running between lodges, smiling, oblivious to want or need, their bellies full, chubby cheeks in healthy glow. The tribe, one of dozens once allied to the French, left on their own, with little hope of any support from the English.

A'neewa recognized their mood; the emotions on their drawn faces presenting a dour view of shattered dreams once held in their arms. She pushed away her own feelings, sliding from the mare, leading it toward a lodge in the center of the camp, then waited until a tall man stepped out, gazing at her, searching her face as if hawk on wing, eyeing its next meal. He nodded, lifting a flap of hide aside, invitation for her to enter. A'neewa tethered the horse, then ducked inside.

The chief settled into place across from a small fire, littered with charred bones around the edge. A'neewa judged them to be from squirrels, bats, or a small rabbit. The village, located on poor hunting lands, lay far outside the resource-laden basin area. The man she was there to speak with was a chief of what remained of a once powerful tribe.

He was the first to speak, his voice higher in tone than she'd imagined it would be. "Your people, they are from the valley of the Big Water."

A'neewa looked straight ahead. "They are."

"Why are you here?"

A'neewa paused, softening her expression. "For your help."

The chief scoffed. "We *helped* the French." He hesitated, his face wrinkling its way into a deep frown. "It did not help us, at the end of the trail." He was silent for a few moments, then smiled. "But how we *prospered* in the beginning, until the English unleashed their bloody *wolf* on us."

"We name him the *Red Fox*." A'neewa noted the man's sudden interest, his dark eyes probing hers again, searching for the meaning behind her direct approach.

"You *know* of him?"

"I *knew* him, but am no longer with the English. My people have returned to our lands, carrying many war-prizes and trade goods."

"We had a man of our own. A close *match* for him. Young, but wise in the ways of fighting. Our own fox, who bloodied *yours*. Burning his tail."

"Yes." A'neewa fixed him with a stare. "The *one* time. A brutal victory, for your side."

"You are not here to speak of battles, won or lost."

"I am looking for a small band of men, known to have raided in the valley of the Whispering Trees. Three men, who have shared the same paths as you."

"How do you know I am not one of those you seek?" His eyes hardened, his expression a slab of smooth oak. "Someone who might be interested in exchange of a—*heated* greeting."

"I have their names. Yours, Chief Matanac, is not one of them." A'neewa watched for his reaction, hand in her lap, hilt of her knife felt beneath the tanned doeskin covering she wore.

Matanac nodded, then leaned forward. "Your journey is almost over. Their lodges are in a small valley nearby, at the further end. Poor hunting there. Poorer than here. Game scarce. Their families, sick."

"I have medicine. For *your* people, not theirs." She paused, considering for a moment. "And metal. White-coat coins. Enough to help you through the winter to come."

"And a *horse*. A fine animal."

A'neewa could taste the man's greed, his eyes hungry for a return to power. The need for it revealed in the flex of his fingers, as if grasping the haft of a war club, gone missing. She nodded. "You will need ride behind me until near the English fort. Then it is yours." Recalling the missing dogs, she added; "Do not *eat* it, or attempt to trade it to the English. It has the burned marks, so you will need to be careful when near their settlements."

"Your gifts will help us to survive. Long enough to recover our names."

"It is a payment offered for your words *and* silence. It is unknown when or *if* anyone will come in search of a final answer to my question."

"A *hard* question, asked. *Harder* still to find an answer to." Matanac licked his lips, his eyes lighting up at the thought of potential violence. "These people you seek, were never *ours*." He paused. "Two of the names are no longer here, sent along the spirit trail during the battle at the white rock. A hard day for many of us. Where I got this." He lifted the edge of his shirt, revealing several puckered scars on the outside of his upper abdomen.

"Only one of them remains?" A'neewa narrowed her gaze. "Does he have a strange eye, with a cloud in it?"

Matanac widened his eyes, his lips pursed. "You know of him? Know what he can do?"

"I know *someone* who does." A'neewa stood up, done with the conversation, the chief exiting the lodge ahead of her, in deference to his position of authority. Once outside, they climbed onto the back of the unsaddled horse. A'neewa nudged the animal, letting it pick its way between a rush of laughing children, who shook their tiny fists at her while running around the horse in tight circles.

George turned the corner of the barracks, almost bumping into A'neewa. He stepped back, hands half-raised as if trying to decide between embrace or defense. "You've—returned."

A'neewa nodded. "I am here to see your sister."

George lowered his hands. "I see." He turned to go, stopping when her voice reached out. "*And* you." He looked at her, eyes narrowed, searching hers. "Why? I mean—what's caused your plans to change?" His face brightened. "Have you decided to stay?"

She shrugged, then looked away. "For a short time. There is something I need to do."

George nodded, the ends of his lips turning down. "Involving my sister. Not me."

"Both, if you will allow it." A'neewa hesitated. "Though I will not go back to your home with you."

George considered, knowing her joining him in Philadelphia would deny any rise to prominence in business, social, and eventually, political circles. The thought of it a bucket of cold water, poured over his ambitions. "And I cannot take you with me."

A'neewa nodded. "Then no clouds hide us from each other's truth." She waited a moment. "Only the clothes we are wearing."

George stared down at the packed earth, understanding her offer. "You said you were here to see Meghan."

"It can wait. She is not expecting me."

George looked up, his face wearing a boyish grin. "Perhaps we could explore our common truth—in private." He took her in his arms, leaning down, finding her lips with his.

"They are two days travel away." A'neewa watched as Meghan studied a small hand-drawn map, detailing the area lying to the east of the fort. "By horse. Four days, if on foot and moving quickly."

"They?" Meghan looked at A'neewa, confused. "You said only one is still alive. The one who led the—the one I left my mark on."

"He has a wife, with two children. And a handful of other women with children he provides for."

Meghan looked up, her face a mix of emotions. "What have they to do with me?"

"Without his support, they will not survive the winter. I thought you should have this knowledge before making a plan holding him accountable for his sins against *you*."

"Does my *brother* know of this?" Meghan stared at A'neewa. "You've lain with him since you returned. I can see it in your eyes. Can *smell* his scent on your clothes."

"I *have* been with him. We have been with each other. I have not spoken of this to him. It is you who must decide the path taken. No one else."

"It might have been better, not knowing how near to hand my solution lies."

"Your grief has faded?"

Meghan shook her head. "No. It hasn't. I carry it with me as if a child in my arms, growing stronger each day. Tears of anger are on my cheeks when I awake. Shed for a boy no longer here. For my—" She stopped, a distant look forming on her face. "Thank you, A'neewa. For this—" She held the map up. "—and for not providing guidance or advice on what comes next."

"This is your path, not mine. Though I will help you to walk it."

"I want him *dead*."

A'neewa shook her head. "It will be difficult to do. He is skilled in—"

Meghan interrupted; her eyes fixed to the map. "This is all that separates me from my revenge." Her finger traced a line from a small symbol representing the fort to where A'neewa had left a red mark. A single drop of blood.

She looked up at A'neewa, her face a mirror to the other's stoic expression. "Thank you, for bringing me this. It's *all* I need or have wanted. Ever since—" She stopped speaking, her eyes in a cold stare as she looked past A'neewa. Her thoughts taking her beyond the wall of the fort, beyond the hills and mountains, left to stare into a place of dark shadows, hidden deep within her memories.

A Life, Overturned

She could not hear, sounds muted by shock-numbed ears. Red-black faces darted in and out of her vision. The sun-burnished faces of husband and child, staring up at the sky, their blue eyes, unblinking. Mouths gaped open in questioning pose with ears as deaf as were her own. Heads misshapen, concave depressions pressed into place. Bloodless wounds, death having arrived between one beat of erstwhile heart and the next. Their final breaths expelled in sudden gasp. Their final thoughts, mirrors to her own. Why?

A gray fog descended from out of a cloudless sky. A colorless world, in tug, toss, and trip. Hands pawing at a body, no longer hers. A rush of pain across her face. Her wrist yanked up, pulled to her feet. Held in a grip as firm as womb's compress in one last squeeze. Delivered from out of a maze of shouting, laughing men. Her savior, a twin to the others, though darker in mood. Angry. Controlling. Hands bound tight before her. A sinewy arm wrapped around her waist.

No, she thought, a moment before her unbound mind swirled away into a bottomless drain. No savior, this one, tearing her from her home. From her family. From a life once held in cupped hands. This one is a demon. Devil. Dangerous, and determined. Deaf to her pleading to be let go of, to go to her man. Her boy. To close their eyes, cover their faces with her tears. Washing their sins away. Loving them into the ground. Wanting to join them there.

A'neewa touched Meghan's shoulder, with no response in return, knowing her friend was no longer there. No words she could offer to help guide her back. She turned away, leaving in silence, needing to find George. To have him wrap his arms around her. Holding her, without explanation. Without the utterance of a single word.

George had fallen asleep, the comfort A'neewa sought from him, gently offered, as if able to read her thoughts. Lying with her as she pressed her head against his chest. Her tears coming from a place of silent pain. Her own memories released, still carried with her, now breaching the surface of her resolve. Too long away from the women of her tribe, who knew what she needed, providing it for one another, ever since the Mother cried tears enough to fill the world with water, Her sigh of pain creating the rush of wind. Her heart, in steady beat, providing rhythm to emergent life. Her moans vibrating from taut-skinned drums. Her footsteps placed to earth in a thundering fall. All. Where women gathered and bound their wounds, together.

A'neewa listened to the beat of George's sturdy heart, clinging to him as she revisited images hidden in the shadows of her past. Her vision opening to herself as a child, once again.

Trail of Spirits

The great dying was over. Men, once vital in bodies, and women, eternal in their hearts, along with children, carrying within them the seeds of the future. Gone. Six fingers of every ten, placed in the earth. Memories of their smiles, laughter, tears, scowls, and considered stares, fading away. Only a few survivors left to try and hold their memories. To honor, respect, and cherish, all. Much too great a burden, placed on quivering shoulders and aching backs as dull-minded members of the tribe dug large pits with bone-blade shovels, formed from the ant-lers of moose and deer. Shattering roots of trees with precious metal blades fastened to wooden handles, gained in trade, along with doz-ens of blankets from fur traders passing through a moon ago. Now used to wrap around the death stiffened forms of people, their voices silenced.

Still here, A'neewa whispered to herself. Words not enough to paint the picture of quiet devastation. The village turned upside down, then shaken. Bits of debris spilled out, formed from strands of dark hair teased from dozens of wincing heads by the teeth of hand-carved combs. Dust motes, hanging in the air, along with wails of broken-hearted lamentations. Smoke, from herb-scented fires, in drift between lodges, plaintive calls for the Mother's blessing, going unheeded. Nothing able to stem the endless flow of death taking half or more from each lodge, each longhouse, from every family. Taking all but two, from her. A father and younger brother.

Women, their gray hair bound in single braids, moved from dwelling to dwelling like geese on a fog shrouded lake. Stooped bodies, slipping through layers of smoke, soft curtains passed through as they poked their heads into and out of pools of shadowed dwellings, each holding dead, dying, or a few surviving members of the tribe.

A'neewa had just come through her fifth winter. Spring in steady approach. The season for birth of fawn, calf, kit, and cub. For children, brought forth into the eternal cycle of life. Grass in poke and probe through warming soil. Acorn sprouts, eagerly seeking the sun. Seeds of every make and shape rising from out of their winter beds. She stared through tear-stained eyes, holding onto herself, trying to contain grief from a mother lost. Too much pain inside her heart to be set free. Watching, in stone-faced silence as wraiths of loved ones, lost, slipped past. Family and friends, appearing in aimless wandering along the edge of the village, wringing their hands. Women, fearing for their loved ones, having to leave them behind. Men, fingering weapons no longer held in their hands, fearing for the safety of all. Feeling the need to hunt, to predate, to defend, causing their jaws to clench as they passed by. A few of them noting her presence, stopping to look at her. Silent. Their thoughts forming in her mind, asking her to make them whole again.

A'neewa closed her eyes, denying them her energy. Turning her back to them. Alone. Knowing they would need to find their own way back to their path. Hers, still before her. A difficult one, but one she would not have to walk alone. Wrinkled hands, on her thin shoulders. Aged voices, in her ear. Warm bodies, held against her own. Mother of her mother, her mother now. Tears, in rain upon the ground. Birds, in sawing call from tree and sky. The world coming awake once again.

CHAPTER EIGHTEEN

Promontory Fort, Early Winter, 1759

Search of a Hard Truth

Aidyn studied the personnel manifest, his lips pursed in consideration. He held a glass of wine in his hand, trying his best to imagine it a fine French vintage. His tongue recoiling with each sip in a reminder it was a bottle of Colonial provide, taken from a straw-packed crate that had recently arrived from Philadelphia. His personal stock had run out a week ago, all non-essential food items in short supply. Most of his forces preparing for imminent departure east once their replacements would arrive.

Aidyn sighed, reading down names on the manifest, making mental notes of who would stay on for transition duties, and who would return to Philadelphia for rest and rehabilitation. A light knock on his office door pulled his attention from the task in hand. "Enter." His aide came over, stopping on the other side of the desk, his narrow face pinched in concern. Aidyn sighed. "What is it? Have discussions about armistice talks broken down again?"

"Not at all, General. At least, not to *my* knowledge. It is a matter of—the loss of a horse, sir. One of your mounts. The small white mare."

"My *little* girl? From the *stables*? How is that *possible*?" Aidyn's face grew red. His aide rushing to explain.

"Missing from the outer *fields*, sir. Your stock allowed to feed there to help recover their tone. As was ordered, sir." His aide paused. "By *you*."

"And you say she's gone *missing*?" The general frowned. "Not by native hands, I hope. We don't need an inquiry rousing feelings of mistrust. The signing of a treaty with the French still some months off, or even years."

"It is unknown, sir, as to an *exact* cause."

"Notify Colonel O'Malley. Or rather, extend a personal invitation for him to join me for dinner. I shall press the matter into his capable hands, leaving it up to him how best to recover my little lady, gone astray."

⌒℮↷

Harold softly closed the door of his room behind him, making his way to the outdoor latrines. He relieved himself, then turned to head back inside, coming to a stop when George came up, a dour look on the man's weather-beaten face. Harold grinned. "A good morning to you, Brother, though it's only just now arrived."

George frowned. "We need to talk."

Harold raised his arms, crossing them on his chest. "A problem, I take it, having arisen along with the sun?"

"Not interested in a witty spin of phrase, Harold. I'm holding a sack of shit, with a large hole in it, staining the very ground I'm standing on."

Harold was about to point out they were near a solution to disposal of said bag, then thought better of it, seeing his friend was in personal turmoil. "Perhaps we should retire to your room and discuss—"

"That is *exactly* where the problem *lies*. In my *bed*." George cursed under his breath, then looked around as if seeking an escape. "She's put her *foot* in it, dragging *me* along with her. Putting at risk *all* I've earned in political coin these past four years."

Harold waited, feeling the chill of the early winter. He wrapped his arms around himself, trying his best to avoid shivering, wishing he'd brought his coat. George attempted to settle his mood with a long sigh, then shook his head as he stared into the distance. "A'neewa took one of the general's horses. Without consideration as to repercussion to herself. Or to *me*."

"How can you be certain? Has she admitted to it?"

"I *know*, that's all. From the moment he told me, the general, I knew I was in it up to my eyes. He asked me to investigate the matter. To try and find some way to make it right, without stirring the waters. As if *that* were possible." George shook his head, lips in a clenched line. "*Damn it!* No matter which way I turn, this is ever in front of me. The end of my *career*. In *disgrace*."

Harold tightened his voice. "Not to mention *peril* to A'neewa, should your instincts prove correct. Theft of a horse, especially a *general's* horse, a serious offense."

George shrugged. "I realize *that*. My anger at potential injury to my reputation has not overwhelmed an equal concern for *her* welfare. It's only frustration at how she follows such a—*singular* approach to things. Without seeking advice on available options. Stiff-necked, *most* of the time." He looked at Harold, taking note of Harold's stiffened posture and made an attempt to ease his own. "I'm going to do *everything* possible to resolve this, my friend. I promise."

Harold nodded, then reached out, taking George by his arm, guiding him back toward their rooms. "I understand your concern and will begin immediate consideration of a plan to remedy the issue."

"It was only a *small* horse. One he never even rides." A'neewa stood near the far wall of the room she shared with George; her expression fixed in a firm stare. "He has *more* than enough animals for one man."

"It's not the *number*, but the *pride* of ownership that is the problem. No different here than it would be with your father, were someone to do the same to him."

"My father has no horses. They are useless in thick woods, and impossible to keep fed."

"That's not the *point*, woman. You *knew* better when you absconded with—"

"I do not *know* that word."

George glared at her, struggling to keep his tone low. "*Stole*, A'neewa. When you *stole* the mare. Without regard for the position you've placed yourself in."

"You mean *your* position. Your eyes filled with dreams of—"

"*Yes, damn it*! *My* position. *My* goals, put in jeopardy because of your—" He came over and put his hands on her shoulders. "You stand in *danger*, A'neewa. That's what it means. You've placed us *both* in danger. You more than me, but they will see it as *our* decision, by those of the general's staff looking to pull me down."

A'neewa frowned. "You are all so concerned with your—your places in the world. With your appearances. As if you—"

"And what of *your* place, as the *daughter* of Chief Tawana? Or of those of the warriors in your tribe, vying with each other to show their courage, their prowess in the hunt, and in the taking of lives? How are *your* people any different from *us*?"

She widened her eyes, then spit on the floor, her anger in full flare. "To the place of *hell* with your General's *pride*. It is an *animal*, nothing more. I will pay the coins needed to buy back his *pride*, if it means so much to him. And to *you!*"

George caught her at the door, his arms wrapped around her as she struggled, though he knew she could throw him off, her strength a close match to his own. "I will make this *right*, A'neewa. For you *and* the general. I swear it." She turned into him, her face pressed against his chest, voice muffled. "With Harold's help?"

"Yes. With Harold's help."

The tracks were in plain sight on the ground. Harold watched as George moved in a slow pace, following them. They ended at the base of a sheltered hill, carefully erased from a soft compress of leaves beneath a thick huddle of oaks. He leaned down, probing the soil.

"She knew what she was doing, making sure to cover her trail." George wiped his fingers against the side of his leg then came over and stood beside Harold, the reins of their two mounts in his hands. "She knew she was *wrong* in taking the mare."

Harold stared into the woods. "Where do you suppose she went, then came back from, less one small mare?"

"Took it to her father as a gift, I would imagine, though she's right about the effort needed in keeping it fed throughout the winter. Small return, against little value found in an occasional ride."

Harold angled his head, staring at the last few tracks. "I'm of a different mind as to that. An itch in my ear whispering a different tale, not that it matters. Do we go there to buy it back?"

"No. I'm for sticking with *your* plan. Finding a small moose to kill, collecting the bones, claim the loss is due to wolves, bringing an end to the story. Removing any further interest in the *damnable* affair."

Harold nodded, handing one set of reins to George. "Then we should ride to the nearest native village, asking them for help in finding an animal small enough to match up."

"We've supplies enough, and three of my best knives to trade for the favor. So, yes." George worked his thick-set neck in a circle, releasing small knots of tension, then looked at Harold with a wide grin. "Besides, a few days in this fair countryside without imminent threat of violence will do us good, my brother."

Meghan considered the elements of the plan, each step carefully designed to provide options, depending on issues encountered along the way. Joined in her effort by A'neewa, who offered an occasional suggestion, helping knit their strategy together, Meghan realized it had been a moment of luck; their two men heading off in chase of the missing mare. A window of opportunity opened, allowing them to slip away, their absence unnoticed for several days. Enough time, she knew, for her to complete her mission of revenge.

A'neewa watched as Meghan studied the map, aware the other woman was planning out each movement made until meeting up with her abuser, again. Face to scarred face, knife in hand, prepared to take his other eye, before pinning his heart with her honed blade. She kept her full lips in a grim smile, aware her friend would certainly lose her life, the one-eyed man able to kill her with a careless shrug of one arm. Her thirst for vengeance left seeping away, with every drop of blood.

A'neewa kept her thoughts to herself, able to feel Meghan's pain, one all women carried within; the burden of pain from bringing in and losing of life. Added to, in having to watch it leave. A special form of heartache, rarely avoided by those choosing to walk the winding path.

Meghan sensed A'neewa's sullen mood and reached over, taking her hand. "It *will* work out. I promise. I've learned from the best how to make plans, then be ready to adapt to sudden changes." She smiled. "No worries—my sister. I *will* have my revenge, with the bastard lying on the ground before me, *dead!*"

The ribs were of the proper size and shape, well gnawed along their edges by a pack of hungry dogs, lurking in the native village. Harold handed a small pouch of coins to the leader, the man accepting them with a thin smile. Then he pointed at thick slabs of meat hanging on green branches over a bed of coals. "You can keep the meat." The heat was helping to cure the meat while keeping flies away. A dense cloud of smoke penetrated its surface, producing a protective glaze. "The bones are all we need."

Several of the natives covered their mouths to hide their smiles, convinced the two men who'd ridden through their village two days earlier were standing outside their bodies. Now they had returned, along with their tribe's best tracker, having followed the tracks of a small horse, losing the trail in a sea of large rocks, tossed down from an ancient slide.

The chief tucked the pouch into his trousers; white, part of a uniform stripped from a dead soldier on one side of the multi-year conflict or the other. They were stained brown with age-faded blood, in evidence along a rip in one leg. He barked an order to the women, then watched as they tied the bones across the back of the larger mount.

Once clear of the village, George guided his horse to one side and waited for Harold to close. "A splendid plan, thus far. Better if the bones were a bit more *aged*, but the general's not known as a man of the hunt, so we should see it through without any issue."

Harold looked at the bones, a scatter of flies working along the edges. "There will be no evidence presented of *when* the beast met its demise, only the *where*. And that we can tell true."

"Over two days slow ride into the hills." George leaned over and spit on the ground. "Enough to keep further questions at bay." Harold took the lead, his mount nudged into an easy trot as he eyed the trail ahead, careful to stay clear of low-hanging branches.

Women in Roam

"Two days, since last report of seeing them *here*." The general settled back in his chair, looking up at the two men standing on the other side of his desk. Their hats were in their hands, confused looks on their faces. "They must have left on foot, as there's no missing stock. Destination, unknown, though a handful of local natives passed through a day or so ago, reporting of seeing two women, heading west. Though too far away to provide identification as to hair color, or height."

Harold glanced at George, then looked back at Aidyn. "Do you know if they are still in the area; the natives?"

"Stayed the night outside the fort, then moved on. Yesterday, I believe, sometime in the morning. Heading to parts unknown."

The two men glanced at each other again, then Harold opened his mouth to address the general. He stopped, seeing Aidyn's finger pointing at the door. "Go, and *find* them, providing whatever help is required to complete this—mission they are about. Each has provided substantial help in patching up of my men's wounds, your own included."

Both men turned around and started toward the door. The general's voice caught them as they reached it. "When you return, Captain Knutt, I've posted orders for transfer of your station to the barracks in Philadelphia. Colonel O'Malley, you're released from your pledge of service to the Crown and now free to go wherever, and with whomever you please."

Women in the Woods

A seep from a mossy ledge was a welcome provider of water to the two women, lost to sweat after another long hike through tangled wilderness, with trails carefully avoided. Hard scrabble sought wherever possible to hide their tracks. Meghan sat in a cloak of shadows, watching as A'neewa finished filling their canteens. She wiped her hand across her forehead, moving strands of damp hair away from her cheeks.

"I do not question the need for caution, only the cost to us in time. We have no way of knowing when the men might return to the fort. They could still be several days away."

"Or a handful of hours behind us, with sharp-eyed scouts leading them, bringing an end to our journey. Leading to pointed questions." A'neewa gave Meghan a searching look. "Are you willing to take the chance?"

Meghan leaned forward, cupping a handful of water from the spring, using it to cool her forehead. The woods were thick, providing ample shade that was mostly insect-free. The weather dry, with moisture wicked from skin, mouths, and lungs. She sighed, tired from the long hours of travel, the two of them rising before the sun and moving on through to dusk. A small tarp used for shelter at night, borrowed from military stores. Everything else they needed, contained in packs on their backs, with food collected along the way. The wilderness a storehouse to A'neewa's practiced eye, providing a host of berries and edible roots. Meghan let out a long, draining sigh. "They'll not stop us. Will not reach us in time."

A'neewa cocked her head, one eyebrow raised. "You have a vision of this?"

"No. Just a sense of it. That it will play out as I've seen it in my mind, a hundred times and more." Meghan looked at A'neewa, her eyes bright with tears. "Those are the times when it stirs within me, like a serpent, squeezing my heart and lungs. Until I can't breathe. My hate—a painful fist in my throat." She lowered her eyes, her voice barely a whisper. "Death is preferable to failure. His death—preferable to mine."

A'neewa shrugged as she capped the second canteen, both straps slung over her shoulder. She moved to where Meghan was sitting, aware her friend was hovering between her true nature, and the seed of hate planted in her heart, years ago. "Would be better to consider this as justice delayed and not revenge. It will help cool the temper, steady the hand. Sharpen your vision."

"I'll not be turned away from my moment of revenge." Meghan's tone had grown icy cold.

"I do not ask it of you—sister. But this is not a righteous act. There is no hand of your god in this, only a reflection of what happened to you and your loved ones. Your hate, if released, will prevent you being able to exact your revenge. This man—the beast in your night dreams, will not be removed from his path by your anger. Yours or mine." A'neewa reached out and touched Meghan's shoulder. "I share your thirst. I do. But this one is of my kind, not yours. It is a divide between us you cannot see."

Meghan looked up, confused by A'neewa's viewpoint. "We're both women, who've suffered greatly at the hands of men."

"No, Meghan." A'neewa shook her head. Her eyes shadowed. "We are not the same. I am a woman who understands—has always understood the Mother's lack of balance in life. Able to accept the good and the bad. Not like you. Not like your kind, seeking fairness in all things. Shocked when you learn your path does not always go the way you want." A'neewa paused, taking a breath, then releasing it. "We do not and can never see this from the same path."

"But we're not so different. We both share the same vision. Have shared the same man."

A'neewa stepped back, turning to look at the face of a ledge, the moss inviting the touch of her finger. "No, my friend. Your need for my help blinds you to the truth. My truth. One Harold could see and accept there was nothing he could do to alter my view of him. Of his people—your people. Each of us rooted in our own soil, native and—" A'neewa clamped her lips together, looking down.

"Native and what?" Meghan stared at the woman whom she considered as much a sister as a friend.

A'neewa turned around. "Invaders. Without ability to find balance in our world. One we have moved through since—from as far back as our stories take us. No marks on paper to guide us, only words shared around firelit circles. Where truth reveals itself as something felt, not seen in letters, scratched out in lines. Most of them by people dead to the world for countless seasons. That is both your blessing and your curse. In equal measure. The lies told then as strong as the truth, today. Leaving you to decide what to believe. That is the difference between us. Our lies die with the one telling them. Yours—live on forever."

Meghan shook her head, her eyes narrowed. "I can't accept you feel this way. Not after what we've been through. What we've shared in the night and spoken of through our tears." Her expression hardened. "You're trying to divert me from doing this."

A'neewa stood up, her knife in her hand, eyes flashing in anger. "I will go! Find him and drag him here, holding his head back so you can open his throat and watch as his life slips away. If it will open your eyes, letting you see what is standing right in front of you. A truth you refuse to accept." She held the blade above her palm, then sliced into it, blood welling into a pool of dark red. "I am your sister in name. I would be your sister in blood. Swearing to be with you when you have your revenge—or your death."

Meghan stood up, hand out, watching as the A'neewa sliced into her skin. The two women clasped hands, blood dripping between the firm press of flesh to flesh. No words needed. None offered. Then they stepped back, busying themselves in gathering up their few possessions before moving further into the shadowed wood.

George spun his horse in a tight circle as he searched the ground. "They could not have done a better job throwing us off their trail if deliberately trying to do so."

"They are." Harold looked ahead; his eyes focused beyond the horizon.

"To what end?" George leaped from his mount, walking back to where he'd lost the faint marks from the women's soft-bottomed footwear. Reins in hand, he bent down and scoured the leaves. "Your ploy in explaining the missing mare worked, the general accepting our story. They had nothing—she had nothing to fear. Why would she have left? My sister, going with her?"

"It's not because of the missing mare. The twists in their tracks are there to keep us at arm's length." Harold frowned. "Until your troubled sibling completes her effort."

George stared at Harold. "Her effort? Effort to do what?"

"To find and then kill the ones who tore her husband and son from her life. Tearing away a large measure of her soul."

George shook his head, wishing it otherwise, knowing there was a hard truth in Harold's words. "You—cannot know that. There's no way she could locate the ones responsible." He paused, his eyes dawning with sudden awareness. "A'neewa. When she left before. She found them, then returned to share the information with my sister." He lowered his eyes, staring at the ground. "A burden, having a sibling like her. Strong-minded. Difficult to dislodge from her path. Ever since childhood, in a wobble of legs trailing after me as I went about my chores. Squalling in anger when I picked her up, taking her back inside. Nothing's changed, except for her being in carry of a knife, preventing my doing that to her now." He shook his head, considering for a long moment before looking up. "They can't be too far ahead of us. We'll catch them up by morning, then put her back on the right side of this—foolish attempt."

George swung into his saddle and gave Harold a sharp nod, falling back into a trail position as they continued to follow the broken edge of a fractured ridgeline. After a few minutes of silence, he eased his horse ahead, pulling alongside Harold's. "In my speaking of siblings, it occurs to me I've never thought to ask about yours." He smiled. "Don't even know if you have any, close as we've been, hours spent sitting around campfires, or standing watch, shoulder to shoulder." He drew in a deep breath, letting it out. "Making me a poor friend, never having taken the time to ask."

Harold gave him a quiet look. "Are you asking now?"

George nodded. "I am. If you're willing to share."

"No sister. A brother; two years younger. Jackson, or my shadow, as our mother always called him. Ever underfoot, watching everything I was doing. Smarter than me, by far. Eager to learn, pestering me to teach him how to read. No stopping him then, books in our father's library left in piles on the floor. Anything he couldn't work out for himself, brought to me to help him decipher the meaning." Harold stopped, remembering the scent of old leather bindings, his brother's eyes bright with excitement, finger trembling as he traced out words as if they were marks on a treasure map, leading to chests filled with gold. "I learned as much from him as was provided in return."

"Same with me and my sister." George cleared his throat, then turned his head and spit. "He's home in England, your shadow?"

Harold nodded. "His remains are. In a family plot, having died of a fever when he was eleven."

"Hard business, that. Knowing how close you must have been."

Harold shrugged. "All deaths are hard." He stared at George, who nodded in reply. "Robert, Jenkins, and all the rest. Your men. Mine. Our native friends. Each one asked to pay the price for the vanity of kings. And that of my own, in leading good men to their ends by orders I've given. Mistakes I've made. Thousands left to die, as a result."

"I too share a similar burden of blame and loss. And will not allow you a claim to vanity. Far from it. Each man you've led understood the odds stacked for and against success. Ready—nay, eager to follow you. Their fates, their own. Freely decided in having signed the forms. Their deaths, ever before them. Met through no measure of intentional fault on your behalf, or mine."

Harold stared back, then lifted his reins, stopping his horse, tossing its head at the unexpected interruption. "You truly believe that?"

"I do. No different from your brother's fate. His destiny to burn bright, if only for a short time. Like—one of those streaks of light in the night sky. His destiny, then. Your destiny, now. With you having helped bring about an end to this damned war, leaving you free to head wherever you will. Back to England or—to stay on, in Philadelphia." George paused, giving Harold a sly look.

Harold sighed. "She rejected my offer. Again."

"As I said before—stubborn."

"No. She's wise enough to know herself, and me. Unwilling to make her burden mine, which is why we're here—" Harold pointed toward a set of hills that framed a host of small valleys, pinched between their humped shoulders. "—and must go there."

∽

Smoke was a thread of irritation in the nostrils, the first sign in four days of man. The woods had thinned, now that the two women were nearing the end of their journey, no longer moving in a wavering line of travel, clinging like leeches to the bottom of cliff faces, working between twisted fingers of gnarled ledges, fire-less nights spent spooning beneath a worn bearskin covering, trying to keep warm. Stomachs left in constant grumble, mollified with small handfuls of cornmeal cakes and fresh berries washed down with sips of water from body-warmed canteens.

A'neewa paused, wiping beads of sweat dampened hair back from her forehead. "Ahead is a place where I am known. Their leader is the one I gave the mare to."

Meghan slid her hand through a pocket in her clothing, her fingers touching the handle of her knife, strapped to her inner thigh. "And you—trust him?" She knew A'neewa was leading her to her destiny, and not into a trap. Her heart beating faster, aware she would soon be face to face with the man she'd hungered to meet again, for a final time.

A'neewa nodded. "I do. He is the one who provided the information."

"What do I do, when we make our approach?"

A'neewa gave Meghan a long silent look, then smiled. "Become a silent woman. Head bowed. Your hair down around your shoulders in disarray. The Bible in your pack, held out in front of you like a torch in the darkness."

Meghan pursed her lips. "As if I am out of my mind."

A'neewa shrugged. "We say it is a person standing outside their body."

"It means the same thing—insane." Meghan sighed, withdrawing her hand from the slit in her dress pocket.

"He will see you as beyond reach of spoken word. Beyond peace, knowing only torment, as if living in the shadow of death."

Meghan murmured something soft-edged that caused A'neewa to look at her, a question poised on her full lips. Meghan raised her voice, repeating the words. "Not exactly a reach, in my portraying that."

"It is not who you are, Sister. It is what he and the others made of you. Once this last one is dead, the mirror of the past will shatter, returning you to your life."

"I—hope you're right." Meghan reached out and squeezed A'neewa's upper arm. "I need to believe it possible."

A'neewa looked at her, covering her fingers with her own. "I have seen it—your face when this is over. Your hair, the color of silver, surrounding you. A peaceful expression on your face."

೮ల౩

He lifted his head, as if having caught a hint of a wayward scent. Something hiding in the shadows. A spirit of an animal or man he'd killed in the past, prowling the outside edge of his awareness. Close enough to raise the hair on neck and arms. His woman came into the lodge, a young child in clasp. Not one of his, though he was a provider for it. An older boy followed close behind, mirror image to himself. Talena, Little Hawk, a singular joy in what had been an unremarkable life of late. The boy's mother dying two winters past from fever, an infant slipping away with her, still in the womb. Its movements slowly fading as her breathing eased.

The loss led him to search for answers from the Mother, seeking them in three days spent fasting. Sitting on a hilltop, staring into the distance, wondering if the death of settler's children beneath his club in raids had cursed him to the fate visited upon him and his people. More than half of them having fallen to blows from an unseen enemy, slipping from lodge to lodge past clouds of smoke, finding the spirits of many of his people. Twisted from their lives, left walking the winding path.

"We will need meat. The last of the dog is in the pot."

He rose to his feet, scowling, knowing food was scarce in the thinly populated hunting lands. He left without a word, staying his young son from following with a raised hand, taking his war club with him, along with a pistol. One pried from the hand of a young boy, similar in age to his own, with red hair and eyes the color of the sky. Left staring into up into it, head crushed in, his body tossed down alongside a father, already dead.

"He is where he was. I traded powder and shot with him for three beaver pelts and a basket of dried berries. Two suns ago." The chief shrugged.

A'neewa raised her eyebrows. "He has a musket?"

"Pistol. His aim is poor, with only one clear eye. Shoots to the left,

when hurried. We tell him to only hunt animals running to that side."
Chief Matanac smiled, though it fell short of his dark, probing eyes.

"Better—if the trade was not made."

He shrugged. "Better if snow would not fall, but the Mother still
sends it."

A'neewa licked her lips, concern showing in her eyes. She glanced
at Meghan, who stood in the shadow of a tree, rocking back and forth,
singing a monotone song under her breath, her eyes fixed straight
ahead.

"The woman is a—speaker for their god?"

"No."

The chief crossed his arms on his chest, then shrugged. "The one you
seek will not move from his path because of the black book. He killed a
man holding one of those. A man who came to live with us many seasons
ago, saying we were to follow him. He will not hear her words now."

"Then she will need to use a more pointed approach." A'neewa nodded, then walked over to Meghan, taking her by the shoulder and gently
guiding her away.

ↄe᷈

"Looking for sign is only slowing us down. Besides, I know where
they're going." Harold watched as his large friend straightened up, a
groan of pain caused by sore knees turned into a stifled yawn.

George knew a return to Philadelphia would provide the rest his
body needed to adjust to the advancement of age. It had been taking
longer of late to ease the stiffness from old wounds. The time having
come to seek easier ways of proving himself to peers and adversaries
alike, while moving into the political arena. Knowing he would face the
same mindless ferocity as found in battles in the wilderness, though with
less outward spilling of blood. Most of the time, he added, allowing for

the occasional duel. "Point the way, though how you can know their direction based on the—"

"In use of my superior wits. And these." Harold pointed to his eyes, looking toward the east. The sky was clear; a full moon an hour away in rise, promising another chilly night to come. "We need to move as if bee from blossom to hive. From where we are, to there." He aimed his finger at one of the small valleys, directly ahead. "Where smoke is rising from yon hollow."

"I cannot see it."

"You're too low. And your eyesight, too dim."

George leapt into his saddle, then gazed in the same direction as his younger companion. "Yes. I see it now. Exactly as described."

Harold grinned. "How many?"

"How many what?" George twisted in the saddle.

"Threads of smoke."

George looked away, squinting. "Hard to say—they're blended together from the wind." He angled his head slightly. "Three—perhaps four."

Harold nudged his horse, giving it its head, letting it find its own way downhill to the mouth of a narrow opening in the forest below.

"How many are there?" George whisper-shouted the question then watched as Harold lifted one arm, his forefinger extended. Muttering under his breath, George shook his head, tugging at the reins as he forced his mount through the tangle of brush and small rocks.

ᐷ

The head of the village stepped into view, blocking the trail with a wide stance. Four of his warriors flanked the narrow path, weapons at their sides, watching with hooded gazes as their leader raised a hand, signaling the two men on horseback to stop.

Harold raised his hand in return, then lifted one leg over his saddle, sliding to the ground. He removed his hat and gave the tall native man a respectful nod. "I greet you, leader of this tribe." He continued, having greeted the man in French, seeing from the man's expression he understood it. "My brother and I come in search of our sister, and a native woman she travels with." He twisted at an angle, nodding to George, who quickly joined him, taking both sets of reins, holding their horses in place.

Harold stepped forward, shifting to one of three native languages he was fluent in, letting his linguistic instincts choose. "I am the man the natives call Red Fox. My brother is a great warrior of my people. We have killed many French soldiers." He paused. "And many of the warriors who fought on their side."

The chief nodded, the men lining both sides of the trail moving to stand behind him. "I know of you. And your brother. He is the one we call Great Bear." The leader paused, giving both a hard stare. Then he smiled. "Your mother favored your brother over you, allowing more time at her breast."

"He is as strong as I am wise."

Matanac hardened his expression. "You search for the women. Why?"

"Our sister is on the wrong path. Her brother and I would have words with her, to help bring her back into herself."

"Your brother has her look. While you—do not."

"He is my blood-brother."

"This woman you claim as sister passed by here, guided by another, not of your people." Matanac man narrowed his gaze. "Your sister. She stands outside herself."

"Our sister wears two faces. One of light, the other dark. It is the face in shadow we wish to turn back to the sun."

"You speak out language, but do not share our vision of the path. You are wise in battle, as we have learned, but she is beyond your god's reach, despite the book she clings to." He stiffened his stance. "The man she seeks will not hear her words."

Harold hesitated, fear in rise. He swallowed it back down, his voice kept low. "We would move her from the path she is on, only needing someone to show us where it begins."

"I will take you there. You will collect your women and leave. And never return."

Night was a quilt of black fabric, needled through with tiny knots of colored stars. A full moon rose in unblinking gaze, as if trying to count each one. Meghan knelt in the center of a narrow path trodden into the ground alongside a winding brook. She shivered, despite wearing a heavy coat, having refused to comply with A'neewa's suggestion of lighter clothing worn to provide for quieter movement.

The other woman had left her own outer clothing cached in the woods, along with their sleeping fur, canteens, and packs, clad only in a dark brown, doe-skin shift, leaving her arms and legs exposed to the chill air. Meghan noted A'neewa appeared to be unfazed by the low temperature, wondering if tales told about native people's indifference to pain and other inconveniences were true, and not just wives' tales shared at church dinners, or among camp followers in constant gossip. She leaned forward to whisper a question, then stopped, A'neewa's posture taking on a more focused form.

Shadows moved on the other side of a wide, shallow stream, slowly resolving into the forms of two deer, a large doe and her yearling, both reaching down to probe the water for a drink before moving on. "They did not scent us. That is good. The wind is in our favor." A'neewa's voice was a breathless whisper in Meghan's ear. Before she could form a reply, A'neewa pulled away and stood up, reaching down to help her to her feet. "We have more ground to cover."

"How can you tell?"

A'neewa pointed with her chin across the shallow water. "The deer, they told me."

◦℮◦

He moved with the stir of wind, his movement timed to the rustle of leaves and limbs, preventing the doe from hearing his approach. Her yearling, still with her from the year before, oblivious to the stalk. Its mouth tracked above the ground, reaching for acorns scattered there, straying closer to where their paths would meet. His polished warclub in hand, the ball and powder in the pistol saved for another time. He would leave the doe unharmed to breed, delivering once more when the season of snow had come and gone.

He noted a flicker of ear from the mother; her head swiveled around, trying to locate the source of her unease. It was not coming from his direction, his muscular frame in a frozen pose, his breathing steady, invisible in the shadows beneath low-hanging limbs. He knew there must be another predator in the area. Bear, wolf, or man. Could feel the focus of its energy on his skin. The smaller deer becoming a priority, the moon in rise exposing its ribs a few paces away. His fingers tightened on the handle of his club, knowing a rush and crush against the animal's skull would be the wiser choice. His mind made up, he slid out from under the limbs of a scrub oak, rushing ahead, delivering the fatal blow.

◦℮◦

A'neewa held out one hand, then knelt, probing the surrounding darkness. A bleat of alarm from one of the deer slipped from a wooded area ahead, followed by a muted thud, then thump of a body falling to the ground. She leaned in and looked directly into Meghan's eyes, shaking her head, letting her know not to speak. Her knife was already in her hand, Meghan copying the action, slipping hers from the sheath beneath her skirt. A'neewa leaned closer, lip to ear, her voice barely a whisper. "He has made a kill. One of the two deer we saw earlier. With a club."

Meghan narrowed her eyes, shaking her head as she came to an understanding of how unprepared she was to meet and then kill the man of her long nightmare. Knowing A'neewa had realized this from the very beginning, when trying to divert or delay her before leaving the fort.

A Final Warning, Made

A'neewa shook her head, determined to get through to Meghan despite her hard-headed denial of the truth. "This will not be the same as before, when you marked him, taking half his sight. He was in control. With you under his knife, appearing dazed and weak. Of no threat to him, your hidden blade a surprise. Allowing you first strike, though failing to kill him, leaving you to suffer—"

"You think I need be reminded of it?" Meghan rounded on A'neewa; eyes wide in anger. "I do not want you to come with me. Only that you point me in the right direction so I can bring this waking nightmare to an end."

A'neewa remained calm, understanding the information she'd provided Meghan had spurred her pain-driven reaction. "I will go with you. We will see an end to this. My advice is meant to avoid your death. Is failure in seeking your revenge an acceptable trade in seeing him again?"

Meghan sat down on her bed; hands filled with clothing as she stuffed it inside a leather pack. She lowered her head, her voice trembling. "No. I will not see his smirk again. I wish only to see fear in his eyes when he realizes it is my knife pressed against his throat. That he will see my smile as he dies."

"Then you will fail, because he is not capable of fear." A'neewa shrugged, her lips pursed. "I will lead you to him. Our journey guided not by revenge but wisdom, along with patience and careful approach. He is skilled, far beyond my knowledge of the hunt." She paused. "Perhaps we should wait, asking—"

"No! I will not lay this on his doorstep. Or my brother's. I accept your terms. And welcome your help."

ᑫᘎ

Meghan shivered again, wishing Harold were there to hold her, knowing it wouldn't make any difference. That she'd never be free of anger until the deed was behind her, only then. She reached out, taking A'neewa's wrist in her hand, silently mouthing her thanks.

ᑫᘎ

"We leave the horses here." Harold tied the end of his horse's reins to a low-hanging branch. George followed suit, no comment made or suggestion offered on what would happen next. He'd slipped into a support role, aware his friend was thinking far out in front of himself again, trying to discover how to recover both women before it was too late.

"The trail is an obvious issue in our being able to make a stealthy approach. I expect A'neewa to have left it, aware of that as well. There's enough light for tracking, so we'll advance along the slope—over there." Harold pointed to a rise leading to a small hill. "The man we're looking for will be near running water. His lodge, among several others."

George raised his eyebrows. "Man? You mean men."

"The chief said a man."

"The one Meghan wounded—with a blind eye?"

Harold shrugged. "He didn't say. I didn't ask. Enough that we're in time to stop her. To stop them both."

George nodded, then narrowed his eyes. "And where and when will we be catching up to our two girls?"

"In time to alter their plan. Where that will happen, I don't yet know." Without another word, Harold turned and started into the woods.

The yearling was field dressed, stripped of its offal, the body placed in the limbs of a tree to drain pooled blood and heat, released to preserve its flavor. The man rinsed his hands in the shallow brook, careful to avoid splashing as he glanced into the edge of woods, looking for any sign of movement. None seen, but he knew someone was out there, focused on finding him. His instincts strengthened over years of stealthy approach in hunts and raids made against other tribes. Against trespassing settlements, when they began to appear, seeking to gain reputation, captives, and arms. He recovered his club and pistol, then slipped away along the edge of woods in search of the one or ones seeking to pin him to the ground.

Meghan waited where A'neewa had placed her. The other woman slipping away, intent on scouting ahead in a careful circle, her lithe movements certain and silent. She was soon out of sight, Meghan left to question how long she should remain still. Her imagination began to tug at the taut string of her growing apprehension, each sound carried on the soft evening breeze magnified in threat, as if coming from the stealthy approach of their intended victim's moccasin clad feet.

She squeezed the handle of her knife, its point held out as if a candle, helping to ease her mood. A stirring began within her, fear replaced by anger. She smiled as she imagined how it would happen. How she would shrink back in fear, then lunge forward, her blade driven into his other eye to secure her revenge. She almost wet herself when A'neewa touched her on her back of her shoulder, coming in from behind.

"I thought it would be safer, making my approach from this way." A'neewa glanced at the knife Meghan was clinging to. "You seem—eager enough. Are you ready to move ahead?"

Meghan nodded, her anger still building, warming her soul. Her breathing had steadied, her hand on the hilt of blade, no longer trembling. "I am. Take me to him, that I may claim one of the two lives owed me."

ᕞ

Two horses stood with their heads down, as if asleep. He watched them as he sniffed the air for the sour-sweat scent of men who were not native to these lands. The cured meat they ate, heavily salted. He noted no such odors where the horses stood, tethered to a tree, ignoring the temptation to claim the animals, leading them away and butchering them. Enough meat from them to get his people through the winter. He turned parallel to the woods path and began to search for their owners. His fingers gripped the polished wood of the pistol in his left hand, handle of his club in the other.

ᕞ

"They're in front of us." Harold pointed toward a dense thicket of scrub oaks that bordered a moon-silvered ribbon of water. George slid up beside him, straining to see the women.

"You're certain?"

"Yes. I saw a shadow leave, then return." Harold nodded, his voice confident. "Your sister left in watch while A'neewa moved ahead, uncertain where the man they're after is hiding, knowing he's somewhere close by."

George held his tongue, aware the game had changed, again. Harold connected in to an energy he himself could barely sense. Having grown more confident since early afternoon, when he'd taken command, leading them to where they were now. The next step, yet to be determined.

Harold leaned in. "I'll move ahead and close the distance. You stay here and watch for movement from the sides, calling out if you see any. Once I reach them, you'll join us there."

George nodded, shifting his pistol into his hand, prepared to fire it, if needed.

∽

"I hear something." Meghan twisted her head around, eyes wide as she searched the woods. A'neewa reached out and stopped the other woman's panicked rise to her feet. "It's Harold. And your brother. I heard them coming along the path behind us, their movements like those of a blind bear, rooting for grubs."

Meghan settled back, wondering what Harold would say when he came to her. What offer he would make to convince her to abandon her mission. Or worse, offer to complete for her. She finally spotted him, a familiar silhouette in the moonlight streaming down from above. "There. I see him."

A'neewa sighed, glad the responsibility would soon shift to Harold's shoulders. Hopeful he could convince Meghan to return to her senses, abandoning the hunt. She searched the shadows Harold had come from, knowing George was there, ready to provide cover. Her heart sped up, seeing his enormous figure separating from the thicket, moving uphill along the slope. Then she frowned, surprised by the movement. She moved to one side as Harold slipped in beside them.

"You're both in danger. The man you seek is out there. Somewhere." Harold wiped his brow, his voice tight with tension. A'neewa touched his arm, drawing his attention.

"Why is George moving up into the hill?"

Harold shook his head. "He's not. Should be right behind me. Must be halfway here by now."

A'neewa's eyes widened as she rose to her feet, knife in hand, making a dash to where she'd seen the shadowy figure step out from.

◦℮◡

He watched the smaller of the two men make his way toward where the two women were hiding, having already marked their location. He frowned, realizing he would have to make the chief of the tribe pay with his life for having betrayed him. Then he smiled, creeping forward, club in his hand as he listened to the white man thrash his way across the broken ground.

◦℮◡

George rose slightly, searching for movement in the edge of woods bordering a steep slope. He felt uneasy, a sure sign of trouble in the offing, his hand on the trigger of his pistol, held against his chest. A slight noise to his right drew his eyes, followed by a soft whinny. It was his horse, standing a few steps away, having slipped its tether and coming to find him, nose outstretched, seeking his caress.

George reached out, then stopped as the animal's eyes shifted to one side then yanked its head back, mouth open and teeth bared. His instincts screamed at him to spin away, to avoid the attack from his left. He turned his head to the side and pulled the trigger, his eyes closed for a moment against the flash of the powder. The pistol fired without marking a target, in an attempt of defense and as fair warning to the others. He opened his eyes, continuing his turn, dropping into a crouch, knife in his other hand.

A native face formed before him, arm moving in a blur. George raised his shoulder to try and absorb the blow. Stars of pain filled his eyes, the point of his knife thrust in an upward slant, striking bone, then sliding away. His assailant spun, then disappeared into the shadows as George stumbled back, tripping on a root, losing his balance, the side of his head impacting an outcrop of rock. His vision faded; his world going dark.

The man looked down as he moved away, fingers clamped to the wound in his side. He knew it was not fatal, though the pain rose from a shocked numbness to that of a burning ember. He forced himself to straighten up, his shoulders squared as he moved away, stumbling as he did so, heading over the nose of the ridge back toward his lodge.

Meghan tried to stand, to follow A'neewa, concerned for her brother's safety. Harold kept her pinned in place, shaking his head. "She can move quicker than us. We'll wait until she returns with George, then gather ourselves and leave."

"I—I'm not leaving."

"This isn't the way, Meghan. It can only end badly, your enemy expert at killing, and this is his home ground. He holds all the advantages. We're but sheep in his lair."

"You know how to kill! And my brother too! It's what you do—so do it now!"

"Not like this. Not in cold blood."

"My blood isn't cold. It burns, seeking his." Meghan reached out, finger in point. Harold turned to greet the other two, but no one was there. He rose, taking several steps toward the thicket, hearing a call for help in the still air. "Something's wrong. That wasn't your brother heading away. We need to go help them!" When Meghan didn't answer, Harold spun around. She'd gone, no movement seen in the sudden darkness, a cloud covered the face of the full moon.

A'neewa cradled George's head, her fingers searching the bruised skin of his lower neck and shoulder where the club had struck. The thickness of his muscles had absorbed most of the blow, though he was fading in and out of consciousness. She felt the side of his head, her fingers coming away sticky with blood from a laceration just above his ear. Concerned, she leaned forward, feeling his throat, measuring his pulse on both sides. It was steady, letting her know she could dare to leave him to his sister's care, calling to the others for help. She heard Harold respond, then stood up, her instinct's urging her to follow the native man into the woods, with a murderous gleam shining in her dark eyes.

He crouched beside the path, hiding by the last turn before it ran straight into the clearing where his lodge and several others were located. He knew the woman guiding those who sought his death would pass by. Soon. The larger man he'd injured left to struggle behind, along with the other man and the taller woman, who was familiar to his eye, the memory of having met before hidden away in the shadows of his memory. He knew it would come to him. That she would come to him. All of them. Knew the smaller of the two men would be the greater threat, one he would eliminate first, then the native woman, acting as their scout. The taller man would not escape his death a second time. The taller woman, left for last, keeping her alive until after dawn. Or the day after, depending on his mood. His son encouraged to watch, as he'd learned from his own father, gaining from the lessons

taught. The thought stirred him, his body feeling warm as pain from the shallow wound faded away. Soon, he whispered to himself, as the moon uncovered its face, light again in a steady wash. Soon.

Meghan ran as fast as she could, determined to reach the pinched end of the narrow valley. She managed to follow the path, its surface a sheen of trampled grass in the light from above. Her breath fogged the air, eyes fastened on a cleared area opening before her. A slim-bodied figure standing there, mouth agape, eyes opened wide in surprise as she closed the distance between them.

The young native boy tried to understand how the strange-looking woman had come to be there, expecting his father to arrive with a fresh kill. He stared as she slid to a stop, then raised his hand to greet her. She reached out, a wide smile on her pale face, grasping his forearm, a yelp of pain forced between his teeth as she wrenched it up behind him, his thin shoulder numbed by the harsh movement. A scream of pain rose from his throat, covered by a warm hand over his mouth. His arm released, the blade of a knife pressed against his throat as a wash of heat ran down his thighs, his bladder emptying as he trembled in fear.

"You have his look. He must be your father. Father and son, like I once had, until he took them from me."

Her words meant nothing to him, low in tone though over-flowing with anger. The knife had cut him; the outer layer of pulsating skin on his throat parted by the honed blade pressed against it. His body stiffened in resistance, held in place by a firm arm around his narrow waist. His eyes bulged out in shock as another, strangely dressed figure came on the run from out of the edge of woods. He watched as the shadow of his father rose from the side of the trail, knocking the stranger to the ground with a swing of his war club.

Meghan shouted, her voice a shriek of fear. "Stop! I have your son! Leave him—leave my man alone—or I'll kill your boy!"

The man hesitated, standing over the prone figure, having struck him down with a glancing blow of his club, the man managing to duck to one side at the last moment, the wooden ball of hard wood clipping the side of his skull, then thudding against his shoulder. He stared over to where the woman stood, knife held to his son's throat, his voice calm as he answered her.

"I can easily make another son. Can you make another one of him?" He pointed with his club, then shifted his feet to swing again, planning to complete the killing blow, then turn and throw the weapon in the woman's direction, risking his son's life against her freezing in place on seeing her man killed before her eyes.

He raised his weapon, stopping at the apex of his stroke, something striking him from behind. Blood flowed across his tongue, his body coming unstrung, legs folding beneath him as the club slipped from his limp fingers. Dead, before his head hit the ground.

A'neewa stepped around the native man's body, kneeling to check on Harold's breathing and heartbeat, sighing when she felt the strong pulse in his neck. "He is all right." She angled his head, squinting to check on his pupils in the bright silver light from above. "He is not concussed, only stunned." She took his hand, helping him to sit up.

Meghan stared, having thought Harold dead, shocked at seeing him rise to his feet while the man she hated beyond any measure of the word lay on the ground. It was too much for her distraught mind to handle, fleeing to a place where death was hers to deliver, not A'neewa's. She screamed in anger. "His death belonged to me! Not you!"

A'neewa walked over and reached for the knife in Meghan's hand.

"It is over, Sister. Finally. Accept the Mother's will and release the boy to me. Harold is going to be fine. I promise. Please."

Meghan screamed, beyond reason. "No! I'm owed another life—this one's life for my Jacob. For my precious boy." Her hand trembled, eyes filling with tears. A'neewa reached for the hilt of the small knife, intending to free the terrified boy. A flash of steel caught her by surprise, Meghan striking out, slashing A'neewa's palm, causing her to step back.

"No! He belongs to me!" Meghan's eyes widened with mindless fury.

"No. He belongs to me." A voice in French came from behind Meghan, who twisted around, the young boy turned with her. A native woman holding an infant pressed against her breast stood a few paces away, eyes fixed in a solemn gaze.

A'neewa clamped her damaged palm with her uninjured hand, looking at the native woman, hopeful she would stay back. Meghan's emotions in turmoil, with A'neewa uncertain what she might do, if not approached with great care.

"He is innocent. You have taken your revenge. Leave my son and go."

Harold struggled to his feet, hand to the side of his head, staggering slightly as he walked over. "She's right, Meghan. The boy is—"

"He's of his father's blood! As my Jacob was of his! Blood cries out for blood. I'm owed and will be paid!"

"Wait." Harold's shout stayed the killing stroke. "Listen to me, Meghan. The boy is yours. He's your son, Jacob. Look at him. He has your eyes. He wears my face. He's ours, yours, and mine. Our son. Can you not see him standing there, in your gentle embrace?"

"Patrick? But you—you can't be here. Nor Jacob. I saw your graves. My brother showed them to me. Two more crosses, nailed into the ground beside my sweet girl. How I longed to join you there."

"No, Meghan. It was only a dream—a terrible dream. One you must now wake from. We need you. Both of us. Let our boy come to me and you'll see. We're alive, and need you to be with us again. Please?"

Harold sensed A'neewa coming over, standing behind him, removing herself as a threat. The native woman froze in place, the child in her arms beginning to stir, a thin mewling cry from its small mouth building in volume. He took another step forward, reaching out for Meghan's arm. "Come to me, my love. Take my hand. It's time to go home. To our home. The three of us."

The young child cried; Meghan's attention drawn to it. "She has my daughter. My Eliza! My precious girl. Give her to me! She needs me to care for her—to keep her alive."

Harold saw Meghan's arm loosen from around the boy's chest. Enough that the young boy tried to squirm free, grabbing her wrist, biting into it, drawing a gasp as Meghan looked down, his features shifting to reveal those of the man who'd haunted her dreams. Harold shouted when he saw the feral look in her eyes, then lunged forward, knowing he was too late.

Meghan slid the blade across the boy's throat, a gush of blood fanning out as she released his flailing body. Then she lashed out, Harold the target, driving the blade through his palm as he reached out, passing through his palm, into his chest.

Harold trapped Meghan's hand in place, his fingers locked around hers. He stared into her eyes, knowing her mind was gone, spittle from her words hitting him in the face. "Liar! You're not my Patrick!" She tried to wrench the blade free, intent on driving it home again. Harold let go, accepting his fate. A click, snap of flint on steel, and thud from behind deafening him. Meghan head snapped back, her unbound hair forming a silvery halo around her face. A dark hole appearing in the center of her forehead, just above her beautiful eyes. Her hand slipped from the knife as she fell back, landing on the ground, a peaceful expression on her face, as if in awe at the thick spray of stars above.

CHAPTER NINETEEN

Promontory Fort, Mid Winter 1759

Pulled Back from the Shadows

Harold could hear faceless voices in murmuring tones, mixed with an occasional whine of protest. One of them gruff, in commanding response. A wash of cool swept across his brow, followed by a brush of a gentle touch against his cheek. He could smell A'neewa's scent, a blend of exotic notes as if a rare wine, newly opened. Familiar. Soothing. Healing. He climbed out from beneath a heavy blanket of fever induced fatigue, his voice a whisper in his own ears.

"I'm. *Still* here."

"Yes." A'neewa leaned down, her lips near his ear.

"Somewhere." Harold's voice was the saw of a raven's croaking call in morning air.

"At the fort."

Harold was silent, wanting to know but afraid to ask. "It has been some—horrible dream?"

"No."

He asked the next question, his voice trembling, afraid of the answer. "Meghan?"

"Gone."

Harold shook his head, the slight movement causing his thoughts to spin, having to wait for them to settle. "She's—gone?"

"Yes."

"George?"

"Here. Escaped with a broken collarbone and minor lacerations to his skull. Back to normal now, at least, normal for him."

Harold felt a river of tears leak from beneath his closed eyelids, slipping down the sides of his face, struggling to accept the nightmare was real and his beautiful Meghan was truly gone.

A'neewa gently wiped his tears away, then leaned down, kissing his forehead. "You *tried*. We *both* tried. But she couldn't find her way back, though she was *close*, because of you. Because of your words."

Harold felt a black wall crash down, knocking him back into the void. A'neewa checked his breathing. It was steady, his heartbeat strong beneath the press of her fingers on the side of his neck. She looked at the two doctors as they continued their protest to the stern-faced general who'd ordered them away, telling them both to leave her to tend her patient as she saw fit.

Harold's wound had been life-threatening, the point of Meghan's knife piercing his hand, passing through to the outer wall of his heart, though not in full penetration of it. The weapon left in place until the surgeon could remove it, with great care. The deep wound cleared of a knotted clot of dark blood, then dosed with A'neewa's elixir to prevent infection. Loosely closed with sutures, not a heated iron, as the hard-headed surgeons had insisted on using.

Aidyn had interceded on her behalf, Harold's life put directly in her hands. His journey back to the promontory fort having been a race between an urgency to reach it and need for careful movement,

Harold's life balanced on a razor's edge during two days of steady travel. Another two days spent in around-the-clock attention, with infection of the wound a constant concern.

George had been able to hire a dozen natives willing to carry Harold in a hastily assembled litter, the men swapping off in three groups, preventing fatigue that could lead to jostle or sudden shock. The four-day journey, completed in two, the men paid double for their tireless efforts. George led from the front; his sister's body tied in place across the back of Harold's horse in trail of his own. A'neewa rode the small gray mare, Chief Matanac eager to swap it back in trade for a handful of coins, unable to keep it properly fed.

The general had ignored the return of his mare, leading A'neewa to believe it had gone unnoticed in the frenzied activities of new recruits arriving from the east. Soldiers who'd seen service throughout the long campaign now heading back to Philadelphia for barracks duty, or a return to England for eventual reassignment.

A'neewa had let George know she would stay on until Harold recovered enough to survive transport back to the large port-side city. Then she would return to her people, leaving the past year and more behind, closing the book on this chapter of her life. She smiled as she recalled the words Harold had written to her on the page torn from his journal. Carried in one of the many pockets in her wide belt. Her participation in this war, now over, with preparations begun for the next one to come.

A Final Parting

George pursed his lips. "I will ask you one last time to go *with* me. Travel back to your people, arranged as often as you wish."

A'neewa shook her head. "The answer is the same."

"Why?"

"Philadelphia is *your* home, George. It will never be mine." A'neewa reached out and shoved him on his uninjured shoulder, urging him toward his horse. She checked on Harold, sitting upright in the back of a wide-bodied wagon. Still pale, but strong enough for a slow trip over an improved road back to the city of Philadelphia.

"You will soon be on your way home. Back to your mother, who will shed tears of joy, seeing you safely there."

Harold nodded. "Yes. After a short stay at George's estate, until they can arrange a ship. You will not be riding there with us?"

"No. We say our goodbyes here, on *common* ground. Me, back to my people. You, back to yours. They deserve you, Harold. More than any of those on *this* side of the—" She hesitated.

"Atlantic Ocean."

A'neewa returned a soft smile. "You have spilled enough of your blood here, *Renard Rouge*." She leaned forward, kissing his tear-stained lips. Then she walked away, head held high, refusing to let him see her own.

The general came over, placing one hand on the side of the transport. He watched A'neewa as she took the reins of the small gray mare, climbing on, giving him a slow wave as she rode off. The animal, presented by Aidyn to her as a gift, having miraculously recovered from its untimely death. Aidyn looked down at Harold, smiling. "The men of the escort are to move at *your* level of comfort and must not be allowed to chivy you. The nights of late cold, and your health is of paramount importance."

"Yes, sir." Harold reached out, taking the general's hand, exchanging a firm shake then letting go.

"Use my Christian name, Harold. You're released from formality of active service, due to your wound. I would have these last words between us be as friends, not fellow officers."

"Have you an idea of when *you'll* be returning home—Aidyn?"

"At some point, with you already on a ship back to England. So—this is to be goodbye. At least, for now. Go and claim what's *owed* you, by all of us, here and back home. Having earned a *full* pension, with disability payments. More than enough of a stipend to set you on a far easier path than has met you *here*. A small place in the countryside with retirement to a life of study and reflection. A book written, based on your experiences. Your vast store of knowledge passed on for future generations to absorb. To use in trying to solve—*insurmountable* problems with *cunning* diversions."

"A captain's pension is hardly enough to provide for that, Aidyn."

"A *colonel's* pension, Harold. With full rank and privileges assigned, courtesy of the King himself. Reward for your sacrifice of health and exemplary service. Arranged by messenger before you headed off on your recent—" Aidyn paused, then lowered his eyes, his voice soft. "I'll never forget Meghan, her loss beyond any measure. Nor will I forget any of you. Even George." He turned his face away, then reached up to wipe his eyes, taking a moment to look toward the fort, remembering how easily they had taken it, preventing a significant loss of lives. All because of the young man's strategic mind. "Anyway—it's the *least* you deserve."

Harold reached out, placing his hand on Aidyn's. "*I appreciate it*, General. And I promise you I'll never forget your efforts, made on my behalf. Nor all the rest of what we went through, and accomplished. I swear it."

"See that you do *not*, Colonel Knutt. Now go, before our lovely A'neewa returns and scolds me for delay of your departure." Aidyn stepped back, then hesitated. "One question, if I may—before you take your leave."

"Of course."

"I find it odd that two men I respect, with *cunning* minds and no small measure of wood-skills between you, should have mistaken the bones of a moose for those of my little mare, gone missing."

Harold shrugged, then managed a thin smile. "Not my only mistake, Aidyn. Nor George's."

Aidyn nodded, then slapped the side of the barge in a signal for it to pull away. He watched as George swung his horse in a tight circle, one arm raised in a wave, leading the way. Aidyn responded in kind, looking over at Harold and tossed him a salute. His recently promoted officer, a man as close to him as any son could ever be, returning the gesture then leaning back, his eyes closed as the wagon moved away.

CHAPTER TWENTY

Philadelphia Port, Early Spring 1760

Homeward, Bound

The port city of Philadelphia was a frenzy of organized chaos, wagons in steady retreat from long, finger-thin docks; ships jammed in on either side allowing for removal of tons of supplies. A line of soldiers with belongings in tow trudged along angled walkways, heading downhill. The men part of a two-way exchange of valuable products. Recently delivered goods heading west, while the ships' holds were hastily reconfigured to support transport of men back home to England, with disembarkation to take place at ports in Hull, London, and Bristol. Each destination a few weeks voyage away on high seas, once the tall-masted ships could clear the river's mouth.

Harold had finished his convalescence at George's estate, his injuries now fully healed, his energy near a full return. Prominent people had constantly dropped by, in attendance by George, visiting to wish him well in his recovery, before pulling the large man aside, engaging in subdued conversations, seeking his input on dozens of issues. Many of the more notable men among them eager to promote his advancement to a seat in Pennsylvania's government, one he was in serious consideration of. Explaining to Harold, when they were finally alone, his thoughts on the subject.

George gave Harold a wide smile. "I'll have my hands on the reins, with the power to guide the beast of politics, serving the needs of *both* sides, colony and crown."

"And those of the *native* territories, as well."

George's face slipped into a pained expression. "A'neewa and her people will *always* be foremost in my thoughts." He paused, giving Harold a questioning look. "Is there any doubt in your heart on that regard?"

Harold shrugged. "Those men slapping your back today may try and nudge you from your path, tomorrow. To one they would *prefer* you to walk, many of them in control of the purse needed to help smooth your way." Harold walked over and stood beside George, looking through the window of his study. "Your wish for the future, as described, is one thing. The means to attain it, another altogether."

"I *would* not—*will* not sell my services, brother." George stared at him; his tone iced with anger.

Harold raised an arm, waving it in surrender. "I did not mean it to sound as such, having no doubts as to your stance on equitable treatment, for all parties. Nor do I harbor any doubts as to your resolute adherence to a strict moral code. It's only the disease of *greed* I sense in the men standing behind the promised seat of power, if you will, that is of concern."

Harold paused, allowing time for his words to pass through the serious-faced man's mind, his lips still set in a firm line. Then he continued, needing to voice his concerns, as his departure was due on the morrow.

"Every civilization that has arisen throughout recorded time, and most likely ever will, has been driven to its ultimate destruction by those caring only for themselves, and not the greater good."

George's face lit up. "But it's a *new day*, brother. One filled with *novel* ideas. There's talk of forming an alliance between the colonies to strengthen trade negotiations with other countries. Along with the creation of mutually supportive militias, protecting our common interests in the outer settlements."

"Protection against *whom*?"

"The Spanish and the French. We've not seen the last of their meddling, I can assure you. And it'll be on *our* shoulders where the burden will fall, protecting our interests. We must prepare for it through *deliberate* consent and decree agreements between men of reason."

"Paid for with *what* monies? The Crown will soon be at your door, seeking repayment for efforts made on your behalf by the King, with an increase in standing taxes, along with imposition of new. Not to mention the impress of free men on open seas to help rebuild their naval forces. A bared fist soon to rise with long fingers, exerting control over any attempt at self-governance, reminding you *who* owes what to *whom*. And exactly how *much*." Harold paused once more, a bead of sweat on his forehead as a wave of weakness passed through him.

George frowned, waving a hand as if to dismiss the idea, confident of a future based on his recent success in having acquired a handful of commercial properties, offered him at a reduced price with attractive terms. He was excited to begin to build on the back of his popularity, with additional opportunities looming near to hand. "Enough for now. We have *other* items in need of our attendance." George's face took on a somber note. He lowered his voice, placing his hand on Harold's shoulder. "My sister's service is scheduled for tomorrow morning, the stone just now delivered. With a private gathering for yourself, before you board ship, per your request."

The earth was rich with the scent of newly turned loam. Dark-black furrows coursed along the tops of the mile long fields of George's estate, recently plowed and planted, green dots of crops beginning to show. The base of a tall elm tree stood on the edge of nearby woods centering a circle of headstones; George's family plot, framed by slabs of carved granite, letters on their faces, forming stiff lines in describe of the identities of those lying below.

Meghan's stone, more plainly formed, displayed her name, etched in stark relief. The measure of her life pinched between date of birth and demise, followed by a line of letters describing her as a loving mother, wife, daughter, and sister, along with four words added below, per Harold's request: *Madonna, Standing in Sunlight.*

Harold was there now, alone, kneeling to place a wreath of mixed wildflowers against the base of her stone, collected during a slow walk along the edge of the woods bordering a variety of flower gardens, his choices limited by the cool spring weather. Enough gathered, he told himself, to let her know his love for her was more than words on cold stone, alone. Tears formed in his eyes, having risen early, a spectacular sunrise letting him know she was still with him; a curl of red-gold hair curled against her cheek, looking into his eyes, her own as blue as the sky could ever hope to be. With a trembling sigh, he leaned down and kissed her name, then rose to his feet and walked away.

Harold stood on a hill overlooking the port, feeling unbound, his service at an end. The future ahead, unfettered by orders or responsibilities assigned, seemed foreign. He took a deep breath, knowing he would return one day, aware this land was part of him now, his blood having stained its soil. Forming a tether between body and soul.

"Excuse me, sir." A voice with a hint of a wheeze coaxed Harold's head around. A short, stout man, with a large portmanteau in tow, stood at his side, one hand half-raised in greeting. "I am seeking one of his Majesty's transport boats. The *Aurora*, bound for Bristol. I have let slip the number of the dock where it is to be found."

"It's the center-most *ship*, of the three just there—to the fore." Harold raised his arm and pointed.

"I fear I've rather *misjudged* the distance to said vessel, as well the overwhelming weight of my bag. A hired cart would have been the wiser choice in conveyance of myself and my belongings to said transport." Harold reached out in a polite greeting. The man smiling then handing him his bag, ignoring the look of surprise on Harold's face. "My thanks, young man. I will happily carry your more *sensibly* sized and *much* lighter rucksack until we reach your—ship *or* mine. My body provided time enough to recover, thanks to your generous spirit."

Harold nodded, then lifted the large piece of luggage onto his shoulder, hiding a wince of pain from his recently healed wound. "It's the same destination—the one we're bound to."

"How *fortunate*, for us both. I shall take the lead and clear the way for you." The man hesitated; his brows drawn close together. "I have neglected my manners. I'm Nathan Brauer, late of Philadelphia."

Harold returned the man's handshake. "My name is Knutt. Harold Knutt, late of—points west." He noted the other man's eyes widen. "Are you all right, Mister Brauer?"

"I'm fine. Just a—moment of flush. My former pace, too quick by half in fear of missing the—the *ship*."

The two of them moved downhill, mixing in with a mill of men and materials to be consigned to dozens of transports. Mules in full bray pulled large carts filled with newly arrived goods uphill, moving alongside them. Nathan raised his voice, in constant regale of every occurrence, small or large, helping Harold to lose his dour expression, his spirit growing lighter with each step, leading him back home.

Uncharted Waters

"Captain Knutt—out of uniform. Not looking at all like the *Red Fox*."

Harold slowly turned, his back placed against the rail of a two-masted barque, a sleek French prize, taken by the British navy, re-flagged with a Union Jack fluttering in a stiff wind atop the forward mast. He nodded at Major Sandersen, the man's thin arms crossed on an expertly tailored uniform, resting below rows of unearned medals gleaming in the sunlight, a condescending smirk on his pale lips.

Harold cleared his throat, his eyes cool above a respectful smile. "Colonel."

The officer frowned. "The General did *not* see fit to approve my request for promotion, though I will remedy the omission once back in London."

"Bristol is some nine hundred furlongs from London." Harold fixed the other man with a considered look. "Strange choice of port, for your triumphant reentry."

The major sniffed, then held up one hand, admiring the play of light on his manicured fingernails. "My family estate is in Melksham, outside of Bath."

"You have a family? Had never considered you—married." Harold paused. "You don't exactly seem the type."

Sandersen drew himself up, chest puffed out. "It is the estate of my father, *Lord* Sandersen. And as I stated before—you are *not* in proper uniform, Captain Knutt."

"And as I corrected you *then*, Major—I'm one who *has* seen recent promotion. To *Colonel*, at the request of my good friend Aidyn. A promotion approved by the King himself."

The other man blanched, his already pale face gone completely white, matching the color of his fine wig. The blood returned in a flush of pink staining his cheeks. "You're *not* a—"

"Caution, *Major.*"

The apoplectic officer fought a war for control, using more strength of will than had been his meek reputation, when under fire. His eyes searched Harold's face for the least sign of falseness; finding none, his hands clenched at his sides in small balls of repressed rage. He spun away, aiming for the aft end of the ship.

Harold stopped him with a softly framed order. "You have not been dismissed, Major Sandersen. Nor have you offered me a—*proper* salute."

It was as if a layer of ice had descended from the overcast sky, settling on the florid features of the flustered officer. His narrow-set eyes blazed in anger; the side of his hand barely reaching his forehead before he spun about and strode away. A violation of military courtesy that Harold let pass, knowing every man had his limits. Certain he'd just found those in the man who would forever be an enemy to him.

"That was—a *delicious* display of leverage, former Captain, now *Colonel* Knutt. An admirable rise in rank if you'll allow me the compliment."

"And so I have, Mister Brauer." Harold paused, giving the man a considered look. "I take it you already knew of me, based on your reaction ashore, when I introduced myself."

"Do call me Nathan, if you would, Colonel Knutt." The shorter man smiled. "I tried my best to suppress any outward sign of recognition, unprepared as I was in meeting a living legend so—*diminutive* in stature. The tales shared by soldiers I'd spoken with, while they were in convalescence from campaigns made against the French, having painted you a man of great height *and* breadth." He frowned, then shook his head. "An important skill, that of hiding one's emotional reaction, especially in *my* line of work. Must be certain to do better, next time I'm caught out, unaware."

"I judge you to be a printer, at least. A publisher too, based on your verbosity."

"You deserve your reputation for keen observation, Red Fox. If I may call you that."

Harold held out his hand. "Harold. And it would please me greatly, if I never hear the other again."

Nathan returned the handshake, his grip as firm as the iron frame of one of his presses back in Philadelphia. His thick fingernails bore stains of black ink no amount of scrubbing could hope to erase. He eyed Harold; his semi-bald head tilted to one side. "You do not miss a thing."

Harold lowered his gaze. "My many scars suggest otherwise, result of numerous mistakes made in the field, with dire consequences for myself. Along with the undeserved deaths of others." He paused. "Too many of them—a burden I will carry the rest of my life."

"All deaths are dire for those who must *bear* them."

Harold's voice dropped as he stared at his hands, measuring the stack of lives lost, placed on the opposite side of life's scale from his own. "A fate I've been fortunate to *avoid*. Thus far."

"The day is young, my dour-faced friend. *Cheer up!* Poseidon may yet send a rogue wave from out of the depths, sweeping you from the deck. Your problem solved, though a poor ending to the legend spun about your superlative exploits, some greater part of them woven from these *very* hands." Nathan held his up, grinning. "*Most* of them, I confess, myself the resident authority in Philadelphia in recount of activities occurring in the western wilderness. Distribution rights sold on to all major cities in the colonies and over there—" He pointed to the horizon. "—in Bristol, Bath, London, and beyond. Based on, with some *minor* elaboration, stories shared with me by the soldiers mentioned before."

Harold nodded. "So, you are both publisher *and* writer."

"As well editor, distributor, procurer of monies owed, errand boy, news gatherer, and—oh yes, the *owner.*"

Harold leaned back against the railing, a large swell in steady approach, crosswise to the bow. He nodded, drawing Nathan's attention to it. "The great sea god has heard you, though it is too small, by half. And as to the small grain of truth in stories told regarding my efforts, I did no more than those standing alongside me. Less so than many others, who gave their all to a—" He sighed, lowering his eyes. "To a worthy cause they believed in, serving country and King with honor."

Nathan shrugged, holding out one hand and examining his stained fingertips. "And were any of *them* assigned titles of native respect?"

Harold fixed the other man with a stare. "They were fortunate enough to avoid such meaningless things."

"And, as such, their names would not have provided a positive effect on *my* sales account, so I made do with you. The public ever in clamor for tales of your strategic ploys, accompanied by my rather artful image of a fox in grasp of King Louis by his ringed nose, leading him from one grand loss to the next."

The wave lifted the nose of the ship, slipping it a point or two off its course, soon corrected by the helmsman standing fifty paces away. Harold gave him a slow wave of his hand. The gesture of respect returned in kind.

Harold looked at Nathan, liking the man for his open and honest self-appraisal. "I recognize the value of providing an optimistic outlook of events, for soldiers and citizens alike. It's a poor thing, men marching into peril with hollow hearts and leaden feet, knowing their loved ones might never see them home again, alive."

"But—?" Nathan looked at Harold, as if he were holding a pen, taking every word down.

Harold squared his shoulders, feet braced, looking the stout man directly in his eyes. "I am *not* the man you've portrayed. Neither hero nor leader. I sought only to prevent loss of life, on both sides, when possible, by use of strategic movement, finding it preferable to the counting of, and subsequent need to bury the dead."

"And where do you stand on whispered rumors made of—killings deemed necessary, in support of field maneuvers without carry of the burden of any prisoners taken?"

Harold tried to hold up before the other man's stare, failing, his eyes dropping to look at the deck. He reached out, clenching the railing. "I—failed to consider in advance the need for additional men to take charge of any of the enemy captured, returning them as prisoners of war, back to our main line."

Nathan nodded. "An oversight. One you've paid for, bearing the guilt of lives taken from surrendered men."

"*One* of them, yes." Harold's voice twisted in a building breeze, barely more than a whisper. "The rest of them—were not provided opportunity to do so. Killed during the ensuant action. Only the first one taken captive, then executed. The look on his face, haunts my dreams to this day."

"Which is why you were, and still *are* the man best suited to represent the cause before you. One that is before us *all*, those capable of seeing it *clearly*."

Harold hardened his expression. "And what *cause* is that Mister Brauer?"

"To try and stop the storm in rise." Nathan pointed to the east. "One that threatens to overwhelm what you've helped to accomplish, based on your considerable contribution to the effort." He stepped forward, placing his hand on Harold's arm. "You have leverage, Harold. Enough to pry open the closed minds of men consumed with the endless counting of coins, eager to recover every one of them gone missing in funding the removal of the French from lands they held sway in these past one hundred years and more. Minds *blind* to the immense wealth lying in abundance throughout the colonies, and lands west, should they only bide their time and allow us to build a new English Empire in the west—eager to deliver it to them."

Harold crossed his arms on his chest. "And what of the people who are already in residence there?"

"They are loyal English citizens, asking only the right of self-determination in—"

"*Native* peoples, Mister Brauer." Harold leaned forward slightly, a small swell lifting the bow of the ship, his knees flexing to adjust. "Are they to be allowed the same right of self-determination?"

Nathan stepped back, touching the railing for support. "Those who've proven themselves to be loyal allies, yes. Deserving *some* measure of consideration in return, pending acceptance of our laws and ways."

Harold shook his head. "And if they are not open to that suggestion?"

Nathan shrugged. "I confess I have not thought on it. Not in its entirety, though I'm certain we can reach an accommodation. Lands set aside with nod made to ancestral claims and traditions."

Harold bored in. "But not a separate and *sovereign* group of protected states, with dominion over its people in accordance with their own beliefs and customs?"

Nathan gaped, his dark eyes revealing his exasperation. "You cannot be *serious*! Indians—*savages* left to rule themselves? With their recorded history of bloodthirsty raids and constant, intertribal conflicts? Of the *butchery* of settlement families? Of women and children? Those who survive, made slaves?"

Harold relaxed his stance, leaning back against the railing, arms still crossed, a slight smile on his face. "They are *natives,* Mister Brauer, not savages. The title of *Indian* a misnomer, given them based on faulty navigation by a piss-poor sailor. One with a deplorable record of slaughtering hundreds, if not thousands of innocent people, including those who met him and his men as friends. The same way the natives here met the early colonists, when they stepped foot on the eastern shoreline."

Nathan was silent, his head turned to one side, staring at the horizon. Then he looked at Harold. "Howsoever you name them, it is an *untenable* idea, one trapping the colonists' between Indian—between *native* lands to the west and eastern development. A tight squeeze, eventually, limiting our right to expansion."

"Yet you would take their lands from *them*, tearing away their ancestral ways, a bible in your righteous fingers, helping justify the attempt." Harold's expression overflowed with fiery determination to protect A'neewa and her people. "You see only one side of this divide clearly, from lofty perch behind printing press, far from the edge of what we name *wilderness*, and the native people call their *home*. Only half the issues they face brought into your line of sight. The others, those faced by the displaced peoples who were forced to melted away from the east, left hidden away in shadows you cannot see into, cannot comprehend, unless willing to go and learn about them for yourself."

Nathan stepped over. He touched Harold's shoulder, his fingers firm, eyes bright with excitement. "Then you are even *more* the man needed *now!* Before the glow of your notoriety starts to fade, which will occur once the two great nations sign a treaty, recognizing our victory over the French. The butcher's bill then to be submitted by King George, insisting on repayment of every copper, made."

Harold shook his head. "*I'm* homeward bound, with little interest, monies, or the energy required to raise myself to a position of political influence."

Nathan stepped back, nodding his head. "Valid point, Colonel Knutt, and if any man deserves time away from the deadly conflict of war, it is you, sir. Please—forgive my ardor just now in pressing my ill-formed opinions on you. Your view on things has—opened my eyes, proving you an excellent tutor on all things native." He bowed, then gave Harold a wide, warm-edged smile. "I bid you good day, hoping to see you at the Captain's dinner tonight. That is, if your appetite for the company of one of the other guests improves."

Nathan moved away with a confident stride, his hand held out to one side, helping maintain his balance against the slow rolling of the hull.

Harold smiled, tight-lipped, knowing he would never allow himself to become part of the other man's political machinations. His only desire, to see home again, with a quiet reintroduction made to family and friends, hoping it would clear him of the latent melancholia, still there. Meghan present in every one of his waking hours, causing a constant turn of his head to find her, to share an observation, listen to her thoughts. The loss of her love, limited as it had been, one that would haunt him the rest of his days. He turned around and stared at the horizon, his breathing falling into a rhythm with the slow rise and fall of the ship's bowsprit, pointing the way home.

A Welcome, in Rouse

The weeks turned one upon the other, the port city of Bristol finally reached at the end of their twenty-third day at sea. The Aurora made to wait at anchor until morning, a small boat sent ashore with news, messages, and retrieval of a copy of the ship's manifest, listing materials and men aboard. All passengers required to stay aboard until allowed to disembark and clear customs, before venturing through the busy port on the morrow. One last night aboard, with Harold standing a lonely watch from the upper deck, unable to remain below except to lie down for short spells, in a troubled sleep.

Harold stared at the lights of the city and wondered if his parents would be there to meet him, announcement of his pending arrival sent in a message ashore, letting them know he would stop by the office fronting his father and uncle's warehouses so his mother could avoid having to greet him at the docks.

"Excuse me, sir." The helmsman was leaning alongside the railing, a few paces away, sailors' cap in his hands. Harold nodding a greeting, a welcoming smile on his face. "Our *gifted* steersman, who's guided us through a peaceful and *precise* passage, safely home to a welcoming port through perilous seas."

The wiry, deeply tanned man touched his forehead in acknowledgment. "My thanks to *you*, sir. An honor, coming from a man such as yourself. I feel you could've done as good a job as me, with all the time you've spent on deck these past few weeks, staring at the sea and stars."

Harold gave a slight nod. "Was there something you wished to ask of me? You have but to name it."

The helmsman shook his head. "Only a shake of your hand, sir, now we're all but home. Captain's orders not to bother you while a'sea. Seeing we've now arrived, I wanted to thank you." The middle-aged reached out and shook Harold hand, with salt-weathered fingers as strong as if formed of wrought iron. "You don't know it, sir—but my oldest son, he served with you. Deciding against shipboard duty, preferring service to the King, ashore. He was with you at *Bloody Rock*, sir. Stood at your shoulder when the bloody *savages* came pouring in. Was fortunate enough to have him aboard ship, on his return home. Injured—but alive, by the grace of God."

Harold let a tight grin lift his compressed lips, his fingers brushing against his coat, touching the scar in his side, just below the starched fabric. "I'm sorry for the wound he suffered. His name?"

"James, sir. James Ramsey." The old salt's voice was full of pride.

"*Little Jim*. Yes." Harold released his smile, letting it find his eyes. "He has your look. Along with your eyesight. Able to see things from afar, the rest of us like bats, in compare."

"I thank you, sir. My Jimmy has the misfortune of bearing my looks but is indeed gifted with fine sight." The man paused, then lowered his voice, a solemn look in his eyes. "So proud he was, sir, of his wounds. Considered them as badges of honor, having served alongside the Red Fox himself. Back when you were first starting out, sir." He raised his eyes. "It's been truly an honor, sir, having shared the late watch with you."

Harold, off-put by use of the title, forced a smile, giving the proud father the respect deserved. "It was *my* honor, serving with men such as your James. As too, in sharing of the deck with yourself these weeks past." He paused, reaching out to touch the man's forearm. "I trust your son was able to make a full recovery?"

"He has, sir, with barely a limp showing. Married now, with a babe on the way. Going to name him after you—Harold Ramsey, if'n it's a boy."

"And if a girl?"

The man pursed his lips, as if the thought had never occurred. "I suppose—Harriet. *Yes!* That would work, sir. Harriet. With your approval, of course."

Harold nodded, then returned the other's salute, watching as the man moved back astern. Then he shivered, the air heavy with a damp chill. A feeling of uneasiness trickled down his spine as he turned around and stared at the city, sensing something lurking in the shadows, licking its lips, waiting for him to step ashore.

"They started gathering just before dawn, the streets now packed with onlookers." Nathan glanced over at Harold, who sat beside him, a sour expression on his lined face. "Extra soldiers were brought in to maintain order at the docks, preventing interference with unloading. The broadsheets having been sent ahead naming our arrival date to the exact day, thanks to pleasant enough weather during the crossing."

The two of them were in an open carriage, Nathan insistent that Harold join him, their baggage stowed in back. The horses shook their heads, drawing them away from the dock through throngs of people clustered alongside, shouting the name of the war hero returned home.

"As you can see from your welcome, leverage is *yours*, if you wish make use of it." Nathan noted Harold's expression tightening. "*After* you have had opportunity to rest and recover in the bosom of family and home, of course."

"Where are we bound? I've sent word ahead to my parents—"

"They've been gathered up, taken to a private establishment nearby. Made guests of a friend of mine. Well—several friends of mine, eager to make your acquaintance and shake your hand."

Harold turned and gave Nathan a hard glare. "You presume *too* much, my friend. Standing as we are on thin acquaint. I'm to be no *puppet* tied to your cause."

"Of course not." Nathan returned a look of calm appraisal. "One would be unwise to hold such low opinion of a man with as much— *honor* on his hands as you, Colonel Knutt, reluctant hero to the English people." He paused; his hands clamped to the side of the carriage as it rocked, dozens of hands clinging to its sides. "And I am anything but unwise, in action considered—or taken."

Harold leaned back, the cries of the crowd begging for him to join in with celebrating his triumphant return. Victory over the French, now assured, awaiting only negotiation and signatures, bringing an end to the sacrifice of thousands of lives and expenditure of great wealth. He noted a dozen or more veterans in partial kit scattered among the throng, their hands to their foreheads in salute, tears in their eyes, some with empty sleeves, or using crutches. Looking at him as he passed by, with the crowd chanting his name, saluting their hero, Red Fox.

Harold stood up, returning the salutes of his men, holding it until they'd passed by. Then he bowed to the cheers of the clamoring throng, removing his hat, and waving it about his head, honoring those among them who'd sent their sons, their husbands, their men off to war. Many of them left buried where they'd fallen, in mass graves scattered through-out nameless battlegrounds. He remained on his feet, honoring the genuine heroes, who would never get to hear the shouts of an adoring crowd.

As he gazed out at the mass of supporters, Harold knew powerful men were already at work behind the scenes, conspiring on how to turn the crowd's affection for him to their own advantage. As the carriage moved further away from the docks, he wondered how long it would be until those same men would turn the mob against him. The waving sea of welcoming hands reshaped into raised fists, calling for his ouster. The portrayal of him as a hero, turned into strident shouts, naming him betrayer to his countries need to expand into the New World. His eventual fall from grace, assured.

ACKNOWLEDGEMENTS:

I would like to thank all the people who helped make this novel possible through their dedication, willingness to work through my initial efforts, and emotional support. Chief among them, my mother, who taught me how to read, opened the door to thousands of her books spanning every area of interest. Her library proved to be fertile ground for a young boy's imagination. She continues to be my favorite reader, willing to peruse each and every draft, seeing the story through the trees of excessive wordiness of a first-time writer.

I give special thanks to my good friends and adopted siblings, Ray and Lorna, who have hung in with me through thick and thin, encouraging, offering insights, keen-eyed editing, and love.

I owe much to many. A woman who deserves all my praise for her willingness to butt heads with a Leo while maintaining her literary idealism, wedging it in wherever she could find a crack in my writer's defensive posture, is my dear friend, Laurie Ellis. A beacon of light, she guided me forward through turbulent waters, believing in my ability to tell a pretty good story, knowing I had something of value to say.

I would like to acknowledge my children, my big sister, family and friends, all of whom provided, as my late grandmother called it, "grist for my mill." Without them, I would not be the person, man, or writer I am today.

I also offer my sincere thanks to David Aretha, who taught me how to form my thoughts into coherent sentences, becoming paragraphs, then chapters. And to two wonderful people he introduced me to Martha Bullen, Christy Collins, and Maggie McLaughlin, each helping to put a professional veneer on the story enclosed.

Finally, I give my eternal thanks to Lyn, my wife of twenty-five years, now deceased, who told me to remain open to love and to continue to pursue my dream, and for sending me a wonderful woman who now shares my life. My Yvonne, a vibrant being of light and love, is helping me make my way into the world and see life clearly again.

ABOUT THE AUTHOR

M. DANIEL SMITH is a prolific author of historical fiction, speculative and literary fiction, mysteries and thrillers. *The Red Path,* the first book in the *Legacy's Road* series, is his debut historical novel.

He particularly enjoys writing about strong-willed, feisty women and the men they love, showing them in moments of emotional turmoil, introspective conversation, and physical closeness. Coming from a blue-collar background, raised with two older sisters and strong female role models, Daniel enjoys exploring the interplay between wives and husbands, siblings, and people meeting, then falling in love.

As a voracious reader who began reading all the books in his parents' library when he was five, he cut his teeth on a wide range of subject matters, covering war, romance, historical novels, and the like.

A life-long Mainer, he is continually inspired by the wild natural beauty of his home state. Now retired, Daniel spends his time writing the type of novels he grew up with, telling his character's stories as clearly and as honestly as possible. Learn more about Daniel and his books at www.bayledgespress.com.